About the Authors

Avril Tremayne is happily settled in her hometown of Sydney, Australia, where her husband and daughter try to keep her out of trouble – not always successfully. When she's not writing or reading she can generally be found eating – although she does *not* cook! Check out her website: www@avriltremayne.com. Or follow her on Twitter: @AvrilTremayne and Facebook: www.facebook.com/avril.tremayne

Stefanie London lives in Melbourne with her very own hero and enough books to sink a ship. She frequently indulges in her passions for good coffee, French perfume, high heels and zombie movies. During the day she uses lots of words like *synergy* and *strategy*. At night she writes sexy contemporary romance stories and tries not to spend too much time shopping online and watching baby animal videos on YouTube.

Kelly Hunter has always had a weakness for fairytales, fantasy worlds and losing herself in a good book. She has two children, avoids cooking and cleaning and, despite the best efforts of her family, is no sports fan! Kelly is, however, a keen gardener and has a fondness for roses. Kelly was born in Australia and has travelled extensively. Although she enjoys living and working in different parts of the world, she still calls Australia home.

Red-Hot

COLLECTION

May 2018

June 2018

July 2018

August 2018

Red-Hot Summer

AVRIL TREMAYNE

STEFANIE LONDON

KELLY HUNTER

MILLS & BOON

Published in Great Britain 2018
by Mills & Boon, an imprint of HarperCollins*Publishers*
1 London Bridge Street, London, SE1 9GF

ISBN: 978-0-263-26636-8

09-0518

MIX
Paper from responsible sources
FSC™ C007454

This book is produced from independently certified FSC™ paper to ensure responsible forest management.

For more information visit: www.harpercollins.co.uk/green

Printed and bound in Spain
by CPI, Barcelona

THE MILLIONAIRE'S PROPOSITION

AVRIL TREMAYNE

For Peter Alati - best brother ever.

CHAPTER ONE

SCOTT KNIGHT TOOK one look at the redhead standing over at the punchbowl and almost swallowed his tongue.

Tall, confident, beautiful…and dyspeptically cynical, judging by the look on her face. He liked every single thing in that package.

So…exactly what *was* the pick-up etiquette associated with divorce parties? Were they like funerals—no hitting on attendees unless you wanted to look like a slimeball?

He pondered that while he took another look at the redhead.

Strictly speaking, of course, this was a little more than a divorce party; it was a celebratory segue to Willa's new committed relationship with Rob. Scott wouldn't normally have advocated a jump from one hot pan right into another—even when the guy in the second pan was Rob, who was several thousand light years ahead of Willa's ex, Wayne-the-Pain—but he was suddenly cool with it if it lifted the party out of the funereal stakes and opened the way…

The redhead turned to the punchbowl for another dip. Scott noted that her body was divine. And he stopped worrying about anything other than getting his hands on it.

He headed over to the punchbowl with great purpose, grabbing a beer on the way—punch being way too girly for him. 'What's that quote about divorce…?' he asked, tilting his head towards her—but it was a rhetorical question.

She turned before the words had finished leaving his mouth and a slap of undiluted lust walloped him. She was even better close-up. A scorching mix of opulent looks, with slanted grey eyes, wickedly arched dark auburn brows, regal cheekbones…and a top-lip-heavy mouth painted blistering red.

She didn't bother answering. Clearly knew she didn't have

to. Knew he was already caught. He could tell by the way she waited, all self-possessed confidence, for him to continue, with the mere hint of a smile on her insanely sexy lips.

'Jean Kerr, it was,' he continued. '"A lawyer is never entirely comfortable with a friendly divorce, any more than a good mortician wants to finish his job and then have the patient sit up on the table."'

The sexy lips parted in surprise…and then the corners tilted up, just a little. She looked fascinated. He took that as a sign—a *good* sign—that his opening conversational gambit had hit the mark. She was with him. *Yes!*

She took a slow sip of her punch and examined him. Down, up. 'Are you in the market?' she asked, and the smokiness of her voice had his libido purring like a tomcat on the hunt.

Mmm-hmm. She'd not only caught him, she was well on the way to hog-tying him and dumping him in a babbling heap at her feet. And he wasn't complaining.

Scott gave her his *I am available for sex immediately* smile, which he liked to call his Number One smile, because it seemed to be the one that got the most use.

'Why, yes, I do happen to be in the market,' he said.

She laughed. Throatily gorgeous. 'I meant the divorce market.'

'I'm not married, if that's what you're asking. Or engaged.' Little step closer. 'Or partnered in any way, shape or form.'

She made a little moue with her luscious lips. 'Shame. Would have been fun.'

Scott wasn't often taken by surprise, but Cool-Hand Red had managed it with five little words. Why was his singledom a shame? Did she only do married guys?

'Still could be,' he said, rallying fast as he figured that simply couldn't be true. 'Fun, I mean.'

'With no money involved?' Little regretful sigh. 'I don't think so.'

What the *hell*? She not only preferred married men, but they had to *pay*? This was *so* not Willa's scene. It wasn't *his* scene either, and he'd thought he was up for most things—

except for all that hardcore S&M business. Inflicting pain—and receiving it—thank you but no! Not his cup of tea.

She put down her punch, reached into the small and sparkly emerald-green evening bag draped via a chain over her shoulder, took out an elegant silver card case, flicked it open one-handed and handed him a plain, crisp white business card.

'"Kate Cleary",' he read. And then, 'Oh…' *Wince.* 'Ouch.'

Another of those throaty laughs. 'Divorce lawyer. Willa's, in fact. And she's not only sitting up on the mortician's table, she's leaping off it and twirling across the floor with a dance partner. And I'm *very* comfortable with that. Now, what's that *other* quote about divorce?' She raised a mischievous eyebrow. 'Ah, yes. Zsa Zsa Gabor. "He taught me housekeeping; when I divorce I keep the house."'

He laughed. Delighted, relieved, intrigued—and *horny*. 'That explains how Willa got the house—who would dare say no to *you*?'

'Lots of people dare—but there can only be one winner. And I like the winner to be me.'

Scott's inner purr became a growl as his libido kicked up a notch.

'Scott Knight—architect,' he said, holding out his hand. 'And expert inserter of foot into mouth.'

She took his hand in a firm, cool grip. Two mid-level shakes—not wimpy, not crushing. Perfect.

'Nice to meet you, Scott Knight,' she said. 'And you're more than welcome to roll out the lawyer jokes. Who knows? There may even be one I haven't heard.'

'Ouch. Again. I'm going to need stitches.'

She retrieved her punch glass. 'Well, I have a needle and thread.' Sipped. 'And a stapler too, if you prefer it a little… rougher.'

His eyes skimmed her the way hers had him. She was covered from neck to mid-thigh in snug black. Plain, plain, plain—and off-the-chain sexy. Naked arms and legs. High heels in nude. The little green handbag. Her red hair loose and gorgeous. And the lips—good God, the lips.

He felt a little shiver of excitement as he caught her scent. Tuberose. His favourite.

'You look like a tearer, not a repairer, to me,' he said, plucking the words more for their innuendo value than anything else. The only important thing was staying near her. He'd talk about knee replacements if that would keep her close.

'That's because I am,' she said. '"Ball-tearer" is the complete phrase, I believe.'

'You're not scaring me.'

'What *am* I doing?'

'You *know* what you're doing, Kate Cleary. You know very well. So let's cut to the chase. Are you hooked up with anyone? I mean, anyone I couldn't take out in a Rubik's cube tournament, obviously.' He held his breath, waiting for the answer. *No, no, no, please.*

'Is that your speciality? The Rubik's cube?'

'Well, I'm better with the cube than I am at hand-to-hand combat—although for you I could get a little gladiatorial. Certainly *with* you I could.'

'Then how fortunate that I am, indeed, single. So…do you need me to demonstrate my Rubik's cube abilities?'

'Exactly how limber are you with those nice, long, slim fingers?'

'Eleven seconds—limber enough.' The tip of her tongue came out, ran across her plump red top lip. 'But I can go slow.'

Scott's nostrils flared with the scent of her, the triumph of it. He edged closer, until they were almost but not quite touching. 'I'd like to see you go fast…*and* slow.'

She raised that eyebrow again. And, God, he knew—just from that—she would be awesome in bed. He was going to have to find out. Maybe tonight…

She tilted her head back. And there was a challenge in that. 'That's going to depend.'

'On…?'

'What you're offering.'

He was about to suggest they consider an early departure to negotiate the 'offer' when—*dammit*—Willa materialised, with Rob beside her. Okay, maybe she hadn't materialised—maybe she'd walked quite normally across the floor and he'd been too busy gagging with lust to notice. But, whatever, the interruption was so ill-timed he wanted to punch something.

'Kate, I'm so glad you've met Scott,' Willa said, all warm and thrilled and happy. 'He's not likely to be a client, though—he's the confirmed bachelor of Weeping Reef!'

Scott only just held back the wince. Because that made him sound either gay or like a player. Rob, at least, had the grace to wince *for* him and clap the hand of sympathy on his back.

Kate couldn't possibly think, even for a second, that he was gay. Not after the conversation they'd been having.

On the other hand… A player? Yeah, he admitted to that. But he liked to do his *own* warning off of women who had happily-ever-after in their sights—with charm and skill and softly negotiated ground rules that meant everyone had fun right up until the goodbye. He didn't need his friends making public service announcements to scare away prospective bedmates before he even got to the first kiss.

'Let's leave it at bachelor, shall we, Willa?' Scott suggested through slightly gritted teeth.

Willa, oblivious, turned to him. 'Oh, are you *not* a confirmed bachelor? I thought you said friends with benefits was as far as you ever intended to go? Not that there's anything wrong with that. At all. Of course.'

Scott stared at Willa, speechless. Rob blew out a *not laughing, I promise* breath. Kate was biting the inside of her cheek, in the same predicament as Rob.

'After what happened in the Whitsundays I—' At last Willa stopped. Blushed very prettily—as Willa did everything.

Scott was still staring, frozen, praying she was not going to finish that.

'Oh,' Willa said. 'Well. Anyway. Kate is the best family lawyer in Sydney, as well as being a wonderful, kind, compassionate—'

'Thank you, Willa,' Kate interrupted smoothly. 'But I'm not quite ready for sainthood.'

Scott, unfreezing, saw the flush of pink that slashed across Kate's high cheekbones—not pretty, *stunning*!—and decided it was time to take control of the conversation and get his seduction back on track.

Leaning into Willa conspiratorially, he said, 'I hear Kate's also a Rubik's cube champion.'

Kate choked on her punch, trying—again—not to laugh.

And somehow that made Scott want her even more. He needed to get her away from everyone immediately. Out onto the deck into that particular corner that he knew from previous forays at Willa's harbourside mansion was very private, screened by a giant pot plant.

But any chance of getting Kate alone was snatched from him by another of the old Weeping Reef gang, Amy, who landed in their midst—because Amy never merely *appeared* anywhere—accompanied by her flatmate Jessica, who'd become an honorary gang member despite never having been near the Whitsundays.

Seduction plans were officially on simmer—but not off the heat. Half an hour—that was all he needed. Half an hour and Kate Cleary would be his.

Amy gave Scott a smacking kiss on the cheek before enveloping Kate in a hug.

'Kate!' she squealed. 'It's been an age.'

Kate laughed as she returned the hug. 'Well, two weeks, anyway—you didn't drink so many mojitos at Fox that you've forgotten?'

What the hell...? Scott wondered if he was the only one of the group who'd never met Kate. Well—him and Willa's brother, Luke, who was still in Singapore. Was this some kind of Weeping Reef conspiracy? Would Chantal turn up at last—because God knew how he'd deal with that—and Brodie? He could picture Brodie sauntering over, snatching the heart of *another* of Scott's women…

Not that Kate was Scott's woman.

Jessica and Kate were hugging now. Okay—this was officially out of control. Even *Jessica* knew Kate?

'It wasn't the mojitos that were news at Fox,' Jessica said. 'It was one very particular martini.'

The blush was back on Kate's cheekbones. 'The less said about that the better,' she said with a theatrical shudder.

Scott was suddenly desperate to hear the story. 'You don't like martinis?' he asked—only to have Willa, Amy and Jessica burst out laughing.

He looked at Rob, who gave him a *don't ask me* shrug.

'It was a *dirty* martini,' Amy said, putting him out of his misery. 'Bought for her by Barnaby, my arch nemesis at work, who just happened to be drinking at Fox too. Blond, blue-eyed and gorgeous—that's Barnaby. Thinks he's God's gift to marketing. *And* to women. And to be honest, he kind of *is*. Just not to Kate.'

Kate shook her head, laughing, as though batting the subject away.

'It was the way he said "dirty",' Jessica put in, helping herself to a glass of punch. 'It's one thing being presented with a dirty martini. It's quite another to have it presented with a slimy pick-up line. *"Just how dirty do you like it, baby?"* Yep—that would make any woman want to jump you. *Not.*'

More laughing from the girls as Kate covered her eyes with a hand.

Rob was practically cringing. 'Seriously?'

Willa kissed Rob's cheek. 'Not all men are as evolved as you, Rob.'

Rob turned to Scott. 'You ever used that one?'

'Dirty martini? Nope. And, given the reaction Barnaby

got, I doubt I ever will. Although in my youth I did once embarrass myself with a comment to twin girls about a *Ménage à Trois*.'

Jessica's eyes bugged. 'Twins? Like…a real *ménage à trois*? Or is that the name of a fancy-pants cocktail?'

'It's a cocktail,' Scott assured her. 'And delicious, apparently—because, as it happens, they both ordered one and made very…*approving*…noises.' He cleared his throat, all faux embarrassment. 'As they sipped, I mean.'

'They ordered one apiece—with a side order of you?' Amy asked, batting her eyelashes outrageously.

Scott smiled. The lazy, teasing smile he reserved for flirty moments with women he wasn't ever going to take to bed. 'A gentleman never tells a lady's secrets.'

He saw something flash across Amy's face. Something like…distress? But it was gone so quickly he wondered if he'd imagined it. And the next moment she was laughing again.

'Well, anyway, enough with the "in my youth" talk. If I've got my arithmetic in order you're twenty-seven—one measly year older than me. And I'll have you know I still consider myself to be in my youth.'

An odd gasping sound from Kate had Scott turning to her. It looked as if she'd spilled punch on her dress, because she was brushing a hand over the bodice. It must have been only the tiniest drop—*he* certainly couldn't see any sign of it—but the next moment Willa was ushering Kate to the guest bathroom and Amy was asking Rob what exactly was in the punch, because she'd never seen Kate's nerves of steel so much as bend before, let alone be dented.

The punch, apparently, was a combination of vodka, white wine, white rum and champagne, with an occasional strawberry waved over the bowl—that did *not* sound girly! It was a miracle everyone in the house wasn't stumbling around breaking bits off sculptures, staggering into walls and pitching face-first into pot plants.

But Scott had a feeling the potency of the brew was not

the problem with Kate. She'd looked sort of *shocky*. Surely not because of that harmless *ménage à trois* talk? She was too sophisticated for that. It would take him two minutes, tops, to explain that away. Which would leave him twenty-eight minutes to charm her out of her panties.

But twenty minutes later Scott hadn't managed to get near Kate. Every time he took a step in her direction she moved somewhere else. As if she was on guard against him—which was crazy. Almost as crazy as what the sight of her loose-hipped, strolling, rolling walk was doing to his testosterone levels. Sexiest walk *ever*.

At the twenty-four-minute mark, as he made what felt like his hundredth attempt to reach her and she replaced the stroll with a dash—an actual freaking *dash*—towards a small group of people whose average age looked to be a hundred and four, he realised she really and truly *was* on her guard.

Oh, my God.

He was chasing her and she was running away. This had never, ever happened to him before.

And as he watched her, trying to figure out what the hell had gone wrong, the last six minutes of his self-allocated thirty minutes' seduction time ticked away…and she was gone.

Disappeared. Like Cinderella, but wearing both of her take-me-now shoes.

He fingered the card she'd given him.

Weird. Very, *very* weird. A mystery. What had he said? Done?

Well, Scott loved mysteries. And challenges. And women who wore red lipstick.

And he was suddenly very certain that this thing between him and Kate Cleary—because there was definitely a thing—was not going to end with a drop of spilled punch and no explanation.

He looked at her card again, noted the address—a block from his city office.

Easy.

CHAPTER TWO

KATE LET HERSELF into her apartment, tossed her bag onto the couch, kicked off her shoes, wiggled her toes…and let out a tortured groan that had nothing to do with her sore feet and everything to do with the divorce party.

Which had been a disaster.

She couldn't believe she'd been smut-talking about a stapler and a Rubik's cube. As bad as Dirty Martini Barnaby! Flirting with that hot, gorgeous hunk like a horny teenager.

And then to discover that the hot, gorgeous hunk practically *was* a horny teenager…

She let out another tortured groan.

Not that twenty-seven really *was* teenaged.

But she was thirty-two, for God's sake! A *my way or the highway* woman of thirty-two!

She opened the French doors and stepped onto the expansive terrace of her apartment. She'd chosen the apartment for the view—not the Harbour Bridge in the distance, even though that was her favourite Sydney landmark, but the boats. Something about them, bobbing gently in Rushcutters Bay, soothed her. The escape daydream, she called it. Sailing away from her troubles to a world of possibilities. A world of adventure…

She tried to bring herself back to earth by reminding herself of the time she'd forced the husband of one of her clients to sell his boat and hand over half the cash and he'd cried like a baby. But even the memory of that less than edifying spectacle couldn't stop her thinking about adventures and possibilities.

And tonight, very specifically, the possibility of an adventure with Scott Knight.

The image of him was so clear in her head. That killer body—tall, broad, strong. The slightly spiky mid-brown hair. The alertness of his cool, pale green eyes. That *I've got a secret* smile that was kind of calculating…and somehow intriguing exactly because of that. She'd wanted to twist him into a sexual pretzel the moment she'd heard his lazy, drawling voice—a voice so at odds with the alert intelligence in his eyes it was almost a challenge.

But…*twenty-seven years old*?

She covered her face with her hands and let fly with one more tortured groan.

Pent up need—that was the problem. It had been a long time between…cocktails. Dirty Martini, Bosom Caresser, Between the Sheets, Sex on the Beach or any other kind. A *damned* long time.

Well, she clearly couldn't be trusted to see Scott Knight again until that pent-up need had been met. She would have to make sure any Weeping Reef gathering was Scott-free before attending. In fact, she'd go one step further and stick to girls-only catch-ups when it came to Willa. So just Willa, Amy, Jessica and the other girl she had yet to meet—Chantal—if she ever showed. No Rob. No Scott. Luke was in Singapore, and the other guy whose name started with a B—Brady? No, Brodie—hadn't turned up at anything yet. So the whole girls-only thing was definitely doable.

And in the meantime she would find some other man to twist into a sexual pretzel. Someone like Phillip, a barrister who was happily divorced, suave, cultured and—at forty years old—mature. In the right age ballpark.

Then she would let the girls know she was taken, word would find its way to Scott, and that would be that.

Yes, Phillip would do very nicely. She would give him a call on Monday and arrange to catch up with him at the bar near her office for a Slow Comfortable Screw. A Strawberry Stripper. A Sex Machine. Or…or *something*.

* * *

Monday morning for Kate began with an eight o'clock client meeting.

Kate always felt like cuddling this particular client. Fragile, timid Rosie, who crept into her office as though she'd like a corner to hide in. Rosie was so intimidated by her husband she couldn't even bring herself to tell him he was making her unhappy—so how she was going to raise the subject of divorce was anyone's guess.

It was not a position a *Cleary* woman would ever find herself in!

Her frustrating meeting with Rosie reminded Kate how happy she was not to be married. And that, in turn, prompted her to get to the task of calling the equally gamophobic Phillip to arrange that bar meeting. A highly satisfactory phone call that took four businesslike minutes.

Two meetings later she made herself a cup of coffee and opened her diary to recheck her schedule…and blinked.

Blinked, blinked, blinked.

She called her no-nonsense, indeterminately aged, absolutely superb assistant. 'What's this appointment at twelve-thirty today, Deb?'

'Hang on…' Keyboard clicks. 'Oh, Scott Knight. He called while you were with your eight o'clock. Said he'd mentioned a lunch appointment when he saw you on Saturday night.'

Kate slumped back in her chair, awed—and depressingly delighted—at the presumption of it.

'Oh, did he?' she asked, trying to sound ominous.

'So he *didn't*?' Chuckle. 'Well, I did wonder why you hadn't mentioned it to me, but he sounded… Well, let's keep it clean and say *nice*, so I made an executive decision and slotted him in.'

'Yes, he does sound "nice",' Kate said dryly, and smiled at Deb's sudden crack of laughter.

'Want me to cancel him, hon? Leave you to your takeaway chicken and mung-bloody-bean salad?'

Kate opened her mouth to say an automatic yes—but into her head popped an image of Rosie that morning. Diffident. Nervous. Panicky. Dodging her husband rather than telling him their marriage was over.

And hot on the heels of that came the memory of her own behaviour on Saturday night, dodging Scott at Willa's party. So unnerved by the force of her attraction to him she'd mapped out an actual plan for seeing only Willa, Amy and Jessica. *Crazy.* She should be able to see her friends whenever and wherever she wanted, without giving a second thought to whoever else might just happen to be in the vicinity.

As if she couldn't handle a *twenty-seven-year-old*!

And on her own turf…in her own office? Easy.

This would not be like the divorce party, where the kick of lust had taken her by surprise. She would be prepared for it today. And she could tell him directly, herself, that she was no longer in the market—so thanks, but no thanks.

'Kate?' Deb prompted. 'Shall I cancel him?'

Kate straightened her shoulders. 'No, that's fine,' she said. 'It will take approximately five minutes to conclude my business with Mr Knight. Plenty of time to eat chicken and mung-bloody-bean salad afterwards.' She nodded, satisfied. 'Now, can you grab me the McMahon file? There's something I need to check before the parties arrive to have another crack at a settlement conference.'

'Mmm-hmm. Settlement conference… That's what they're calling World War III these days, is it?'

Scott, no stranger to wooing women, brought flowers to Kate's office. Nothing over the top. Just simple, colourful gerberas that said *I'm charming so I don't have to bring roses.*

Not that he saw any softening in Deb's face as he handed over the bunch.

'Seems a shame to spend money on flowers when you're only going to be in there for five minutes,' she said.

'Oh, they're not for Kate,' Scott said. 'They're for you.'

'Even so…' Deb said, but he didn't miss the tiny sparkle that sprang to life in her eyes. 'Her meeting is running over time. Take a seat, if you'd like to wait.'

Scott angled himself so he could see through the glass wall of the boardroom. Could see *her*. Kate.

She was sitting at a long table, her back to him. Beside her was an overly blonded, expensive-looking woman wearing lime-green. The client, obviously. On the opposite side of the table was a man who epitomised lawyerdom. Pinstriped suit, white shirt, conservative tie. Beside Pinstripe was a man who looked as if he'd spent too long on the tanning bed, wearing an open-necked shirt with a humungous gold chain visible against his chest. Gold Chain was holding a dog. A furry little dog. Which he kept petting.

Amongst the four of them—five, if you included the dog—there were frequent vehement headshakes, very occasional nods, hand gestures aplenty. At one point Kate ran a hand tiredly over her hair, which was tied in a low ponytail. It made Scott want to touch her.

And that reminded him that their only physical contact on Saturday night had been a handshake. So it was kind of nuts to be so obsessed with her. But obsessed was what he was.

Suddenly Kate stood. She put her hands on the table and leaned forward—making a particular point, he guessed. She was wearing a cream skirt suit. Beautifully, tightly fitted.

Scott was appreciating the view of her really superb backside when she stretched just a little bit further forward and her skirt hitched up for one split second. Just long enough to give him a tiny glimpse of the lacy band at the top of one of her…*ooohhh…stockings*.

She was wearing *stockings*.

All the blood in Scott's body redirected itself in one gush, straight to his groin. The sudden ache of it made him clamp his jaws together.

Stockings!

Stay-ups? Suspenders? Hell, who cared which?

Then she was back in her seat. Scott realised he'd been holding his breath and exhaled—very, very slowly.

He forced his eyes away from her—scared he'd start drooling otherwise—and saw Gold Chain give the dog a kiss on the nose while keeping his eyes on his wife across the table.

That seemed to incense Blondie—which Scott could understand, because it *was* kind of gross—who leapt to her feet and screeched so loudly her voice bounced straight through the glass wall. Next moment all four of them were standing. There were waved arms, pointed fingers, even a stamped foot. The stamped foot was from Blondie, who was then subtly restrained by Kate, who seemed serene in the midst of chaos. Pinstripe was using a similar restraining movement on Gold Chain, but was somewhat hampered by the dog snapping at him.

Scott heard a few words shouted—hurled. *Custody. Holidays. Missed drop-offs.* Interspersed with an occasional ear-sizzling foul-mouthed curse.

Shocked, Scott looked at Deb. Shouldn't she be calling the cops before someone threw an actual punch? But Deb just kept typing, unperturbed. Which would have to mean that Kate put up with such crap routinely, wouldn't it? Did that explain Kate's air of cynicism at Willa's divorce party? Because if this was divorce, it sure wasn't pretty.

He tuned back in to the screeches. A custody battle? Had to be. The antagonists were…what?…in their early thirties, maybe? So the kids had to be young. How *many* kids?

Scott wondered how his own parents would have handled a custody battle. Not that his parents would have done anything so undignified as get divorced. The joining of two old families, the merging of two fortunes, had been destiny working the way it was supposed to—even if he'd never seen his parents kiss, let alone hold hands. Their merger was too perfect ever to be classified as a mistake, so that sucker wasn't getting dissolved.

But if they *had* divorced he couldn't imagine them getting into a raging custody battle. Over *him*, at any rate. They would have come up with a simple, bloodless schedule of visits, complete with taxi pick-ups and drop-offs.

Custody of his older brother would have been a different story. There would have been nothing amicable about sharing the 'perfect' son. Maybe that was the real reason they'd stayed together—the inability to satisfactorily halve his brother.

And what an opportune moment for the boardroom door to be opening, so he could stop thinking.

Gold Chain was coming out, carrying the dog, speaking furiously to his solicitor. Pinstripe had a grip on his client's dog-free arm and was dealing admirably with dodging the growling dog's snapping jaws as he walked Gold Chain past Deb's desk and out of the suite. Kate and her client stayed in the room talking for a few minutes, but then they too appeared. Kate was nodding, her red-lipsticked mouth pursed in sympathy.

Kate caught sight of him—and slashes of pink zapped along her cheekbones as if by Magic Marker. And then she returned her concentration to Blondie.

'It's not good enough,' Blondie was saying. 'He keeps returning her late. If it doesn't stop I'll be rethinking the money. Make sure he knows that, Kate.'

A few soothing words, an unrelenting shepherding towards the suite exit. Out through the door.

And then…silence.

Deb looked at Scott. Raised her eyebrows. That little sparkle was in her eyes again.

Scott raised his eyebrows back, a little shell-shocked and a lot awed at what Kate had just put up with. And still somewhat gobsmacked that such a small dog could be so nasty. He'd back that dog against a pitbull.

And then Kate was coming back. Smiling coolly—very lawyer-like and professional.

'Scott,' she said, and held out her hand.

Scott shook it. 'Kate,' he said, and could hear the laughter in his voice. Less than forty-eight hours ago they'd been heading for sex. Today he got a handshake.

No. Just...*no.*

Kate gestured to the office next to the boardroom. Scott walked ahead of her, opened the heavy wooden door and stood just inside, taking in the dignified space. Carpeted floor. Big desk. Behind the desk a large tinted window on the outside world. Large window on the inside world too—untinted—through which he could see Kate speaking to Deb, because the Venetian blinds that were there for privacy were open. Neat, modern filing cabinets. Two black leather chairs in front of her desk. Vivid knock-out painting on one wall—the only splash of colour.

And then Kate was entering, closing the door behind her. He turned to face her. She was close. So close. Cream suit. Red hair. Those other-worldly grey eyes. Tuberose scent.

Just for a second the memory of the top of her stocking burst in his head.

And drove him wild.

Which had to be why he grabbed her by the upper arms, backed her up a step, pushed her against that nice solid door and covered her mouth with his.

CHAPTER THREE

FOR ONE FRANTIC SECOND he felt Kate stiffen.

God, don't stop me. I'll die if you stop me.

He licked her mouth—her gorgeous, red, luscious mouth—and with an inarticulate sound that was half-moan, half-whimper she opened to him.

Thank you, thank you, thank you.

His tongue swooped inside, tangled with hers…and she was everything he'd hoped she would be. Delicious, and hot, and desperate—as desperate as he was. She tasted so good. Smelled like heaven. Felt lush and ripe against him as he pressed her to the door. He wished he could get her closer—although that was knuckleheaded. If he pushed any harder against her they'd be through the wood, spilling onto the floor at the base of Deb's desk. And exhibitionism wasn't high on his must-do list.

Then Kate's arms circled him and he *was* closer. *Miracle.* She tore the shirt loose from his pants and then her hands were under the cotton, sliding up his back, down, then up. Rushing over his skin. No finesse, just raw, hungry possession. Restless, seeking, sweeping…

He heard her whimper, low in her throat, and it set off a flare in his head. He wanted every part of her in his hands all at once. Impossible lust. Outrageous. He grabbed the back of her head, bringing their mouths together so furiously their teeth clashed. But he didn't stop and neither did she. They were straining together. He could feel her heart thudding against his own rocketing beats. He wished he could see her naked. Needed to touch her bare skin.

Alone. He needed them to be alone.

Keeping his burning mouth fused to Kate's, he reached,

one-handed, grabbing for the cord that controlled the Venetian blinds. He scrabbled there, cursing inside his impatient head until he found it, yanked. *Close, dammit, close!* And then the blinds came clattering down and they were invisible—just him and Kate, wrapped together—and he was going to take her in some way, by God!

Next second they were spinning, fast and clumsy, and with one rough push it was *his* back jammed against the door, and he was sucking in gasping breaths with every tiny *get it while you can* break in their hungry kisses. Her hands were under his shirt again almost before the thud against the wood sounded his willing submission. Skating, racing up to his shoulders, over his chest, across his sides, down his stomach. Then she was reaching for his belt, undoing, unbuttoning, unzipping, her hands diving to touch, to grip him through his underwear.

He cradled her head, hands digging in to keep her mouth fused to his. Felt her hair—cool silk against his fingers. He must have wrenched the band from it because it was loose. They were almost at eye level—and that reminded him she was wearing high heels. The thought of those heels, her legs, made him groan. The memory of the top of her stocking—that one hot glimpse—was ferocious in his head. He wanted to see those stockings, wanted her legs wrapped around him.

His hands moved to her perfect backside. Tight and sexy and…*covered*. Not good enough. Not now. His hands went lower, down to her thighs. He stopped for a blinding moment as her hand squeezed him and he thought he'd lose it, but determinedly he moved on. The stockings. He had to feel them…touch them.

The instant his fingers reached the hem of her skirt he yanked it up. Out of the way. Out of *his* way. *God, God, God*, he'd reached that lacy edge. He could feel the band, snug against her slender thigh. *Oooohhhhh. G-o-o-o-d.* So damned *hot*. Fingers toyed at the edge for long moments, tracing the skin at the very top, then sliding up, over her bottom, now covered only by soft, slippery silk. He groaned into her mouth. He had to have her—*now.*

She spread her legs to accommodate his straining erection between her thighs, pulled him hard into the cradle of her, wordless and panting.

'I want to see you,' he said.

But before she could respond he was backing her further into the room. Step, kiss…step, kiss…step, kiss. And then they were at her desk, her thighs hitting the desktop. Her amazing, stockinged thighs. Just the thought of them had his fingers twitching to touch.

'Open your legs,' he said, and she did.

And then his fingers were there, feeling the damp silk. He was too desperate to be gentle, wrenching the covering aside so his fingers could dip into her. Urgently slipping inside her, then out, circling, then in, out, circling again. She cried out and he plastered his mouth to hers, bending her backwards at the same time as his arm swooped, scattering everything off the desk onto the floor.

He heard the thump and clatter—didn't care. Her back was on the desk, her bottom at the edge, her legs splayed and dangling, her feet in their sexy high heels just touching the floor. He was between her thighs, fingers still working, resolutely wringing wordless cries from her. He hadn't stopped kissing her, scared to break that mouth-to-mouth bond in case she told him to stop. He couldn't stop now—didn't want to stop.

Fingers still moving against her, he used his other hand to wrench her skirt higher until he knew—even though he couldn't yet see—that she was exposed to him.

He imagined the picture: pale fabric bunched around her hips, silky knickers covering her except for the slight skew at her core where his fingers played, the stay-up stockings in an understated nude that just made them that much sexier. *Steam.* He thought he must have steam coming out of his ears. Hell, he wanted to see that picture.

Okay—he would have to risk freeing her mouth just so he *could* see that picture.

He pulled back and Kate reached automatically to push her skirt down, but his hands stayed hers.

'No. I have to see. I *have* to, Kate.'

Throwing her head back, she let her hands drop to her sides, open to him.

He pulled back, looked long and hard, while his heart threatened to leap out through his eyeballs and he thought he might actually come on the spot. Violet. A flash of purple amongst the cream and nude. That delicious part of her just peeping out at the side. She was the most gloriously sexy thing he had ever seen in his life. He had a feeling the image of Kate Cleary on the desk, spread for him, would be the hottest memory of his life.

He made some low, growling noise—like an animal, because he *felt* like an animal—and knew he had to get at her the fastest way he could. No condom—because why would he need a condom just to see her briefly in her office on a Monday afternoon? *Idiot—don't leave home without one ever again.* So it would be his fingers and his mouth.

Even before the thought had finished he was on her, his fingers there, renewing their endless dipping slide. He dropped to his knees, watching each undulating movement of her hips. And when that wasn't enough he tugged that violet silk a little further off centre and put his mouth on her.

She bucked, cried out, as his tongue replaced his fingers, as his hands moved to grasp her hips and bring her closer to his mouth, angling her so he could explore every delicious fold and crease. The taste of her was intoxicating. The scent of her arousal, the feel of her as he suckled the pearly clitoris he'd freed from the silk…

'Delicious,' he said, between long, slow pulls. 'I knew you would be.'

And then she was whimpering in earnest, soft mewing cries as he alternated the pressure, building the fire in her with every scrap of skill and care he had, building, building… One last, long, endless, sucking kiss there and her hips bucked off the desk.

And then a low, throaty moan was torn out of her as she came and her hands fisted convulsively in his hair, dragging him into her moist heat, and he was breathing her in as he laved her with his eager, lusting tongue, so damned *hot* for her.

He stayed there, his mouth on her, until the waves receded.

And then her legs relaxed and she lay like an exhausted doll, legs spread, limp hands slipping from his hair as he stood back and looked at her. She was so wantonly beautiful to Scott's still hungry eyes that he had to cover his face with his hands—because he wanted to be inside her so badly the sight of her was painful.

A heartbeat later he heard the soft sounds of her getting herself together—sitting up, adjusting her clothes. He dropped his hands a millimetre at a time, gauging his control as he went.

Okay.

She was covered.

He could breathe.

Sort of.

That spectacular blush was on her cheekbones. 'What about…about you?' she asked. 'I mean…you. You know…'

Scott winced. 'That's what I get for not packing a condom,' he said, and pulled up his gaping pants, refastening the openings Kate had wrenched apart earlier. He tucked in his shirt. 'Not that I expected… Well, not that I expected *that*.'

Her eyes darted to the Venetian blinds as she edged off the desk and he read her relief as she puffed out a little breath. Had she not even noticed that he'd closed the blinds? That said something about the passion between them.

'So, Kate, I'd say you owe me,' he said. 'And I have an inkling you're not the kind of woman who likes to be in anyone's debt, so I'll collect tonight. Name the place. Name the time.'

She bent to pick up the various objects Scott had so unceremoniously shoved off the desk. Including her laptop, which she didn't even bother checking for damage.

Ordinarily he would have helped. But not now. Now he just watched. She was doing something inside her head. Calculating. Planning. So best to be a spectator, gathering clues from her demeanour. What was she thinking?

She picked up a box of tissues, but instead of putting it back on the desk she held it out to him. 'Lipstick,' she said, gesturing to his mouth

He plucked a tissue from the box. '*Still* there?' he asked, giving her his most wicked smile. 'After my mouth was so busy between your '

'Yes, still there,' she cut in.

Her voice was curt, no-nonsense…but he saw the shiver tremble through her body as she put the tissue box back in its place on her desk.

And then she checked her watch. Followed that with a stride over to the Venetians to open them with one sharp tug of the cord.

'Oh, no, Katie,' Scott said at that point. 'We don't get back to normal and move on to our next appointments after *that*.'

She looked at him. 'Kate. Not Katie.' She licked her top lip. Again. Eyes closed. Then opened. And then she threw her hands out with a *you win* sigh. 'All right—fair enough. Let's talk.'

She waved him to one of the black leather chairs as she walked around behind the desk and settled into her own intimidating, high-backed number.

'That was a mistake,' she said, very direct.

'I made one mistake—I didn't bring a condom. Otherwise that went pretty much as I would have liked.'

'I don't do relationships,' Kate said, ignoring that.

'Really?'

'Really.'

'Perfect.'

'What does that mean?'

'You don't do relationships. I don't do relationships. But I *do* do sex…and so, obviously, do you. And very well too.'

She stared at him for a long moment. Then that little lick of the top lip again—God, he wanted to be the one licking it.

'I have someone,' she said.

That brought a frown—fast and hard and very displeased. 'You told me at the party you didn't.'

'I'm seeing him tonight. We're working out an arrangement.'

'What kind of arrangement?'

She looked at him out of those clear eyes. 'A mutually satisfactory "friends with benefits" arrangement.'

'Work out an arrangement with me instead.'

'Phillip is forty.'

'Past his sexual prime.'

'Closer to my age.'

'How old are you, Katie?'

'Thirty-two. And it's Kate.'

'Then he's not closer to your age—I am. Five years versus eight years. And I want you more.'

'How could you possibly know that?'

'Because nobody could want you more than I do.' He leaned forward in his chair. 'And you owe me. One orgasm.'

'I'm not interested in having a toy boy.'

'And I'm not interested in being one.' He stared at her, wondering… And then he relaxed back in his chair. 'Aha! So *that* was it.'

'What are you talking about?'

'What happened at the party to make you run away. Amy said I was twenty-seven.'

'I don't do relationships.'

'Yeah—we covered that one.'

'People who are twenty-seven are in the prime age bracket for relationships.'

'Newsflash—so are people who are thirty-two.'

'I'm not like other thirty-two-year-olds.'

'And I'm not like other twenty-seven-year-olds. Remember? I'm the confirmed bachelor of Weeping Reef.'

'You said bachelor, but not *confirmed*.'

'I lied because I didn't want to scare you off.'

'Not exactly honourable.'

'That's because I'm not honourable. I have not one honourable intention when I look at you. Which won't bother you since you're not interested in relationships. So, Katie, you're going to have to tell your forty-year-old he's too late. Unless you didn't like what just happened…?'

Kate leaned back in her chair. Licked her top lip again, which was now almost bare of lipstick. It was heavy, brooding. He wanted it on his body.

'There's no reason I won't like it with Phillip just as much,' she said.

'What—you'd let Phillip go down on you on your desk during business hours, would you?'

'He wouldn't want to.'

'And that's why I'm the man for you. Because I would. I *did*. And I would do it again in a heartbeat, Katie.'

'Kate. And it's not a matter of liking. It's a matter of being clear what the end-game is so nobody gets hurt.'

'I don't get hurt.'

She looked startled. 'Everyone gets hurt.'

'Not me.'

'You've never been hurt?'

Scott's body tensed. *Redirect.* 'Let me put it this way. There's no need for either of us to get hurt. You mentioned the end-game. Why can't the end-game be sex? Pure and simple sex?'

Kate had picked up a pen and was tap, tap, tapping it on the desk. 'Pure and simple sex,' she said slowly. 'No strings?'

'You got it.'

Long moment. Tap, tap, tap. 'And if I were to lay some ground rules…? You wouldn't have a problem with that?'

'Lay away.'

'I'd need time. To think it through. Come up with an agreement.'

'I'm sure you already have the ground rules worked out for old man Phillip.'

'He's not old.'

'So your age fixation only works one way?'

No answer.

Scott smiled the Number One smile—*I am available for sex immediately*—as he got out his business card and tossed it onto her desk. 'You've got until I see you tonight to work out whatever rules you want—but, just to be clear, whether we come to an agreement or not, you owe me. If I leave this office and you suddenly have second thoughts about embarking on an affair with me, you still owe me. You. Owe. Me. And I'm not leaving until you give me a time and a place for tonight where you're going to pay me back. Katie. So let's have it.'

She was thinking—he could almost see her brain fizzing.

And then, 'Seven o'clock,' she announced. 'Come to my apartment.' She scribbled something on a sheet of paper and held it out to him. 'That's the address. And it's Kate.'

Scott reached for the paper, pocketed it.

Kate stood, walked around the desk to the door, opened it.

Scott got to his feet more slowly and followed her. But something about the controlled expression on her face got to him—so instead of walking out and heading merrily on his way, he stopped beside her, grabbed her upper arms, tugged her close and slammed his mouth hard on hers. Long, hot moment. Framed in the doorway for anyone who happened to be in the suite to see.

He released her just as suddenly, and smiled to see the combination of shock and desire on her face as he drew back.

'You've got no idea how much I'm going to need that debt paid when I see you at seven tonight,' he said softly.

And with that, he turned to wink at the unabashedly staring Deb and sauntered towards the exit.

As he reached it he heard Deb's voice. 'That was some five minutes, Kate. So, what will it be? Chicken and mung beans? Or do you need something more substantial—a chunk of raw meat, perhaps—to get your strength back?'

CHAPTER FOUR

RACING HOME AFTER WORK that evening, Kate was kicking herself for not going with her first instinct and simply supplanting Phillip with Scott at the bar. A quick twist of an arrangement already in place. Same bar. Same purpose. Just a different model.

She didn't know why the invitation to her apartment had popped out of her mouth instead.

Although, thinking back to that hot scene on her desk—God, her *desk*!—she figured it was probably just as well she'd gone for a more private option. If she couldn't control herself with Scott in her place of work, with Deb sitting just outside the door, how could she trust herself not to perform her payback sex act in the bar, on her knees under the table?

An image that got her so turned on she switched the water temperature of the shower to cold before getting under the spray.

Lust was still fizzing under her skin when she got out, so choosing something to wear took on a whole new meaning—because it had to be something that could come off easily.

Forgoing underwear, she grabbed a loose, tissue-thin shift in a rich russet colour. *Very* easy to take off when the moment came. And she hoped the outline of her body under the fine silk would drive Scott a little crazy in the meantime—payback for how crazy he'd driven *her*.

She left her hair loose. Put on a minimum of make-up. No lipstick—her mouth was going to be all over him, and she didn't want to leave a trail over his clothes or his skin.

She was so full of nervous energy, she caught herself pacing the floor while she waited for him. At this rate one touch of his clever fingers would have her unravelling—and she was *not* going to unravel twice in one day! She poured herself a glass of very cold white wine and forced her fidgety limbs onto the couch, trying to summon at least a semblance of composure.

The intercom buzzed at six fifty-nine p.m. and she closed her eyes, taking a deep breath. *This was it.*

As she let Scott in she ran her eyes over his body—white T-shirt, jeans. Very cool, very gorgeous. Her eyes kept going. Down to his…

Oh.

Converse All Star sneakers.

Cool, gorgeous… and *young.*

Those sneakers were *not* something forty-year-old Phillip would wear.

Twenty-seven. Okay, wake-up call. What the hell had she been thinking? She forced her eyes away from his feet, up to his eyes, preparing to tell him the deal was off.

But the look on his face gave her pause.

Kate had never seen such taut grimness—and she'd seen some very grim faces in the courtroom. His look got more taut and even more grim as he ran his eyes over her dress, all the way down to her bare feet and back up.

'Is something wrong?' she asked, alarmed.

'Yes,' he said, and his voice was every bit as grim as his face. 'I've been replaying that scene in your office in my head all afternoon, and I'm so desperate to get my hands on you I can't think straight. So let's skip the pleasantries.'

He nodded at the glass of wine on the coffee table.

'I don't want the drink you're probably going to offer me. I'm not into mood music, so don't bother asking me what I want to listen to. No need for a tour of the apartment—I can see it's nice and modern and open-plan. Don't give a rat's about the view. And the only thing I want to eat is you. *Again.*' Strained smile. 'Now, are we doing the ground rules before or after I get my orgasm?'

'Before,' Kate said, any thought of backing away from

their agreement obliterated by the heat of his words, the wild rush of desire that bolted through her.

'Then let's do it fast. Before I explode.'

The air was thick with lust as she guided him to the dining table, handed him the pages she'd prepared for their signatures.

'So we're—what?' he asked. 'Signing a contract?'

She nodded. 'With a contract we'll both know where we stand, what we can expect. It keeps things uncomplicated.'

Scott laughed, but didn't refuse, so Kate started running through the clauses.

She didn't even make it through the first one before Scott cut her off. 'Katie—you want a contract, then a contract it is. But it's a sex contract—not a pre-nup or a business merger. And it's not even legally enforceable, as we both know. So can you just give me the basics? Then I'll sign—there's no way I won't—and we can move on to implementing it. Because if I have to see your nipples poking against that dress for much longer without touching you, I am going to go freaking insane.'

The sudden throb between Kate's thighs had her squirming on her chair.

'I see I'm not the only one eager to get to the implementation stage,' he said, and with an inarticulate *I give up* growl reached out to cup one of her breasts through the silk.

She felt her nipple tighten even further. He pinched it gently, once. She gasped, he groaned, and then he wrenched his hand away and shot out of his seat.

'Going to need a drink after all,' he said. 'No—don't get up. Faster if I get it myself while you start going through the rules.' He headed for her kitchen, with a final prompt. 'Come on, Katie. Get it done for pity's sake. I can hear you, I can see you—go.'

'Right,' she said. *Basics*. Basics were good. Fast was good. The sooner they agreed on the terms, the sooner she could have him.

Cupboard opening…clacking of a glass on the kitchen counter.

'Two nights per week,' she said.

Fridge door opening…closing. 'What if I want more?'

'Two per week is the minimum. We can negotiate additional days as required.'

He was pouring. 'Okay. Next.'

'Any costs incurred in pursuit of mutual sexual pleasure to be split fifty-fifty.'

He was back with his wine. 'I can live with that.'

'No public displays of affection.'

He was sitting. 'Done,' he said. 'Nauseating stuff, PDAs.'

'No kissing unless it's sex-related.'

Scott held up a 'stop' hand. 'Hang on. When is kissing between an unrelated man and woman ever *not* sex-related?'

She was blushing—she could feel it. Because this was an embarrassing clause. It presupposed he would *want* to kiss her outside of sex. But kisses led to affection. And trouble lay down that road. So, embarrassing or not, it was best to have it covered in advance.

'I mean no kisses hello, goodbye—that sort of thing,' she said. 'Only kisses that lead to or are the result of sex.'

Scott looked at her mouth for a long moment. She thought he was going to object. But then he shrugged.

'Okay,' he said. 'Go on.'

'Fantasies,' Kate said, and felt the blush deepen.

'We get *fantasies*?' Scott asked reverently. 'Yee-ha!'

Kate rolled her eyes, but she was smiling. 'I thought you'd like that part of the deal. There are still rules, however. I'm suggesting a start phrase—if one or the other of us decides to enact a fantasy, a text message with "Play Time" is all that's required—along with the date, time and place. And, of course, any outfits, devices and accessories will be provided by the fantasy's owner.'

'If you could see inside my mind…'

Kate laughed. 'I'm sure I'll be seeing what's inside it very soon. But in addition to a start phrase we'll need a trigger word which, when said, will stop the activity should one of us become uncomfortable with what's happening.'

'Why not just "stop"?'

'Because that might be part of the fantasy—either a version of "stop" or "don't stop". Or it could mean "pause" or "wait" just as easily as it could mean "no more". Better to have something unambiguous. Like...maybe...a name? Something that couldn't be mistaken for anything else and wouldn't have anything to do with sex.'

Scott smiled—a particularly cool smile that made his eyes look like ice. 'Let's go with "Hugo", in that case,' he said.

'Hugo?'

'I can assure you that will stop me in my tracks.'

'Fine,' Kate agreed. 'I don't know any Hugos, so it won't be confusing for me.'

'What else?' Scott asked, hands clenching and unclenching with impatience.

'We're up to confidentiality. The details of this contract must remain confidential.'

'Okay. Are we done?'

'Last point. Fidelity is assumed—'

'Absolutely,' Scott agreed promptly. 'I don't share.'

'I haven't finished. Fidelity is assumed, but should an unforeseen sexual encounter occur with someone other than the two parties covered by the agreement—if you or I—'

'Yes,' he interrupted. 'I know what you mean. If you sleep with someone other than me; if I do someone other than you...'

'Yes. If that happens it must be confessed prior to the resumption of any contracted sexual activity between us.'

But it seemed Scott had reached his limit.

He whipped the pages out of Kate's hand, grabbed the pen, flipped to the final clause, scratched out some words, added something and initialled the changes.

'That's my input,' he said. 'No infidelity or the contract is null and void.'

Kate thought about insisting that it remain, because fidelity was for real relationships and this was not one of those—but in all honesty it was a relief. She'd seen too much of the aftermath of infidelity to be sanguine about it under any circumstances.

So... 'All right,' she said. 'Should one of us seek our pleasure elsewhere, the agreement is broken.'

'You won't need to look elsewhere, Katie. I'll keep you so busy you'll be begging for a break.'

He picked up the pen again, ready to sign.

'Wait,' Kate said, snatching the pen from him before he could put it to paper. She licked nervously at her top lip. 'Scott, I think you should read the contract properly before you sign. You've found one clause you didn't like—there may be some wording that's unclear, or something else you're uncomfortable with when you have time to think about it. And I don't want to feel like I'm taking advantage of your youth.'

Scott's eyes narrowed. 'I'm twenty-seven—not stupid,' he said. 'And I hope we're not going to waste a lot of time talking about my age. Otherwise I'll be calling "Play Time" pretty damned fast and spanking you—and that's not even a fantasy of mine.'

'Not? Really?'

'Really. Not into pain—giving or receiving.'

'No spanking. Got it. Good. But, back on topic, you're not as experienced with the law as I am, so—'

'Boring subject. And not *germane*—there's a lawyer word for you, to prove that not all twenty-seven-year-olds are ignorant morons. I just love lawyer words.'

'Yes, but—'

'Am I deeding my firstborn child to you?'

'No.'

'Am I beholden to you for the rest of my life?'

'No—just a month. Through to the twenty-eighth of February.'

'Maybe I'd better read the contract, then, because that's not going to work for us unless there's an automatic rollover in there. Considering the size and intensity of my hard-on all three times I've been near you, I'm going to need longer than a month to do you every way I want to.'

Kate took a long, slow, silent breath. She'd never been with a man who talked so blatantly about sex. It should have been a turn-off—so why did it have the opposite effect? She had the feeling that if Scott Knight had bought her a martini and asked *'Just how dirty do you like it?'* she would have offered to show him on the spot.

'Yes,' she said, 'there is a rollover option in there.'

'Right—so give me the damned pen.'

Kate watched as he scrawled his signature.

It made a funny feeling erupt in her stomach—almost as if she owned a part of him with that one dashed name. For a moment it frightened her. She didn't want to own him. Didn't want him to own *her*. Not in any way, shape or form.

He handed her the pen and she hesitated.

'They're your rules,' Scott said, reading her easily. 'So sign.'

She signed.

And then Scott pushed his chair back from the table, looked across at her. All that grimness was back, tenfold.

'Now, come here,' he said.

CHAPTER FIVE

KATE WALKED OVER to him.

'I love that dress,' he said. '*Love* that dress. But take it off.'

Kate forced herself to go slowly as she reached for the sides of the dress and started to roll the fine silk between her fingertips, raising the hem gradually. Their first experience, in the office, had been frantic and fast, sudden and shocking and blind. This time she wanted to control it. To offer herself to him one piece at a time. Tease him. Wow him.

Payback.

Scott leaned forward in his seat, eyes intent on the hem inching upwards, until she reached her upper thighs. She paused there as Scott's breathing became harsher, choppier. One more roll. Another. Bringing the hem higher up, up—until she was exposed from the hips down.

She saw Scott swallow as his eyes focused. 'Like fire…' he whispered. 'Come closer.'

Kate took two steps until she was standing an arm's length away. He reached out to touch, smoothed his fingers over the narrow strip of dark red hair.

'Let me in.'

She adjusted her stance and Scott slipped his fingers between her legs, playing there until she was gasping.

He looked up at her. 'Keep going. I want to see all of you.'

With that, Kate lost any desire for taking things slowly—so much for control!—and reefed the dress up and off. She tossed it to the floor and stood naked before him.

He kept his fingers moving in the moisture between her thighs while he looked up at her. He swallowed again as she pulled her hair back over her shoulders. The movement tightened her breasts, as if she was offering them to him.

His fingers stilled, slipped out of her, and Kate almost protested.

He sat back, eyes all over her. 'You are the sexiest thing I've ever seen,' he said hoarsely, and with a determination that was almost intimidating bent to remove his sneakers.

He got to his feet, reached into his back pocket for a condom, held it out to her.

She took it and instantly started ripping the packet. Scott—with sharp, efficient movements—took off his T-shirt, unzipped his jeans, pushed them and his underwear down and off.

And, God, he was gorgeous. Hard. Huge. Perfect.

He reached for her, pulled her in, groaned long and low as their naked bodies connected, slid together.

'I'm sorry, but this won't take long,' he said. 'We're not going to make it to the bedroom. Not this first time.'

He pulled back, jaw clenched tight. Nodded at the condom in her hand. 'Put that on me and I'll try not to come while you do it.'

Trembling, eager, Kate complied, while Scott uttered a string of low-voiced curses. And then he basically stumbled back, pulling Kate with him, until he was sitting on the chair again.

'Straddle me,' he said. 'I can get more deeply into you from this position. And I want to go deep. Deep and hard. Okay?'

'Okay,' Kate said, in a breathy voice she hardly recognised as her own.

She slid onto his lap, wrapped her legs around him, around the chair. He held her hips, settling her, then shifted so her bottom was in his hands, manipulating her so she was more perfectly positioned for his entry. Another groan, this time against her neck, followed by a sucking kiss there. Then, with one almost vicious thrust, Scott was inside her, pulling her closer, closer. Another sucking kiss on her neck and then his mouth was on hers, kissing her deeply, tongue plunging within, licking her top lip, back inside her mouth.

'Best—the best ever—to be inside you,' he said against her lips.

And somehow those not very romantic words pushed Kate over the edge and into orgasm. She grabbed his face. Pulled his mouth closer, too close for words, and fed him gasping kisses until he followed her, with one long, last, deep thrust, into an explosive orgasm.

Best. Ever.

Those two small words were all Scott could think of as he came back to earth after the most mind-blowing release of his life.

Kate. So jaw-droppingly sexy. Looks that were almost taunting, they were so hot. She'd met him thrust for thrust, taken him as deep and as hard as he wanted to go, kissed the wits right out of his head.

He snuggled her close for a long, quiet moment, stroking her hair gently now that the first rampage of lust had passed. He felt her heartbeats and his, in unison, starting to slow. But he figured he'd never have a normal heartbeat around Kate. She fired his blood like nothing he'd ever experienced. Everyone else he'd ever been with paled in comparison. Every other one was a girl. But Kate was a woman.

And, for now at least, *his* woman.

At the thought, he felt himself start to harden again, still inside her.

She laughed, low and deep. She'd felt that, then.

She pulled back and looked into his eyes. Kissed him again, lush and soft, and he got harder still.

He stood, bringing Kate with him. Her legs wrapped automatically around him.

'Bedroom's back there,' she said with a head movement.

'I hope it's a single,' he said with a laugh as she squirmed against him. 'Because anything wider than that is going to be a waste of space.'

* * *

Three hours later Scott got quietly out of Kate's bed, pulled on his jeans and T-shirt, and looked down at her.

She was deeply asleep, no doubt exhausted after what he'd put her through. Even when he hadn't been able to get it up after that third time he hadn't stopped touching her. Mouth, hands…all over her.

Best. Sex. Ever.

He thought about leaving and going home—but that felt… wrong. Sneaking away as though he'd got what he came for and didn't have to linger. Not that Kate would mind, given the contract. Sex—just sex. The end-game. He could sneak away and it wouldn't be regarded as sneaking by either of them.

But they hadn't had dinner and he was too hungry to leave. She would be too if she woke before morning. He padded into the kitchen, checking the contents of the cupboards and fridge. Not overly stocked, but he could fix omelettes.

Making himself at home—as he always seemed to do in kitchens—Scott got busy with eggs and whisk and was soon sliding his perfectly cooked omelette onto a plate. He grabbed a glass of wine—making a mental note to bring some beer to leave in Kate's fridge—and pondered where he should sit to eat.

But it was no contest—and he knew it in his heart.

He'd said earlier that he wasn't interested in the view from Kate's apartment. And in that first hot burst of screaming desire it had been true—she was the only thing of interest to him.

But he knew what the view was, and now that the edge had been taken off his caveman libido he wanted to see it.

Rushcutters Marina, where he'd boarded his first yacht as a child and learned to sail. Sailing had become a passion. His one and only rebellion had been taking that year to sail in the Whitsundays rather than go straight to university the way his parents wanted, the way his perfect, by-the-book brother had. For Scott, sailing had been…*freedom.* And even though he'd given up sailing, there was something about boats that just kept pulling at him.

So he settled himself at Kate's girl-sized outdoor table and looked out at the water as he ate. It should have been peaceful but, as ever, he found peace elusive.

He finished his omelette and walked over to the edge of the terrace, looking out at the water, listening to the gentle lap of it against the boats.

It was so different from the Whitsundays, and yet it made him remember that time eight years ago at Weeping Reef. The six of them—Willa, Luke, Amy, Chantal, Brodie and him—had formed what they'd imagined would be a lifelong bond, when their lives had been just beginning, only to see that bond disintegrate before that one summer was over.

All because of a love triangle.

One moment Chantal was Scott's girl; the next she was Brodie's. No words needed. Because everyone had been able to see it, just from the way they'd looked at each other.

Brodie was the only person Scott had ever confided in about all his childhood crap—and it had been hard to deal with his best friend slipping straight into the place his brother usually occupied in his tortured mind: the best, number one. As the white-hot knowledge had hit, Scott had lashed out, and everything had crashed and burned.

Scott and Chantal, both stuck working at Weeping Reef for the summer, had never recovered the friendship that had been between them before they'd become lovers.

Brodie had simply disappeared.

And Scott had missed him every single day. He *still* missed him.

The fight seemed so stupid, looking back. But that was what happened when you combined too many beers and too much unseasoned testosterone.

Chantal was just a girl—albeit it a smart, beautiful, wonderful girl—and what they'd had was a romance of proximity. They'd arrived at the resort before the others, and everyone had automatically assumed they were an item because they looked perfect together. A default relationship. With occasional sex that had been fun but hardly earth-shattering.

The fight hadn't been about Chantal. Scott knew that with hindsight. That fight had been all about *him*. About never being quite good enough to win the prize. Never being quite good enough to *be* the prize.

At least he'd learned from the experience. Learned not to trust. Learned to take control of his emotions and hang on to that control at all costs. Learned to keep his pride intact. Learned not to care too deeply. About friends…or lovers.

Now, if only he could work out how to deal with the restlessness that had followed him ever since, he'd be happy. But it was as if he was in a constant battle with himself: *let go and just be; don't ever let go; let go; don't let go; just be...*

'Couldn't you sleep?'

The soft question from behind him startled him out of his heavy thoughts. Scott took a moment to school his features. And then he turned, dialled up a smile—one that was a little bit naughty, a little bit *sex me up*—which he routinely used on women he'd just laid.

Kate was wearing a loose, light dressing gown, and looked tousled and natural and lovely.

'You wore me out, Katie,' he said. 'I needed fuel, so I made myself an omelette. I'll make one for you too—because if you tell me I didn't wear you out in return, I'll die of shame.'

She chuckled. 'Oh, I'm worn out, I promise. We're equal.'

She came over to stand beside him and he found himself drawing her close, tucking her against his side, under his arm.

'I think that qualifies as a PDA,' Kate said.

'We're not in public, so how can it?'

He felt her sigh at his dodge-master answer but she didn't say anything, so he kept her there, under his arm. It was… restful, somehow.

'I love this view,' she said after a long moment.

'Best harbour in the world.'

'Yes,' she said slowly. 'But it's more about the boats for me. The thought of sailing away from your troubles, beginning a wonderful adventure. The freedom of it. I've often dreamt about stealing a yacht and just going.'

She must have felt the slight jerk he gave, because she turned her face up to his, frowning.

'What?'

'A lawyer? Stealing? *Sacré bleu.*'

Her eyes narrowed. 'Yes, but that's not really it, is it?'

Pause. And then he laughed—even managing to make it sound natural. 'What you said just reminded me of my own sailing adventures, that's all. And not that I want to burst your bubble, but reality will bite you on the arse wherever you are.'

'Ah, of course—I forgot you were a sailing instructor at Weeping Reef. You and the other guy I haven't met yet. Brodie?'

That was all it took for Scott to tense up. Brodie's name coming out of Kate's mouth. He didn't want to talk about Brodie. It was too personal, too…raw. God, *still.*

'So what part of it bit you?' Kate asked.

'Let's just say I was too young to appreciate the experience,' he said, and forced himself to smile down at her. This smile meant *go no further*—and he didn't have to use it often because he didn't let people get close enough to push his buttons.

'And, no,' he added quickly, thinking to nip in the bud any other question she might have brewing, 'that's not an invitation to tell me I'm still too young. I'm old enough to have made the sensible choice: sail back to Sydney, go to university, become an architect. All grown-up—just like you. Now, are you ready for your omelette?'

He could sense her slight hesitancy. Another question…? A comment…? But Kate finally shrugged, smiled. And thankfully gave up.

'How lucky am I?' she said. 'A man who sizzles in bed *and* in the kitchen.'

'I like cooking—the orderliness of it. You put a set number of ingredients together and, as long as you combine them in the right order, they come out at the other end in perfect formation.'

Kate grimaced. 'My cooking doesn't do that!'

'Mine does. I insist on it.'

He leaned down and kissed her.

'No kissing,' Kate said, pulling away awkwardly after a moment. 'Not outside of sex. Remember the rules.'

'Oh, yeah, the rules.'

Well, Scott happened to think parts of her contract were ridiculous, as *well* as not being legally enforceable. So not only was he *not* going to be controlled by her rules, he was going to enjoy flouting them. The kissing clause was a case in point. He liked kissing Kate, so he was going to keep kissing her. Simple.

'You know, Katie, a kiss isn't a declaration of honourable intentions, if that's what's bothering you. I assure you my intentions are still *entirely* dishonourable—so relax. It shouldn't surprise you, as the owner of that sexy-as-hell mouth, that men want to kiss it.'

'But—'

Scott swooped before she could get another word out, kissing her again, drawing from the deep well of expertise he'd amassed during an impressive career of seduction. And this time it took her longer to pull away.

'Scott!'

'Hey, this is pre-contract,' he argued. 'We're still on payback sex, by my reckoning.'

'I owed you one orgasm. And I paid that back on the dining room chair. We're on the clock now—and I can't believe you're blurring the rules on day one.'

'Then if it makes you feel better,' he said, grabbing her hands and pulling her in close, '*this* kiss is going to lead to sex.'

And with that, he lowered his head once more, put his mouth on hers. He felt her melt, melt, melting into him. *That* was control. He would control this. Control *her* through her precious contract. Take what he wanted when he wanted it with a clear conscience and no hard feelings when they said goodbye at the end. He'd finally achieved perfection in a relationship!

Not that this was a relationship.

Scott nudged her legs apart, settled himself between them, thrust against her. 'See? I'm ready for you already.'

'Is that perma-erection of yours a benefit of youth?' she asked, leaning into him.

'I could be a hundred years old and five days dead and still want you, Katie,' he said in return. 'Let's go to bed and I'll show you how much. And *then* I'll make you an omelette before I head home.'

CHAPTER SIX

KATE DIDN'T KNOW if it was youthful vigour or if Scott just had more testosterone than the average man, but he'd been at her apartment nine nights in a row. He'd only skipped the tenth night because he had a pre-scheduled poker night—and he'd bemoaned not being able to get out of *that*!

Each time they'd both been insatiable, from the moment he stepped inside to the moment he staggered out, bleary-eyed, in the wee hours.

By tacit agreement Scott never stayed the night. That would have been too...intimate. And, okay, that seemed ridiculous, given the extent to which they'd examined each other's bodies—she'd seen the kitten-shaped birthmark on Scott's right butt cheek, for God's sake, so cute it hurt—but there was something 'next step' about sleeping together. And the contract didn't allow for next steps.

Their nine encounters had included two Play Times.

The first Play Time Scott had turned up as a doctor making a house call. Doctor/patient had been hilarious, to start with. But it had quickly progressed to hot, hot, hot as he'd gloved up and examined various parts of her body, sounding cool and professional with his 'How does that feel?' and 'Is that helping?' while she squirmed and gasped and orgasmed in a long, crazy, unending stream.

Their second Play Time, on their ninth night together, he'd opted for master/slave—but with a midway role-swap.

For the first part of the evening Kate had been the master. Which was just as well, because her phone had been running so hot she would have made an unsatisfactorily preoccupied sex slave. Her client Rosie was in crisis mode, having finally asked for a divorce, and was calling Kate every fifteen minutes for advice. Another client was desperate for help because his ex-wife was threatening to move interstate with their two children. And a colleague wanted advice on a property settlement.

None of it had seemed to faze Scott, who'd taken to his slave role like a duck to water and lavished attention on her as she'd stressed on the phone. Making her tea, massaging her shoulders and feet, rubbing her back, stroking her hair...

And when the phone had finally stopped ringing he'd reduced her to a state of orgasmic bliss. By which time she'd been *dying* to be his slave and would have agreed to anything he asked.

But Scott had issued only one command: that she accompany him to the Visionary Architect Awards dinner.

Which was how now, two nights later, Kate found herself in her best evening gown—a modernised cheongsam in royal purple satin—her hair pinned into a complicated bun, her face flawlessly made-up, essentials stuffed into a glittery silver evening bag...

And feeling all kinds of weird.

A date that wasn't a date.

With a lover who wasn't a boyfriend.

And, despite her being Scott's 'slave' tonight, he'd insisted on coming to her door to get her, like an old-fashioned gentleman caller.

It was...*confusing*. And Kate knew she wouldn't be any less confused by the end of the night. Because not only was Scott a master manipulator, adept at getting her to do whatever he wanted, he was also a champion question-deflector. If she asked him something he didn't want to answer he would just kiss her! And if she complained about kissing being against the rules he would insist the kiss was going to lead to sex, and the next moment they'd be in bed.

Kate had never had so much sex in her life! Or so few answers.

And the upshot was that she wanted to know...well, *everything*!

She was even insanely curious about what Scott would be wearing tonight—something she'd never, ever contemplated ahead of dates with other men…*not* that this *was* a date. How ridiculous was that? It was a black-tie event: ergo, Scott would be in black tie. No need to be curious because all men looked pretty much the same in black tie.

A thought that went straight out of her head—along with the rest of her grey matter—when she opened the door to him and her heart did a thudding swoon.

He was just *so* gorgeous.

Tux in navy blue. Formal shirt in black, not white. He'd forgone the bow tie. Shoes that were buckled, not laced. He looked modern and edgy and scrumptious. Exactly the way an award-winning architect should look.

'Wow!' she said, after a moment of stunned silence.

'Wow yourself!' he responded, and kissed her. 'I wish I'd come over after the game last night, because now I think I'm suffering withdrawal symptoms. I don't know how I'm going to keep my hands off you during dinner.'

And as Kate's heart swooned again—at the kiss, at his words—she wondered if she could invoke *her* first Play Time and whisk Scott off at some stage of the evening for some restroom sex. And she'd *never* wanted to try that before.

Scott took her hand—hmm, PDA or just giving her some support for her five-inch heels?—and didn't let go until they reached his car. When Kate did a double-take, because it was a red Mini—not at all what she would have expected. Not that she'd given a lot of thought to what car Scott would drive, but shouldn't it be a little less…well, *cute*? A little more macho? Like maybe a black off-road truck. Something that did not remind her that he had a kitten-shaped birthmark she would love to see *right that second.*

Scott opened the car door for her and helped her in before getting behind the wheel.

'I hate these events,' he said as he buckled his seat belt. 'So thank you for not leaving me sad and dateless.'

'I'm your slave, remember? I didn't have a choice.'

'Hey, yeah—I forgot!' he said. 'So in that case I would like a kiss for the road.'

'Your wish...my command,' Kate said, and leaned over to give him a steamy, lingering kiss. Even though that kiss was not going to lead to sex. *Uh-oh.* She was getting as bad as him.

But at least he was looking suitably scorched when she eased back.

'Definitely not going to keep my hands off you during dinner,' Scott said fervently.

Kate laughed. 'Not that I believe for a moment that a phone call to the first name in your little black book wouldn't have snagged you a date.'

'Not wishing to sound like an egomaniac, but that is true. The fidelity clause, however, is a killer,' he said. 'How ungallant it would have been, beating off my lascivious companion at the end of the night.'

'You're not telling me your dates always end in sex?'

'Aren't I?'

Kate dutifully laughed—but the idea of him even thinking about sex with another woman was somehow unsettling. And the fact that it unsettled her was...well, *that* was unsettling too.

'You're the one who got fussy about that fidelity clause,' she reminded him, aiming for a nonchalance she just couldn't make herself feel. 'If it's a hardship to give up all those women out there panting for you, you only have to say the word.'

'I'm not risking you ditching me that fast.'

'Who says I'd ditch you? Maybe I wouldn't care.'

He shot her a curious look. 'You honest-to-God wouldn't have minded if I'd done the deed elsewhere tonight?'

'We'll never know, will we?'

'Yeah—not buying it,' he said. 'You wouldn't have liked it. And—just to remind you—I definitely *would* mind, so no going there for you.' Quick, cheeky grin at her. 'Not that you need to.'

'Oh, the confidence of youth.'

Another grin. 'Not youth—*skill*, Katie. And, for the record, it's not that I couldn't have resisted Anais—she's the first A in my black book, by the way—because I could have. It's that I didn't want to hurt her feelings with a knockback she wouldn't have been expecting. So, you see, you had to come to spare the poor girl's feelings.'

'Oh, so this is all about me doing Anais a favour!'

'Well, you can't deny you've got a soft spot for the oppressed.'

'Has Willa been talking about my imminent canonisation again?'

'Nope. I just know, Saint Kate. When you were on the phone two nights ago I sensed weeping aplenty and a fair amount of teeth-gnashing at the other end of the line—and I heard how you dealt with it.' Scott reached for her hand, brought it to his mouth, kissed it. 'All class.'

Kate, uncharacteristically flustered, had to swallow twice before she could force herself back into banter mode and once more to actually find her voice.

'And poor Anais is oppressed *how*, exactly?' she asked—and was relieved the question had come out light and amused.

'All right, you got me,' Scott said, rueful. 'Anais is not oppressed. In fact, she tried to oppress *me*!'

'You? Oppressed? *Puh-lease.*'

'She *did*! Bondage and discipline. *Ouch.* Evil. I cried like a baby.'

Kate couldn't help it. She laughed. 'So that's what I have to do to keep you in line, is it?'

'No. I told you—I'm not into all that. All you have to do to keep me in line, Katie, is redirect your soft spot where it's needed.'

'And where would that be?'

'Well, to me, obviously. Haven't you been listening? I'm oppressed.'

'You need a little more oppression,' Kate said dryly, and when he laughed, sounding boyish and completely irresistible, she found herself wanting to kiss him again.

She decided a subject-change was required for her own sanity.

'So, what are the chances of Silverston taking the prize tonight?' she asked.

Scott waited a moment. 'Did you look it up?'

'Well, yes, of course. What kind of slave would I be if I didn't know what award my master was up for? Creative Residential. Five finalists.'

'I'm not expecting to win.' He sounded offhand—but his hands had tightened on the steering wheel.

'Why not?' she asked.

A shrug, but no answer. Just one of those smiles that she thought he must have stacked up like a jukebox—pick one and play it.

'I hope the food is good, because I'm starving,' he said. 'What's the bet it'll be smoked salmon out of a packet, followed by overdone steak with three vegetables on the side, then chocolate mousse?'

Which, of course, was not an answer. And it seemed she wasn't going to get one, because Scott kept the conversation flowing around a host of boy subjects—which Kate suspected had been deliberately chosen—for the rest of the drive.

Sports results—*please, kill her*—action movies, gory television shows.

By the time they arrived at the five-star hotel where the event was being held, Scott had a new jukebox smile pasted on—a smile that said *I'm here! No big deal!*

But it became obvious very quickly to Kate that his arrival was, in fact, a *very* big deal—to everyone except him. As pre-event cocktails were served outside the ballroom people made their way to Scott in a steady stream, drawn as though by a magnet. But although Scott smiled, chatted, shook hands, kissed a score of female cheeks, he held everyone at bay...and they didn't even realise he was doing it. He was effortlessly, carelessly charismatic, and people clearly wanted to be in his orbit, but he was essentially untouchable.

What the hell...?

Kate remembered what he'd said that day in her office. *I don't get hurt.* She was starting to believe it was true. To get hurt you had to be close to someone. And dial-a-smile Scott wasn't close. To *anyone*. The question was: why not?

'Bored?' Scott asked her, leaning in close.

'No. Why?'

'You were staring off into space.'

'Oh, just…thinking. But not bored.'

'Well, *I'm* bored. Slave or not, I'm going to have to think up a way to reward you for sacrificing your night to this tedium.'

'Just win the prize,' she said.

Instantly his eyes shuttered. 'Hmmm.'

That was all he said. *Hmmm.*

What the hell...?

'Have the organisers already notified the winners?' Kate asked, puzzled. 'Is that why you're so sure you're not going to win?'

'No. It's not— No.'

'Then…what?'

One of those dismissive shrugs. 'I just don't.'

'Don't what?'

'Win. That's the way it is, Katie.' He looked over her shoulder. 'Ah, the doors are opening. Let's go in and try not to…' His eyes widened, his voice trailed off. Then, 'Damn,' he said under his breath. 'He *is* here.'

Kate turned to see what he was seeing. 'What? Who? Oh! He looks like—'

'Me.'

'Only—'

'Taller.'

'Well, yes, but—'

'Better-looking.'

'I was going to say "older".'

His eyes zoomed to her. 'Are you going to tell me he's more

age-appropriate for a thirty-two-year-old? Because if you are—don't. I'm not up to another discussion about my age.'

Kate could only blink. She seemed to be thinking *What the hell?* a lot tonight but…well, *what the hell…?*

His eyes roamed behind her again. 'Oh, for the love of God!'

Kate turned again as Scott's lookalike descended on them.

'Who *is* he?' she asked.

'My brother. His house is one of the finalists.'

That was all he had time to say before he was enveloped in a bear hug.

'Scottie!' his brother boomed out.

Scott stiffened, before giving his brother an awkward pat on the back.

Edging back as fast as he could, he took Kate's elbow and brought her closer. 'Kate—my brother Hugo.'

Hugo? As in Play Time? The word that would stop Scott in his tracks? *What the freaking hell…?* This evening was turning out to be very…instructive.

The resemblance between the two men wasn't as strong close-up. Hugo was like a more refined version of Scott. His eyes were brown, not green. And he spoke with a slightly British accent—very different from Scott's Aussie drawl. Kate thought the accent was an affectation until Hugo confessed, with the fakest attempt at self-deprecation Kate had ever heard, that he'd been to medical school in England.

He looked more conservative than Scott—from his sharp, perfect haircut to his traditional black-tie get-up. Hugo was more talkative, more…accessible. But there was something missing. That indefinable something Scott had in spades—that mix of charm and wit and sexy intrigue. Hugo was obviously smart. He was good-looking. A little stuffy, maybe, although he seemed like a decent guy. But nobody would rush to Hugo's side the way they rushed to Scott's.

Kate was on the point of filing that description away when Hugo raised the subject of the award, with a look at Scott that could only be described as *pitying*—and Kate's hackles rose, sharp and hard. Okay, description revised. Hugo was *not* a decent guy; Hugo was a bastard.

'So—Creative Residential! Who would have thought we'd end up competing *again*, Scottie?' Hugo asked, with a heavy clap on Scott's back. 'I checked out Silverston on the website. Good job, Scottie. *Really* good job.'

'Thank you,' Scott said with a smile that was definitely forced.

Kate, *hating* that smile, blinked innocently up at Hugo. 'You're not a doctor *and* an architect, are you, Hugo?'

'Well, no, but—'

'So your *architect* is the finalist?' More wide-eyed *I don't understand* innocence.

'Yes, my man Waldo.'

'Oh, your *man*. I see. Scott's client is leaving the honours to him. Credit where it's due, right?' Kate asked, and hoped Scott's client wouldn't embarrass her by appearing out of nowhere!

Hugo chuckled, oblivious to any insult. 'Ah, but I had considerable input into Waldo's design,' he explained. 'So when I asked if I could come along this evening, of course Waldo was only too happy. Especially when I told him there would be a little friendly family rivalry for the prize.'

Scott, whose eyes had frosted in a way that did not look at all friendly, raised his eyebrows. '*Waldo* let you have a say? Waldo *Kubrick*?' He turned to Kate. 'Waldo is brilliant—actually, the best. But he's more temperamental than a busload of French chefs.'

Hugo gave Scott another pitying look. 'Yes, he *is* the best, isn't he?' Then came an apologetic and yet not *at all* apologetic cough. 'Sorry, Scottie.'

'Sorry?' Scott asked. 'Why?'

There was something in Hugo's eyes that Kate didn't like. Something malicious.

'Let's just say Knightley is pretty special,' he said. 'The buzz is there.'

Kate felt a laugh building and had to bite the inside of her cheek hard. Knightley? His house was called *Knightley*?

'Yes, it is,' Scott said coolly, and gestured towards the ballroom. 'Well, good luck, Hugo. We're heading in.'

And then Scott turned to Kate—who was trying not to laugh and at the same time silently communicating to Scott that she knew why the name *Hugo* would stop him in his Play Time tracks—and something lit in his eyes as he took in the expression on her face. And his smile, for the very first time, was in his eyes.

And it was absolutely devastating.

Scott felt a little off-balance.

It had been a lightning-fast emotional shift—from the normal feeling of inadequacy he always experienced around his brother to wanting to take Kate in his arms right there in front of Hugo, to whom he never, ever introduced *anyone*. And not only take her in his arms but breathe her right into his body. All because she'd wanted to laugh. It didn't seem to matter that he didn't even know what had amused her. Not that Kate didn't usually laugh—she did, a lot, and he loved that. But there was just something different about it tonight.

'What's so funny?' he asked as he pulled out her chair.

She sat. Waited for him to sit beside her. 'Not that I want to disparage your brother, *Scottie*—'

He groaned.

'Sorry, but I owe you for all the Katies,' Kate said.

Wince. 'Yeah. I get it. No more Katies. Hand-on-heart promise.'

'But what is *with* that house name? Is Hugo an *Emma* fan? Or maybe his wife? Naming the house after Mr Knightley, perhaps?'

'Emma who?'

Kate rolled her eyes. 'Never mind. I think the explanation is simpler. He named it after *himself*, didn't he? Like one of those British stately homes?' She was biting the inside of her cheek again. 'Maybe he got the idea at med school…'

'Knightley,' Scott said slowly. '*Knightley.* Oh, my God. I didn't even think— It never occurred— I mean—God!' He sat, stunned, for a moment, and then he started laughing. '*God!*'

'It's not a laughing matter,' Kate admonished, but Scott could see she was struggling to keep a straight face. 'It's *de rigueur* to name your home after yourself, you know.' Her mouth was starting to twist. 'My own apartment is c-called C-Castle C-Cleary.'

And then Kate was laughing too, and the sound of it was just so sexy he had to touch her. Needed to share this delicious absurdity with her physically.

He reached for her hand and she twined her fingers with his, still laughing. Even her eyes were laughing. What must that be like? To have eyes that laughed? Eyes that were warm like molten silver. Beautiful.

His throat closed over and the laughter jammed. Stuck in his throat. All he could think about was kissing her until she was breathless. As breathless as he felt just looking at her. Breathless. And perfect. For once, perfect…

Kate stopped laughing too, and then she reached out with her free hand. Touched his face as if she felt it too. The connection.

And then panic hit.

No! No connection. He didn't want that.

He jerked back, away from her touch.

He looked at their joined hands, and the sight of their linked fingers jolted him like an electric shock. He let go.

He picked up his wine glass, took an urgent swallow. And then, eyes sliding away to some distant point, he cleared his throat.

Kate cleared her own throat, picked up her own wine glass, sipped. He heard the quick breath she took.

'So…um…what's it like?' she asked, putting the words out hesitantly into the sudden, excruciating void.

Wine. He needed another sip. Took it. Put the glass down. 'What's what like?'

'Knightley?'

Shrug. 'I know as much as you do about Knightley. Just what I've seen on the awards website.' He waved at someone across the room.

'So it must be… Is it…? Is it brand-new, then? I mean that you haven't seen it?'

'No,' he said. 'I just haven't. Seen it, I mean.'

Their first course arrived, and Scott almost sagged with relief. He pasted on a cheerful smile, and at last he could look at her again. 'Well, Kate—as you can see, I was on the money with the smoked salmon.'

From that point the seemingly endless procession of award presentations, cheesy entertainment and bland food courses proceeded exactly as Scott had expected. Except for one thing: a burning awareness of Kate beside him. Something he'd never felt with Anais or any of his other black-bookers at one of these insipid evenings.

And that bothered him.

Even the way she was captivating the architect on her other side was getting to him. Thank God Miles Smithers was sixty years old and happily married, or he'd probably want to smash the guy's tee—

Whoa! Pull up. There was no thanking God required. Or teeth-smashing. It didn't matter if Kate was captivating a sixty-year-old married architect or a thirty-two-year-old billionaire Greek god! If she was physically faithful she could captivate whomever the hell she wanted to captivate. None of his business.

And it wasn't as though he was being a scintillating conversationalist himself. If not for Miles, Kate would be catatonic! He was being a first-class boor, barely grunting a reply when she asked him anything.

All because of that…that moment. That intense connection which he hadn't bargained for and didn't bloody well want.

Having Hugo sitting two tables away, already looking every inch the victor, wasn't helping either.

Scott had known his brother wouldn't be able to stay away tonight, wouldn't be able to vacate the space, just for once, and let Scott occupy it. But he'd been anticipating a hand-wave and a superior nod across the room—that was their usual interaction. It must have been the sight of Kate that had prompted Hugo to dial it up a notch.

Kate. So glamorous and secure and beautiful. Out of his league. Which Hugo would have seen at a glance. So he probably should have guessed Hugo wouldn't have been able to resist coming over in person to foreshadow his win.

And Knightley *would* win.

Because Hugo *always* won, even if he had to win via a third party like Waldo.

When the Creative Residential category was announced Hugo looked directly at him. There was a tiny narrowing of his eyes, an oh-so-poignant smile—a look Scott had being seeing all his life. A look that said *Sorry, I just can't help it that I'm so much better than you, little brother.* Even more insufferable than usual because Kate saw it. And, God, how he wished he could get her out of there so she didn't have to see it again when he lost. Why, why, *why* had he brought her?

Knightley was the second finalist announced. Pictures flashed up on the huge screen at the front of the room and—yes—it was a knockout. Hugo turned to clink glasses with Waldo, who had the grace to look uncomfortable about such precipitate celebration.

Two more finalists.

Then Scott's name was announced. Silverston was being described in admiring detail and Kate turned to him, radiant, looking as if she was proud of him or something. She took his hand in hers as though that were entirely natural, held on.

PDA, Scott wanted to say—but couldn't get it out of his tight throat. This was embarrassing. He wasn't going to win. Kate would be giving him one of Hugo's pitying looks in a minute, and having her hold his hand while she did so would only make it harder to stomach.

He wanted to disengage his hand, but couldn't seem to let go. So he concentrated, instead, on making his hand go slack and dead. Let her interpret that. She'd be letting go of his hand any moment now. Any moment… Any…

Nope.

She wasn't letting go. And everything was starting to blur in his head until he forgot why he shouldn't be holding her hand.

Flashing images on the giant screen… The MC leaning into his microphone, saying something… A short blare of music… Spotlights swirling…

Scott found that, far from going slack and dead, his hand was gripping Kate's. Hers was gripping right back.

And then she leaned in and kissed him briefly on the lips, and he thought, *What?*

And the applause was ringing out.

And the spotlight—it had stopped on him. It was shining on him. On *him*!

He blinked. Shook his head.

Kate laughed. Nodded.

And Scott knew. He'd won. He'd really won.

He was too shocked even to smile, let alone move. But Kate nudged him and somehow he got to his feet, started heading towards the stage—only to realise he was still holding Kate's hand. He looked down at it, looked at her. She was laughing as she raised his hand to her lips, kissed it—the way he'd kissed hers in the car. And he needed exactly that, right at that moment. *Exactly.*

And then he was walking to the front of the room, up onto the stage.

'Wow,' he said when he got to the microphone. 'Like… *wow!* Okay, this is like one of those moments where the award-winner says they never really expected to win…and then pulls out a *just in case* speech.'

General laughter.

Deep breath.

'But I don't have a *just in case* speech. So…so…um… thank you. I mean—to my client, to the team at Urban Sleek. The other finalists! So amazing. And…and Kate. Just…for… well. Thanks again. And…well, wow.'

Trophy in hand, Scott made his way back to the table, where Kate kissed him again, and he sat in a daze for the rest of the presentations, embarrassed at having given the worst speech in the history of all awards ceremonies everywhere in the world. But he'd just never expected to win. Why would he have prepared a speech? He never won. *Never.*

It wasn't until the final award was being presented that he remembered Hugo. He looked over at Hugo's table, saw his empty seat—bathroom visit?—and then forgot all about Hugo as formal proceedings gave way to the dancing and socialising part of the evening and what felt like a horde of people headed over to congratulate him.

He figured Kate must be longing to escape by the time the throng of well-wishers had dissipated, but when he opened his mouth to suggest they make a run for it, she smoothed a hand over his lapel and smiled at him—and his brain cells scrambled.

'Don't you think we should have a celebratory dance?' she asked.

Scott looked from her to the dance floor, then back.

'Scott?' She smiled. 'Dance?'

'Er…'

Really? 'Er…' is the best you've got? Get it together.

Clearing of the throat. 'Actually, I'm not much of a dancer, Kate.'

'That's all right, neither am I.'

'No—I mean I don't. Dance. Ever.'

She seemed startled by that. 'You mean you never *have*?'

He checked his watch. 'I was thinking… It's late. I should get you home. You've suffered enough.'

Kate was watching him. Curious, a little wary. She seemed

on the verge of asking something… But then she gave her head a tiny shake and said, 'Sure.'

Scott was silent on the drive to Kate's. Because the tension he'd been feeling all the way up to the announcement of his win was back. Tenfold. And it must have rubbed off on Kate because she was silent too, staring through the windscreen.

He pulled up outside her building and Kate unbuckled her seat belt. Then she just sat there, looking at him, waiting for him to turn off the ignition.

'Aren't you coming up?' she asked at last.

'I thought…it's late…I thought…'

'*I* thought you said all your dates ended with sex?'

Silence. Awkward.

'Ah, but not tonight,' Kate said. 'Well, we only specified two nights a week, didn't we? And we've hit that target. But, just so you know, slave girl ends now.'

With that throaty laugh he loved a little too much, she opened the car door and got out. But then she leaned down to look in at him. 'Congratulations again, Scott. That was some house you designed.'

'Thanks. And…and…' Shrug. 'Goodnight, Kate.'

Door closed.

Night over.

Thank God.

Scott drove off, up the street, around the corner, heading home.

Ordinarily he would have helped his date out of the car. That was what he always did, because that was the gentlemanly thing.

Ordinarily he would have walked his date to her front door—again, gentlemanly.

Ordinarily he would have followed his date inside, all the way into her bed. Gentlemanly? No. But expected. On both sides.

Ordinarily.

But with Kate…?

Well, it wasn't a *date*.

It was supposed to have been just an easy fix for the night. Because he really *hadn't* felt like going the black-book route and he really *hadn't* wanted to do the sexual brush-off at the end—which he definitely *would* have done, because fidelity really *was* a sticking point for him and he really *wasn't* interested in having sex with anyone except Kate. *For now*, he added, just to be clear on that. And, aside from all of that, it had been fun to manipulate Kate's rules by negotiating her role tonight as part of Play Time.

An easy fix, a non-date, a fun manipulation.

But it had turned into something…*else*.

Because with her there, the award had been somehow more important than it should have been—and that had surprised him.

Because Hugo had tried to show off to her and she hadn't thought he was anything special—in fact, she'd thought he was a little bit ridiculous.

Because they'd laughed together like…like *that*.

Because she'd had to go and get all proud and lovely about his award.

None of which had anything to do with the end-game.

And it was the end-game he wanted—not the something… *else*.

So it was best to re-establish some distance between them before he had sex with Kate again. And as for walking her to her front door…? He just hadn't trusted himself to get that far and no further. Not with her.

Anyway, it wasn't as if she was his responsibility. He didn't have to usher her protectively behind locked doors. She wasn't some vulnerable girl who couldn't take care of herself. She *could* take care of herself. She *wanted* to take care of herself. She'd been arriving home from all kinds of dates—and this wasn't even a date—for years. She'd laughed when he'd insisted on going to her door to pick her up tonight. She hadn't looked at all put out that he wasn't getting out of the car to walk her to her door at the end of the night. She didn't want that kind of attention. She didn't need—

Oh, dammit to hell!

Swearing fluently and comprehensively, Scott did a U-turn and sped back to Kate's. He screeched to a stop, leapt from the car, raced to the apartment block and followed a semi-familiar resident into the building without having to press the intercom. Which was fortuitous, because he had no idea yet what he was going to say to explain his reappearance.

His heart was thumping when he reached Kate's apartment and knocked on her door.

He still had no idea what to say, but he was suddenly so desperate to see her he was happy just to wing it. *So answer... open the door...come on.*

Kate opened the door cautiously.

Well, of course she was cautious! He could have been anyone.

'You shouldn't open the door without knowing who it is,' he said. Yep, he had lost his freaking mind.

Her only response was to raise her eyebrows. God, he loved the way she did that—all haughty and amused.

She was still wearing that stunning dress, but her hair was half down and her feet were bare.

Scott cleared his throat. 'I should have walked you to your door.'

'Why?'

'Because it's the right thing to do.'

She shook her head, laughed as though to say *silly boy*—and that riled him.

So he reached for her, pulled her close and did what he'd been wanting to do all night.

He kissed her.

CHAPTER SEVEN

SCOTT WAS STILL kissing her as he backed her into the apartment and kicked the door closed.

And Kate really wished he didn't have the ability to turn her to mush—because *she'd* wanted to be the one closing the door. *Slamming* it. Right in his face.

Because…because… Well, because how *dared* he make tonight the first date in his life that wasn't ending with sex? *Not* that it was a date, but still!

Pride might have forced her to laugh it off out there in the car, but she was furious. His first date not to end in sex and it was *her*? On *this* night of all nights? An important night he'd *shared* with her? A night when he'd finally shared *something*?

Yep—one hundred per cent furious.

But with Scott kissing her as though he wanted to suck her right into his soul, she felt the anger drain away. Because she could feel that it was more than a kiss. There was something there—something he wanted from her that he couldn't, wouldn't, articulate. Something that made her ache for him, *long* for him.

'Scott, what's wrong?' she asked when he broke away to take a breath. 'Tell me. Please tell me.'

But he kissed her again. 'Just let me…' he said. *Kiss.* 'I want…' *Kiss.* 'I just…'

He didn't finish those sentences. Kate wondered if he'd even finished them in his own head. Because he kept kissing her, for the longest time, as though there *were* no thoughts, just the kissing.

And for tonight, she decided, it was enough.

'Come with me,' Kate said, and led him to the bedroom.

Scott undressed her. First, the cheongsam—falling to the floor in a purple crumple. Next came her underwear. Her most expensive, coffee-coloured silk and lace, removed like an inconvenience. She smiled, remembering the excitement with which she'd donned that underwear, thinking to drive him wild tonight—and now he just didn't care.

He reached into her hair, gently removed the remaining pins, tossed them to the floor. Ran his fingers through the red mass of it, seemingly more interested in her hair than the sight of her naked body.

It felt strange…and thrilling. The way his eyes stayed on her face, her hair.

'Take my clothes off,' he said, and his voice was a throb.

Kate chose first to put her mouth on his, to let it cling there. She took a moment to snuggle against him, feeling both vulnerable and wicked as his arms closed around her and she was held, naked, against his fully clothed body.

Not until he started to shake did she step back, slipping her hands under his jacket, over his shoulders, smoothing it back and off so that it dropped to the floor behind him. Next came his shirt buttons, slipped through their holes as Scott breathed out a long, slow prayer of a breath. Then she eased his cufflinks out.

They looked expensive, so she glanced towards her dressing table, thinking to put them somewhere safe—but Scott stopped her before she could step away.

'Don't leave,' he said.

'But I only—'

He took the cufflinks from her and tossed them over his shoulder as though they were no more valuable than her hairpins. He didn't even blink as they hit the wall.

Kate slid the shirt from his body, stopped to kiss him again, her breasts against his chest, almost moaning at how wonderful that felt.

Next, she undid his pants. Eased them down. Knelt at his feet, unbuckled his shoes. She paused, rose on her knees.

Perfect position for taking him in her mouth. She wanted to do that so badly.

But Scott, reading her mind, drew her up. 'Not tonight,' he said.

A minute later his shoes were off, his pants and underwear kicked away, and she was back in his arms, being held against him, while his hands smoothed down her back, over and over, as he breathed her in, his mouth against her hair. 'Kate…' he said. 'Kate.'

But Kate didn't think he even knew he was saying her name. He seemed to be in a kind of trance.

So she let him lead her to the bed, let him pull the covers back, draw her gently down beside him. He kissed her again, so softly. And then he eased slowly back, taking Kate with him. Wrapped her in his arms. Kissed her eyelids, her mouth, her neck, nuzzled into her hair.

She simply held him, opening to him in any way he wanted. Even the simple act of sliding a condom onto him, his hands lightly covering hers while she did it, seemed like a sensual discovery.

And when at last he positioned her beneath him and slid inside her welcoming heat, it was as though his body sighed and relaxed and just…*was*. For the longest moment he stayed still, taking her face between his hands, laying his mouth on hers, kissing her with an intensity that pierced through to her burning heart.

Tears started to Kate's eyes and she didn't even know why. She closed her eyes, knowing it would change things if he saw her cry. And she wouldn't have changed this slow, sweet loving for anything.

She knew what was happening, and she wanted it. She was giving herself to him: *I'm here, yours.*

His. For tonight she was his. And Scott was hers. Hers alone. For tonight.

And when he spilled himself inside her, with a gasping, luscious groan into the mouth he was kissing so deeply, Kate held him tight, so tightly against her, and wrapped her legs around him, let herself join him in her own flowering release.

'Thank you,' he whispered into her ear.

For what? she wanted to ask, but she dared not break the spell by seeking answers he wouldn't give.

And in any case Scott was holding her close, kissing the top of her head, stroking her back. And it really was enough.

So beautiful… Soothing… Lovely…

Ahhhh...

When Kate woke early the next morning she turned, smiling, to face Scott—only to find his side of the bed empty.

A quick walk through the apartment showed that all he'd left behind was a note, on the kitchen bench.

Saturday night?
S

Two words. One question mark. One initial.

Which brought home to Kate that last night had been just…well, just last night.

He hadn't stayed until morning, the way she'd thought he might. She wouldn't see him tonight, the way she'd hoped. And their relationship hadn't metamorphosed into anything other than what it was: contractual sex.

Which brought her to Saturday night. Yes or no?

She sighed as she looked at the calendar on her fridge. Today was Friday the thirteenth—hopefully that wasn't an omen!—and Saturday, tomorrow, was…

Oh.

Ohhhhh.

Saturday. The fourteenth of February.

Not that the momentousness of that date would have entered Scott's head. He wasn't a Valentine's Day kind of guy.

And in this instance it was a moot point. Because her sister Shay, and Shay's partner Rick—who *were* Valentine's Day kind of people—were leaving their two gorgeous daughters with Kate while they went out for a romantic dinner.

So she should just get straight on the phone and tell Scott she was busy on Saturday. No need to embarrass herself by mentioning Valentine's Day. She didn't want him to think she was angling for something other than sex. Something like… Well, something Valentine-ish.

Even if she had a lump in her throat about the whole stupid day.

A lump so big it was physically impossible to get a word out of her clogged-up throat. Which made a phone call impossible.

Okay, she would email.

Got your note, Scott.
I'm babysitting my nieces, Maeve and Molly, on Saturday night. I'm free Sunday if that suits?
Kate

There. Cool, businesslike. Contract-worthy.

Three hours later, back came a two-word response: No problem.

And Kate released a big, sighing breath.

Right.

Good.

Good…right?

Because Valentine's Day actually sucked. If Kate had a dollar for every now-divorced couple who'd managed either their proposal or their actual wedding on February the fourteenth, she'd be retired already! Valentine's Day was all about spending too much on wilted roses and eating overpriced restaurant dinners.

Stupid.

The worst possible day for scheduling a date with a sex-only partner.

Valentine's Day? *As if!*

Kate went to her kitchen, looked again at the calendar stuck on her fridge.

Yep, there it was. February the fourteenth. With a nice big red heart on it, courtesy of whoever printed stupid refrigerator calendars. A big red heart. A *love* heart.

And, to her absolute horror, Kate's eyes filled with tears.

Kate had a hectic day of meetings, followed by a catch-up with the girls for drinks after work, and by the time she clambered into bed that night, she was sure she was over the whole weepy Valentine's Day phenomenon that had blindsided her.

So when she woke on Saturday morning to find that depression had settled over her like a damp quilt, she went the whole tortured-groan route. What had happened to her brain during that awards dinner on Thursday night to have resulted in her losing all her common sense?

Sex-only partners *did not celebrate Valentine's Day.* Sex-only partners scheduled sex on days like the *fifteenth* of February. A perfectly legitimate, much more appropriate day for having no-strings sex with guys who left two-word notes on your kitchen counter.

A *two-word* note. And a *two-word* email. That encapsulated her relationship with Scott very nicely—two words: *sex contract.*

Imbued with a burst of *damn your own energy*, Kate got out of bed and on the spot decided to clean her apartment. An activity that was *not* some kind of displacement therapy twisted up in her need to wash that man right out of her hair, but a simple household activity. A spring clean—just in summer.

She got underway with gusto.

Gusto that lasted approximately fifteen minutes.

Which was how long it took for the first memory to sneak in.

Kate was wiping down the dining table—and there in her head was the memory of that first night…Scott reaching across to hold her breast…and then the whole dining chair thing. *Ohhhhhhh.*

It was like a switch, throwing open the floodgates—because the memories started pouring in, room by room, after that. Plumping up the couch cushions—that night when he'd thrown the cushions off and dragged her on top of him… Cleaning out the fridge—Scott, coming up behind her, hands all over her… Bathroom—three separate shower scenes.

Her bedroom—*holy hell.* So vivid it was painful. And the most painful of all that last time… Scott drawing her gently down onto the bed…kissing her as if he wanted them to merge.

Okay, enough cleaning.

She hurried to the laundry to dump the housekeeping paraphernalia, only to be hit by another memory. *Oh. My. God.* Had she—? Yes, she had! She'd had sex with Scott Knight in *every single room* of her apartment—*including* the damned laundry room! What normal person had sex in the laundry room? Sitting on top of the washing machine, with the vibrations adding a little extra hum to proceedings as you wrapped your legs around—

Arrrggghh.

She had to get out of the apartment. Maybe even *sell* the apartment.

She took a cold shower, changed into *I am not in need of antidepressants* clothes and hurried out of the building.

The boats were what she needed. Up close and personal. Escape. So she crossed the road to the marina and breathed out a sigh of relief as she reached the jetty. The boats would float her stress away as they always did—on a tide of dreams. Adventure. Possibilities.

One day she would hire a sailing instructor and she would learn… She would learn…

Uh-oh.

Her eyes darted from yacht to yacht…and on every deck she could picture Scott Knight eight years ago, young and free, teaching people to sail. Scott as he was now, teaching *her* to sail.

One of those now-familiar tortured groans was ripped out of her and she turned her back on the boats.

Coffee—she needed coffee.

She hurried to the marina cafe and was horrified when Dean the barista's eyes popped at her as if she was a crazy person. 'You okay, Kate?'

What the hell did she *look* like?

'Fine, fine, fine,' she said reassuringly—before realising that two more 'fines' than were strictly necessary did not denote 'fine'. 'I just need coffee, Dean.'

'Really? Because you seem a little wired.'

Forced smile. 'Really, Dean. Just the coffee.' Subtext: *Give me the damned coffee and shut up.*

But as she took her coffee to one of the tables and sipped, Dean kept giving her concerned glances from behind the coffee machine. As if she had a neon sign flashing on her forehead: *Beware of woman losing her marbles.* Thank heaven her coffee of choice was a nice little macchiato. If she'd had to put up with a cappuccino's worth of *Are you okay?* looks she might have gone over and slapped Dean!

As it was, she could chug it down quickly and flee back to her apartment. Where she would look up the official definition of 'pathetic'! Just to be sure she *wasn't*.

Fifteen minutes later she had the dictionary open, her finger running down the column...*paternalism*...*paternity*... *paternoster*...

Aha!

Pathetic: arousing pity, especially through vulnerability or sadness.

In other words, *Kate Cleary: sexless on Valentine's Day.* The usually imperturbable Dean, the barista, had instantly clocked her out-of-character vulnerability. And she didn't need a dictionary to know that she was arousing pity—in *herself*!

How very…well, *pathetic.*

Although at least she could dispute the 'sad' part of the definition. Because she was not *sad.* She was sexually frustrated! Completely different from sad. Not that two whole nights without sex was going to kill her. She'd gone way longer than two nights before! *Waaaaaay* longer. She wasn't a nymphomaniac! Or…hell! *Was* she a nymphomaniac?

Nylon…nymph…nymphalid…nymphette… Nymphette? Good Lord—nymphette? *Nympholepsy…*

Nymphomaniac: a woman who has abnormally excessive and uncontrollable sexual desire.

Ohhh, crap. Maybe she *was* a nymphomaniac. At her age! That was just…sad.

Oh, God! Sad!

She was a fully-fledged pathetic nymphomaniac.

Kate fled to the terrace—the only place in the apartment she hadn't had sex with Scott. And the only reason she hadn't had sex with him on the terrace was because exhibitionism wasn't exactly his 'thing'. And, even though it wasn't her 'thing' either, the realisation that she probably would have gone there, *in full view of any passersby*, flashed through her mind and shocked her.

Depraved pathetic nymphomaniac! That was her. And it was Scott Knight's fault. Because she'd never been this desperate for sex in her whole life.

And now she wouldn't even be able to enjoy the view from her terrace, because one quick look at the boats confirmed that Scott was now firmly entrenched as part of her escape daydream.

When the intercom finally buzzed that evening and she heard her sister's calm voice, she almost cried with relief.

Her family always anchored her. And you *had* to get it together when you had two children to entertain.

When Shay and Rick had left she pushed the coffee table out of the way so the girls could take up their preferred positions on the rug—seven-year-old Maeve leaning back against the base of the couch, engrossed in a book about cake and cookie decorating, and five-year-old Molly stretched out on her stomach, leaning on an elbow and drawing her version of a fairy house in her sketchbook.

Kate was just about to pick up the phone to order pizza—the girls' favourite meal—when the intercom buzzed again. Shay and Rick should be sipping champagne at the restaurant and surely could have telephoned if they were having a last-minute panic—but nobody needed to tell a family lawyer that parents could be irrational!

She pushed the 'talk' button. 'Yes, Shay?' she said with an exasperated laugh.

'Um…nope. It's me, Kate.'

CHAPTER EIGHT

SCOTT.

Kate's vocal cords froze. *God help me, God help me, God* help *me.*

'Kate? Come on—buzz me up. My arms are going to fall off in a minute.'

Kate buzzed the door and then just stared at it, paralysed.

Something was swelling in her chest—a mixture of joy and yearning and uncertainty. What did it mean that he'd come when she'd told him not to? He shouldn't be doing this. She was glad he was here. No, she wasn't—because they had rules. But it was Valentine's Day. No, that meant nothing. She couldn't let him get away with breaking the rules. No matter how glad she was that he was doing it.

Mmm-hmm. She sure was making a lot of sense!

She heard Scott's voice vibrating through her door like a tuning fork. That disarmingly lazy drawl, addressed to some stranger. A laugh. Yep—he'd hooked a new fan in under a minute.

She rested her palms against the door, could almost *feel* him through it.

Breathe. Just breathe.

One knock.

Breathe!

She opened the door and Scott stepped over the threshold as though he owned the place.

'What are you doing here?' she managed to get out.

'Why wouldn't I be here?'

He handed her two bottles of wine—a white and a red—and carried a six-pack of beer and a paper bag containing who knew what into the kitchen.

Kate followed him, put the red wine on the counter, the white wine and beer in the fridge.

'You can't just buzz the intercom whenever you feel like it,' she said, in her *Don't disturb the children* voice.

Scott shrugged. 'If the intercom annoys you, give me a key.'

Which, of course, was *not the point*. 'I am *not* giving you a key.'

Another one of those shrugs of his. 'Then it's the intercom.'

'You can't stay,' she said. 'I'm just about to order pizza.'

'I love pizza.'

'Not for you, Scott. You shouldn't be here. I told you I was babysitting Maeve and Molly tonight.'

'And I emailed you back to say that wasn't a problem.'

'That wasn't—? I mean… Huh?'

'Oh,' he said. 'Were you trying to tell me not to come? Tsk, tsk, Kate—you have to be more specific, in that case. Lawyers shouldn't be leaving loopholes. So, to be clear…it's not a problem that you're babysitting tonight, which is why I'm here. And, yes, Sunday is fine too.'

Kate thought back to her email, his reply, acknowledged the ambiguity…but knew very well he was playing her.

'You knew what I meant, Scott. And we're supposed to negotiate if we have a problem with dates.'

'Okay, let's negotiate.'

She closed her eyes, took a deep breath. Opened her eyes to find him looking all woebegone.

'Don't you like me any more?' he asked.

She stared at him as laughter and frustration warred inside her. 'No.'

'But why?'

'Because you're—' She broke off, laughed because she just couldn't help it, damn him. 'Just because. And I hope you like entertaining children—because that's the only action you're getting tonight. I can't—won't—leave two little girls eating pizza while you and I go for a quickie in the bedroom.'

He leaned in close, snatched a kiss. 'One—that's just a kiss, not a proposal of marriage, so don't complain. Two—I'm not *asking* you for a quickie in the bedroom while the girls eat pizza. And three—it won't be quick; it will be nice and slow…*after* Maeve and Molly's parents have picked them up.'

One more rapid-fire kiss.

'You really have the most sensational mouth in the world.' Another kiss—quick and scorching. 'And make mine pepperoni.'

He had the nerve to laugh at the tortured look on her face.

'What? Is it the money? I'll pay you half, as per our contract, if that's what's worrying you. Honestly—you lawyers are so tight!'

And with that, he liberated three red foil-wrapped chocolate hearts from the paper bag and presented one to her. 'Happy Valentine's Day.'

And there she went—crumbling. 'Oh, you…you *know* it's Valentine's Day?'

'Well, *yeeeaah*! Multiple cards. Even one present—a cute little cat o' nine tails from Anais that you and I will *not* be trying out. But nothing—*nada!*—from you. And, Kate, I'm warning you—if you haven't had the common decency to buy me a chocolate or a cupcake or at the very least a soppy card, I'm eating half of that chocolate heart.' Quick unholy grin. 'And I'll take mine molten…off your tummy.'

And with that gobsmacking pronouncement, Scott swaggered into the living room while the last of her resistance disintegrated.

'Which one's Maeve and which one's Molly?' he asked. 'No, don't tell me. My friend Willa told me Maeve is seven, so that would be…you.' He pointed to Molly, who giggled. He did an over-the-top double-take. 'Not you?'

Head-shake from Molly.

'I'm Maeve,' Maeve said, and Scott plonked himself down on the rug and leaned back against the couch next to her.

'Okay—will you be my Valentine?' he asked and handed over one of the hearts.

Her eyes lit as she shyly took the heart and nodded.

'Ohhhhh!' That came from the rug. 'What about me?'

Scott nodded sagely at Molly. 'Well, it just so happens I'm in the market for two Valentines tonight.' He produced the other chocolate heart and a beaming Molly came over for long enough to take it from him and give him a sweet little hug before she resettled on the rug.

He turned to Maeve. 'So, Maeve, what's so interesting?'

Maeve flashed her book's cover.

'Ah, you're going to be a chef,' he said.

Maeve nodded, still shy.

'I'm not bad in the kitchen myself,' Scott said, and proceeded to talk about biscuits.

Biscuits? That was just so…random. Biscuits! And chocolate hearts on Valentine's Day. And asking Willa about the girls. Kate didn't know what to make of it all. What to make of *him*.

Unless it was that he was completely irresistible.

She called for pizza, then set the dining table, while Scott charmed her nieces—looking absolutely nothing *like* a confirmed bachelor as he did it.

The man knew his baking. The pros and cons of shortbread, ginger snaps, honey jumbles, chocolate chip cookies and macaroons were all discussed at length. And the absolute deliciousness of…what?…whoopie pies?…was being extolled? Kate had never heard of a whoopie pie.

'They're like little chocolate cookie sandwiches, with a creamy filling,' Scott explained to Maeve—who'd never heard of them either. 'Next time you're here, we'll bake them together.'

'Can I bake too?' Molly asked.

'You sure can. Three of us can make three times the pies! What have you got there, Molly?'

In no time Scott was lying next to Molly on the floor, having the picture explained to him. Maeve abandoned her book to lie on Scott's other side.

Scott gave a bit of improvement advice, explaining that it was his job to design houses, and as Kate paid for the pizzas she heard the girls asking him to redraw the house for them.

'I'd be honoured,' Scott said, and then got to his feet and helped the girls up. 'But first—pizza!'

It was adorable the way he got the girls drinks, helped them choose the biggest pizza slices, chatted about the most beautiful houses he'd designed in a way that made them sound like magic castles. After dinner he stayed with Maeve and Molly while Kate cleared up, drawing in Molly's sketch-book and making the girls *ooh* and *ahh*.

Yep, bona fide adorable.

And Kate just *had* to see the drawing. So she peeked over Scott's shoulder.

Oh. *Ohhhhh.*

It was the perfect little girls' house. Towers and turrets. Winding paths. A secret entrance to an underground treasure cave, a private elf garden, a sunken pool with a waterfall. He'd sketched two bedrooms, labelled 'Molly' and 'Maeve', with fairytale beds and magic mirrors and spiralling staircases.

When Kate took the girls off to clean their teeth and get ready for bed, each of the girls kissed Scott goodnight—one per cheek—and he blushed.

Scott Knight, who could talk more boldly about sex than any man she'd ever met, *blushed.*

Kate felt her heart do one of those swoons inside her chest, and thought, *Uh-oh. This is bad. Very, very bad.*

She read to Maeve and Molly until they drifted into sleep, and then—a little apprehensive—went to find Scott.

He was on the terrace, where he gravitated every time she left him alone.

'I poured you a glass of wine. It's there on the table. And sorry, Kate, but that table's going to have to go, along with the chairs,' he said. 'It's so fragile I feel like I'm going to break something every time I'm near that furniture.'

She had to agree it looked like a children's toy set next to Scott's imposing frame. Everything did. But she forbore from pointing out that she was not going to change her furniture for a man who wouldn't be in her life for long.

Whew. That hit her. This was finite. It had a start date and it would come to an end. She couldn't let herself forget that just because he'd smiled at her once as if he saw something wonderful in her. Or because he'd made love to her once as if he was embedding himself inside her.

Scott took a long pull of beer from the bottle in his hand, gazing out at the marina as Kate fetched her glass and joined him at the edge of the terrace.

'What's it like? Sailing?' she asked.

'It was fun.'

'Was?'

'I don't sail any more.'

'But...why? I mean, why not?'

'It was just...' Shrug. 'Time to concentrate on the important things in life.'

'Fun is important.'

He looked down at her. 'I *am* having fun. With you,' he said, and leaned down to kiss her.

'I know why you do that,' she said, when he pulled back.

'Do what?'

'Kiss me.'

'Well, *duh*, Kate! I do it because I like kissing you.'

'You do it to distract me. So you don't have to answer my questions.'

'And does it? Distract you?'

'Yes. But why are such simple questions a problem for you?'

Pause. 'Prying into my past is not part of the deal, Kate.'

Kate felt it like a slap—not just the words but the *keep your distance* tone. She found she was gripping her glass too hard, so put it on the broad top of the terrace railing.

She heard Scott sigh. Then he was smoothing his hand over her hair like an apology. 'Kate, the sailing… It's just something I set aside to focus on the realities of life—like studying and working. And look at me now—I'm an award-winner!' Low laugh, with all the self-deprecation his brother lacked. 'It's enough for me.'

'If it were enough you wouldn't spend every moment I leave you alone out on the terrace, watching the boats.'

'Pry-ing…' he sing-songed.

'It's not prying to ask questions about a person you… you're…'

'Having sex with,' he supplied. And sighed again. 'You drew up the contract, Kate. There wasn't a clause for fire-side chats in there.' Slight pause. 'Right?'

'Right.'

'So has anything changed for you?'

She wanted to say yes. That things *had* changed. Because of the way they'd made love two nights ago. The way he'd presented her with a chocolate heart. And blushed when two little girls had kissed him. The way he tried to pretend that the boats bobbing on the harbour held no fascination for him when she knew they did.

But if things changed he would go. She knew it instinctively. *Not yet. Not...yet.*

'No,' she said quietly, and picked up her wine glass, sipped. 'Nothing's changed.'

They stood in silence, side by side, staring across at the dark water, the city lights in the distance.

And then Scott cleared his throat. Just a tiny sound. 'Good. Because the whole fireside-chat thing… It would be like me asking you…' Shrug. 'I don't know…' Shrug. 'If you wanted…maybe…to have children. One day, I mean.'

Another clearing of the throat. 'Because you're so good with the girls anyone would wonder about that.'

What the hell? Kate slanted a look at him. He was looking out at the Harbour.

But then he turned, looked at her. Eyes watchful. 'And you wouldn't want me to ask you that, would you?'

'If you wanted to ask me that, Scott, I'd answer. Because it's no big deal.'

'Ah, but I don't need to ask. I already know the answer is yes.'

And for the first time in a long time, Kate thought, *Yes.* The answer, very simply, *was* yes. Except of course she'd lost that simple answer somewhere along her career path.

She turned back to the boats. Long moment.

'You know, Scott, I've seen fathers who say they've been tricked into pregnancy and shouldn't have to pay child support. Divorcing parents using child custody as carrot and stick to punish or bribe. Surrogates who decide to keep their children when those children are the last hope of desperate couples. Fathers pulling out all the stops to avoid their children being aborted. Twins separated and fostered because of financial pressure. Unwanted children, abused children, ignored children. I'm not sure that's an enticement to parenthood.'

'But you wouldn't be like any of those parents.'

'No. But a lot of women are good at choosing the wrong man.'

'Then don't choose the wrong man.'

'Oh, simple!' She turned to him. 'So simple that I suppose if you found the right woman it would be a case of *Bingo, let me impregnate you immediately!*'

He laughed softly. 'Since the longest I've been with a woman is two months, I'd say I'm hardly father material.'

Two months. The equivalent of one contract rollover. *Consider yourself warned, Kate.*

'Well, at least you've got the uncle routine down pat,'

she said. 'Judging by how you were with Maeve and Molly. Where did you learn that? Does Hugo have children?'

'Yes, he does. One girl. One boy. Twins. A perfect set. My brother does all things to perfection.'

Kate caught the wryness—but before she could even wonder at it Scott had tugged her under his arm, leaned down for another *that's enough talking* kiss.

'I can't wait to touch you,' he said.

'You *are* touching me,' she said, all breathless—because that was what it did to her every time he kissed her.

'I'm calling another Play Time next week, Kate.'

'What do you want to do?'

'Uh-uh. Secret. But you're not keeping up. Come on—don't you have a fantasy *you* want to try out? I'd love to indulge you.'

'I do have something in mind for next week,' Kate said, because since it was a damned sex contract, and she'd put that stupid clause in there herself, it would look strange if she didn't have even one scenario in mind. But the truth was she could think of nothing she wanted more than just taking him into her body, holding him close.

'Woo-hoo, I'll be hanging out for that,' Scott said. 'But remember—no S&M, no B&D. I wasn't kidding about that stuff. It creeps me out, the pain thing. I don't enjoy it, and I sure as hell can't see myself inflicting it on you. Oh—and while fruit and veg is acceptable, under certain circumstances, no wildlife, no livestock. I'm not *that* kinky.'

'Wildlife?' Kate spluttered out a laugh. 'That is just disgusting. Is your black book annotated? Because maybe I'd better take a look at what you expect. I might have to rein you in.'

Scott grinned at her. 'Just making sure we're on the same page after seeing the way that guy in your boardroom was patting and kissing his little dog like it was his girlfriend.'

Another spluttered laugh. 'Please! You're going to give me nightmares. And Sugarplum isn't a dog. She's a shih tzu.'

'The dog is called *Sugarplum*?'

'Yep.'

'Well, *that* is an abomination.'

Kate bit the inside of her cheek. 'Actually, I have another name for her. *Hostis humani generis*.'

'Is that a legal term?'

'It is. It means "enemy of the human race". Which I think is very apt in Sugarplum's case.'

'I'm going to have to kiss you for that. Because legal terms get me so damned *hot*! Can you say something with *functus officio* in it?'

She was laughing helplessly. 'Not offhand, no.'

'Then *hostis humani generis* it is.'

Kate was still laughing as Scott planted his mouth on hers…but not for long. By the time he slipped his tongue inside her mouth, she was tingly and dazed. And Scott seemed equally affected.

'I love kissing you,' he breathed against her lips.

'People do tend to love doing things they're particularly good at.'

'You're no slouch yourself—but even if you were, Kate, one look at your mouth is all I'd ever need to get me ready to dive inside you.'

She shivered. Closed her eyes briefly. He could turn her on too easily. So easily it was dangerous.

Change the subject.

'Anyway, Sugarplum's family is sorted. You won't be seeing her around the office again.'

'Who ended up getting the kids?'

'Kids?' Kate asked.

'That couple. You know—the kids?'

'Ah,' Kate said, and winced.

'Not kids?'

Another wince.

'You're not telling me that fight was about that evil little yapper, are you?'

She could see the horror—almost comical and yet not. The disbelief.

Kate shrugged.

'So they don't have kids?' he asked.

'I'm not saying that.'

'So they *do* have kids, but the fight was over…' Stop, stare. 'You're not serious?' he said.

She raised her eyebrows.

He shook his head, stunned. 'I hope they're paying you a lot, because from where I'm standing your job sucks.'

'Lately…yeah, it *does* suck.'

'At least your family must be proud of you, though. Lawyers are like doctors—they've got the parental-pride market cornered.'

'Actually, my mother would probably prefer an architect to a lawyer! She's an artist, so creative stuff is more her speed.'

'Your mother's an artist?' And then his eyes widened. 'Oh! *Ohh!* Cleary! *Madeline* Cleary? Yes! Of course! The painting in your office and the one in your bedroom. Wow.'

'Yes—wow. And my father is a playwright, but not as well known. What about *your* parents?'

'Doctors times two. So…your mother… She's not happy about you being a lawyer?'

'She thinks I get too emotionally invested in my cases. Whenever I stress out, she says, *"Kaaaaate, I warned you how it would be."* And then she adds something about thanking heaven for divorce—which is her way of telling me I'm doing the world a favour, and to just get on with the next uncoupling. It's the Cleary way, you know—fight like hell, then move on.'

'Now, you see, *my* mother would see divorce as an admission of failure. Which is why Knights don't divorce. Failure is not an option.'

'Even if the alternative is to stick with someone who's horrible? Someone abusive? Divorce has got to be a better alternative.'

'Then why do you stress out about it, Kate?'

'I've just…' She paused, sighed. 'I've had a run of nasty ones lately. And seeing people ripping each other apart, seeing the kids on the sidelines…' Another pause. 'It can make you cynical.'

'Cynical. Now, *that* I understand.'

'Which is when I start thinking about boat theft.'

'I'm surprised you haven't done it already.'

'Maybe I would have—except for one small thing.' She slanted him a glinting smile. 'I can't sail!'

He touched her face. Gentle, soft. 'Ah, well—definitely a problem!'

'And, you know, my job has compensations.'

'Money?'

'Yes, that's one.'

'And meeting handsome architects through your clients.'

'Handsome *egomaniacal* architects, even,' Kate said, and laughed. 'But I'd definitely classify meeting Willa as compensation. It was…*satisfying* to fight for her.'

'Yeah, I get that. From what I know of Wayne-the-Pain, he would have tried to screw her out of everything just to pay her back for wanting to be something more than an arm bauble. She said you fought like a demon. That it was your way—to fight to the death.'

'Yes, like I said—the Cleary way. And definitely *my* way. Even more so for people I love—and I love Willa. She's… special. Strong. So much tougher than people think. I admire her more than I can say. She deserves everything good and fine in the world. Joy. Peace. Security. And love. She deserves love.'

'I think you're a secret romantic, Kate.' He nudged her playfully. 'So where's my Valentine's Day card?'

'It's in the mail,' Kate said, nudging him back. 'Along with a few tools of oppression—handcuffs and hot wax to go with Anais's whip, because I think she's on to something there.'

Scott gave an exaggerated shudder. 'I promise you, she

is *not*.' Pause. 'Mind you, for a B&D aficionado, Anais has some remarkably pedestrian notions about love.'

'What's pedestrian?'

'Let's just say the idea of a straight up and down sex contract would never have entered her head. You and I… We're… *different*. We know what we want and what we don't. And we go for it.'

Kate thought about that for a moment. 'Are you saying Anais believes in love, and that that's pedestrian? Because I hate to break it to you, Scott, but I'm pedestrian in that way too. It's impossible *not* to believe in love in my family. They throw it at you in great gooey clumps, whether you want it or not.'

'Ah, but that's a different kind of love to the romantic stuff.'

'The principles are the same. Real love, of *any* kind, glories in a person's strengths and talents and…and their flaws too. *Especially* their flaws. It accepts and it…it heals. It lets you just…*be*. Be who you are. A lot of divorces happen because that's *not* the kind of love on offer.' Stop. Breath. 'And that's when the lawyers come in—earning thousands of dollars negotiating whether it's Mr or Mrs X who gets five hundred dollars' worth of groceries in the settlement. And that's a true story.'

'But it's not about the groceries, is it?'

'No. It's about power. Punishing someone because they can't love you enough, or don't need you enough, or won't give you enough.' She shivered. 'It makes you wonder…'

'Wonder?'

'Why you'd ever let someone have that power over you.'

'And that is why you and I—two sex-crazed cynics—are meant for each other.'

'For the grand total of two more weeks.'

'Rollover clause, remember?' He eyed her closely. 'You're not finished with me yet, are you, Kate?'

'No, I'm not finished with you.' She clinked her glass

against Scott's beer bottle. 'Here's to not having to get divorced. Not that Clearys get divorced any more than Knights.'

'But—' He broke off, shook his head. 'You said your mother's in favour of divorce.'

'And so she is—for all those people silly enough to get married in the first place.'

'You mean…? Hang on, I'm not getting this.'

'Clearys don't get divorced because they don't get married.'

'You mean like…ever?'

'Not in recent history.'

'Your mother?'

'Nope.'

'*Her* mother?'

'Absolutely not—Gran was all about free love.'

'Molly and Maeve's parents?'

'No. It's easier, you know, not to rely on a man. Or, in reverse, a woman. But don't misunderstand me—our fathers were in our lives as much as they wanted to be, and it worked very well.' She smiled. 'Gus—my father—and Aristotle—Shay and my other sister Lilith's father—even get along well together.'

'So it's one of those weird, blended, out-there families that are going to be the ruin of civilisation? The Knight family would be horrified!'

'Are *you*? Horrified?'

'I said the Knight family. I'm not really part of that.'

She looked at him sharply. 'What does that mean?'

He shrugged. 'I need another beer,' he said, and went into the apartment.

Kate followed him inside. Waited while he grabbed a beer from the fridge.

'What's your family like, Scott?'

'Doctors.'

'No—I mean, what are they *like*?'

'Well…doctors.' He hunched a shoulder. 'You've met

Hugo. He's pretty up and down perfect. That's the standard. My family is *not* weird, blended and out-there. More like stultifyingly conventional.'

'So you're...what? The black sheep?'

'More like the sheep with second-grade wool.'

'Okay, what does *that* mean?'

He took a pull of his beer. 'Nothing. Just that growing up as a Knight is... Well, it's nothing a Cleary would understand.'

'Try me.'

He paused. Looked at her. Opened his mouth. Closed it. Shook his head. 'Forget it, Kate.' One of those infuriating smiles that meant nothing. 'It's not *germane*. And— Ah, the intercom. Better go let your sister in.'

If Shay and Rick were surprised to find a man at Kate's they didn't show it. And Scott—well, he was all smooth charm. But in that closed-off, *keep your distance* way. A way that made Shay, who was unusually perceptive, narrow her eyes at him.

As Shay and Rick went to get the girls there was silence.

Kate racked her brain for a way to break it—a way to break through the sudden wall of reserve that was between them.

But in the end Scott was the one to break the silence. 'So, Kate, I owe you.' He reached in his pocket for his wallet.

'Wh—What?'

'Money for the pizza.' He handed over some notes.

Kate stared at the money in her hand as he returned his wallet to his pocket. 'Scott...?'

'Fifty-fifty, remember?' he said with a meaningless smile. 'And now I'd better hit the ro—'

He broke off as Rick and Shay reappeared, carrying Maeve and Molly, who were drowsy and tousled and lovable.

Kate kissed the girls. And then watched, fascinated, as they each in turn leaned towards Scott for him to kiss them too. She saw Scott blush as he did so. The cool reserve was gone for those few moments, replaced by something perilously close to tenderness.

Scott…and children.

Something he couldn't have because he never stayed with a woman long enough? Or because he was a Knight. Or… or what?

Shay, won over in that instant, smiled at him, and Scott blushed again.

And then Kate and Scott were alone again, and she wondered what was going to happen next. Given the way he'd kissed her out on the terrace, by rights she should have been flat against the door with Scott all over her the moment it closed behind her family…but Kate had a feeling that was not going to happen.

Scott took her face between his hands and she waited, breathless and curious.

'You're so beautiful, Kate,' he said, but that fact didn't seem to make him happy.

He leaned close, put his forehead on hers and just stopped. Not moving, not even breathing.

Kate wanted so badly to wrap her arms around him and tell him everything would be all right, even though she didn't know what was wrong. But she stayed exactly as she was. Soaking in this moment where nothing happened, nothing changed.

And then Scott released her, stepped back. Smiled one of those smiles that didn't reach his eyes.

'I hope you appreciate that I did *not* kiss you then,' he said. 'Please note for future reference that I am capable of obeying the rules. No kissing if it isn't going to lead to sex, right?'

'But I thought—'

'I just—I just think I'd better go home tonight.'

'But you can still go home tonight. I mean, after…'

But at the look on his face—closed-off, determined—Kate forced herself to stop. She wasn't going to beg. Not any man. Ever. And especially not this one, who was already running rings around her in every possible way.

Ring-running. For her own mental health, it was going to have to stop.

So she smiled, as remote as he was. 'Yeah, we're over our target, right?'

'Right,' Scott said. 'I'll see you tomorrow, then—new week, new target.'

'Not tomorrow,' Kate said.

'But you said Sunday.'

'And now I'm saying no.'

His eyes narrowed. 'That sounds like pique, Kate. And we don't have room for pique in our contract.'

'No, we don't have any allowances for pique in our contract, Scott,' she said, very cool. 'This is not pique. I wasn't expecting you tonight—as you know very well. I was, in fact, planning to do some work once I'd put the girls to bed. Now I have to play catch-up tomorrow. So thank you.'

'Ouch. I'm going to need that stapler,' Scott said.

Then with a mock salute he was gone.

Kate looked at the door, wondering exactly what had happened out there on the terrace.

She crossed her arms against a chill premonition that things between them were not going to work out the way either of them expected.

CHAPTER NINE

THE NEXT MORNING Scott was back at Rushcutters Bay, his finger frozen just short of the intercom buzzer, wondering what the hell he was doing.

Kate had made it clear she was going to be busy today, doing the work she'd planned to do the previous night if not for his inconvenient arrival. Code—and not exactly secret—for *I don't want to see you.*

And yet here he was, trying to work out how to charm his way into her apartment, how to apologise for the way he'd run away last night. The way he *kept* running away.

But how did you tell someone you'd run because you were in too deep and wanted to pull back—even as you were fronting up for more?

He hadn't intended to see her last night after she'd sent that irritatingly dismissive email about babysitting, but... well, he'd *wanted* to see her, dammit!

And he'd also known that if he *didn't* see her he'd be looking down the barrel of another sleepless night. Because his frazzled brain kept circling round and around everything that had happened on Thursday night, urging him to prove to himself that the way he'd been feeling was a one-off, all caught up in the unforeseen angst of the occasion—Hugo; that shared moment when they'd both just *got* it; his winning—*winning*! *That* was why he'd smiled at her—okay, he smiled a *lot*...he even smiled at *her* a lot...but not like that. And *that* explained the sex too—so straighty one-eighty that it should *not* have seared him like a barbecued steak, and yet it had been on fire, plated up, skip the garnish, *delicious*.

So, yeah, last night, he'd intended to prove the one-offness of it all to himself. To turn up off-schedule, joke about Valentine's Day, dazzle her with a little light-hearted banter, with the girls there to run interference and put the kybosh on anything emotional. Then they'd have sex in a manner in keeping with their contract—he'd thought of something highly technical that would mean they'd have to concentrate on not breaking a bone, so no time for losing themselves in the moment—and *voilà*: back to normal. Head back in the right place, heart untouched.

No watching her sleep or tracing his finger over her eyebrow, no sniffing her damned perfume when he was alone in her bathroom. None of that creepy stuff.

But instead his dumbass brain had started shooting off on tangents until he'd started thinking about kids. Redheaded, grey-eyed kids. How it would be to bring up kids the Cleary way, with people flinging gooey clumps of love at you—not the Knight way, where you had to prove yourself every damned day just to get a frosty nod. And then had come the blinding knowledge that he'd have to be married to the mother of his kids, so maybe the Cleary way would never work for him.

And then it had hit him that he was really, actually, contemplating fatherhood. *Fatherhood! Him!*

In too deep—caring too much—needing more—*run*.

He should have been happy to be barred today, so he could get his brain out of his gonads and back where it was supposed to be. But after one more sleepless night, thinking about that look on her face as he'd left, here he was.

Because... Well, what had that remote smile of hers meant? That she was finished with him? Well, no. Not happening until *he* was ready. So he was going to charm her into *not* finishing with him—while simultaneously stepping away from the too-deep chasm that was yawning at his feet.

Simple, right?

Yeah, simple. Sure.

Oh, for the love of God, man up*!*

He let his finger land on the buzzer. Waited, drumming his fingers on the wall.

By God, she'd better be at home after spinning him that line about work. She'd better not be out somewhere, with someone, doing something. Or he would— Would— Well, he'd...explode! Or...or something.

'Hello?' Her voice, husky and gorgeous—and for a moment his breath caught.

Get a grip. Get a damned grip!

'It's me,' he said, and winced—because that aggressive tone of voice was not charming.

Long pause. Followed by an arctic, 'Yes?'

'Can I come up?'

'Why?'

'Because I want to see you.'

'You saw me last night. That will have to tide you over until I can spare the time.'

Pause. Pages being riffled. What the hell—? Was she checking her schedule?

'Probably Tuesday.'

Yes, she'd been checking her schedule! Scott felt his temper start to simmer.

'No,' he said, and there was *absolutely* nothing charming about that snapped-out word.

'I beg your pardon?' Past arctic and heading towards ice age.

'Let me come up and explain.'

'The contract doesn't require explanation.'

The freaking *contract*. They didn't *need* a contract to have sex. He hadn't *asked* for a damned contract, had he? She'd *forced* it on him.

'All right, I won't explain,' he said through clenched teeth. He made a mammoth effort to rein in his slipping temper. Charm. Charm, charm, *charm*. 'So...since I'm obviously not coming up, why don't you come down and keep me company while I have a cup of coffee at the cafe across at the marina? Ten minutes and you can get back to work.'

Long, long moment. He heard the breath she sucked in. Waited for the breath out—waited, waited…

And then the breath whooshed out and she said, albeit grudgingly, 'All right.'

Not exactly effusive, but Scott closed his eyes in relief.

Five minutes later she was there, wearing a maxi-dress in sky-blue and a pair of flat silver sandals, her hair swinging in a ponytail. Delectable Sunday-morning fare.

His temper disappeared as if by magic just at the sight of her. He wanted to kiss her so badly he automatically leaned in—but Kate flinched backwards.

'No kissing, remember?' she said.

'Sorry, Kate,' he said, trying to look chastened but not quite managing it. He was just so happy to see her. God, what was happening to him?

They walked in silence to the cafe. Ordered coffee at the counter. A long black for him; a macchiato for Kate. Took their cups to one of the tables closest to the jetty.

'About last night…' Scott said, diving in.

Kate stirred sugar into her coffee. 'I thought you weren't going to explain.'

He ignored that. 'It just got a little…a little…heavy. Talking about children—'

'A subject *you* raised.'

'And about… Well, about all that stuff.' Shaky little laugh. 'Love.' Grimace. 'And…and stuff. I didn't sign up for deep and meaningful. Neither of us did. So I'm not sure how all that came spewing out.'

'It happens,' Kate said. 'It's normal.'

'No, it's not. Not for me. It's not what we—'

'Signed up for,' she cut in dryly. 'Got it. No need to labour the point. And no need to explain, remember?'

'Anyway, I thought we needed a breather—that's all,' he mumbled, and hurriedly picked up his coffee, took a sip, burned his tongue and refused to show it. Because people in control didn't burn their tongues on coffee. And he was. In control. Definitely.

'And yet here you are, the very next morning. That's a breather, is it?'

'I just— I wanted to—'

'Explain. Yep. Got it.'

Kate looked at him—the epitome of inscrutability. She drew in a breath. Seemed on the verge of speaking. But then something behind him caught her attention and her eyes widened.

'Isn't that…? Yes, surely…'

But it was a murmur directed at herself, not him.

She refocused on Scott. 'That's Brodie, isn't it? He really is as gorgeous as his photo.'

CHAPTER TEN

Brodie.

Gorgeous Brodie.

Instinctively Scott hated that combination of words coming out of Kate's mouth.

But then the reality of her words hit.

Brodie. Here.

They were about to come face to face. *If* he could make himself turn around.

But for that first moment he was robbed of the ability to breathe, let alone move, as eight years of feelings rushed at him.

That one hot moment. The sense of betrayal. The bitterness. Shame at what he'd done. Regret at what he'd lost. And…loneliness. A confusing, potent, noxious mix he just couldn't seem to control the way he'd since learned to control everything else.

Kate was watching him. Any minute now she'd ask him what was wrong. It was a wake-up call to get it together—because he did *not* want to be asked.

He took a breath, pushed the feelings away, forced himself to turn.

Recognition in a split second. Brodie's walk. Unmistakable. A loose-limbed, relaxed amble. He was as beach-blond as he'd always been. Tanned. Wearing sunglasses. Boat shoes, jeans, pale blue shirt with the sleeves casually rolled up to the elbows. And a tattoo—an anchor—on the underside of one forearm.

Scott remembered that tattoo. He'd been impressed by it. And a little bit jealous. Because Knights didn't get tattoos—and yet when he'd seen Brodie's he'd wanted to be the kind of guy who *did*. Not that he couldn't have had one—

then *or* now. But deep down he'd always known it wasn't his thing. It was the rebelliousness of a tattoo that had appealed to him, not the reality of ink in his skin. Everything about breezy, laidback Brodie had appealed to Scott—who was the exact opposite.

He knew the instant Brodie recognised him from the slight hitch in his stride. The sunglasses were whipped off, the eyes widened, a smile started…then stopped. Replaced by wariness. Then the sunglasses were shoved into the pocket of his shirt—Brodie was not the kind of guy to hide behind sunglasses or anything else—and Brodie walked on, heading straight for them. He stopped at their table.

'Scott,' he said.

'Brodie.'

Okay, it was all a bit ridiculous. *Scott. Brodie.* Kate would be coughing up her name in a minute. Maybe the barista would pop out and give them a *Dean.*

Scott laughed—couldn't seem to help it. And he had the satisfaction of seeing surprise replace the wariness. It felt good.

'Join us for coffee?' he asked.

'Sure,' Brodie said, recovering from the surprise, and snagged a spare seat from the next table.

Kate reached out a hand to shake. 'I'm Kate. A…' Tiny, tiny pause. 'A friend of Scott's.'

Brodie smiled as he took her hand, said nothing—but Kate blushed.

She flicked a glance at Scott, then back to Brodie. 'I'm a friend of Willa's too. And Amy's.'

'Ah, you're *that* Kate.'

'Oh, dear, you're not going to make a lawyer joke, are you?'

'Fresh out of lawyer jokes, sorry!'

'Well, isn't *that* a breath of fresh air?' she said with another of those flicking looks. At Scott, then Brodie.

Scott felt the sting. So he'd made one lawyer joke—just

once! That didn't put him ahead of Dirty Martini Barnaby in the woeful pick-up line competition, did it?

'I'll go and get the coffee,' Kate said. 'What'll it be, Brodie?'

'Black. Same as Scott.'

Nod. Smile. And she was off.

'Girlfriend?' Brodie asked, once Kate was out of earshot.

Scott crossed his arms over his chest. Shook his head. 'Nothing like that.'

Pause. A long one.

Okay—they were back to ridiculous.

Time to suck it up and move on.

'Are we going to get all girly and talk about things?'

Brodie winced. 'God, I hope not.'

'Right. Good. Great.'

Arms were uncrossed. His hand held out. Brodie took it. Shook.

'That's it?' Brodie asked.

'Well, let's see…' Scott frowned, looking as if he was thinking deeply. 'We were best friends. A girl who never loved me—a girl I didn't really love—fell for you. I punched you. You got an attack of nobility and took off. She stayed and was miserable.' He shrugged. 'I'd say between the three of us we royally screwed that up. It's sure felt screwed up for the past eight years, and I'm kind of over everything about it. So, yeah—that's it. From my perspective at least.'

'I've missed you, you know—you bastard.'

'Hey—we're not getting all girly, remember?'

Brodie laughed. 'That's why I added the "bastard".'

'Yeah, well, "bastard" doesn't make it any less girly.'

'Still an uptight control freak, then.'

'And you're still…what? King of the hair braids?'

'The sisters have outgrown the braids.' Brodie shuddered, but he was laughing too. 'Thank God.'

Slight pause. But not uncomfortable.

And then the question just came out of Scott's mouth, as though it was just…time. 'So, have you seen her?'

'No.'

'Do you want to?'

Long pause. 'Eight years,' Brodie said.

And somehow Scott understood the world in those two words. 'Okay, enough said. But just so you know—it wouldn't bother me. Not any more.'

Brodie jerked his head backwards towards the cafe counter. 'Because of Red?'

Brodie looked over Scott's shoulder, saw Kate coming towards them with a coffee-laden tray. That rolling walk. So damned sexy.

He blinked. Swallowed a sigh. Shook his head. 'That's just an…arrangement.'

Kate arrived, distributed the coffee. Sat down. 'So, how's the luxury yacht touring business?' she asked Brodie. 'In Queensland, right?'

'I should warn you,' Scott broke in. 'Kate's main goal in life is to steal a boat and sail off on an adventure—except she can't sail.' He smiled at Kate, expecting her to share the joke. But she merely looked steadily back at him.

Brodie was smiling at her too, and she *did* smile at him—and Scott found himself gritting his teeth. *A contract. Just a contract—and this is why.*

'Well, Kate, I'm down for a couple of weeks,' Brodie said. 'I'll take you sailing. Unless…?' He glanced at Scott. 'Are *you* going to teach her?'

Scott shook his head quickly. 'I sold my boat.' He looked at Kate; she was still smiling at Brodie. *Just a contract.* 'She's all yours.'

He caught—just—an infinitesimal flinch, the blink of hurt on Kate's face, and wanted to call the words back. But it was too late. Her smile went megawatt—straight at Brodie. And Scott wanted to claim that wide, gorgeous mouth of hers right there and then, in front of Brodie and everyone else in the vicinity. Screw the no-kissing rule.

'If you're still here next Saturday, Brodie, I'll take you up on that,' Kate said, and then she was tossing back her macchiato—and that *had* to burn her damned tongue. Not that you could tell from the next blinding smile she beamed at Brodie!

Brodie and Kate discussed timing, swapped numbers, while Scott sat there like a statue—ice on the outside, volcano on the inside.

And then Kate put some money on the table and Scott had to grit his teeth again. Because—come *on*!—couldn't he even buy her a damned cup of coffee?

The contract. Fifty-fifty. No, you can't buy her a damned coffee.

'Work calls,' she said, all cheery and unconcerned. 'Bye, guys. See you Saturday, Brodie.'

Gone.

Brodie looked at Scott, who had yet to take a sip from his fresh cup.

'Are you insane?' Brodie asked conversationally.

Scott laughed, and if it had a slight edge of insanity he wasn't going to acknowledge it. 'Tell me about your business,' he said instead.

When Kate got back to her apartment she was so furious—and disillusioned, and…and *hurt*, she couldn't think straight.

God, she hoped Scott hadn't seen the hurt.

Not that Scott, who didn't *get* hurt, would ever understand it. He'd just think she was *piqued*. The way he had last night just because she'd finally taken a stand and told him not to turn up today.

Well, that had sure worked!

And she really *must* be a pathetic nymphomaniac. Because she'd been so glad to see him when she should have been annoyed. So very glad…right up until he'd told her he hadn't *signed up* for deep and meaningful.

Nobody signed up for deep and meaningful. It just…*happened.*

But not, apparently, to Scott.

Well, what had she expected? That two weeks of rock-your-hormones sex would somehow make her special? That the guy she was sleeping with might want to teach her to sail rather than palming her off on someone else? That he might actually introduce her to his friends so she didn't have to introduce herself, when she didn't have the remotest idea how to categorise their relationship for public consumption? That he might, somehow, claim her as someone just a little bit special?

The way she wanted to—

Ooohhhh.

She shuddered out a breath as reality hit her like a truck. She wanted to claim him. *Mine, mine, mine.*

Great! Just freaking great. Because Scott had made it pretty clear this morning that he was reading from a different script—and it wasn't a romance. To Scott she was a collection of body parts, transferable to his friend for any non-bedroom stuff!

She's all yours!

Well, *quid pro quo. There* was a legal term for Scott to mull over.

If she was nothing but a collection of body parts to him then he would be nothing but a collection of body parts to *her.*

Scott Knight: Kate Cleary's stud.

No more kissing. No dates that weren't really dates. No unscheduled drop-ins. No fireside chats. Nothing except sex. Only twice a week, because she was no longer in a negotiating mood. Starting with a Play Time that would fry his nether regions!

Before she could think twice she grabbed her phone, pulled up Scott's number and got texting.

Play Time. Tuesday. 9 p.m. Ellington Lane.

That would shock him. He'd be sitting there with Brodie, never dreaming she'd text him so soon after that dismal coffee catch-up. He probably expected her to be lying face-down on her bed, crying into her pillow because she was *piqued.* Well, he could just—

Ding.

Text message. She grabbed her phone. Opened Scott's text message.

Roger that.

With a smiley face.

A…a *smiley face*?

Now, you see—that was why he wasn't the right man for her.

Or maybe why he is.

'Yes, thank you, subconscious. Not helpful.'

Scott was champing at the bit as he approached Ellington Lane on Tuesday night.

He had no idea what fantasy Kate had dreamt up to carry out in this dingy, narrow, deserted laneway, but hopefully it didn't involve his murder—because Ellington Lane certainly looked as if it regularly saw a dead body, and Kate surely must want to kill him after Sunday.

He wasn't even certain she was going to turn up, given she hadn't bothered answering any of his thousand calls since then.

But he was here waiting anyway—he who *never* had sex in public places—so hungry for her he'd do anything.

He was going to make tonight *so* damned good for her. Use his body to show her he didn't mean what he'd said—because clearly he couldn't trust his malfunctioning brain to choose the right words.

He still couldn't believe he'd said it. *She's all yours.* Just because she'd smiled at Brodie and he'd wanted to grab her and demand she stop. Because she was his, his, *his*, and she was supposed to smile at *him*—got it?

God, he was a moron! *You're mine—so go with that guy instead, why don't you?*

He *deserved* to be standing here, lust-starved and desperate, in an ill-lit, deserted alley, wondering if she'd turn up, shivering at the thought of what she'd do to him, and just… well, *longing* for her.

He took a deep breath, trying to steady himself.

And suddenly there she was.

CHAPTER ELEVEN

SCOTT'S HEART LURCHED as Kate took one step. Stopped.

She was backlit by a street lamp just outside the lane. Standing with her legs slightly apart, looking tough. Tight pants, high boots, hands on hips, wearing some kind of cap.

She started walking towards him—very slowly, very deliberately. Halfway, he could see she was wearing a police uniform—but a sexed-up, skintight version.

His mouth went dry—so dry that when she asked, 'What seems to be the problem?' he couldn't answer.

And then she was in front of him, and he could smell tuberose, and he wanted to throw himself at her feet and beg.

'Not talking?' she asked, and there was a snap in her voice. 'Then I'd say you're up to no good. Turn around, hands wide on the wall.'

He did as he was told.

She kicked between his feet. 'Spread 'em.'

He *spread 'em* with alacrity, and then breathed out a long, silent sigh of surrender as she plastered herself against his back.

'So... Are you behaving yourself?' she asked, and chuckled, low and breathy, right in his ear.

'Yes, Officer,' he said—or at least he tried to, but it came out as a half-strangled gargle.

'Now, why don't I believe you? What's in your pockets?'

'Nothing.'

'I think I'll check for myself.'

Next moment her hands were diving into the back pockets of his jeans.

'Condom,' she said. 'Not exactly "nothing". Not soliciting, are you?'

'No.'

'No *what*?'

'No, Officer.'

'I'll hold on to this,' she said, and he imagined her sliding the condom into the back pocket of her tight, tight pants.

'Right. Let's check your other pockets,' she said.

And her hands were *there*, digging into his front pockets, making his heartbeat go off like a cracker as she 'accidentally' nudged against the erection straining fiercely against the denim.

'All clear,' she breathed against his ear. 'So—why don't you just tell me what you've been up to so I don't have to keep searching?'

'But I've done nothing wrong, Officer.'

'So let me ask you, buddy: do you know the meaning of the term *ignorantia juris non excusat*?'

Oh, God. God, God, God.

'No. But it sounds…sexy.'

'Well, it's not sexy,' she said, despite the fact that she was unbuttoning his jeans, sliding his zipper down, sliding her hands inside, over his erection, squeezing, stroking. 'It means ignorance of the law is not an excuse.'

He groaned.

'Am I hurting you?' she asked.

'No. No, Officer, you're not hurting me.'

'Then why are you groaning?'

'Can't…*ahh*…help it. Sorry. J-Just what law am I ignorant of?'

'The law that says you're not allowed to bribe a police officer.'

'But I'm not,' he said, just as her hands went beneath his underwear, cool and silky and freaking *wonderful*. Another groan slipped out. Could a man die of lust? Because he was on the way.

'Then maybe you should *think* about bribing me, so I'll let you off the hook.'

'Um... Um... Um...' Seriously, his brain was fricasseed.

'Something that doesn't involve a condom, since I've confiscated that,' she said.

'Um...'

'Turn around.'

He turned fast enough to give himself a corkscrew knee injury. Reached automatically for her.

'No touching an officer,' she barked. 'Just stand there. Stand there and take it like a man.'

Before he knew what was happening she'd shoved him against the wall. And then she was on her knees in front of him, dragging his jeans down, just low enough to free him. Holding the base of him with one hand, cupping his balls with the other, she licked the very tip of him. Delicate, fluttery...gradually moving down the shaft, back up, down, then up. Alternately kissing and licking. Gradually increasing the pressure of her tongue, her lips.

He wanted to touch her hair, but she'd wound it up under the police cap. And looking at that cap as she worked on him was getting him more excited than he'd ever been in his life.

She tilted her head back, replaced her mouth with her hands, looked up at him, parted her lips, licked that heavy top lip...and with a quick, wicked smile closed her mouth over him.

Scott let loose with a whole string of groaning cries as she sucked him, using her lips, her tongue, her teeth, even the roof of her mouth. Stretching him, laving him, devouring him. Her hands were moving everywhere her mouth wasn't until he was half insane with need. He felt the orgasm building, clawing to get out.

And then she did something with her tongue, and he looked down at the police cap, caught a glimpse of pale skin as she angled her head and her mouth performed a twist he'd never experienced before, and it was rushing at him.

'Kate! Kate, I'm going to come!' he said in urgent warning.

But she just kept right on going, shifting so that her hands were gripping his hips, keeping him inside her mouth, and he thought for a moment he was going to pass out with the pleasure of it. She kept up the pressure right through his explosion of a release, as his hips jerked under her hands and he spilled himself to the point of exhaustion.

And then she got to her feet. Looked at him as she licked that top lip again. 'So, whatever you were doing tonight before I caught you—' as though she'd just written him a ticket '—don't do it again.'

And then she turned, started walking away.

Scott couldn't believe, at first, that she would just leave him like that—but she kept going.

'Kate!' he called out, pulling up his jeans.

Stop. Turn. 'It's Officer Cleary.'

'I'll come with you. I owe you.'

'Is that another bribe?' She shook her head. 'Now, you see, that's why I don't associate with criminals.'

'But—'

'You'll receive a message from the station in a few days, once I've cleared your name, and then we'll see.'

She turned again, walked briskly down the lane. And was gone.

He finished tucking in his shirt. Feeling both incredibly sated and hugely unsatisfied.

Because she was gone. Without having let him touch her once.

Gone. Just like Sunday morning.

Gone.

One thing Scott knew was that he wasn't a fan of this 'gone girl' thing. He was going to have to let her know he didn't appreciate her just leaving. Like, *bang*, leaving.

Even if it *was* essentially what he'd done to her on Saturday night—and without giving her any kind of release at all. But he'd had a *reason*. Self-preservation! Her? Tonight? What possible reason could she have had?

Bang. Gone.

Nope. He didn't like it one bit.

The next day Scott left two phone messages for Kate.

Her response was to text him back.

Play Time. Thursday. Your house. 7 p.m.

He swore long and loud. Play Time was all very well, but he wanted to talk to her. That interrupted conversation from Sunday morning was still heavy on his mind and he wanted to fix it. Because things didn't feel…*right*.

He tried to call her again—she didn't pick up. So he called her office, spoke to Deb. Received the message that Kate was interstate, working on a child custody case.

'And it's a messy one,' Deb told him. 'So you've got no chance of getting hold of her and please don't try. She's…'

He could feel the hesitation. Teetering, teetering… *Go on, tell me, tell me.* But no.

'Look, just leave her to it,' Deb said, and hung up.

He found himself hanging on to the phone, reluctant to let it go. As if it was some line of communication he didn't want to snap.

Which was just plain stupid.

He forced himself to disconnect.

He worried about what Deb had said. *'She's…'* Just the one word. Hesitant, hanging, worrying.

She's…what? She's…not interested in you any more? She's…having a meltdown? Having a biopsy? Eating chicken for lunch. What, dammit? *What?*

He paced around his office, needing to speak to her, knowing he couldn't.

Focusing on the first thing that had popped into his head—that she wasn't interested in him any more—calmed him a little. Because if that were true she wouldn't have sent him that Play Time text.

And they had a *contract*—which might be stupid but at least meant that even if she was over him she still had to see him for another week and a half. So he had time to work on her, get her back onside. Time to make the sex so phenomenal she'd be sorry she didn't have a clause demanding seven nights a week instead of a lousy two.

Starting Thursday, when he saw her again. At *his* house, this time. In *his* bed

He never brought women home, because...well, *because*. But Kate...?

He sucked in a breath as the image of her in his house shimmered in his head.

Would she like it?

In his bed?

How would she look there?

Not that those thoughts were *germane*! The *germane* thing was that it would be the perfect opportunity to gauge whether the wattage of their sexual attraction needed to be amped up. Although, frankly, much more wattage might just finish him off.

A new image popped into his head. Kate on her knees in that dark alley, going down on him. Refusing to allow him to touch her. Just leaving him there.

Okay, so he *hadn't* calmed down.

He wouldn't be calm until he spoke to her. Until he knew what was going on with her.

He wouldn't be calm until *she* was calm.

Because he knew, *knew*, she wasn't calm. He'd heard the worry in Deb's voice. A child custody case. The kind that hit Kate the hardest. She would be stressed. And...and *grieving*. Interstate—on her own. With nobody to hold her and tell her it was going to be all right, even if it wasn't. Just to *be* there. With her—for her.

And then he stopped himself. She had a family to turn to. A large, loving family. She didn't need him.

Sex. No strings. That was what they had. She'd made that plain by responding to his voicemail messages with a text. She was going through hell…but for him she offered Play Time. Because that was the deal. He'd teased her that she was falling behind on the fantasies, so she was dishing them up. Twice in one week. Any man would want that. Phillip the aged barrister would be *thrilled* with that.

Scott found that his hands had balled into fists and determinedly unclenched them. Flexed them. Took a deep, calming breath.

Better.

It was no good getting bent out of shape over Phillip. Over Play Time. Or over Kate being alone dealing with hell. No damned good.

So he would take Deb's advice. He would wait until Thursday. He would see what fantasy she came up with. He would respond sexually.

And that would be all.

CHAPTER TWELVE

KATE TOOK EXTRA-SPECIAL care getting ready for Play Time on Thursday. Her hair was swinging loose, artfully dishevelled, and she had on her favourite red lipstick—which was fine for today because there would be no kissing.

She was wearing her sexiest underwear. Nude mesh and lace, complete with suspender belt—and she'd gone for ultra-sheer black stockings as a contrast. Achingly high black stilettos. A taupe trench coat, tied but not buttoned.

That was it. Not one thing more. Perfect for the role she was playing.

A role that would not involve any of those pesky *deep and meaningful* fireside chats.

Scott would be happy about that. And, frankly, she was happy about it too. Having spent two soul-destroying days fighting to get her client's little boy back, 'Kate Cleary' deserved the night off. Tomorrow she would take up the legal cudgels again—but tonight, Kate wanted to be someone else.

When Kate arrived at Scott's house in East Sydney she had to recheck his business card to make sure she had the right address—because she was standing in front of an old church. She'd already guessed Scott's house was going to be special, if Silverston was anything to go by. But this was something else. She couldn't wait to see inside.

No! She caught herself up. She wasn't a starry-eyed girlfriend, about to get a guided tour of her boyfriend's architectural wonder of a home. Scott—who hadn't even invited her here—was probably in there pacing the floor, hating the idea of her invading his private space. So she wouldn't give him the satisfaction of being interested.

She noted the intercom in place of a doorbell, which reminded her that his house doubled as a second office. Perfect, since she was here on 'business'.

She waited outside for seven o'clock to hit, using the time to layer on the persona she'd chosen, mentally steeling herself to resist the first heart-melting look at him, the first touch. And then, on the dot, she pushed the button.

Instant answer.

'Kate?' Sounding anxious. 'There in two seconds.'

'Oh, Mr Knight, has there been a mistake?' she asked, all breathy and flustered.

Pause. And then, 'Kate? It *is* Kate, right?'

'It's *Lorelei*, Mr Knight. Don't you remember? You booked a home visit. Are you going to buzz me in?'

Another pause. Longer.

He would be processing that. Kate's voice giving a name he'd never heard, referring to a job he hadn't booked.

And then the intercom clicked off. So...was he *not* going to buzz her in?

But less than ten seconds later the door opened and he was there. He took her arm, drew her in. Tried to kiss her.

'Oh, sorry, Mr Knight. Miss Kitty doesn't like her girls to kiss the clients.'

His jaw tightened, but he said nothing.

Despite Kate's best efforts she couldn't help giving the space just one sweeping glance. Soaring arched ceilings, like a...well, like a *church*. Stained-glass windows, stark white walls, honey wood floors, a staircase that provided a pop of colour, with steps painted a vivid red, leading up to a mezzanine.

Enough! Stop!

'Where do you want me, Mr Knight?' she asked.

He gestured to the staircase. 'Go up.'

She walked quickly to the stairs and ascended. She paused at the top, needing direction—and had to close her eyes to stop herself peering over the half-wall. She was not going to look again. Not, not, *not*.

'There,' Scott said from behind her—and she opened her eyes to find him pointing to a long, intricately carved wooden screen at one end of the mezzanine floor.

Her heart started to race as she approached the screen. She was so excited to see what was behind it. And when she stepped around it she gasped. Just couldn't keep it in.

More stained-glass windows—taking the place of a fancy bedhead—dominated the space. The walls were painted a dull gold. A huge bed of dark wood with a blood-red coverlet sat on a raised stone dais. There were Persian rugs on the wood floor surrounding the dais. Antique chairs—grand and austere—were positioned either side of the stone slab, with candlesticks as tall as Scott beside them. The room was heartbreakingly, unexpectedly beautiful.

Kate schooled her features to show nothing as she turned back to Scott and smiled—a professionally vacant smile.

He was watching her with a hint of disapproval that she forced herself to ignore. Conservative Scott Knight *would* disapprove of a prostitute—but that didn't mean he wouldn't enjoy the experience.

She undid her belt, held the coat wide. 'Do you like what you see, Mr Knight?'

He swallowed, hard, as his eyes slid down her body and stuck at the tops of her black stockings. 'Yes,' he said. 'I want to touch you.'

'You can touch. Just no kissing.' And with that, she shrugged out of the coat and went to lay it on one of the chairs.

But she didn't make it that far. Because Scott was after her in a heartbeat.

Kate shivered as he grabbed her, as he spun her to face him, as he yanked her hair back to give him access to her neck, as he licked the pulse beating there.

And then he lowered his head, going straight for her nipple, taking it into his mouth through the mesh of her bra, sucking hard, harder, until she cried out. He didn't stop, just moved to the other nipple, then back again. Back and forth.

She was a quivering mess of nerves and need by the time he stepped back, took her coat and threw it at the chair.

He swallowed hard again as his eyes dipped to her breasts. Her nipples were dark and distended, the mesh covering them wet. His hands moved to her breasts, fingers pinching where his mouth had been. Pinching, rolling. And then he was digging into the thin cups, tearing them down so that her nipples popped over the tops, and his mouth was back, suckling and nipping and licking her.

Her hands were in his hair, pulling hard enough to hurt—but to keep him there, not to drag him away. She could feel the unbearable wetness between her thighs, wanted his hands there, his mouth.

As though he'd divined that, he dropped to his knees, kissed the tops of her stockings—one, then the other—and licked, *slooowly*, along the top of each, where her thighs were naked. Kate was scared she'd collapse on the spot, it was so erotic.

And then, completely at odds with the languor of that, he yanked her panties down to her knees and shoved his tongue between her legs. Her tangled underwear trapped her and limited Scott's access, forcing him to concentrate his tongue in one ravaging line. *So...damned...good.* She heard his ragged breathing, felt his fingers digging into the backs of her thighs, hard enough to bruise.

He growled something, impatient, and next moment was dragging her down onto the rug, ripping at her underwear, manoeuvring her onto her hands and knees. And then he was behind her, his mouth on her again, sucking her, forcing his tongue inside her until she was panting and whimpering with need.

A quick rustling sound, but his mouth didn't stop. Condom. She heard the packet tear. Zip opening. She imagined him sheathing himself. Knew he would be inside her soon.

She pushed herself back against his mouth, urging him wordlessly to hurry, to fill her.

He moved, covered her, his mouth at her ear. 'You're going to have to ask me,' he breathed.

'Please...*please*.'

'Please what?'

'I want you inside me. Do it. Inside—*now*.'

The words weren't even out of her mouth before he'd shoved himself into her. Holding her hips, screwing into her as though he had to get close, closer, closer still. Up to the hilt. Over and over. Pounding, pounding, pounding. And then he tensed, coming with a loud cry. His hands reached for her waist, yanked her upright, her back against his chest, and he was feeling for her clitoris, fingers forking either side, perfect pressure.

Ah, ahh, ahhhh.

'Come for me, Kate. Come now...come.'

And, in a blast of almost excruciating pleasure, she exploded into orgasm.

Slowly, Scott withdrew from her. Sat back, turned her, hoisting her onto his lap

He tried again to kiss her, and she drew back. 'No kissing,' she said, but was horrified to find her voice wobbling.

Even worse—he'd heard it too.

He looked at her—sharp, concerned. 'What is it, Kate?'

'Lorelei. And no kissing.'

'I'm not kissing Lorelei. I'm kissing Kate,' Scott said.

He coaxed her to open her mouth, took his leisurely time, letting his tongue move from licking her lips to sliding inside.

After a long, delicious moment he stopped, edged a fraction away, smiled into her eyes. That smile she'd only seen once—that night—but it was even more devastating now, because it was layered with gentleness.

I am in such trouble here.

'Kate...' he said, and his voice shook.

Such trouble. And she didn't need trouble.

Steeling herself, she smiled back. 'Lorelei,' she corrected. 'And that will be two thousand dollars, Mr Knight.'

The shock on Scott's face had her shrinking inside, but she forced herself to hold his eyes.

And then he smiled again—but it was back to the juke-box, pick a smile and whirl. 'Your prices are too low. I would have paid five. In fact, I *will* pay five. Because, as I recall, I booked Lorelei's services for a full night.'

'We don't stay overnight, Scott...you and I.' *Uh-oh*, the wobble.

'Miss Kitty says Lorelei *does*. And if you want your five thousand dollars that's what you're going to have to do.' He gave her a boost off his lap. 'So up you go. Whatever you've still got on, get it off. Then get into that bed.'

The next morning, after *Lorelei* had belted herself into her trench coat and left, Scott threw down three cups of coffee. He needed the caffeine to get his brain and his body functioning again.

But it didn't work.

Something was bothering him. Very deeply.

And it was... Well, it was Play Time.

The whole 'Lorelei' thing was eating at him. After that one frenzied bout of lovemaking on the rug, when he'd kissed Kate, he'd felt such an overwhelming burst of joy. Kate...in his arms, in his house, and he'd wanted her so damned much.

And she'd responded by asking him for her fee.

So he'd decided to get his money's worth. All night long he'd been at her, taking her with lips, tongue, fingers, his never-ending hard-on. And she'd met him move for move, always receptive—as 'Miss Kitty' expected—never saying no, opening her arms, her legs.

Everything but her mouth.

Because he'd tried to kiss her many times, and each time she'd pulled away with a coyly admonishing slap on the wrist, the shoulder, the butt, and a reminder of Miss Kitty's rules.

He'd tried to talk to her in those respite periods while they'd recharged their burnt-out batteries. About the child custody case. Her mother's art. Maeve and Molly, Shay and Lilith, Gus and Aristotle. Even about Deb. But every time he'd been frozen into crunchable cubes by her vacant 'Lorelei' stare.

The end result was that although he could have written his own sex manual after experimenting so comprehensively with Kate's body during the night, he wasn't satisfied.

And the flat fact was he didn't *like* Play Time.

There. He'd admitted it.

He must be certifiable, but he couldn't seem to whip up enthusiasm for any more fantasy-land stuff. It was like the sexual version of Brodie's tattoo—nice in theory, but just not him. He must be more of a Knight than he'd thought. Conservative. Boring, even.

Did Kate find him boring? In bed? Out of it? Both? Because she was suddenly very interested in Play Time. No kissing. No talking. Just role play. Was Play Time the non-nautical equivalent of a yacht heading to the Whitsundays? Taking Kate away from humdrum in the bedroom?

He put his coffee cup down with a clatter.

She'd made him *pay* for it! He almost hadn't believed it when Kate had demanded his cheque for five thousand dollars—and then had actually taken it when he'd jokingly written it out, before breezing out of the house.

A house she hadn't expressed the slightest interest in.

And his house was worth *some* level of interest from the woman he was exclusively sleeping with, dammit.

Not good enough, Kate.

He wanted to know what she thought about it. And he was going to force her to tell him. Did she like it? Hate it? Want to change it? *What?*

Scott gave her three hours—time to slough off that annoying Lorelei—then called her mobile. No answer. So he called her office.

Deb picked up the phone—and told him in no uncertain terms he wouldn't be getting a look-in that day because Kate was in back-to-back meetings.

Well, he wasn't going to put himself through the embarrassment of having his call go to voicemail, as had been happening with monotonous regularity. He would email her instead. And if she didn't respond he would… He would… He would do something as yet undetermined! But *something*, at any rate.

Calmly, rationally, unemotionally, he tapped out a message suggesting they catch up for dinner that night and fired it off, knowing she'd pick up the email on her smartphone whether she was in a meeting or not.

And then he waited, refreshing his emails every thirty seconds, working himself into a lather over the fifty-fifty rule she'd probably insist on when the bill came tonight. Well, screw her stupid fifty-fifty rule—*he* would be picking up the tab. Like a normal guy who *wasn't* a complete arsehole would do when he took a woman out for dinner.

Refresh, refresh, refresh…

Come on—respond!

Fifteen minutes later his phone buzzed.

Text message.

His stomach clenched as he reached for his phone. Because he just knew.

And, yep, there it was.

Play Time. Sunday. Noon. My apartment.

Scott hurled the phone across the room.

CHAPTER THIRTEEN

KATE SAW THE Whitsundays girls in their usual corner table at Fox on Friday night, cocktails already in hand, and thought, *Thank heaven.* A rowdy, uncomplicated girls' night out was exactly what she needed.

Jessica, who was facing the entrance, was the first to notice her across the crowded floor of the bar area, and she waved enthusiastically as Kate squeezed her way across the floor.

Willa slid a Manhattan—Kate's favourite cocktail—to her as she collapsed into her seat.

Kate, surprised and touched by Willa's prescience, kissed her.

'I knew you'd need it.' Willa's smile was full of sympathy. 'How did the case end up?'

Kate eased the elastic from her hair and ran a tired hand through the strands. 'Victory for Team Cleary.'

'Fantastic!'

'But it was harrowing, even for a jaded cynic of a lawyer.'

'You're not a jaded cynic,' Willa said. 'Or you wouldn't care so deeply.'

Kate felt a little prickle of tears—and that just underscored how wrung-out she was, because she never let her emotions show in public. She blinked the tears away, smiling determinedly.

'Whatever I am, I sure need this!' she said, picking up her glass and half draining it. 'And now—a *fun* topic of conversation, please.'

Amy laughed. 'Well, you're just in time to hear Willa tell us about her most romantic moment with Rob. Will that do?'

'That will do very, very nicely!' Kate said. 'But first…' She drained the rest of her Manhattan and signalled to a passing server for another round of drinks for all four of them. 'Better! Okay, Willa darling, spill it!'

'I'm not sure you guys will think it's romantic, but…oh, God, it *is*!'

'Don't make us beg!' Amy said.

'Well…Rob recommended me to a chief financial officer…'

'And…?' Amy urged.

'For a vitamin distribution company.'

'And…?' Jessica prompted.

Willa sucked her mojito through a straw. 'Rob told him I was super-bright!'

'And so you are, my darling,' Kate said.

'And…and brilliant!'

'Nice,' Jessica added.

'And that I knew about foreign-owned entities, so maybe I could help find a creative solution to a problem the company was having.'

Kate laughed. 'Okaaaay… That's not exactly floating my boat just yet, but I'm hoping something juicy is coming up.'

Willa beamed around at them, glowing with love. 'The CFO said they'd had a dozen accountants try to find a solution and fail. He said Rob had assured him I would be able to help. And I *did*! And I got *paid*!' She sighed, all satisfaction, and sucked up another mouthful of mojito. 'Isn't that romantic?'

Kate, Amy and Jessica stared at her, and then Amy burst out laughing.

One by one the others started laughing too.

'Hey, it's not funny,' Willa protested, but she had a smile lurking too.

Jessica said, 'Well, it's not exactly rose petals strewn over the bedcovers.'

Amy looked at Jessica. 'Seriously? *That's* your romantic fantasy? I would never have picked it, Miss I-can-play-basketball-and-change-a-car-tyre-when-the-game's-over.'

'Well, I *can* change a car tyre,' Jessica said. 'But I'd like a rose-petal-strewn-bed for afterwards. With candlelight. And being hand-fed ripe strawberries in the midst of it all. Lovely.' She raised her eyebrows at Amy. 'Why? What's yours, Miss Personality-plus?'

'Easy. A defender,' Amy said definitely. 'Someone who will ride in like a medieval knight on a destrier, catch me up and save me from…from…' She stopped, smiled a little sheepishly. 'Well, from danger,' she finished, then sighed. '*That's* romance.'

All three looked expectantly at Kate.

'Oh, no,' she said.

'Come on,' Amy begged.

Jessica sniggered. 'I'll bet it has something to do with Big Burt the handy vibrator.'

Kate felt herself blush—and then blushed harder when three jaws dropped simultaneously as the girls took in her colour change.

'No way!' Amy said.

'Not…not exactly,' Kate said, and then she threw in the metaphorical towel. 'Okay, you asked for it. It *does* happen to involve Burt. Not *Big* Burt, but his namesake. Burt *Lancaster.* And Deborah Kerr. And, no, Jessica, that does *not* mean I want to be in a three-way with Burt and Deborah, who are, in fact, both deceased. And, no, I never wanted to have sex with Burt Lancaster when he was alive either.'

'So what *does* it mean?'

'It means— Oh, dear, this is kind of embarrassing! Okay, it's all about my obsession with *From Here to Eternity*, which I really need to outgrow. And you have *got* to watch that movie, Jessica! It should be mandatory viewing for all women.'

'Okay—it's on the download list!' Jessica said promptly.

Kate ran a finger around the rim of her empty glass. 'When you get to the scene at the beach their passion is just so…so *strong…* And there's nothing they can do about it except acknowledge it and know that it's going to happen. They've been swimming, and they're at the shore, and she's lying on the sand, and then he's there with her, and she's in his arms. And he's kissing her like he can't help himself, with the waves breaking over them… And when she runs for drier ground he follows her, and drops to his knees, and basically…basically *falls* on her—like he's so damned hungry for everything about her… Well, *whew*!' She waved a hand in front of her heated face. 'That is *some* scene.'

Jessica was, likewise, fanning herself. 'It beats Willa's chief financial officer and my rose petals, that's for sure. And it gives Amy's destrier a nudge too.'

Kate laughed. 'Well, suffice to say if a man kisses me like that in the surf I'm his. From here to eternity.'

There was a moment of respectful silence.

And then Willa smiled. 'There's one thing I need to add to my own account,' she said, all smug. 'When Rob spoke to that vitamin-company CFO he said…' Pause. Blink. 'He said…' She paused again, went all dreamy-eyed. 'He said he'd trust me with his life.'

'Oh…' said Amy.

'Oh…' said Jessica.

'Oh,' said Kate. Deep breath. 'In that case, you win.'

Willa was glowing. 'Yes, I do, don't I?' she asked, delighted.

'I wonder what Chantal would say?' Amy mused. 'About *her* most romantic moment, I mean.'

Willa pondered that, eyes half closed. 'It would be something to do with dancing. The romance of swaying against a man, having him hold you close, showing you just by the way he looked at you that you were his…'

Four sighs as their fresh round of drinks was deposited—and then four dreamy sips.

'So Chantal's in your camp, Willa. She's already had her moment,' Amy said. 'With Brodie, I mean, at Weeping Reef.

Because that's what happened, right? The dance, the look that everyone could see?'

'It *was* sizzling,' Willa said.

Amy drained her glass. 'No wonder poor Scott got bent out of shape.'

Kate felt the blood drain from her face. What? *What?* 'Scott?' she said, and thanked all the saints in heaven that her voice had come out halfway normal.

'Oh, yeah—you don't know the story,' Willa said, sounding sad. 'Scott and Chantal were an item at Weeping Reef. *The* item. Until Brodie came on the scene. Actually, they were an item even after Brodie arrived. Chantal and Brodie didn't seem to like each other—except that they *did*, if you know what I mean, and just didn't recognise it. I think I was the only one who saw what was happening. Scott certainly didn't, and he was blindsided. Chantal was dancing with Brodie—which was no big deal. She loves dancing. Lives for it. But she could never get Scott onto the dance floor, and he never had a problem with her dancing with other men. But that night it was…*more*. Like a…a flash. The way they moved together…the way they looked at each other. Everyone knew in that one moment that Chantal and Brodie belonged together.'

Kate remembered asking Scott to dance at that dinner. Him telling her he didn't. Ever. Remembered him insisting on absolute fidelity in their contract.

'So what happened?' she asked through her aching throat.

'A huge argument—which ended with Scott slugging Brodie. Brodie took off, leaving Scott and Chantal at the resort together…but *not* together. Not *at all* together. Looking back, it all seems so needlessly dramatic, given nothing actually happened between Chantal and Brodie. But Scott and Brodie haven't spoken since.'

Uh-oh. Awkward. 'Actually, they…they *have* spoken,' Kate said, and took a quick silent breath to steady her nerves for the inquisition.

The three girls stared at her, waiting.

Kate took a slow sip of her Manhattan. 'I was having coffee with Scott, at the marina across the road from my place, on Sunday morning. And Brodie walked past. His boat's moored there.'

'Oh, my God!' Amy squealed. 'I don't know what part to ask about first. Coffee with Scott? How did *that* come about?'

'We've seen each other a couple of times since Willa's party.'

There was a long pregnant pause.

'It's nothing,' Kate said.

More silence.

'Really nothing,' she insisted. 'There was an…an attraction there, and we wanted to see if there was anything worth exploring. That's all.'

'And is there?' Jessica asked.

Kate took another sip. 'No. There really isn't,' she said, and felt the truth of that, the pang of it, pierce right through her heart. It took her a moment to recover from that certainty, to find her voice again. 'Anyway, Sunday morning he was in the area, so—'

Amy choked on her drink. '*In the area?* Are you *sure* there's nothing worth exploring?'

'Yes, in the area, and, no, there's nothing worth exploring,' Kate insisted, but she could feel the heat slash across her cheekbones. 'He buzzed my apartment and I went down to meet him.'

Very important to get the message out that he hadn't stayed the night at her place. She was a little embarrassed about hiding what was a straightforward arrangement from her friends, but she couldn't seem to up and confess. And it wasn't only the confidentiality clause stopping her. It just felt too…*painful*, somehow, to share.

'And what happened?' Amy asked.

'While we were sitting there drinking our coffee along came Brodie.'

'And then…? Come on, Kate,' Amy urged. 'The suspense is killing me.'

'All right. I'm just trying to remember it.' *As if she didn't!* 'There was some…tension. Yes, now that I think back there was definitely tension between them to start with. But I left them talking while I went to order, and by the time I returned, it was all quite amicable between them.'

'Thank God,' Willa said. 'They were so close, back in the day. Closer than brothers. It hasn't felt right, their estrangement.'

'So what happened next?' Amy asked. 'Is Brodie still here? I'd love to see him. And did they talk about Chantal?'

Chantal. The name whipped through Kate's bloodstream, breath-stealing.

Jealous. She was jealous—of something that had happened *eight years ago*. Because one woman had sneaked past Scott's defences, where *she* couldn't go. Where she was resolutely *blocked* from going. She picked up her glass to take another sip of her cocktail, realised it was empty but had no recollection of drinking it. Too much, too fast.

'I don't know what happened then because I left them to it,' she said. 'I knew they hadn't seen each other in a while, and I…I had work to finish. I haven't spoken to Scott since.'

Which wasn't strictly correct…but was still true. Officer Cleary and Lorelei had spoken to Scott—not Kate.

'Nobody was throwing punches, if that's any comfort to you,' Kate added. 'And one thing I *do* know is that Brodie is still in Sydney, because he's giving me a sailing lesson tomorrow.'

'Oh! You are *so* lucky!' Jessica said. 'I'd love to learn to sail.'

'Well, it's only one lesson,' Kate said. 'All I can really expect is to find out if I've got what it takes or if it will be like the time I tried Tai Chi—nice idea, but not going to happen. Why don't you come too, Jessica?'

Jessica sighed. 'Nah—I've got kickboxing tomorrow.'

'Why don't you ask Scott to teach you if you're really interested, Jess?' Amy suggested. 'He's the absolute best. Better than Brodie—even though Brodie's the one who's made it his career.' She turned to Kate, looking quizzical. 'In fact, Kate, I don't know why *you* don't ask Scott to teach you. At least he lives in Sydney, so you'll get more than one lesson out of him.'

Kate busied herself snagging a server and ordering more drinks. By the time she'd done that, she had her poker face on. 'From what I've gathered, Scott doesn't sail any more.'

'That's true,' Willa said. 'You know, Weeping Reef was so beautiful, and we were all so excited to be there, but a lot of things went wrong. Things that…that changed us, I guess.'

'Ain't that the truth,' Amy murmured. And then she took a deep breath, seeming to shake off a thought. She smiled—very brightly. 'But that was then and this is now, so let's drink to moving on. Onwards and upwards, ladies. Onwards and upwards.'

The girls clinked glasses, although Kate wondered if her empty glass actually counted.

'The music is starting and they're opening the bar off the dance floor,' Jessica said. 'The crowd should spread out soon.' She looked at the packed bar area. 'I wonder if there's a rose-petal-sprinkler in amongst that lot who might be persuaded to ask me to dance.'

And then Jessica gasped, her eyes wide as saucers.

'Well, bite me!' she said. 'Maybe I *will* come along tomorrow, Kate. Because Brodie looks mighty hot.'

'Huh?' Amy swivelled in her seat and squealed.

Willa was the next to look. 'Oh, my God. I told Rob to join us here, but…but…how…?'

Kate turned very, very slowly as a cold finger of dread trailed its nail down her back.

Rob, Brodie…and Scott. Heading across the floor towards them.

CHAPTER FOURTEEN

'LOOK WHO I roped in!' Rob said as the three men reached the table.

And then everyone was standing, exclaiming, hugging, laughing. Even Jessica, who'd never met Brodie, was in there.

Everyone except Kate, who stayed in her seat with a fixed smile on her face, watching the reunion.

There was a general scrabbling for chairs while Brodie went off to the bar for beer and the next round of cocktails was delivered.

Rob sat and drew Willa onto his lap. 'Scott called to see if I wanted to go for a beer with him and Brodie, but I persuaded them to join us here instead,' he explained.

'I'm so glad you did,' Amy said. 'Because we were just talking about them.'

Scott sent Kate a brooding look, which started her heart thudding.

But all he said was, 'I'll go and find some extra chairs,' before stalking off.

Brodie was soon on his way back, carrying three beers as he cut across the small, still deserted dance floor rather than squeeze through the crush of drinkers spreading out from the bar.

He slid the beers onto the table and Rob snatched one up.

Jessica looked up at Brodie conspiratorially. 'We've been talking about our favourite romantic moments, Brodie. What do you think is better? Impressing a CFO with your business acumen—and no prizes for guessing who *that* one belongs to—strewn rose petals on a bed, a knight on a charger or *From Here to Eternity*?'

Brodie laughed. 'Are they the only options?'

Amy slapped her hand over Jessica's mouth—no doubt staving off any mention of dancing cheek to cheek in the Whitsundays.

'Can't take her anywhere,' Amy said, and quickly redirected the conversation.

Kate was relieved. Not only did she not want to hear the Chantal story again—not with Brodie at the table and Scott on approach—but she didn't want to let any red-blooded male into her guilty *From Here to Eternity* secret. And especially not Scott, who would laugh himself into apoplexy over it.

Scott had one of his false smiles in place as he handed a chair to Brodie. 'I had to promise to go back and have a drink with a group on a hen-night bender to get that chair, Brode!'

Brodie laughed as he took the chair. 'Don't pretend that's a hardship,' he said, and then grimaced an infinitesimal apology as his eyes flickered in Kate's direction.

Great. Brodie had seen her with Scott for all of ten minutes and yet he knew. Or maybe Scott had shared all the salacious details—perhaps with an offhand *And soon she'll be* all yours, *Brodie.*

Scott carefully didn't look at her—just positioned himself between Amy and Willa.

Brodie slotted his chair in beside Kate. 'Ready for tomorrow?' he asked, raising his voice a little over the rising sound of music that was being cranked up to encourage dancers to take to the floor.

'I'm still game if you are,' she said, leaning in close so she could be more easily heard.

'Oh, I'm game,' he said with an easy smile.

Such an *easy* smile. A *natural* smile. A smile that reached his eyes. Green eyes, like Scott's—but deep and warm, not cool and cautious.

Amy nudged her shoulder against Scott's. 'I told Kate she should have asked *you* for lessons.'

Scott cast Kate another brooding look and she felt herself blush almost by reflex. Everyone at the table would be working it out any minute if he kept that up.

'I sold my boat,' he said.

'Well, you could hire one, couldn't you?' Amy asked. 'What would it cost? To hire you and a boat and learn how to sail?'

'Well…' Scott said, and rubbed a jaw darkened by raspy shadow.

It was the first time Kate had ever seen him anything but clean-shaven. His eyes looked strained too. Tired. And she was an idiot, with no instinct for self-preservation, because she wanted to hug him, and kiss him, and tell him to take better care of himself—

'I'd say…' Scott began again, with another look at Kate '…five thousand dollars? Or the barter system is okay. Trade a service for a service.'

—and kill him. She wanted to *kill* him.

Amy looked shocked. 'Man, that's expensive.'

'But worth it,' Scott said. One more look at Kate, and then he turned to Willa to say something.

The conversation ebbed and flowed around Kate as, silent, she pondered the way her evening had started—four friends sharing their secret longings for romance. But Willa's was real. Whereas Kate's…? Pure Hollywood. Never going to happen.

And it was probably time she admitted that she wanted it to be real. Wanted what Willa had. Wanted someone to trust her with his life.

Because she *could* be trusted.

People trusted her with their lives every day. They trusted her to extricate them from bad marriages with a whole skin and the means to live. They trusted her to do the best thing for their children. They trusted her to find a way for them to achieve closure, and keep their dignity, and get a fair deal.

They trusted her…before moving on with their lives without her.

And that wasn't enough any more.

She wanted someone who trusted her but didn't *want* to move on with his life without her. She wanted someone complicated and creative, and strong and principled, and smart and funny, and sexy and…and…*hers*.

She wanted love. She wanted, specifically, *Scott Knight* to love her. Not just the scent, the taste, the feel of her…but the whole of her. Wanted to trust him with her life and wanted him to trust her with his.

She wanted him to tell her about growing up never feeling quite good enough, and she wanted to make sure he knew that he *was*. Good enough for anything—for everything.

She wanted *Scott* to tell her about Weeping Reef. About Chantal and Brodie. How he'd felt, what it had meant, what it had done to him to feel so betrayed, if it still ate at him.

She wanted to tell him she would never, ever hurt him like that. That she would never betray him. *Couldn't* betray him. That she—

'Kate?'

Brodie—pulling her back.

'Refill?' he asked, nodding at her glass, which was empty again.

'No,' she said, and tried to smile. 'And that's my last—so don't worry. There'll be no heave-hoing over the gunwales tomorrow.'

'It wouldn't be the first time I've held a girl's hair out of the way, so don't sweat it for my sake, Katie.'

Scott clunked his beer glass on the table. Loud enough to make Amy, sitting beside him, jump.

'Kate—not Katie,' he said. And then he turned back to Willa as though he hadn't just bowled that out loud and livid enough for everyone to marvel at, and asked, 'When's Luke coming home?'

After a stunned moment, Willa gathered herself enough to speak. 'No immediate plans, as far as I'm aware. He's in the middle of a deal in Singapore he won't tell me anything about. Confidential, apparently.'

'Confidential,' Amy repeated, but the tone of her voice—all dark, when Amy was basically the brightest, shiniest girl in the world—made Kate wonder if perhaps she wasn't the only one hitting the cocktails a little too hard.

'Yeah,' Willa said, a little uneasily. 'He's like a clam about stuff like that.'

Amy looked straight at Scott. 'But *you* know.'

'About Singapore?' Scott asked. 'Nope.'

'Not Singapore. I mean what happened at Weeping Reef.'

Kate wondered what she was missing and looked around at the others. Willa was looking startled—everyone else confused.

Scott half sighed, half laughed, winced. 'I think we all know what happened at Weeping Reef.'

'I *knew* he'd told you. You know—at Willa's party—when you said that…that thing about a gentleman never telling a lady's secrets.'

Nobody spoke.

'Amy,' Scott said into the awkward pause, 'if you think I have a lady's secret to tell—one that *doesn't* involve me getting up to no good with a hooker called Lorelei…' He waited while everyone at the table except a cringing Kate and a startled-looking Amy laughed. 'Then please fill me in. Otherwise I'm going to go and fulfil my obligation to that clutch of hens—or flock, or brood, or whatever the hell a group of chickens is called. The ones who donated a chair to our cause when I first arrived.'

He waited, watching Amy, who was blinking, stunned.

'Right, I'll take that as a no, then,' he said, and stood. 'Give me fifteen minutes,' he said to the group at large.

'Yeah—as if!' Jessica said as he was sucked into the crowd. 'It will only take him five minutes, max, to sort out his next one-night stand. He has the gift.'

But Amy was looking at Willa, dazed and confused. 'Luke really didn't…?'

Willa slid off Rob's lap and into Scott's vacated chair,

right next to Amy, and took Amy's hand. 'No, Amy. He really didn't.'

'Well…*wow!*' Amy said.

Brodie turned to Kate. 'We seem to be a little out of this loop, Kate. Shall we join the few brave souls venturing onto the dance floor?'

Kate had a feeling Scott wouldn't like her dancing with Brodie.

But, then again, Scott was in the process of picking up a drunken bed partner on a hen night.

And he'd told Brodie she was *all his*.

And Scott didn't love her.

And he never would.

And she wanted to die.

What was one dance stacked against all that?

'Sure,' she said.

Brodie led her onto the small dance floor. Without any hesitation—and completely ignoring the fact that every other couple on the floor was dancing without touching—he took Kate in his arms.

'What's going on?' Brodie asked, without preamble.

'What do you mean?'

'You and Scott. Am I going to get my teeth smashed in for dancing with you?'

'No. But I don't think the threat of that scares you or you wouldn't have asked me to dance, would you?'

No answer. He simply pulled her a little closer.

'So, Brodie, why *did* you ask me to dance?'

'Because I love Scott.'

'I don't—'

'And don't tell me you don't know what I mean, because you do.'

There was a pause as she silently acknowledged the truth of that. 'He won't care that I'm dancing with you. He's not the jealous type. Not with me anyway.' She sighed and settled her head on Brodie's comfortable shoulder. 'We're not…*meant*.'

'Why not?'

Kate ran through the reasons in her head and chose the least painful one she could think of. 'For a start, he's too young for me.'

She heard the laugh rumble through Brodie's chest. 'Scott hasn't been too young since he popped out of the womb—when he no doubt emerged *not* crying, just calmly looking around and wondering how to get fed without having to ask for help.'

Kate choked on a sudden giggle. 'That does sound like him.'

'Yep—everything calculated, everything his way, no drama, no demands, keep your distance. He has more self-control than anyone I've ever met. Too much.' Pause. 'I've only ever seen him lose it once.'

'I know about Chantal,' Kate said, looking up at him.

'Yeah, I figured you did. And if he told you that—'

'No,' Kate interrupted. 'He didn't tell me. He doesn't get personal. Not with me.'

'Ah.'

'Yes, *"ah"*.'

'But you want him to?'

'What would be the point, when he's off picking someone up for the night?'

'Except that he's not.'

'Well, who knows?'

'I do. Because if he was doing that he wouldn't be heading this way looking like he's about to deck me, would he?'

'What?' Kate squeaked, and Brodie spun them so she could see Scott as he approached.

'I wonder if he's about to cause the second scene of his life?' Brodie asked, not seeming at all concerned. 'Let's hope so.'

CHAPTER FIFTEEN

SCOTT HAD NO IDEA what he was doing, but he was doing it anyway.

He reached Kate and Brodie, then stood there like an idiot while he tried to contain the savage burst of possessiveness that was urging him to tear Kate out of Brodie's arms. This was beyond that drunken punch at Weeping Reef. Because this wasn't about Brodie, either as a love rival or as a Hugo substitute. This was about Kate and him. About wishing he *did* dance so it could be him dancing with her. Wishing it was *him* teaching her to sail. About hating himself because of all the things he wasn't—but wanting to demand, anyway, what the *hell* she thought she was doing dancing with another man when she belonged to him.

He barely noticed Brodie melting away as he reached for Kate, yanked her into his arms and kissed her. Right there on the dance floor. A scorching kiss, which he hoped said *I want you*, but suspected said something else. Something about need and desperation and all the things he didn't want to risk.

When he stopped, pulled back, looked down at her, she shivered. He felt it rip through him as though they were connected.

'I think that qualifies as a PDA,' she said.

'That had nothing to do with affection. That kiss was not *affectionate*, Kate.'

'That kiss is not going to lead to sex either.'

'Yes, it is.'

'No. We have an appointment, and it's not for tonight.'

'We can negotiate, remember?'

'You don't negotiate. You do whatever the hell you want, whenever you want.'

'That's because your rules are stupid.'

'You agreed to them.'

'I shouldn't have.'

'But you did. And now you've gone and broken the confidentiality clause.' She nodded towards their table. 'Because your friends just saw you kiss me.'

His only response was to grab her hand and drag her off the dance floor, out of the bar, into the night, around the corner into an alleyway that was only a step above Ellington Lane in terms of desolation. Without a word he took her in his arms again, kissed her almost savagely. He wanted her so much—so *much*.

Her hands grabbed the front of his shirt, clutching fistfuls of it, anchoring her as she kissed him back, and he thought, *Thank God.* She wanted him. She still wanted him. Everything else would fall into place as long as that fact held. Because without it why would she keep seeing him?

There was a burst of sound as the bar's main doors opened, disgorging a group of people into the night, and sanity returned. The doors closed again. A low conversation, a trill of laughter from the departing patrons. Scott pulled back, waiting to see if he and Kate would be discovered, but the group passed by. All was quiet again.

And Scott suddenly felt utterly, utterly miserable.

He stepped away, shoved his hands in his hair, looked at Kate.

'What was *that* about?' she asked—as usual, going straight to the point in the way he just bloody loved.

'I wanted to kiss you, that's all.' Could he sound any more defensive?

'So what happens if I ask you—now—to come inside and dance with me, in public, in front of your friends?'

Tight, fraught pause. Scott stuck his hands in his pockets. 'I don't dance.'

'No, you *don't* dance, do you? But that doesn't mean *I*

don't, Scott, if I'm lucky enough to be asked. And I *was* dancing. Why did you drag me out here?'

'Because—' He broke off with a muffled curse.

'Because…I was dancing with *Brodie*, perhaps?'

One heavy heartbeat…two, three.

And then, 'Why is that a problem, Scott?'

No answer. Because how could he explain without revealing everything that was wrong with him? All the reasons she would soon find someone better—whether it was Brodie or that barrister or someone else? How could he tell her that he needed to push it? Push it while he still had it in him to get over her when the inevitable happened?

'Do you think I prefer him?' Kate persisted.

He shrugged as his hands dug a little deeper into his pockets. 'If you do, that's okay. Women…lots of women…do.'

He said the words but his heart was threatening to leap into his brain and cut off his blood supply, oxygen, his synapse control—everything. Because it *wasn't* okay. It would kill him.

'Not *lots of women*, Scott,' she said. '*Chantal.* And that's what this is all about, isn't it? Chantal. The only woman who ever got to you. Enough to make you lose that prized control.'

Scott registered the fact that she knew about Chantal. Who'd told her? Did it even matter? He tested that in his brain. No, it didn't. Because Chantal didn't matter. It had been *Brodie* who'd mattered all those years ago, not Chantal. And now…only Kate mattered. *Only Kate.*

'I'll teach you to sail,' he said, which was so far from an adequate response as to be classified as a non sequitur.

'You don't have a boat, remember? And I don't have five thousand dollars since I ripped up your cheque—which, in case you're too stupid to realise it, was only ever a Play Time prop. So no need to trade sailing lessons for my services like I'm a *real* prostitute. I'm already under contract. You're getting the goods for free. Until the twenty-eighth, anyway.'

She turned to walk away and his temper surged, hot and

wild. His hands came out of his pockets and he grabbed her, spun her, gripping her upper arms, furious. 'Don't talk about yourself like that.'

'Then stop making me feel like that by trading me to your friends,' she shot back. '*"She's all yours."* Remember?'

'All you have to do is tell him no. No, you're not going sailing tomorrow. Tell him, Kate,' Scott said, wanting to explode with the emotions churning in his gut, but hanging on…and on, and on.

'I *am* going sailing tomorrow,' she said. 'As planned. Because he *offered*, without having to be shamed into it. But don't worry, Scott. If anything happens between me and Brodie I'll advise you. As I expect you to tell me if you hook up with one of those giggly hens. And that will be that, won't it? Agreement null and void, as per the contract. Okay?'

They stared at each other. Scott's hands unclenched, slipped down her arms to her hands, held. The words were there in his chest. *Not okay. Don't do it to me. Don't. Please, please don't.* Choking him.

'Kate. Oh, God, Kate. I just—'

But the bar doors opened again and Scott let go, stepped back, re-jamming his hands in his pockets at the sudden burst of sound. People were walking past, talking, laughing.

And up popped his shield, like some automatic reflex. 'Okay,' he said.

'Okay?' she said, incredulous. And then, 'Okay…'

Her eyes closed.

Long moment, and then she opened her eyes. 'I don't understand any of this. Why did you let Rob talk you into coming here when you knew I'd be here? It's not what we're about, is it? Drinks with friends?'

'I wanted—' Stop. Swallow. *Confess.* 'I wanted to see you.'

'You're seeing me on Sunday. At noon. Remember?'

'I remember. But who'll be opening the door? Kate? Officer Cleary? Or Lorelei?'

'Who do you *want* to see, Scott?'

Silence. Because the answer had stuck in his throat. The way words always did.

He saw her shoulders slump, as if she was defeated. Knew he wasn't handling this. Wasn't handling *her*. Wasn't handling *anything*.

'Surprise me,' he said, and forced a smile. His *I'm cool with that* smile.

Except he *wasn't* cool with it. He wanted her to call him on what he'd said. To fight with him. Rage at him. Slap him if she had to. To demand more. *More!* To tell him that she *deserved* more and she *wanted* more. And she wanted it from *him*. To say, *So step up to the plate, Scott Knight, and if you can't give it to me I'll find it somewhere else. I'll find someone else. Someone...else.*

Say it—say it, Kate. You want someone else. Say it!

But she gave him smile for cool smile instead. 'Fine,' she said. 'I'll make sure it's memorable for you.'

And then she patted her hair into place. Twitched at her dress.

'But now I'm going to go back inside to get my things. I've had a big week. A bad week. And I need to go home.'

He wanted to take her hands again, but he couldn't seem to get them out of his pockets. 'Tell me. What happened with the case?'

She looked at him. And the tears in her eyes almost undid him. But when she spoke her voice was like crystal. Clear and smooth and cold.

'No fireside chats, remember?'

'But I—'

'Stop, Scott. Just *stop*. I came out to relax with a few girlfriends and instead I'm standing in a dark alley with a man who's not saying anything that makes sense. I just want to go in, pay my bill, grab my things and leave. You go back to that hen party, and text me before Sunday if you've been unfaithful.' Short, strange laugh. 'How quaint that sounds. Let's say, instead, if you've adhered to the clause.'

And with that, she stalked out of the alleyway.

By the time Scott had himself enough under control to return to the table, Kate had been and gone.

He picked up the fresh beer that was waiting for him because Brodie, who had his back like in the old days, had known he'd need one.

'Want to borrow my boat in the morning?' Brodie asked.

Scott smiled—his *all okay here* smile. 'No, I'm good. She's all yours.' *Oh, God, no!* He'd said it again. *All yours.*

'I think we both know, Scott, that she's all *yours*. But if you'll take my advice you won't take too long to claim her—because Kate doesn't strike me as the type to wait forever.'

CHAPTER SIXTEEN

KATE WOKE ON Sunday with full-blown jitters.

Because she didn't have a clue what she was going to offer Scott for Play Time at noon.

It was almost more than her tired, slightly sunburned body could manage just to get out of bed, let alone plan a fantasy, because yesterday's sailing lesson had been the most full-on physical three hours she'd ever spent.

Sailing was as freeing, as exhilarating, as wonderful as she'd always thought it would be—with an excellent side benefit: all that hauling of sheets and dodging of booms, being ordered around and shoved all over the deck by Brodie and his two cohorts, had left her with no time to think about Scott. Or about their upcoming Play Time either.

The guys had taken her out for a congratulatory drinking session afterwards, because apparently she had what it took, and by the time Kate had got home, she'd been so tired she'd fallen into bed.

She'd slept for a full three hours before thoughts of Scott had niggled her into wakefulness. And then had come the night-long tossing and turning she was learning to expect.

Fractured sleep, painful dreams, tortured thoughts. Wondering how Scott had felt, knowing she was on the water with his best friend. Rethinking every look, every word from Friday night. Trying to figure out what was behind the anger Scott refused to unleash—was it the way he felt about her, or residual mistrust from the eight-year-old Chantal/Brodie situation? Hoping he hadn't—*please, please, please*—voided their contract by touching another woman.

After all that it was no wonder she was devoid of ideas.

Arabian nights, pirate and tavern wench, boss and secretary—all of which she'd considered—just seemed stupid.

How she wished she'd never thought of writing fantasies into the contract. She hated Play Time. *Hated* it!

So much so that in a fit of pique—yes, *pique*!—she decided to wear her most complicated dress. Buttons *and* zips *and* ties, with an exotic fold or two. An origami nightmare of a dress. Because Scott *deserved* to have to fight his way through to her for a change, rather than have her laying it all out for him to take.

He'd said the first time they met that for her he could get a little 'gladiatorial'—so let him prove it by fighting his way past her dress! In fact, she would make it harder. She would blindfold him! And what was more, she would give him a time limit.

That was a good enough Play Time for her.

Scott buzzed on the dot of noon—he was nothing if not punctual—and she let him into the building without waiting to hear his voice.

'We only have an hour,' Kate said, all brisk and businesslike as she opened the door to him, holding two silk scarves at the ready.

His eyes narrowed. 'Why?'

'Nothing to do with Brodie, if that's what you're wondering.'

'I'm not wondering. Are you wondering?'

'About Brodie?'

He just looked at her.

'Oh, do you mean am I wondering about you and the hens on Friday night?' she asked, and eked out a tinkling laugh. 'No. You would have texted me, wouldn't you, if anything had happened?' She was forcing the panic back. 'And anyway...well, *pacta sunt servanda*, right? Agreements must be kept. And as I recall, that was your sticking point. Fidelity.'

'Pacta sunt servanda,' he repeated. 'You *do* remember how that legal talk turns me on, don't you?'

Her breath caught in her throat. 'Yes.'

'Is that why you're doing it?'

'The more turned on you are, the faster we'll be, right?'

He didn't like that—she could tell by the way his whole face tightened. He walked past her and laid a flat parcel on her dining table.

'Stand still while I do this,' she said, coming up behind him.

And, although he stiffened, he let her tie the scarf over his eyes.

'Play Time,' she announced.

The set of his mouth was grim as she led him carefully into the bedroom, over to the bed. 'Sit,' Kate said.

But Scott did more than sit. He flopped onto his back, lying there as though he didn't give a damn what she did to him, and Kate hesitated, wondering if he didn't want her today. If he didn't want her any more, period.

Pulse jittering, she looked at his body, laid out on the bed for her, wondering how she would be able to bear that…and saw that he was hard. She hadn't even touched him and he was aroused—whether he wanted to be or not.

It took the edge off her sudden panic to know that whatever his *I give up* attitude was about, it wasn't a lack of desire. She could work with that. She would make this so good for him he wouldn't be able to pretend he didn't want her.

'I'm going to blindfold myself now,' she told him, knowing how disorientating it must be for a control freak like Scott not to know what was happening. 'No peeking today—by either of us. And no speaking either.'

'No—?' Short, tense pause. 'No *speaking*, Kate?'

'No. Just…feeling…'

Scott's lips tightened but he said nothing.

And then Kate tied her own scarf and felt her way onto the bed. She lay next to him, turned to him, kissed him. A long, lush moan of a kiss. Not being able to see, she was even more conscious than usual of the uncompromising firmness of his mouth as he stayed stock-still for her to explore. The warmth of it, the taste, the way it fitted so perfectly against her own.

Slowly the tension left him, and at last he kissed her back, his tongue sliding into her mouth, and then he was taking over, reaching everywhere. Thank *God.*

A moment later his hands were wandering over her fully clothed body. Traversing the cotton of her dress. Pausing, testing, assessing the fastenings, the barriers.

Kate's task was easier. She slid her hands under his T-shirt, smoothing them over his chest. She loved his chest. The breadth and strength of it, the texture of his warm skin, the spread of hair. The picture of him, flat on his back on her bed, was so strong in her mind...but the fact she couldn't see it with her eyes somehow made the drug of touching him more potent. As if she could reach right through his chest and into his heart with nothing but the pads of her exploring fingers.

A push, a nudge, and his T-shirt was up, over his head, off. She checked quickly that the scarf was still secure around his eyes, and then her hands moved to his jeans. Unbuttoning, unzipping as his breathing turned harsh and laboured. She loved the way his breaths came like that when he was excited, almost past bearing but trying to control it—control himself, control everything.

She straddled him, facing his feet—which might have felt weird if they hadn't both been masked, but now felt perfect. Her core was on his warm skin, just above the band of his boxer briefs. Just that was enough for her to long to have him inside her. She started pushing his jeans down his legs, hands stroking as she leaned further forward with each push. She loved his legs. Long, hard, strong, the perfect amount of hair. Down, down, down. And then—*stop.*

She'd forgotten about his sneakers. Well, blindfolded or not, she could undo a shoe. She fumbled with the laces, wrenched the sneakers off, threw them. They landed on the floor with a soft thud. Next she pushed his jeans off, threw them too. Started to turn around.

But Scott kept her exactly where she was with a hand on her back. She got the message and stopped, on her knees, one either side of his hips. Stayed…waited. What was he going to do?

And then the hand on her back was gone and both Scott's hands were under her dress, reaching between her spread thighs, snagging against the French knickers she'd put on today before she'd come up with a plan that meant he wouldn't actually *see* the frothy pink lace.

He didn't seem to care about the lace, because his fingers were impatient, almost rough, as he yanked the knickers aside, his fingers sliding into her drenching wetness, in and out, until her breaths were nothing more than rasps and she was trembling. She felt so hot, so lush, aching as those fingers continued to dip in and out of her while the fingers of his other hand joined the action, circling her clitoris, precise, constant, inexorable.

She hadn't removed his underwear, but that didn't stop him thrusting hard against her bottom as he circled and slipped and probed every millimetre of her sex until she was coming in a luscious roll.

She didn't know how it had happened, but a moment later she found herself flipped onto her back. She waited, breathless, for what Scott would do—regretting the damned dress, deciding she would help with her own unwrapping.

But before she could lift a finger to even one zipper, Scott had gripped the cotton at her neck and torn the dress right down the front, spreading the two halves wide.

'Scott…' she whispered, shocked.

'No talking,' he said, and reached for her bra straps, accurate despite the blindfold.

He yanked them down her arms until her breasts were bared. Unerringly, his mouth found her nipples, sucking, licking, building the pressure from barely there to strong and demanding, unrelenting as his cotton-clad erection strained against her.

She reached down to try to push his underwear off him, clumsy because of her bra straps, but he knocked her hands aside and kept up the suckling. Next moment he was scooting down her body, between her legs. The French knickers were shoved down and his mouth was there, licking fast and frantically, and she was coming again with a loud cry.

He kept his mouth there through the last undulation of her hips and then he came back up her body, kissing her almost brutally. He fumbled with the scarf over her eyes, ripping it away. Rising up over her, on his knees, he tore off his own blindfold. Stared down at her for a scorching moment.

Before Kate could reach for him he was off the bed, throwing his clothes on helter-skelter.

'But— But— What about you?'

'Owe me,' he said, zipping up his jeans.

'I can do it now.'

'You should have grabbed a condom before the blindfolds went on. Because now I've ripped the masks off, Play Time's over. We're seeing...we're talking. And that's not in the rules for today, is it? You don't want to *talk* to me today. You don't want to *see* me today. I'd say you didn't even really want me to *touch* you, or you wouldn't have worn that chastity belt of a dress. You wanted it over with *quickly* today.'

He grabbed his sneakers, shoved his feet inside them, yanked on the laces.

'Well, you're done—all sorted, all serviced with time to spare—and now I'm going.'

'Scott...'

But he was out of the room, and her curse was floating behind him.

'Scott—wait,' she said as she got off the bed, impatiently shedding her ruined dress, wrenching up her bra.

The door slammed before she was even out of the bedroom.

He was gone.

Eyes swimming, she walked over to the dining table, picked up the parcel he'd left there. Opened the brown paper. Removed a…a *plaque*? Yes, a simple metal plaque. Black type on dull silver. Two words: *Castle Cleary.*

Her swimming eyes overflowed.

To hell with Play Time, Scott thought savagely as he got into his car. And to hell with being made to feel like a male prostitute with an allocated time slot.

Not that the whole blindfold experience hadn't been intense. He'd been insane with need by the end of it. So needy it had made no sense to run out when he did. She would have serviced him even without the blindfolds.

Serviced him.

And didn't that say it all?

She would have *serviced* him. The way he'd *serviced* her.

Scott Knight, Escort Service, at your beck and call.

So what? his sane self asked.

It was perfect, wasn't it? Exactly what he'd wanted? A sex contract. Month to month. No strings. No emotions. Complete control. No pretending they were forever. No need to call her unless it was to schedule a hot bout of sex. No deep and meaningful conversations. No conversations at all, lately—not with Lorelei, not with Officer Cleary. And not with Kate.

And today not only no speaking, but no looking either!

Just feeling—which was a good enough euphemism for *just sex.*

Just sex.

Perfect.

And he was a freaking idiot not to just take that and run with it.

Scott pulled out his phone. Stabbed the buttons.

Play Time, my house, Tuesday, 7 p.m.

Half a minute later, back came a reply.

Fine.

'Right,' he said out loud to his face in the rearview mirror.

But something about his face wasn't normal. He looked like a freaking psycho killer!

Well, to hell with that too! He was *not* going to see that every time he glanced in the rearview mirror on the drive home. He'd have a crash if he had to see that.

He had to calm the hell down.

Cursing, he banged out of the car, strode across to the marina, focused on the boats.

Which made him feel even crazier. And just miserable again.

Kate had had her first sailing lesson yesterday. With Brodie. How had it gone? What had they talked about? Fireside chats aplenty with Brodie, for sure. Because Brodie was easy to talk to—easier than Scott. Easier, kinder. Better all round.

Everything inside Scott clenched—including the growl that he wouldn't let loose from his chest.

And then he put his face in his hands—because the sight of the boats was suddenly unbearable.

CHAPTER SEVENTEEN

KATE WAS PREPARED for the Monday morning *What the hell was that kiss about?* calls from Willa and Amy. She offered up a perfectly nuanced laugh as she blamed the lethal combination of Scott's beer and her Manhattans, positioning it as a Dirty Martini Barnaby moment gone a step too far. And if the girls didn't sound exactly convinced, at least they let the subject drop.

She was *less* prepared for Deb's darting, anxious eyes as she kept a steady flow of peppermint tea—her favourite stress remedy—pouring into Kate's office—while very carefully *not* asking about 'that nice Scott Knight'. Not that Deb had to ask; Kate was convinced she had psychic powers.

And she was not *at all* prepared for her mother's visit on Tuesday morning.

Madeline Cleary swept into Kate's office the way she swept through life: grandly, wearing a caftan, hot-pink lipstick and high heels.

She took a seat, fixing Kate with one of her *don't mess with me* stares. 'Okay, Kate, what's this Deb's been telling me?'

Deb! Psychic and *traitor*!

'"This"?' Kate asked, closing the door sharply—knowing it would drive Deb crazy not being able to listen in, which served her right.

'Scott Knight,' her mother said.

'He's an architect.'

'Well, isn't that lovely? Much more interesting than a barrister. But not really the pertinent fact at the moment, is it, Kate? Don't bother with any of your legal obfuscation. Just tell me what's happening.'

'No.'

'Okay, then bring him to dinner on Sunday and I'll ask him instead.'

'That won't be happening. It's not like that with us. I mean the…the family thing. It's just…just…' The words trailed off and she shrugged.

Her mother looked at her—very long, very hard. 'It's just that he's the one, perhaps?'

Kate tried—failed—to laugh. 'Nothing that romantic.'

'So *make* it romantic.'

'You can't make these things happen.'

'Not if you're pussy-hearted. Which, of course, is *not* the way I raised my daughters. I raised lionesses.' She leaned forward. 'Kate, remember when I tried to dissuade you from going into family law?'

Eye-roll. 'Yes.'

'Not because I don't like lawyers—'

Another eye-roll. 'Although you don't!'

'But because you're so tender-hearted. I knew you'd be running yourself ragged, fighting for the downtrodden and then bleeding all over the place when you lost a case.' She sat back again. 'And do you remember what you told me to do?'

Kate smiled—it blossomed despite her hideous mood. 'I told you to shove it.'

Her mother beamed at her. 'And I was so proud of you.'

Kate ran her hands over her face, laughing helplessly. 'You're a weirdo, Mum.'

'It's an artistic thing. So what?'

'So I love you.'

'And I love you. And I think you deserve a reward for all the crap you put up with day after day. And if he's the reward you want, then you're going to have him.'

'He doesn't want…that. The whole forever thing.'

'From what I hear, he's had plenty of what *he* wants.'

Arrgghh. Going to kill Deb. Boil her in a vat of peppermint tea.

'So, Kate, it's time for what *you* want. Which just might turn out to be what he wants too.'

'He doesn't.'

'How do you know? Have you asked him?'

'No, of course not.'

'Why "of course not"? Because he's a boy and they have to ask first? Don't make me slap you. Just *ask* him.'

Silence.

'Kate, the reason I was so proud of you that day when you told me so eloquently to shove it was because you threw it all at me. How you felt, why you felt it, what it meant to you. You said you would move heaven and hell to do it. And that if it all came to nothing, or you couldn't hack it, at least you'd have no regrets about not *trying*. And, really, Kate? If it's *you* asking for something, fighting for something...' She smiled—a smile so completely proud and understanding and just so *family* Kate wanted to cry. 'Well, Kate, who would ever say no to you?'

Who would ever say no to you?

Oh, God. God! Scott would say no. *He* would.

'So, Kate, *tell him*. What you feel. Why you feel it. What he means to you. And move heaven and hell. Because, of all of my daughters, *you* can. And then, whatever happens, at least you'll have no regrets.' She paused again, shrugged. 'The alternative is that I tell your father what he's done to you—and he and Aristotle have been playing with a new set of throwing knives, so I'd prefer not to go that route. At least not yet.'

Kate arrived at Scott's on Tuesday ten minutes late.

She stayed in her car for another ten minutes, with her mother's words going through her mind. *Tell him, tell him, tell him.*

But she couldn't help feeling it would be like pulling the rug out from under him. *I said it was only going to be sex, Scott, but it's love.*

What would he say?

Big sigh. Because she had no idea.

He'd sent so many mixed signals her way she was beyond knowing what he expected of her, what he wanted from her, how he felt about her. He'd been everything from distant to demanding, from impassioned to indifferent. From flippant to furious. Agreeing to the rules—and breaking them.

The way he'd looked at her in that alley on Friday night, when he'd taken her hands in his—that was not about sex. And that last Play Time, when he'd been so angry with her—irrational, emotional…

Wasn't that a bit like love?

She sucked in a breath, because just saying that in her head made her heart flutter. Running a hand over her stomach, which was similarly fluttery, she wondered, maybe, if she *should* ask him.

But *after* Play Time. Because if Play Time involved her getting into a PVC cat suit or wielding some kind of implement…? Well, she couldn't see herself talking about love after a dose of kink.

Sighing, she started to push the intercom button—but Scott opened the door before the chime even sounded. He took her in his arms, kissed her as though he'd been waiting a year and was starving for the taste of her.

And *everything* in her fluttered. Nervous and hopeful and a little bit terrified.

Releasing her slowly, Scott gestured for her to move into the house, and she was struck again by the magnificence of what he'd achieved—even more so today, when she was seeing it as Kate, who'd been invited, not Lorelei, who'd invited herself.

It was stylish, lavish, unusual. A manifestation of all those parts that made Scott who he was. The coolness, the control, the hidden fiery core.

Kate cleared her throat. 'So… Play Time?'

He put his arm around her, led her into what she supposed was the living room—or living *space*, more correctly, since there were no internal walls, only strategically placed columns.

'Yep,' he said. 'I'm calling it "The Architect and the Lawyer".'

She halted as her hopes started to soar. 'That sounds…normal.'

'Ah, but with a twist. The way I'm seeing it is that the architect gives the lawyer a tour of his house. Along the way the lawyer tries to find a legal term appropriate for each space—extra points for Latin. And if the lawyer likes what she sees, she gets to touch the architect. And if the architect likes what the lawyer says…same deal. He gets to touch her. And then the architect—because he is multi-talented—prepares dinner. And they eat. And drink wine. And then, if all that touching has meant anything at all, they go upstairs to bed and negotiate the rollover of their contract for another month.'

'Oh,' she said as her hopes stopped soaring and started plummeting. The contract. One more month. Not exactly forever.

Scott took her briefcase, threw it onto his glamorous coffee-coloured couch with no regard for the potential damage its buckles could do to the fabric, and slowly turned her to the living area. 'So—what do you think?' he asked.

She tried to smile. 'I guess I'll start with…*ab initio*.'

'Well, I'm going to have to kiss you for that.'

'Do you even know what it means?'

'No.'

And then he drew her close and kissed her cheek. Just her cheek…but she felt it tingle all the way through her body.

'So what *does* it mean?' he asked when he released her.

'"From the beginning",' she said. 'It's commonly used to refer to the time a contract, statute, deed or…or marriage becomes legal.' *Oh, God—why had she mentioned marriage?* She cleared her throat. 'But in this instance we'll use it for the start of the house tour.'

'Suits me,' Scott said. '*Ab initio.* We can use it for the start of our new month too.'

'Hmm…' Kate said. A vague, *nothing* noise. 'Where to next?'

'Library—which, you will be interested to note, used to be an altar.'

She could already see it, and walked slowly across the wooden floor and up the three steps. So beautiful. Coloured rugs. A fireplace—unlit in the heat of February. Books nestling in custom-made shelves; armchairs—some leather, some fabric—low wooden tables. She turned to face the main space, looking out at the expansive floor, partitioned into discrete zones via the columns—all spectacularly clean and modern, which made the library feel like an oasis of plush comfort.

'It could do with a few of your mother's paintings, but otherwise what do you think?' Scott asked.

Mother. Her mother. *Tell him, tell him.* 'Umm…' She turned to him. '*Ad coelum.*'

Scott drew her in and kissed her eyelids. First one, then the other.

'If you like it…aren't you going to touch me?' he asked, all husky.

Kate reached a hand up, cupped his face, ran her thumb over his cheekbone. 'Want to know what it means?' she asked.

'Yes, as soon as you touch me again—you owe me for the living room.'

She brought up her other hand and now both hands cradled his face. She leaned up, kissed him gently on the mouth. And then she smiled into his eyes.

'To the sky. It's actually abbreviated from *cuius est solum eius est usque ad coelum et ad inferos*—which basically means whoever owns the soil owns that space, all the way up to heaven and down to hell. And this is just heavenly. Which seems apt for a converted church.'

'You've got no idea how much you are turning me on, Kate.'

'That's the whole idea of Play Time, isn't it?'

He frowned slightly, but said nothing. Simply took her arm and continued the tour.

Scott showed her all over the masterpiece that was the lower floor. And it was obvious why his renown as an architect was growing.

The huge arched panels of stained glass juxtaposed against the ultra-modern use of materials and neutral colours in most of the spaces were startling and lovely. The structure of the zones, flowing one into the next, was incredible. Scott's stark office and the state-of-the-art kitchen and guest bathroom were top-notch contemporary. The surprising pops of colour, like the scarlet staircase and the chartreuse relaxation nook off a plant-filled atrium, were brilliantly eccentric. How could such disparate elements combine into something so blow-your-head-off gorgeous? But that was...*Scott*.

Kate had to concentrate hard in order to be able to spit out Latin legal phrases, only to have her thoughts scatter every time Scott chose a different part of her to kiss. It was agonising, this falling in love. Feeling it dig itself more deeply inside her with every gentle, lavishing touch of Scott's fingers, his mouth, on her lips, her cheeks, her ears, her eyebrows—her damned *eyebrows*!—and her hair. Wishing so hard it meant something, the way his eyes closed, the way he held his breath as she touched him in turn. Shoulders, hands, neck, chest.

She was in torment by the time they circled back to the library, where Scott settled her with a drink while he finished preparing dinner. He was so jaunty as he left her—even whistling, as though he had everything he could possibly want.

But then, Scott *did* have everything he wanted. *Exactly* what he wanted. *She* was the one who didn't have what she wanted. And she still had no idea how to get it—except to ask for it...and risk losing even the little of him she had.

Kate didn't know how long had passed when Scott came to escort her through to the dining area. But she could feel time just generally slipping away. Four days until the twenty-eighth of February. When their contract would be terminated—or rolled over.

Scott held out a chair for her at the sleek wooden table and waited for her to sit.

'You didn't have to cook dinner,' Kate said.

'Well, you see, Kate, the fifty-fifty rule wasn't working for me. So this—' charming little shrug '—is my way of taking you to dinner. And before you tell me I'm breaking the rules, I'm going to remind you that extras are allowed in Play Time.' He sat opposite her. 'Cucumber soup. Perfect for a Sydney summer.'

But Kate was beyond taste as she silently filled her spoon, raised it to her mouth, swallowed. Time after time. Until her bowl was empty.

Scott—who'd done an excellent job of keeping up a flow of small talk—cleared the plates, then returned with something that looked so delicious Kate's heart sank. He'd taken such care—but how was she supposed to eat it when her heart had swelled so gigantically it threatened to choke her?

'Korean-style pork tenderloin with wild and brown rice pilaf and steamed pea pods,' Scott announced.

As Kate doggedly forced the food down Scott explained a house design he was currently working on. Presumably she offered appropriate rejoinders, because he didn't make an issue of her lack of vocal enthusiasm.

But then, why would he? It wasn't *conversation* he wanted.

He cleared the plates a second time, and while he was gone Kate had a mini-meltdown, remembering her mother's words. *Make it romantic.* How did a person turn a contract into something romantic? *Move heaven and hell.* How? What was the trigger? What would it take to make him love her?

And then he was back, carrying a tray. On the tray was a plate piled high with cookies of some kind and two exquisite boxes—one pink, one purple—decorated with fluttery fairies, shimmering with glitter, finished off with gauzy bows.

'Whoopie pies,' Scott said, depositing the tray in front of Kate and taking the seat beside her.

Unable to stop herself, Kate reached for one of the boxes, ran suddenly trembling fingers over the top, pulled the end of the ribbon through her fingertips.

'Do you like those boxes?' Scott asked.

She looked at him, said nothing.

'They're for Maeve and Molly. Because...' He shrugged, blushed. 'Well, you know... I spoke to them about baking whoopie pies and I... Well, since I didn't know when I was going to see them again, and I was baking anyway, I thought they... Ah, hell, I thought they'd like them. That's all. And I saw the boxes in a store near my office, so I...' He cleared his throat. 'I bought them. No big deal.'

Nice and defiant. Still blushing.

And everything surged in Kate—wrenching at her heart, racing through her blood, shattering every thought in her brain...flooding her with absolute crazy love. She was insanely, wildly in love with him.

She couldn't pretend any more. Not for one more moment.

And the next moment of her life started precisely *now*.

'Hugo,' she said.

CHAPTER EIGHTEEN

SCOTT REELED BACK in his chair. 'What's he got to do with anything?'

'I don't know, Scott. Why don't you tell me what he has to do with you, with us, or indeed with anything? Because you've told me precious little so far. So—Hugo.'

'Oh, I get it. Is this—? This is about…about Play Time. Stopping Play Time, right?'

'Yes, Scott, it is.'

'But…why? What was so bad? Do you want to…to go back and start again?'

'No.'

He blinked. 'Okay, then, let's skip it altogether and just go upstairs and—'

'Hugo,' Kate said again.

He tried to smile, but didn't nail it. 'You don't know what I was going to suggest.'

Kate didn't bother even trying to smile. 'The fact that you said we should go upstairs—to bed, no doubt—tells me all I need to know. It tells me we don't have a relationship.'

'Sure we do.'

'No, Scott, we don't. We have a contract.'

'You're the one who wanted the contract.'

'Semantics. With or without the signed piece of paper, we have an *arrangement*. An arrangement is *not* a relationship. And if you're happy with that then I'm calling "Hugo". As in *enough*. No more Play Time. No more anything.'

Scott shoved a hand into his hair. 'Kate, if it's the subject of my brother that's bothering you—'

'Didn't you listen? Hugo—as in *I'm finished.*'

'—he has nothing to do with us.' Right over the top of her. 'I never thought you'd meet him.'

'Well, I did meet him, Scott, so how about you explain now?'

Silence. Scott's jaw tightened.

'Scott?'

'You're the smartest person I've ever met, Kate. I'm sure you worked it all out the night of the architect awards. Why do you need to wring the words out of me?'

Kate stared at him.

He stared back.

And then he shoved *both* his hands into his hair. 'Dammit—all right. It's no big deal.'

He took a moment. Placed his hands on the table, palms down. Very specific. Controlling them.

'Very simply: my brother was the perfect child. Better than me at school, better than me at sport, better than me at everything. My parents let me know it in a thousand ways when we were growing up. And when Hugo hit the doctor target…? Big bonus points, there. Now he's hit all the personal targets too—getting married, providing grandchildren. Long story short—Hugo is *family* all the way. And I'm…*not*. I'm number two. All the way.'

Kate reached for his hand but Scott pulled it back, out of the touch zone.

'All the way,' he repeated. 'Want an example, Kate? What about that time I was in the Whitsundays, goofing off, teaching holidaymakers to sail, making a fool of myself over a girl who didn't love me? What do you think my brother was doing?' But the question was rhetorical. 'He was one-upping me spectacularly by sailing solo around the world.'

'So what?' Kate asked, but it was hard to get that out because she wanted to cry.

'So *what*?' Scott laughed—harsh and awful. 'So sailing was *my* thing. Why did he have to take that too? I swear, if he knew I liked cooking he'd go and get himself a publishing deal for a cookbook.'

'Hugo didn't win the architecture prize. You did.'

'Wait until next year's awards,' Scott said. 'He'll pull a rabbit out of someone's hat.'

'Exactly, Scott! Out of someone *else's* hat! Unlike you, wearing your *own* hat. Because you can't tell me you simply follow blindly—not your parents, not your brother, not anyone. Otherwise you'd be a doctor like the rest of your family—you're certainly smart enough.'

'There's no mystery there, Kate. I just wanted to be an architect.'

'I know that. And I know why. Because it's *you*. Creativity—and order. The perfect career for *you*! And I think your brother hates how good you are at it. Because you can bet that although you could be a doctor if you wanted to—'

'Not as good as Hugo.'

'Maybe...maybe not—but you could be *some* kind of doctor. Hugo, however, could never be *any* kind of architect.'

'You can't possibly tell that.'

'Sure I can—because he wasn't the one in the navy blue tux that night. He doesn't have it. *It.* That thing you have. And what does it tell you that he didn't even have the grace to come over and congratulate you when you won that award?'

Scott said nothing.

'That he was jealous,' Kate said. '*Is* jealous. Of you.'

Scoffing laugh. 'He has nothing to be jealous of.'

'Really? Because the way I see it, you have something Hugo wants badly but will never, ever have. I'll bet your parents don't have it either. I'll bet none of them even understands it—which is why it's three against one in the Knight family. You have creativity, and charisma, and wit, and decency, and...and adventure in your soul, and so much more. *That's* why you went to the Whitsundays, and why Hugo had to make do with what he *thought* was one better. Except it *wasn't* one better. He had to *follow* you to one-up you. And he had to one-up you because that's the only way he can feel better than you. He can't bear your success because he wants it *all*—all for himself. He can't *be* you, so he *steals* from you. But he can't steal the one thing he really wants because that would make him…you. And, no matter what he tries, he never *will* be you.'

Scott shook his head, wearing one of those smiles that meant nothing.

'And the sailing thing?' she said urgently. 'I'd tell you to make it your thing again, if it bothers you, but you don't *have* to make it your thing. Because it *is* your thing. It always was—and it will be waiting for you when you're ready to let it all go and just be, Scott. Just *be*. Without comparing yourself to anyone.'

'I've given up comparing myself, Kate.' Scott took a deep, visible breath. 'Number two is fine with me.'

Heart. Breaking.

'You're not number two. Not with me, Scott.'

'Not yet. But give it time. Someone else will come along. Someone older, like that Phillip guy. Someone smarter, like Hugo. Someone not as stitched-up and closed-off and conservative, like Brodie. That's why you danced with him. Why you went sailing with him. I'll bet you even told him about your custody case.'

She was silent.

'Did you, Kate?' he asked, and she heard the edge of danger in his voice.

'I don't talk about my cases. Not in…in detail.'

'Obfuscation? How very…*legal*.' He shook his head, disgusted.

'You sound like my mother. She really would like you, Scott.'

'Did you tell him, Kate? It's a simple question—one of those simple questions you say you don't have a problem with.'

She took a quick breath. 'Then, yes. That's the answer. I did. I told him.'

Scott's hand fisted, banged on the table, and Kate flinched.

'Why?' The word shot out like a bullet.

'Because he asked. As a friend.'

'I can't *believe* this.' Scott shot to his feet, paced away, then back. 'What the hell am *I*, Kate? I've been trying to talk to you about it for a week.'

He banged both fists on the table this time.

'Tell *me*!' Another bang. 'Tell *me*, Kate, dammit!'

Kate's heart had jumped right into her throat as his fists hit the table, and for a moment all she could do was stare at him. He looked a heartbeat away from breathing fire.

Out of control—at last.

And now she had to find words, when all she wanted to do was fling herself at him and wrap herself around him and beg him to let her love him, to love her back.

She realised she'd left it too long to speak when, cursing, Scott started to pace away again. One step…two.

'Wait,' she said, standing, grabbing his swinging arm so fast her chair toppled backwards. 'I'll tell you.'

He was shaking his head as he turned, wrenched his arm free. 'Don't bother, Kate. Just…just *don't*. It's too damned late.'

'I'm representing the father,' she rushed out. 'Who's been sitting on the sidelines going slowly out of his mind while his ex-wife's new boyfriend slaps his three-year-old son around. Something he's reported over and over and over. But nobody believes him. Because there's been enough mud slung to cast all sorts of doubts about him. His little boy screams and begs every time he has to go back to his mother after a scheduled visit.'

Kate's breaths were heaving in and out and she'd started to shake with the fury of it.

'My client ended up so desperate he kidnapped his own

child to protect him. And what did he get for caring like that? No more visits. At all. That's what.'

Her throat was clogged and swollen. The injustice of it was raging out of her, even though she'd won. Why? *Why* did it still get to her? No answer—it just did. And it was all too much. The case…Scott…her damned life.

'So you want to know why I didn't tell you, Scott?' she asked as the tears started. 'Because you didn't sign up for deep and meaningful, remember? And that's deep and meaningful to me. I needed you. But how could I tell you? What could I say? When you said—made it clear— Oh, God. I can't. I…can't. I…'

But she couldn't go on. She was choking on tears. And suddenly she gave in to them, sobbing into her hands.

And then she was in Scott's arms, held tightly against his chest. 'Shh, shh, Kate…I'm here.'

'No, Scott, you're not,' she sobbed into his shoulder. 'You're not here. Your body's here—that's all. Just your body.'

She tried to pull away but Scott held on. 'I'm not letting you go, Kate, so stop struggling.'

'And if I do? If I stop struggling?' She looked up at him. 'Then what? You'll ask me to spit out a few legal terms and take me to bed?'

'Yes,' he said simply.

'That's not enough,' she cried, and buried her face in his shoulder again. 'I want more.'

'So do I. That's why we're rolling it over.'

'No, Scott, we're not.'

'You just said you wanted more.'

'Not more sex! More…*more*.'

'I don't— I don't—'

'No, you *don't*,' she cut in, half-despair, half-rage, as she pulled out of his arms. 'That's the problem. Well, I'm not hanging in limbo any more, like a suspended piñata, waiting to have the crap beaten out of me.'

'A piña—?' He stopped. Incredulous. 'I'm not beating anything out of you. I would never hurt you.'

'Oh, you're hurting me, all right.'

'I'm *not* hurting you,' Scott said furiously. 'I *won't* hurt you. You won't hurt *me*. That's the whole point!'

'And I'm telling you—you *are* hurting me. Because I love you. And you don't love me back.'

The shock of it was plain on his face. 'You don't love me. Kate, you *know* you don't.' Pleading, almost. 'You can't. You don't want love.'

She laughed, shrugged, helpless.

Waves of panic were emanating from Scott. 'You said you'd never give someone that kind of power over you.'

'Except that now I would give it to you.'

'Cynical. We're both cynical. It's what made us perfect. *Makes* us perfect.'

'I'm *not* cynical, Scott. Or if I am it doesn't last—not if I have someone…' she swallowed '…someone who'll say to me, "Shh, I'm here", like you just did. Putting things right for people is what I do, what I *want* to do, even if sometimes it gets too much. And perfect…? I don't want to be perfect. And I don't want you to be perfect either. I want to be *im*-perfect—with you. I want children who are perfect or imperfect—who are *anything* as long as they're yours. And I want to say to *you*, *Shh, I'm here*, when things get too much for you. Because I'm in love with you. And I would do anything—*anything*—for you to love me.'

His eyes were wild. 'I…can't do this.'

'Why not?'

'I don't. Do this.'

'You loved Chantal. Why can't you love me?'

'I didn't love Chantal, Kate. And I don't blame her for choosing Brodie. I never did. Anyone would choose him.'

'Not me. Because I chose you. I'm *choosing* you. No—it wasn't even a choice. It just happened. Love. I didn't even know I was waiting for it. But I was. I was waiting for the right man to come along. Then there you were. And suddenly you were mine. The perfect imperfect man. The right man for me. Uptight…beer not cocktails…hell, no, to dancing… sport and poker games…with a kitten on your backside… wearing a blue tux and driving a red Mini…baking for two little girls. How could I *not* love you? And now, Scott, I want us to just…just *be*.'

He was shaking his head. His face was white, stark fear in his eyes. 'I'm not the right guy for anyone, Kate. I'm the "friends with benefits" guy, with a bulging black book. I've never had a relationship—don't you see? *Never!* And there's a reason for that—because I know what I'm good at. Sex—no strings. My speciality. I've got more tail than I know what to do with. That's me. And I'm fine with that.'

It was like a punch direct to Kate's heart, killing it—that was how it felt. As if her heart was dead. A swollen lump she wished she could rip out of her chest.

'T-T-Tail?' Kate stammered over the word, her teeth chattering with reaction.

He looked at her, all hard-eyed. 'Tail,' he repeated.

God, the ache of it. Crushing. Ravaging. 'So here I am, opening myself to you, telling you I would move heaven and hell and everything in between—*everything*—to have you—*you*, Scott. Not Brodie, not Hugo, not Phillip, but *you*. And your response is to tell me I'm a piece of *tail*?'

He stood there like a block of granite, silent.

'Right,' she said, and swallowed. 'Right.' She looked blindly around, head spinning. 'Right.' Was the blood draining out of her? That was what it felt like. 'Saturday is the twenty-eighth of February. End of contract. We've had one session this week—Sunday. And we have tonight. We'll make this the last one, because I'm not inclined to negotiate any extras for the week. *Cadit quaestio*—a settlement for our dispute has been reached. Sex—once more—and the issue is resolved.'

'It's not resolved.'

Agony twisted through her. He didn't love her, but he wouldn't let her go either. 'What more do you want from me?'

'I want… I want…' His hands were diving into his hair again. But no more words emerged.

Kate took an unsteady breath. 'Well, given everything you've just said to me, and all the things you can't seem to say, I finally know what *I* want. I want out. I'm saying no to the rollover option. No to everything.'

'You can't do that.'

'Now, you see, you should have read the contract when I told you to. Because I *can* do that. I *am* doing that. I'm not going to turn into one of those bitter people I see in court—hating you, trying to punish you because you don't love me or need me the way I love and need you. If you don't love me then I don't want you.'

'You do want me. I know you do.'

Kate started removing her clothes.

'What the hell—? Kate, what are you doing?'

'Getting undressed.' She was down to her underwear in record time. 'I'm taking back my "Hugo" and we're restarting Play Time. As I recall, it was a dining experience you offered me—you bent the fifty-fifty rule to get it…clever you. So I'll get on top of the dining table, you can put those whoopie pies all over me, and then—'

But whatever she'd been about to say was whoomped out of her as Scott grabbed her by the arms. 'You're not lying on top of anything except my bed.'

She greeted that with a nice, brittle laugh. 'How conservative of you.'

'Yes, I *am* conservative. And I'm over all this Play Time stuff. I don't want you on your knees in alleys, or stripping for me like a hooker, or blindfolding me like we're in a B&D room, or any other kooky stuff.'

'That's exactly what you wanted—why do you think I was giving it to you?'

'Well, I don't want it now. Got it, Kate?' He shook her, once. 'Got it? I. Just. Want. You. As agreed. In bed. Okay?'

'As agreed,' she repeated. And the tears came. 'No, Scott, it's not okay.'

'Why not? Why *not*, dammit?'

'Because I love you. And loving you hurts like hell.'

He let her go, stepped back as though she'd struck him.

'Come on, Scott. Look on the bright side. You never liked all those rules. Anais is going to make you a much more *beneficial* friend.'

'I don't want Anais.'

'And after tonight I won't want *you*. So here I am, offering you one last time. Take it…or leave it.'

'They're the only two options?'

'Yes.'

'Then I'm taking it. Get on the table, Kate. Let's say goodbye in style.'

CHAPTER NINETEEN

SCOTT KNEW HE would never forget the sight of Kate lying on his dining table, letting him take her as tears leaked from the corners of her eyes.

He'd been so sure she would stop crying. That he could *make* her stop crying with the power of his depthless passion for her. But even as she'd succumbed to his body, as she'd soared with him into orgasm, her tears had kept coming… slow and silent.

Scott had been frantic. Scooping her off the table afterwards into his arms, holding her against his shaking body.

Wordless, she'd tried to leave. But he'd whispered that he wanted more, that he *needed* more. So she'd let him carry her upstairs to his bed. He'd kissed her for what felt like forever. But the tears had just kept coming. And even hating himself for her pain and his own desperation, he hadn't been able to let her go.

He'd watched her as she slept. The frown on her face. The tear tracks. The divine mouth, swollen from the way he'd devoured her.

She hadn't spoken one word to him—not since that last, 'Take it…or leave it.'

And he'd taken it, all right. Taken, taken, *taken*. Hoping, selfishly, to sate himself at last. Hoping he would wake up and not want her any more. Hoping he'd be able to let her go in the morning.

But when he'd woken she was already gone and he'd had no choice to make; she'd made the choice for both of them.

He hated his bed—because she wasn't in it.

So he went downstairs.

Where he decided he hated his house—because she wasn't there.

In the dining room were the girls' glittery boxes, waiting to be filled with whoopie pies. But the whoopie pies were nothing but a heap of broken biscuit and smeared cream on the floor, surrounded by shards of shattered plate. The plate he'd shoved off the table in his urgency to get to Kate.

As he looked at the mess and remembered how joyful he'd been, waiting for Kate to arrive, it hit him that what he hated most of all was his *life*—because she'd walked out of it.

And ringing in his ears, over and over, were her words. *'I would move heaven and hell to have you.'*

That was just so…*her*. Direct. Laying the argument out. Fighting to win. The way she always fought. To the death. To win the prize.

To win…the prize…

His breath hitched as he repeated that in his head. *Fighting to win the prize.*

The prize—*her* prize—was…him.

His heart started to thump. Loud, heavy, dull.

Why was he so scared about being her prize when she was everything that was wonderful? When *she* wasn't scared to claim *him* even though he wasn't anything wonderful at all?

But wasn't that exactly it? That time on her terrace, when they'd talked about love, she'd said that real love—of *any* kind—gloried especially in a person's flaws. She'd told him last night that she wanted to be imperfect…with him. She wanted them to just…*be*.

She knew everything. Chantal, Brodie, Hugo, his parents. Knew about all the times he'd lost. Had been with him when he'd finally won. She'd seen the very worst of him—because, God, he'd shown it to her—and she loved him anyway. He didn't have to be perfect. He just had to…*be*.

Eyes stinging.

She'd said she would move heaven and hell to have him.

Chest aching.

That had to make him the best man in the world. Not second-best—*the* best.

Sweat ran down his back.

There might be smarter men, funnier men, better-looking men, more successful men, easier men—but not for Kate.

Breaths coming short and hard.

She would move heaven and freaking *hell* for him.

Whole body throbbing.

Exactly what he would do for her. Move heaven and hell.

Because she was his. Only his. And he wanted, at last, to reach for the prize, to claim the prize for himself—the only prize worth having. *Kate.*

The simplicity of that, the peace of it, burst in his head and dazzled him—but then the enormity of what he'd done to her, what he'd said, hit him and he staggered, grabbing for the closest chair.

Was it even possible to fix what he'd done?

Terrified, he grabbed his phone, called her mobile.

No answer.

Called her office.

Got Deb. Who had only two words for him: *'Drop dead!'*

He emailed Kate. Texted. Called her again.

He risked the wrath of Deb and called her again. *Three* words this time: *'Drop dead, arsehole.'*

So he tracked down Shay, because for sure Kate would have told her sister—she was a Cleary, not a Knight, and they were close—and maybe he could grovel by proxy.

And, yep—she'd told her sister, all right.

Dropping dead would have been a kindness compared to what Shay told him to do to himself, with a casual reference to Gus and Aristotle throwing knives at his corpse wrapped around a collection of four-letter words. She followed that up by telling him the most diabolical thing he could possibly hear. That Kate had never been in love before—but she was a Cleary, so that wouldn't stop her from ripping the love out of her heart and stomping it to a violent death. The Cleary way: fight like the devil—but when you lose, move on. No second chances. No going back.

Shaken, Scott hung up and did the manly thing.

He called Brodie and suggested they get drunk.

It was only beer number one but Scott didn't mince his words. There was no time to wait for the anaesthetising effects of booze. No time for tiptoeing.

'I'm in trouble,' he said.

Brodie took that with equanimity. 'I think what you mean is *I'm in love.*'

'Yep,' Scott said, and swallowed a mouthful of beer.

Brodie took his own long, thoughtful sip. 'I don't see the problem—unless she doesn't love you back.'

'She said she does.'

'And the problem, therefore, is…?'

'I told her I had more tail than I knew what to do with.' He grimaced. 'And that that was how I wanted it to stay.'

Brodie said an enlightening, 'Aha…'

'Well?' Scott demanded belligerently.

'Well, basically…' Pause for a swig of beer. 'You are an idiot.'

'Yeah, but what do I *do*?'

'Call her.'

'Tried. All day. Tried everyone. Her…her office…her sister. Her assistant told me to drop dead. And I won't tell you what her sister told me to do with myself because it's anatomically impossible but will still make your eyes water. I tried Willa. Then Amy. Just subtly, to see if they knew where she was going to be tonight. At least they don't seem to have any idea there was anything between us, so I haven't ruined *that* for her.'

There was a moment of stunned silence, and then Brodie hooted out a laugh. 'Are you *kidding* me? Nobody who saw you kiss Kate on that dance floor is in any doubt that you're a goner. The *bartender* knew, you moron.'

'Well, why didn't *I* know?'

'Idiot, remember?'

'So what the hell am I going to do?'

Long, thoughtful pause. 'Scott, I'm going to share something with you, even though you don't deserve it—you big clunk. Four words: *From Here to Eternity*.'

'Huh?'

'That night at the bar, before we got there, the girls were talking about their idea of romantic moments.'

'And...*what*?'

'Four scenarios were mentioned. One was Willa's—so let's discount that, because it was something financial.'

'Yep, that's Willa.'

'Then there was one about rose petals being strewn around the bedroom.'

Scott snorted out a laugh. 'God!'

'Yep. You wouldn't say *that* was Kate, would you?'

'Er—no!'

'What about a knight on a white charger?'

'What the—? I mean— *What?*' Scott burst out laughing.

'Not Kate?' Brodie asked, his mouth twisting.

'Hell, I hope not.'

'Sure?'

Scott shook his head. Definitive. 'No—that's not her.'

Brodie gave him a sympathetic look. 'Then I'm pegging her for *From Here to Eternity*.'

'What the hell *is* that?'

'A movie.'

'About what?'

'How the hell would I know? It's got to be a chick flick. I mean, come on—*eternity?* But I'm guessing there's a clue in that movie.'

'How's that going to help me?'

'Well, dropkick, I'm going to download the movie and we're going to watch it together. And—sidebar conversation—you are *so* going to owe me for this!'

'Okay, okay—I'll owe you. But what exactly are we going to do *after* we watch it?'

'I don't know—not yet. Which is why we're watching it in the first place. To figure out what her most romantic moment is. And then, mate, you're going to *give* her that moment—because words are not going to be enough. Action is what's needed.'

Two hours later—mid-bite of a slice of seafood pizza—Brodie paused the film. 'And there you have it,' he said.

'Have what?' Scott asked warily.

'That's the scene.'

'That? I mean…*that*? Seriously?'

Brodie replayed it. Nodded, very sure of himself. 'That. Believe me. I know women, and that's it.'

'Looks…sandy…'

'Suck it up, buddy. Suck. It. Up.'

'I can tell you right now I am *not* writhing around in the surf on Bondi Beach surrounded by a thousand people.'

'If that's what she wants that's what you're going to do.'

'Aw, hell…'

Brodie laughed. 'I'm just messing with your head, Knight. Nothing that public will be required. I have a friend down the coast who, as it happens, lives near a beach that is chronically deserted.'

'And just *how* am I going to get Kate to drive for hours along the coastline with me when I can't even get her to pick up the phone?'

Brodie held up a hand for silence. Grabbed his phone off the coffee table. Dialled. Then, 'Kate?'

Scott leapt off the couch, waving his hands like a madman and trying to grab the phone out of Brodie's hand.

Brodie punched him in the arm. 'Nope—haven't seen him.' Lying without compunction. 'Why?'

Scott made another mad grab—got another punch.

'No,' Brodie said, holding Scott off with a hand on his

forehead. 'I just wanted to offer you another sailing lesson on Saturday.'

Pause while Scott almost exploded—but in silence.

'Great,' Brodie said into the phone. 'Eight o'clock. See you then.'

Brodie disconnected and turned to Scott, grinning.

'*I* want to teach her how to sail,' Scott said.

'So do it.'

'Do it *when*, *genius*?'

'After the beach clinch. I'm going to drop Kate off at a particular inlet down the coast on Saturday, just after lunch. You—having bought a neat little yacht I happen to know is for sale—will have sailed down there and will be waiting to drive her to that deserted beach.'

'If I sail down there I won't have a car.'

'So *hire* one!'

'And then what?'

'And *then* you will roll around like a dumbass in the surf with her.'

'And…?'

'And you will sail her back to Sydney, teaching her the way you should have offered the first time she mentioned sailing to you. Honestly—do I have to do *everything* for you?'

Scott stared at Brodie. A grin started working its way across his face as he picked up a piece of pizza. 'I should have known a guy who'd order a seafood pizza would know all about girly stuff,' he said. 'Pepperoni is where it's at, mate. *Pepperoni.*'

'Shove your pepperoni where the sun doesn't shine, *mate*—and get me another beer.'

Scott laughed, and started to get off the couch to go to the fridge.

But Brodie stopped him, one hand on his forearm. 'You're it for her, you know? Don't let that mangy brother of yours keep getting away with making you feel like second-best. Because he is *not* better than you.'

Scott gripped Brodie's hand where it rested on his arm. 'I know he's not. She wouldn't love me if he was.'

Brodie smiled. 'And neither would I.'

'Brode—mate—*please*!' Scott said.

'You are *so* uptight—I'm not at all sure I shouldn't try to cut you out with Red,' Brodie said.

'You can *try*,' Scott said, and then he laughed.

CHAPTER TWENTY

KATE COULDN'T DRUM UP any enthusiasm for the sailing lesson, but she was waiting at the jetty on the dot of eight o'clock, with a fake smile worthy of Scott himself pasted on.

Because it wouldn't do for Brodie to report back to Scott that she was looking wan and miserable.

She climbed aboard and darted a look around the deck. Half expecting… Maybe hoping just a little…?

'He's not here, Kate,' Brodie said.

She looked at him as the hope died. 'You know?' Short, unhappy laugh. 'Of course you do. Best friends, right? You don't have to badger confidences out of him.'

'Are we going to talk about it?' Brodie asked.

'No,' Kate said, and heard the dangerous wobble in her voice.

'Okay, then.' He took her bag, stowed it. 'Remember I said we were sailing down the coast and going swimming when we got there?' He gestured to her long cotton pants, her long-sleeved T-shirt. 'You got your swimmers on under there?'

'Yes,' she said.

'Then we're off.'

Kate tried to recapture some of the joy of her first sailing lesson, but that sense of freedom, of escape, was elusive. She was just so…so heartbroken.

Nevertheless, she threw herself into it—and if Brodie was a little less didactic this time around she wasn't going to complain about getting special treatment. He was that kind of guy—the kind who read anguish and allowed for it. Not the kind to tell a girl she was a piece of tail…even if she *was*.

Hours passed, and Kate started to wonder if they were going to turn around any time soon—because at this rate they wouldn't make it back to Sydney before Sunday morning. But they finally stopped at a calm, protected inlet for lunch.

Slowly Kate started to relax. But with relaxation came those horrible, useless, helpless tears. She hurried over to the bow of the boat, away from the others, trying to stem the flow. But it was no use. They welled in her eyes, clogged the back of her nose. Thank heaven she was wearing sunglasses, so Brodie wouldn't see.

But almost before the thought had formed Brodie was there, standing just behind her. She knew it, but she couldn't turn. Just couldn't move. Because the tears were flowing freely.

'He's not good with words,' he said. 'Not the *important* words.'

Kate covered her face with her hands, dislodging her sunglasses.

Brodie turned her, took off her sunglasses, hugged her. 'At least he didn't punch you. That's what he did to me the first time I told him I loved him.'

Kate started laughing then—and it was the weirdest thing, mixing laughter with tears.

Brodie tilted her face up. 'You going to give him another chance?'

'No. That doesn't happen in my family.'

'Well, at least you gave him *one* chance, I guess,' Brodie said. 'It's more than his own family gave him.'

'Oh, God. Don't say that.'

'It's true. He needs a family, Kate. A new one. A *real* one.'

She was crying again.

'And he's over there on the shore, waiting for you to be it.'

Kate, stunned, turned to look.

And there he was. Tall and bulky, in jeans and T-shirt and aviator sunglasses, hands jammed into his pockets. Waiting for her.

Waiting…for *her*…

But waiting for what?

Kate didn't even notice when Brodie took his arms from around her. Barely heard him call to one of the guys on the boat. Dinghy… Something about a dinghy…

Next thing she knew she and her bag were *in* the dinghy, heading towards the shore. Scott took off his sunglasses as she got closer, flinging them away as if he didn't care what happened to them.

And then she was there, and he was reaching for her, helping her out of the dinghy, holding out his hand for her bag, wrapping her in his arms, holding on to her, holding tight. It felt electric—like a massive, hungry jolt—so different from the calm comfort of Brodie's embrace.

And she knew it would always be like that with Scott. Because he was *it*. The only one for her. It was a thought that scared her so much she almost couldn't breathe. Because it meant that without him she would be alone—forever. And she didn't want to be alone any more.

But being alone was better than loving a man who didn't love her back.

She took a deep breath, pulled out of his arms. 'Scott, I meant what I said.'

'Kate, please—just bear with me, okay? You'll see.'

Without waiting for her to respond, he took her hand, led her away from the water, up to the road.

He opened the door of a nondescript car—where was his Mini?—and helped her in.

'Where are we going, Scott?' she asked tiredly as he got behind the wheel, started the car.

'Don't ask, Kate. I'll stuff it up if I talk.'

So Kate simply sat as Scott drove—a total mess, almost ill from the way her heart was hammering.

He parked, got out of the car and came around to her side to help her out. He took her in his arms again and she couldn't bring herself to pull away. She felt him shaking. Like a leaf.

'Scared, that's all,' he said with an embarrassed shrug as she looked up at him.

'Why?'

Short half-laugh. 'You'll see,' he said again, and led her off the road towards a patch of scrub.

Her eyes widened. 'In *there*?'

Scott winced. 'Yep. In there. God help us.'

He led the way in until the thick scrub morphed into sparsely vegetated dunes. She could hear the roar and rush of surf, and then it was there. A tiny jewel of a beach, waves breaking in a constant sucking stream.

'A surf beach?' she said, poised on top of a dune.

'Yeah, a surf beach,' he said, grimacing, and trudged with her down onto the sand.

'It's beautiful,' Kate said, trying to understand the grimace—trying to understand *something*. Anything. 'And not a soul here except for that one surfer. Amazing.'

'It's a local secret,' he said. 'And apparently a little dangerous for swimming.'

'So why are we here?'

Scott screwed his eyes shut and blushed. '*From Here to Eternity,*' he said.

Kate's mouth dropped open. It took her a moment to find her voice, but at least by the time she did Scott had opened his eyes.

'Is this a joke?' she asked icily.

'No.'

'Who told you?'

'Brodie.'

She sucked in a tortured breath—felt the heat rush along her cheekbones. 'And who told *him*?'

'He figured it out. Something Jessica said that night at Fox.'

'Jessica?' she said ominously.

But Scott wasn't listening. He looked a heartbeat away from a nervous breakdown.

'Well, Kate, we're here,' he said. 'Let's do it.'

He stripped down to a pair of well-worn board shorts—in

which he looked mouthwateringly good. And then he came to her, took her face in his hands. Licked slowly along one cheekbone, then along the other.

‘I’ve wanted to do that for the longest time,’ he said. ‘You are so absolutely beautiful when you blush.’

‘Scott, this is not going to work,’ she said a little desperately, hanging on to her resolve by a thread. ‘I told you. No rollover. I’m done.’

‘It’s not about the rollover and we’re not leaving until we do it—so get your gear off.’

‘That surfer ’

‘I can handle one surfer.’

‘But anyone could come past.’

‘Yeah—I know. It’s a bit like the night Officer Cleary frisked me in Ellington Lane.’

‘That was different.’

‘How so? Did you know we wouldn’t be caught?’

‘No, I didn’t know. But it was dark and I…’ She huffed out a breath, aggravated. ‘Really, I just didn’t care.’

‘And there I was, thinking you were law-abiding!’

‘I am. But I’m not conservative. And *you are*, Scott.’

He touched her hair. ‘And yet here I am, trying to get you out of your clothes on a beach in broad daylight,’ he said, and smiled—and his whole face lit up with it.

Her heart lurched. That smile. *Devastating.*

‘Scott, don’t do this to me,’ she said shakily. ‘Stop doing this to me.’

‘I have to do it. Kate, please. You’ve got to let me. Just this one thing. For you. Please, Kate. Please let me.’

Kate looked into Scott’s eyes—they were warm and serious and…and *desperate*. Looked at the waves. Back into Scott’s eyes.

Why was she fighting it? The man she was in love with was offering to make her a gift of her ultimate fantasy. She’d be like Willa and Chantal—her most romantic moment would be real. And she could pretend, couldn’t she, that it was love?

'All right,' she said, and wondered if he'd finally driven her mad as she stripped down to her one-piece black swimsuit.

Scott took her hand. Gave her a look redolent of bravery. 'Shall we?'

She nodded, but wondered if this memory—precious though it would be—was going to be worth it, given that every time it surfaced in the future her heart would break all over again.

Scott led her into the surf, just far enough for them to duck under the water and get wet.

'No further,' he said. 'I can feel the water tugging, and this is going to lose all its romance value if we get swept out to sea and either drown or get eaten by a shark.'

He pulled her into his arms.

'And in any case…' he said, backing her towards the shore. Backing her, backing her, backing her, and then dragging her to her knees, where the waves were breaking. 'This is the money shot, right?'

And with that, he eased her flat onto the sand, and then he was on top of her, kissing her as if he'd happily drown as long as his mouth was on hers.

The water surged over them. Receded, surged, receded. For the longest time they stayed there, waves breaking over them, Scott's mouth on hers, tongue thrusting, mirroring the breaking of the waves over their bodies. Over, over, over. Way longer than the scene in the movie.

Eventually he pulled back, just a fraction, smoothed her hair off her face, gazed down at her. And something was shining in his eyes that made her long to have him inside her. She wasn't supposed to want it any more—she was supposed to have ripped him from her heart—and yet she did want it…did want him. She ached with need.

A sudden strong wave took Kate unawares and she choked on sea water. Scott grabbed her hand, dragged her out of the wash and up the beach to dry land, where she dropped to the sand and rolled onto her back, spluttering, laughing, coughing, eyes streaming.

And despite the fact that she was half drowned, deranged, probably a little snotty, Scott dropped to his knees beside her and looked at her as though she were the most wondrous thing he'd ever seen.

He was smiling, and there were tears—*tears!*—in his eyes as he rolled with her on the sand until she was on top of him.

She snaked her fingers into his wet hair, wanting him so much she thought she might seriously burst with it.

He looked up at her, so serious. 'So, Kate, what's the Latin for *And so endeth the contract*?'

She froze. *And so endeth...?*

Oh. Ohhh. Her breath caught as the pain hit.

It all made sense. Today was the twenty-eighth of February. The last day of their contract. She'd given herself to him at his house on Tuesday, fulfilled the contract to the letter, but he had to wring that little bit extra out of her—even after breaking her heart. Probably thinking she'd let him get away with this latest manipulation because he was using her secret fantasy to do it. And who *wouldn't* want their ultimate Play Time, right?

Hating herself for letting him do this to her—hating *him*—Kate shoved herself off him, got to her feet, started pulling on clothes over the dampness and sand.

Scott had felt the change in Kate that split second before she'd rolled off him.

'Did I stuff it up?' he asked, getting to his feet. 'Because I thought… I mean I watched the movie… I…I thought that was…'

The words tapered off as Kate skewered him with a glare.

Was this the part where she told him he was too late? That she didn't love him any more? No, he couldn't face that. Didn't—*wouldn't*—believe it.

Scott started dressing, just to keep his hands occupied

while he waited for her to speak, to give him a clue about where he'd messed up. But she didn't speak and he couldn't take the silence.

'Are you going to tell me what I did wrong, Kate?'

'You know.'

'No, I don't.'

'The twenty-eighth of February,' she said coldly.

Scott looked at her blankly.

'February *twenty-eighth*!' she snapped. 'You couldn't resist having the last word, could you, Scott? One last Play Time—and using my deepest, most secret fantasy to do it. Good job. For someone who said he would never hurt me, you sure wield a sharp knife.'

What the hell—?

She picked up her bag. 'So when is Brodie coming back for me?'

'Brodie's on his way to Sydney,' Scott said. 'I'm taking you back.'

The blood drained out of Kate's face.

'What?' he asked urgently. 'What did I do?'

She laughed—and it wasn't the joyful laughter they'd shared in the waves. 'Today. Last day of the contract, right?'

'Yes…' Still bewildered.

'I've spent three days tearing you out of my heart, and thanks to your little stunt today all that work is lost. I'll have to start over.'

Scott's mouth went dry—a dryness that had nothing to do with the ton of salt that had swirled in and out of his mouth with all that sea water. 'I thought you wanted the contract to be over?'

'I did. But not like— Oh, just forget it.'

He grabbed her arm. 'No, tell me, Kate. If you don't tell me, how can I explain?'

She wrenched free. 'Under the terms of our contract you don't have to explain.'

'Dammit, Kate, I've had a gutful of the contract. It's over! *Over!*'

'It was over on Tuesday, but that wasn't good enough for you, was it? Because *I* decided that. I decided it out of love. But you had to control the ending—out of...of...*pique*! And so here you are, controlling it—like you've controlled everything since the moment we met.'

'That's *crap*, Kate. I've *never* been in control. Not from the first moment I saw you. I don't— I don't *want* to be in control with you. And that—' He shoved irritably at his hair. 'That is not an easy thing for me to admit.'

'Oh, you've been in the driver's seat all the way along. Running rings around me. Flouting the rules. Turning up any time you wanted. All those calculated kisses to get me to shut up when I asked you a personal question—when I *told* you kissing was dangerous.'

'You never told me that!'

'It was *implied*! Because it's obvious! To everyone except you. Kissing—no problem for Scott Knight, because Scott Knight doesn't care and Scott Knight doesn't feel.'

'But I did—I mean I *do*—'

'Shut up, Scott. Just *shut up*. Because I *do* feel. And every time you kissed me I felt more—and more and more. Wanted you more and more. But all you wanted was Play Time! So I gave that to you too, because I figured I could *sex* you into loving me. I would have done anything. *Anything!* But you wouldn't even let me protect myself by sticking to a few simple rules.'

'Kate, stop. I—'

'You know what's the stupidest thing of all? I started to think that maybe you were breaking all those rules because you didn't *want* the contract.'

'I didn't. I wanted—'

'I thought you just wanted to kiss me, see me, be with me—take it however it came. The more you broke the rules, the more I hoped. But you were breaking them because it was a game to you. *I* was a game.'

'No, that isn't—'

'And that last night—what you said to me. *Tail.* A piece of tail. That's what I was. *All* I was. All the way along. And you, with more tail than you know what to do with, could have anyone—so why me? Why did you still take and *take* from me that night? When you knew how…how painful it was for me to love you like I did? You knew I wanted to leave and you wouldn't let me go.'

'Okay, that's *enough*, Kate!' He grabbed her then, dragged her in. 'I didn't let you go because I couldn't. I can't, Kate. I *can't*.'

'But you will—because tomorrow is the first of March and we are done.' She jerked out of his arms. '*Done!* Do you get it? *A mensa et thoro*—legal separation without divorce.'

'Don't talk Latin to me now.'

'*Res judicata*—the final adjudication. No further appeals. Goodbye.'

Scott blanched. His shoulders were tight enough to snap his spine. Head drumming. Heart hammering. Hands clenching and unclenching.

'Except for one thing, Kate,' he said. 'You love me.'

'Well, you see, I'm going to let Phillip the barrister help me get over that. Tomorrow—the first of March—when there will be no possible suggestion that I am still under contract to you. Time for a *new* contract. This time I might even get the *friend* part of "friends with benefits". Someone who w-won't h-hurt me.'

'I won't hurt you.'

She turned away, breath hitching. 'You already have, Scott.'

'Then I'll make it up to you.'

'You can't. You wouldn't know how. Because you've never been hurt and you've never been in love.'

'I have been hurt. When you left me. When you wouldn't

speak to me. More hurt than I thought was even possible. And you're hurting me now. And I'm letting you because I deserve it. Hurt me all you want. Any way you want. But just don't leave me, Kate.'

He came up behind her.

'Because I *am* in love. Right now. With you. First love. Last love. All in one. I'm here with my heart bleeding, aching for you, so in love I can't even find the words to tell you how much.'

She turned slowly. 'No…' she breathed. 'You don't love me.'

'Kate, if you think *anyone* else, in their wildest dreams, could have got me to watch a damned chick flick, let alone re-enact a scene from one… Well, you're insane—that's all I'm saying.'

'That was Play Time.'

He glared at her. Shouted. 'Newsflash, Kate. I. Hate. Play. Time. *Hate* it. Got it?'

'Then why—'

'And if you think rolling around in the surf like a lunatic is my idea of a sexual fantasy, you are wide of the mark, my girl. I've got sand in every nook and cranny of my body and it's bloody uncomfortable. A piece of seaweed is sticking somewhere I don't even want to think about—it may require medical intervention to get it extricated. And it's driving me nuts. But you know what? I will go back and roll around in that surf until we shrivel into prunes—with salt water pouring out of my ears, and snot streaming out of my nose, and that surfer out there laughing himself into convulsions, if it's what you want. Hell, I'll take you to Hawaii and we'll try it on the original beach!'

'I didn't *ask* you to roll in the surf!' Kate shouted back.

'You didn't have to ask! I did it because I'm not good with words, so I had to *do* something. I watched that movie for you. I'm on this beach because I love you. I *love* you! And, so help me God, if you don't call that weasel Phillip and tell him to back the hell away and stay the hell away, I am going to *kidnap* you.'

'Kidnap me?' she sputtered.

'On the yacht I bought.'

'You bought a yacht?'

'And I bought *music*—so I can dance with you on it. And I'm going to teach you to sail, and take you to the Whitsundays, and…and… What's so funny?'

'You,' Kate said, and laughed so hard she dropped to her knees. 'The way you said "m-music". Like it was p-poison.'

'Kate,' he said dangerously, 'you *do* realise how many women would swoon to have me tell them I love them, right? But you're the only one I'm ever, *ever* going to say it to.'

'Egomaniac,' Kate said, and kept laughing.

'It's not funny.'

'No, it's not. It's a serious condition, egomania,' she said, and laughed again.

Pause. He was confused. But…hopeful.

'Is laughter…? Is it good under these circumstances?' he asked tentatively.

'Accedas ad curiam.'

'Yeah, smartarse—going to need a translation,' he said, but a smile had started to stretch his mouth and he could feel it—*feel* it!—in his eyes too.

'You may approach the court,' she said. 'That's all I will say for now. And, Scott—just so you know—I have sand in every nook and cranny too.'

'Well, I think I'm going to have to take a look at your crannies, in that case,' Scott said, and dropped to his knees beside her.

He kissed her, long and hard, until they were both breathless.

'Are you going to take me to see your yacht?'

'It's not a *yacht*—it's a Jeanneau 36. If you're going to be a sailor you need to know these things.'

'Does it have a name? Like…you know…a *real* name?'

'It does,' Scott said, and started laughing.

'Which is?'

'Which is...drumroll...*Scottsdale*.'

Kate started laughing again and it reminded Scott of that night—the awards dinner—when they'd laughed about Knightley and he'd wanted her more than he'd wanted to breathe. He should have known right then that she was meant to be his. That she *would* be his.

'Wait until Hugo hears I've copied *him* for once,' Scott said, and then he stopped. Cleared his throat. 'Kate, just one thing... About my family...'

'That would be me,' she said softly. 'Just me.'

'Oh, God, Kate, I love you,' he said, and pulled her down to lie with him on the sand again. 'But you have to know that I have a bit of a conservative streak, like all the Knights.'

'You don't say?'

'So...divorce parties, break-ups, custody battles... They don't apply to us.'

'Don't they?'

'Because Knights don't divorce. And I will not let you go.' He stopped to kiss her. 'If you try to end it I'll make your life hell. I will fight tooth and nail—move heaven and hell and everything, *everything*, in between—to keep you. Exactly the way *you* fight. To the death. So better not to go there. You get all freaked out when marriages end badly. We don't want you stressing.'

'No more stress. Got it. But...Scott? Was that a proposal? Because we're not exactly marriage-minded in my family.'

'But I am. And, sorry to break it to you, but I have to be married to the mother of my children—conservative, I'm telling you, I hope your mother is going to cope. And one more thing. You're not getting any younger, so we'll have to get cracking on the kid thing.'

With that, Kate pushed him away, got to her feet, ripped her T-shirt over her head. 'My *age*? Are you seriously going there? Because if you are we're going another round of *From Here to Eternity*.'

Scott didn't argue. He simply stood up and took off his clothes. And then he turned to Kate and held out his hand. 'Or, as we like to say in legal circles, *ad infinitum*,' he said. 'Which means—'

'Forever.'

And then Scott grinned. 'Okay, let's put on a show for the surfer dude, and see how much more sand we can pack into our nooks and crannies.'

* * * * *

THE TYCOON'S STOWAWAY

STEFANIE LONDON

To my wonderful husband for supporting me from the very first time I wrote 'Chapter One'. Thank you for always understanding my need to write, for keeping me sane through the ups and downs, and for holding my hand when I took the biggest leap of my life.

I love you.

Always.

PROLOGUE

HOT. LOUD. CRUSHING.

The dance floor at the Weeping Reef resort bar was the perfect way to shake off the work day, and for Chantal Turner it was the perfect place to practise her moves. She swung her hips to the pulsating beat of the music, her hands raking through her hair and pushing damp strands from her forehead. A drop of perspiration ran in a rivulet down her back but she wouldn't stop. At midnight, the night was still in its infancy, and she would dance until her feet gave out.

She was enjoying a brief interlude away from her life plan in order to soak up the rays while earning a little money in the glorious Whitsundays. But the second she was done she'd be back on the mainland, working her butt off to secure a place at a contemporary dance company. She smiled to herself. The life in front of her was bright and brimming with opportunity.

Tonight the majority of her crew hadn't come out. Since Chantal's boyfriend wasn't much of a dancer he stood at the bar, sipping a drink and chatting to another resort employee. No matter—the music's beat flowing through her body was the only companion she needed. Her black dress clung to damp skin. The holiday crowd had peaked for the season, which meant the dance floor was even more densely packed than usual.

'Pretty girls shouldn't have to dance on their own.'

A low, masculine voice rumbled close to her ear and the scent of ocean spray and coconut surfboard wax hit her nostrils, sending a shot of heat down to her belly.

She would know that smell anywhere. A hand rested lightly on her hip, but she didn't cease the gentle rolling of her pelvis until the beat slowed down.

'Don't waste your pick-up lines on me, Brodie.' She turned and stepped out of his grip. 'There are plenty of other ladies in holiday mode who would appreciate your cheesy come-ons.'

'Cheesy?' He pressed a hand against his well-muscled chest. 'You're a harsh woman, Chantal.'

The tanned expanse of his shoulders stretched out from under a loose-fitting black tank top, a tattoo peeking out at the neckline. Another tattoo of an anchor stretched down his inner forearm. He stared at her, shaggy sun-bleached hair falling around his lady-killer face and light green eyes.

He's off-limits, Chantal. Super off-limits. Don't touch him...don't even think *about it.*

Brodie Mitchell stepped forward to avoid the flailing arms of another dancer, who'd apparently indulged in a few too many of the resort's signature cocktails. He bumped his hip against hers, and their arms brushed as Chantal continued to dance. She wasn't going to let Brodie and his amazing body prevent her from having a good time.

The song changed and she thrust her hands into the air, swinging her hips again, bumping Brodie gently. His fingertips gripped her hips like a magnet had forced them together. Every touch caused awareness to surge through her veins.

'You can't dance like that and expect me not to join in.'

His breath was hot against her ear. Her whole body tingled as the effects of the cocktails she'd downed before hitting the dance floor descended. The alcohol warmed her, giving her limbs a languid fluidity. Head spinning, she tried to step out of his grip, but stumbled when another dancer knocked into her. She landed hard up against Brodie, her hands flat against his rock-hard chest. He smelled good. So. *Damn*. Good.

Against her better judgment she ran her palms up and down his chest, swinging her hips and rolling her head back. The music flowed through her, its heavy bass thundering in her chest. She probably shouldn't have had so many Blue Hawaiians—all that rum and blue curaçao had made her head fuzzy.

'I can dance however I like,' she said, tilting her chin up at him defiantly. 'Mr Cheese.'

'You're going to pay for that.' He grinned, snaking his arm around her waist and drawing her even closer. 'There's a difference between charming and cheesy, you know.'

'You think you're *charming*?' she teased, ignoring the building tension that caused her centre to throb mercilessly. It was the alcohol—it always made her horny. It was absolutely *nothing* to do with Brodie.

'I do happen to think I'm charming.'

His lips brushed against her ear, and each bump of his thighs sent shivers down her spine.

'I've had it confirmed on a number of occasions too.'

'How *many* women have confirmed it?' She bit back a grin, curious as to the number of notches on his bedpost. Brodie had a bit of a reputation and, as much as she hated to admit it, Chantal could see why.

It wasn't just that he had a gorgeous face and a body that looked as if it belonged in a men's underwear commercial. Hot guys were a dime a dozen at the resort. Brodie had something extra: a cheeky sense of humour coupled with the innate ability to make people feel comfortable around him. He had people eating out of the palm of his hand.

'I don't kiss and tell.'

'Come on—I'll even let you round up to the nearest hundred.' She pulled back to look him in the eye while she traced a cross over her heart with one finger.

He grabbed her wrist and pulled her hand behind his back, forcing her face close to his. 'I'm not as bad as you think, Little Miss Perfect.'

'I doubt that very much.'

The music switched to a slow, dirty grind and Brodie nudged his thigh between hers. A gasp escaped her lips as her body fused to his. She should stop now. This was *so wrong.* But it felt better than anything else could have right at that moment. Better than chocolate martinis and Sunday sleep-ins…even better than dancing on a stage. A hum of pleasure reverberated in her throat.

'I bet you're even worse.'

'Ha!' His hand came up to cup the side of her jaw. 'You want to know for sure, don't you?'

Her body cried out in agreement, her breath hitching as his face hovered close to hers. The sweet smell of rum on his lips mingled with earthy maleness, hitting her with a force powerful enough to make her knees buckle.

Realisation slammed into her, her jaw dropping as she jerked backwards. His eyes reflected the same shock. Reality dawned on them both. This was more than a little harmless teasing—in fact it didn't feel harmless at all.

How could she possibly have fallen for Brodie? He was a slacker—an idle charmer who talked his way through life instead of working hard to get what he wanted. He was her opposite—a guy so totally wrong for her it was almost comical. Yet the feel of his hands on her face, the bump of his pelvis against hers, and the whisper of his breath at her cheek was the most intoxicating thing she'd ever experienced.

Oh, no! This is not happening... This is not *happening.*

'You feel it, don't you?' Worry streaked across his face

and his hands released her as quickly as if he'd touched a boiling pot. 'Don't lie to me, Chantal.'

'I—'

Her response was cut short when something flashed at the corner of her eye. *Scott.*

'What the *hell* is going on?' he roared. His cheeks were flushed scarlet, his mouth set into a grim line.

'It's nothing, man.' Brodie held up his hands in surrender and stepped back.

He was bigger than Scott, but he wasn't a fighter. The guilt in his eyes mirrored that in Chantal's heart. How could she have done this? How could she have fallen for her boyfriend's best friend?

'Didn't look like nothing to me. You had your hands all over her!'

'It's nothing, Scott,' Chantal said, grabbing his arm. But he shook her off. 'We were just dancing.'

'Ha!' The laugh was a sharp stab of a sound—a laugh without a hint of humour. 'Tell me you don't feel anything for Brodie. Because it sure as hell didn't look like a platonic dance between friends.'

She tried to find the words to explain how she felt, but she couldn't. She closed her eyes and pressed her palm to her forehead. She opened them in time to see Scott's fist flying at Brodie's face.

No!

CHAPTER ONE

REJECTION WAS HARD ENOUGH for the average person, and for a dancer it was constant. The half-hearted 'Thanks, but no thanks' after an unsuccessful audition? Yep, she'd had those. Bad write-up from the arts section of a local paper? Inevitable. An unenthusiastic audience? Unpleasant, but there'd be at least one in every dancer's career.

Chantal Turner had been told it got easier, but it didn't feel easy now to keep her chin in the air and her lips from trembling. Standing in the middle of the stage, with spotlights glaring down at her, she shifted from one bare foot to the other. The faded velvet of the theatre seats looked like a sea of red in front of her, while the stage lights caused spots to dance in her vision.

The stage was her favourite place in the whole world, but today it felt like a visual representation of her failure.

'I'm afraid your style is not quite what we're looking for,' the director said, toying with his phone. 'It's very...'

He looked at his partner and they both shook their heads.

'Traditional,' he offered with a gentle smile. 'We're looking for dancers with a more modern, gritty style for this show.'

Chantal contemplated arguing—telling him that she could learn, she could adapt her style. But the thought of them saying no all over again was too much to deal with.

'Thanks, anyway.'

At least she'd been allocated the last solo spot for the day, so no one was left to witness her rejection. She stopped for a moment to scuff her feet into a pair of sneakers and throw a hoodie over her tank top and shorts.

The last place had told her she was too abstract. Now she was too traditional. She bit down on her lower lip to keep the protest from spilling out. Some feedback was better than none, no matter how infuriatingly contradictory it was. Besides, it wasn't professional to argue with directors—and she was, if nothing else, a professional. A professional who couldn't seem to book any decent jobs of late...

This was the fourth audition she'd flunked in a month. Not even a glimmer of interest. They'd watched her with poker faces, their feedback delivered with surgical efficiency. The reasons had varied, but the results were the same. She knew her dancing was better than that.

At least it had used to be...

Her sneakers crunched on the gravel of the theatre car park as she walked to her beat-up old car. She was lucky the damn thing still ran; it had rust spots, and the red paint had flaked all over the place. It was so old it had a cassette player, and the gearbox *always* stuck in second gear. But it was probably the most reliable thing in her life, since all the time she'd invested in her dance study didn't seem to be paying off. Not to mention her bank accounts were looking frighteningly lean.

No doubt her ex-husband, Derek, would be pleased to know that.

Ugh—she was *not* going to think about that stuffy control freak, or the shambles that had been her marriage.

Sliding into the driver's seat, she checked her phone. A text from her mother wished her luck for her audition. She cringed; this was just another opportunity to prove she'd wasted all the sacrifices her mother had made for her dancing.

Staring at herself in the rearview mirror, Chantal pursed her lips. She would *not* let this beat her. It was a setback, but only a minor one. She'd been told she was a gifted dancer on many occasions. Hell, she'd even been filmed for a documentary on contemporary dance a few years back. She *would* get into one of these companies, even if it took every last ounce of her resolve.

Despite the positive affirmation, doubt crept through her, winding its way around her heart and lungs and stomach. Why was everything going so wrong now?

Panic rose in her chest, the bubble of anxiety swelling and making it hard to breathe. She closed her eyes and forced a long breath, calming herself. Panicking would not help. Thankfully, she'd finally managed to book a short-term dancing job in a small establishment just outside of Sydney. It wasn't prestigious. But it didn't have to be forever.

A small job would give her enough money to get herself through the next few weeks—*and* there was accommodation on site. She *would* fix this situation. No matter what.

She clenched and unclenched her fists—a technique she'd learned once to help relax her muscles whenever panic swelled. It had become a technique she relied on more and more. Thankfully the panic attacks were less like tidal waves these days, and more like the slosh of a pool after someone had dive-bombed. It wasn't ideal, but she could manage it.

Baby steps... Every little bit of progress counts.

Shoving the dark thoughts aside, she pulled out of the car park and put her phone into the holder stuck to the window. As if on cue the phone buzzed to life with the smiling face of her old friend Willa. Chantal paused before answering. She wasn't in the mood to talk, but she had a two-hour drive to get to her gig and music would only keep her amused for so long.

Besides, since her divorce Chantal had realised that real friends were few and far between, so she'd been making more of an effort to keep in touch with Willa. Ignoring her call now would go completely against that.

She tapped the screen of her phone and summoned her most cheerful voice. 'Hey, Willa.'

'How's our favourite dancer?'

Willa's bubbly greeting made a wave of nostalgia wash over her.

'Taking the arts world by storm, I hope?'

Chantal forced a laugh. 'Yeah, something like that. It's a slow process, but I'm working on it.'

'You'll get there. I know it. That time I saw you dance at the Sydney Opera House was incredible. We're all so proud of you for following your dream.'

Chantal's stomach rocked. She knew not everyone Willa referred to would be proud of her—especially since it was her dancing that had caused their group to fall apart eight years ago.

Besides, they only saw what she wanted them to see. If you took her social media pages and her website at face value then she was living the creative dream. What they *didn't* know was that Chantal cut out all the dark, unseemly bits she wasn't proud of: her nasty divorce, her empty bank account, the reasons why she'd booked into some small-time gig on the coast when she should be concentrating on getting back into a proper dance company…

'Thanks, Willa. How's that brother of yours? Is he still overseas?' She hoped the change of topic wasn't too noticeable.

'Luke texted me today. He's working on some big deal, but it looks like he might be coming home soon.' Willa sighed. 'We might be able to get the whole gang back together after all.'

The 'whole gang' was the tight-knit crew that had formed when they'd all worked together at the magical Weeping Reef resort in the Whitsundays. Had it really been eight years ago? She still remembered it as vividly as if it were yesterday. The ocean had been so blue it had seemed otherworldly, the sand had been almost pure white, and she'd loved every second of it… Right until she'd screwed it all up.

'Maybe,' Chantal said.

'I think we might even be getting some of the group together tonight.' There was a meaningful pause on the other end of the line. 'If you're free, we'd love to see you.'

'Sorry, Willa, I'm actually working tonight.'

Chantal checked the road signs and took the on-ramp leading out of the city. Sydney sparkled in her rearview mirror as she sped away.

'Oh? Anywhere close by?'

'I'm afraid not. I'm off to Newcastle for this one.'

'Oh, right. Any place I would know?'

'Not likely, it's called Nine East. It's a small theatre—very intimate.'

She forced herself to sound excited when really she wanted to find a secluded island and hide until her dancing ability came back. God only knew why she'd given Willa the place's name. She prayed her friend wouldn't look it up online.

'Look, Willa, I'll have to cut you short. I'm on the road and I need my full concentration to deal with these crazy Sydney drivers.'

Willa chuckled. 'I forget sometimes that you didn't grow up in the city. Hopefully we'll catch up soon?'

The hope in her voice caused a twinge of guilt in Chantal's stomach. She didn't want to see the group. Rather, she didn't want them to see how her life was not what she'd made it out to be.

'Yeah, hopefully.'

There was nothing like being surrounded by friends, with the sea air running over your skin and a cold drink in your hand. Add to that the city lights bouncing off the water's surface and a view of the Sydney Harbour Bridge against an inky night and you had a damn near perfect evening.

Brodie Mitchell leant back against the railing of his yacht and surveyed the group in front of him. Champagne flowed, music wafted up into the air and the group was laughing and reminiscing animatedly about their time working at the Weeping Reef resort. A long time had passed, but it made Brodie smile to think the group was no less lively now than when they'd all been fresh-faced kids, drunk on the freedom and beauty of resort life.

'Hey, man.' Scott Knight dropped down beside him, beer in hand. 'Aren't you drinking tonight?'

'I'm trying to be good for once.' Brodie grinned and held up his bottle of water in salute. 'I'm training for a half marathon.'

'Really?' Scott raised a brow.

Brodie shoved his friend and laughed. 'Yes, really.'

As much as he wanted to be annoyed that his friends would assume him incapable of running a half marathon, he kind of saw their point. Running competitively required a certain kind of routine and dedication that wasn't Brodie's style. He was a laid-back kind of guy: he thrived on surf, sand, and girls in bikinis. Abstaining from alcohol and waking up at the crack of dawn for training… Not so much.

'You have to admit it doesn't seem to fit in with the yachting lifestyle.' Scott gestured to the scenery around them.

The boat was a sight to behold—luxury in every sense of the word from its classy interior design to the quality craftsmanship out on the deck.

Growing up in a big family had meant the Mitchells' weekly grocery shop had needed to stretch across many mouths, and schoolbooks had always been passed down the line. They hadn't been poor, but he'd never been exposed to fineries such as yachts. Now he owned a yacht charter business and had several boats to his name.

'I didn't exactly come up with the idea myself,' Brodie admitted, taking a swig of his water. 'There's a guy at the marina back home and he's always on my back about taking up running. He bet me a hundred bucks I couldn't train for a race.'

'So you started with a half marathon?' Scott shook his head, laughing. 'Why not attempt a lazy ten k to begin with?'

Brodie shrugged and grinned at his friend. 'If I'm going to waste a perfectly good sleep-in, it might as well be for something big.'

'Says the guy who once chose sleep over judging a bikini contest.'

'And lived to regret it.'

Scott interlocked his fingers behind his head and leant back against the boat's railings. 'Those were the days.'

'You look like you're living the dream now.' Brodie fought to keep a note of envy out of his voice.

A slow grin spread over Scott's face as his fiancée, Kate, waved from the makeshift dance floor where she was shaking her hips with Willa, Amy, and Amy's friend Jessica. The girls were laughing and dancing, champagne in hand. *Just like old times.*

'I am.' Scott nodded solemnly.

Just as Brodie was about to change the topic of conversation Willa broke away from the group and joined the boys. She dropped down next to Brodie and slung her arm around his shoulders, giving him a sisterly squeeze as she pushed her dark hair out of her face.

'I'm so glad you're back down in Sydney,' Willa said.

'And where's your man tonight?' Brodie asked.

'Working.' She pouted. 'But he promised he'd be here next time. In fact I think he was a little pissed to miss out on the yacht experience.'

Brodie chuckled. 'It's an experience, indeed. My clients pay an arm and a leg to be sailed around in this boat, and she's an absolute beauty. Worth every cent.'

The *Princess Jo* certainly fitted her name, and although she was the oldest of the yachts his company owned she'd aged as gracefully as a silver-screen starlet. He patted the railing affectionately.

'Guess who I spoke to this afternoon,' Willa said, cutting into his thoughts with a faux innocent smile.

Brodie quirked a brow. 'Who?'

'Chantal.'

Hearing her name was enough to set Brodie's blood pumping harder. Chantal Turner was the only girl ever to have held his attention for longer than five minutes. She'd been the life of the party during their time at the Whitsundays, and she'd had a magnetic force that had drawn people to her like flies to honey. And, boy, had he been sucked in! The only problem was, she'd been Scott's girl back then. He'd gotten too close to her, played with fire, and earned a black eye for it. Worse still, he'd lost his friend for the better part of eight years over the incident.

Brodie's eyes flicked to Scott, but there was no tension in his face. He was too busy perving on Kate to be worrying about what Willa said.

'She's got a show on tonight,' Willa continued. 'Just up the coast.'

Brodie swallowed. The last thing he needed was to see Chantal Turner dance. The way she moved was enough to bring grown men to their knees, and he had a particular weakness for girls who knew how to move.

'We could head there—since we have the boat.' Willa grinned and nudged him with her elbow.

'How do you know where she's performing?' he asked, taking another swig of his water to alleviate the dryness in his mouth.

'She told me.'

'I don't know if we should…' Brodie forced a slow breath, trying to shut down images of his almost-kiss with Chantal.

It was the last time he'd seen her—though there had been a few nights when he'd been home alone and he'd looked her performances up online. He wasn't sure what seeing her in person would do to his resolve to leave the past in the past.

The friend zone was something to be respected, and girls who landed themselves in that zone never came out. But with Chantal he seemed to lose control over his ability to think straight.

'We should go,' Scott said, patting Brodie on the shoulder as if to reassure him once again that there were no hard feelings about that night. 'I'm sure she'd appreciate the crowd support.'

By this time Amy, Jessica, and Kate had wandered over for a refill. Scott, ever the gentleman, grabbed the bottle of vintage brut and topped everyone up.

'We were just talking about taking a little trip up the coast,' Scott said. 'Chantal has a show on.'

'Oh, we should definitely go!' Amy said, and the other girls nodded their agreement.

All eyes lay expectantly on him. He could manage a simple reunion. Couldn't he…?

'Why the hell not?' he said, pushing up from his chair.

* * *

When Chantal pulled into the car park of the location specified on her email confirmation her heart sank. The job had been booked last-minute—*they'd* contacted *her*, with praise for the performance snippets she had on her website and an offer of work for a few nights a week over the next month.

A cursory look at their website hadn't given her much: it seemed they did a mix of dance and music, including an open mike night once per week. Not exactly ideal, but she was desperate. So she'd accepted the offer and put her focus back on her auditions, thinking nothing of it.

Except it didn't look like the quietly elegant bar on their website. The sign was neon red, for starters, and there were several rough-looking men hanging out at the front, smoking. Chantal bit down on her lip. Everything in her gut told her to turn around and head home—but how could she do that when it was the only gig she'd been able to book in weeks? Make that months.

Sighing, she straightened her shoulders. *Don't be such a snob. You know the arts industry includes all types. They're probably not criminals at all.*

But the feeling of dismay grew stronger with each step she took towards the entrance. She hitched her bag higher on her shoulder and fought back the wave of negativity. She *had* to take this job. Her ex had finally sold the apartment—meaning she had to find a new place to live—and this job included on-site accommodation. It would leave her days free to pursue more auditions, *and* it was money that she desperately needed right now.

One of the men hanging out at the front of the bar leered at her as she hurried past, and Chantal wished she'd thrown on a pair of tracksuit pants over her dancing shorts. The sun was setting in the distance but the air was still heavy and warm. She ignored the wolf-whistling and continued on, head held high, into the bar.

The stench of cheap alcohol hit her first, forcing her stomach to dip and dive. A stage sat in the middle of a room and three men in all-black outfits fiddled with the sound equipment. Chantal looked around, surveying the sorry sight that was to be her home for the next month. The soles of her sneakers sucked with each step along the tattered, faded carpet—as if years of grime had left behind an adhesive layer. Though smoking had long been banned inside bars, a faint whiff of stale cigarette smoke still hung in the air. A small boot-sized hole had broken the plaster of one wall and a cracked light flickered overhead.

Delightful.

She approached the bar, mustering a smile as she tried to catch the attention of the older man drying wineglasses and hanging them in a rack above his head. 'Excuse me, I'm here—'

'Dancers go upstairs,' he said, without even looking up from his work.

'Thanks,' she muttered, turning on her heel and making her way towards the stairs at the end of the bar.

Upstairs can't possibly be any worse than downstairs. Perhaps the downstairs was for bands only? Maybe the dancers' section would be a little more…hygienic?

Chantal trod up the last few steps, trying her utmost to be positive. But upstairs *wasn't* any better.

'Oh, crap.'

The stage in the middle of the room sported a large silver pole. The stage itself was round with seats encircling it; a faded red curtain hung at the back, parted only where the dancers would enter and exit from. It was a bloody strip club!

'Chantal?'

A voice caught her attention. She contemplated lying

for a second, but the recognition on the guy's face told her he knew *exactly* who she was.

'Hi.'

'I've got your room key, but I don't have time to show you where it is now.' He looked her up and down, the heavy lines at the corners of his eyes crinkling slightly. 'Just head out back and get ready with the other girls.'

'Uh...I think there's been some kind of mistake. I'm not a stripper.'

'Sure you're not, darlin',' he said with a raspy chuckle. 'I get it—you're an *artist*. Most of the girls say they're paying their way through university, but whatever floats your boat.'

'I'm serious. I don't take my clothes off.' She shook her head, fighting the rising pressure in her chest.

'And we're not technically a strip club. Think of it more as...burlesque.' He thrust the room key into her hand. 'You'll fit right in.'

Chantal bit down on her lip. Perhaps it wouldn't be as bad as she thought.

But, no matter how hard she tried to convince herself, her gut pleaded with her to leave.

'I really don't think this is going to work,' she said, holding the key out to him.

'You *really* should have thought of that before sending back our contract with your signature on it.' His eyes hardened, thin lips pressing into a harsh line. 'But I can have our lawyer settle this, if you still think this isn't going to work.'

The thinly veiled threat made Chantal's heartbeat kick up a notch. There was no way she could afford a lawyer if they decided to take her to court. How could she have made such a colossal mistake?

Her head pounded, signalling a migraine that would no doubt materialise at some point. What kind of club had a lawyer on call, anyway? *The dangerous kind...the kind that has enough work for a lawyer.*

'Fine.' She dropped her hand by her side and forced away the desire to slap the club owner across his smarmy, wrinkled face.

She was a big girl—she could handle this. Besides, she'd had her fair share of promo girl gigs whilst trying out for dance schools the first time. She'd strutted around in tiny shorts to sell energy drinks and race-car merchandise on more than one occasion. This wouldn't be so different…would it?

Sighing, she made her way to the change room where the other dancers were getting ready. She still had that funny, niggling feeling that something wasn't quite right… and it wasn't *just* that she'd somehow landed herself in a strip club.

She concentrated for a moment, analysing the feeling. It had grown stronger since her audition—an incessant tugging of her senses that wouldn't abate. She unpacked her make-up and plucked a face wipe from her bag. Smoothing the cloth over her face, she thought back to the director. He'd looked so familiar, and he hadn't seemed to be able to look her in the eye.

A memory crashed into her with such force she stopped in her tracks, hand in midair. An old photo, taken a few years before she'd first started dating Derek—*that* was where she'd seen his face before. He was a friend of her ex-husband's, and that *couldn't* be a coincidence.

Rage surged through her. Her hands trembling, she sorted through her make-up for foundation. That smarmy, good-for-nothing ex-husband of hers had put her name forward for this skanky bar. He probably found the idea hilarious.

If I ever come across that spiteful SOB again I'm going to kill him!

* * *

An hour and a half later Chantal prepared to go on stage. She looked at herself in the mirror, hoping to hell that it was the fluorescent lighting which made her look white as a ghost and just as sickly. But the alarming contrast against her dark eye make-up and glossed lips would look great under the stage lighting. She'd seem alluring, mysterious.

Not that any of the patrons of such a bar would be interested in 'mysterious'. No, she assumed it was a 'more is more' kind of place.

She sighed, smoothing her hair out of her face and adding a touch of hairspray to the front so it didn't fall into her eyes. The other dancers seemed friendly, and there *were* actually two burlesque performers—though they didn't look as if they danced on the mainstream circuit. When she'd asked if all the dancers stripped down she'd received a wink and an unexpected view of the older lady's 'pasties'.

Well, *she* wouldn't be taking off her clothes—though her outfit wasn't exactly covering much of her body anyway. She looked down at the top which wrapped around her bust and rib cage in thick black strips, and at the matching shorts that barely came down to her thighs. She might as well have been naked for how exposed she felt.

It wasn't normal for her to be so filled with nerves before going onstage. But butterflies warmed her stomach and her every breath was more ragged than the last. She pressed her fingertips to her temples and shut her eyes, concentrating on relaxing her breathing. After a few attempts her heart rate slowed, and the air was coming more easily into her lungs.

Her act would be different—and she wouldn't be dancing for the audience…she would be dancing for herself. Taking a deep breath, she hovered at the entrance to the stage, waiting for the dancer before her to finish.

It was now or never.

CHAPTER TWO

'ARE YOU SURE we're in the right place?' Brodie looked around the run-down bar and shook his head. 'She can't be dancing *here*.'

'I double-checked the address,' Willa said, her dark brows pinched into a frown. 'This is definitely it.'

'Looks like there's an upstairs section to this place.' Kate pointed to a set of stairs on the other side of the room.

A single guy sat in the middle of the stage, playing old country-and-western hits, his voice not quite up to par. The bottom half of the bar was crowded and Brodie stayed close to the girls, given a few of the patrons were looking at them a little too closely for his liking. The group wove through the crowd until they reached the staircase at the back of the room, filing one by one up to the next level.

The music changed from the twangy country-and-western songs to a more sensual bass-heavy grind. The crowd—all men—encircled the stage and were enthusiastically cheering on a blonde dancer performing on a pole. She wore little more than a glittering turquoise bikini and her feet were balanced precariously on the highest pair of heels Brodie had ever seen.

'We *must* be in the wrong place.' Brodie rubbed his fingers to his temple, forcing down the worry bubbling in his chest.

Willa shrugged, looking as confused as he felt.

Chantal was a magnificent dancer—he'd often sneaked away from his duties at the Weeping Reef resort when he'd known she'd be using her time off to practise. She had innate skill and passion when she danced, no matter if it was in a studio or on the resort's packed dance floor. He couldn't understand why on earth she would be wasting her talent performing at some dingy dive bar.

The blonde left the stage to a roar of approval from the crowd and the music faded from one song to the next. His eyes were riveted to the space between the red curtains at the back of the stage. Heart in his throat, he willed the next dancer to be anyone else in the world other than Chantal. But the second a figure emerged from the darkness he knew it was her. He felt her before his eyes confirmed it.

No one else had a pair of legs like hers—so long and lean and mouth-wateringly flexible. She took her time coming to the front of the stage, her hips swinging in time to the music. Each step forward revealed a little more as she approached the spotlight. Long dark hair tumbled in messy waves around her shoulders, swishing as she moved. The ends were lightened from too much sun and her limbs were bronzed, without a tan line in sight.

Her eyes seemed to focus on nothing, and the dark make-up made her look like every dirty, sexy, disturbing fantasy he'd ever had. A jolt of arousal shot through him, burning and making his skin prickle with awareness.

He was in a dream—that *had* to be it. It was the only plausible explanation for how he'd ended up in this hellish alternative universe where he was forced to watch his deepest fantasy come to life right in front of him. He'd never been able to keep his mind off Chantal at the resort, but now she was here, the ultimate temptation, and he had to watch a hundred other men ogle her as though she were a piece of meat offered up for their dining pleasure.

His fists balled by his sides as he fought the urge to

rush up onto the stage and carry her away. She wasn't his responsibility, and the more distance he kept the better. He'd learnt that lesson already.

A wolf-whistle erupted from the crowd, snatching Brodie's attention away from his inner turmoil. Chantal had one hand on the pole, and though she wasn't using it as a prop, the way her fingers slid up and down the silver length made the front of his pants tighten. He shut his eyes for a moment, willing the excitement to stop. He shouldn't be feeling as if he wanted to steal her away and devour her whole…but he did.

When he dared to open his eyes he found himself looking straight into the endless depths of Chantal's luminous olive-green gaze. Emotion flickered across her face and her mouth snapped shut as she continued to dance, her eyes locked straight onto him.

Was it his imagination or were her cheeks a little pinker than before? For a moment he let himself believe she danced only for him, each gentle curve of movement designed to bring him undone.

In that moment she was *his*.

Dancing barefoot, she moved about the stage as though she owned it. Her feet pointed and flexed, creating lines and artful movement. Her arms floated above her head, crossing at the wrists before opening out into a graceful arc. Brodie's body hummed as though she played him with each step, with each look, each flick of her hair.

Her eyes remained on him. She seduced him. Broke apart every brick of resolve that he'd put in place until the wall crumbled around him like a house crushed by a tidal wave.

She capsized him. Bewitched him.

Her eyes glimmered under the spotlight, energy building with the climax of her performance. His body tensed and excitement wound tight within him. A coil of wanting, ready to be released at any moment. It was so wrong. He'd thought he'd moved on. Forgotten her. What a joke. He'd never get Chantal out of his head. *Never.*

The spell was broken as soon as her song finished. Her eyes locked on him for one final moment before she retreated behind the red curtain. The catcalls and cheering only made Brodie's pulse increase and tension tighten in his limbs. She should *not* be dancing in a place like this. Wasn't she supposed to be married? Where the hell was her husband and why wasn't he protecting her?

'That wasn't quite what I expected,' Willa said, looking from Amy to Brodie and back again. 'I mean, she's a gorgeous dancer—but this place is…'

'Wrong.' Brodie gritted his teeth together.

'Don't be so judgmental, you two.' Amy folded her arms across her chest. 'I'm going to see if I can find out what time she finishes.'

She wandered off in the direction of the stage but Brodie hung back with the others. Scott and Kate were chatting and laughing amongst themselves; Willa and Jessica were discussing the outfit of the next performer. Brodie leant back against the wall and ran a hand through his hair. His heart thudded an erratic beat and he wasn't sure if it was from the desire to protect Chantal or from the fact that her skimpy black outfit had worked his libido into overdrive.

No, it had to be concern over her safety. He had four little sisters, and the need to protect was ingrained in him as deep as his need to breathe. Sure he was attracted to Chantal—what red-blooded man wouldn't be? But it was nothing more than that. It had *never* been more than that.

Somehow the lie was no more believable now than it had been eight years ago.

Chantal had thought it wasn't possible for the night to get any worse. Dancing in front of a room full of people who wouldn't know art if it hit them over the head was bad enough, and the catcalls and leering were the proverbial cherry. But then she'd spotted Brodie and a good chunk of the Weeping Reef gang. Her stomach had felt as if it had dropped straight through the stage floor.

She braced her hands at the edge of the make-up bench and looked at herself in the mirror. All she wanted was to wash off her make-up and lock herself away until humiliation lost its brutal edge…though it was possible that would take a while. The shock on his face had been enough to destroy whatever confidence she'd managed to build up. He'd looked at her with an unnerving combination of disbelief and hunger.

She was about to remove her false lashes when her name rang out amongst the backstage hustle and bustle. Amy bounded towards her, arms outstretched and shiny blond hair flying around her face.

'You were fantastic!' Amy threw her arms around Chantal and gave her a friendly squeeze.

'Thanks.' Chantal forced a smile, wishing for possibly the hundredth time since she'd met Amy that she could have even an ounce of her vivacious confidence. 'It's a small gig in between a few bigger things.'

She hoped the lie didn't sound as hollow out in the open as it did in her head, but she couldn't let go of the false image she'd constructed. If they knew how bad things were right now… She wouldn't be able to handle the pity. Pity was the thing she detested most in life—possibly due to the fact that it had been doled out in epic proportions throughout her childhood.

The teachers had pitied her and her borrowed schoolbooks, the other mums and their suit-and-tie husbands had pitied the way she'd had to wear the same clothes week after week, and as for the students…pity from her peers had always stung the most.

'No judgment here.' Amy held up her hands. 'You have to come for a drink with us, though. We've got everyone together...well, almost everyone.'

'Oh, I would love to, but...' Chantal's smile wavered. 'It's been a long day and I've got an audition tomorrow.'

She scrambled for an excuse—something that Amy wouldn't question. There was no way she could go out there and face them—no way she could keep her head held high after what they'd seen. Heat crawled up her neck, squeezing the air from her throat. *Not now, please don't fall apart now.*

'Is your audition in Newcastle?'

'No, Sydney. So I've got quite a long drive.'

Amy grinned and grabbed her hand, tugging her towards the door. 'I've got the perfect solution then. Brodie got us here on his yacht, but he's supposed to be docking at The Rocks. If your rehearsal is in the city it would be perfect. You won't have to drive there, and Brodie can sail you back here after your audition.'

'I really *am* tired.' She shook her head and pulled her hand from Amy's grasp.

'You just need a drink or five.' Amy winked. 'Come on—it'll be like old times.'

Chantal stole a glance at her reflection. She'd have to change. There was no way she'd go out there and stand in front of Brodie wearing mere scraps of Lycra. *It's not like he didn't notice you dancing half-naked on that stage.*

'Just one drink,' she said, sighing. 'I need to be on good form tomorrow.'

'Great.' Amy bounced on the spot. 'I'll let you get changed. Meet us out the front in a few minutes?'

'Sure.'

With Amy gone, Chantal could let the fake smile slide from her lips. Why the hell had she agreed to a drink with the old gang? She was supposed to be keeping her distance—at least until her life had started to match the image she'd presented online. No doubt they'd ask about her marriage: fail number one. They'd want to know about her career: fail number two. And she'd have to act as if it wasn't awkward at *all* being around Scott and Brodie: fail number three.

Willa had told her that they'd recently repaired the rift she'd caused, but that didn't make her any less squeamish about having the two of them in the same room as her.

She contemplated looking for a back exit to slip out of. Maybe if she disappeared they might get the hint that she wasn't feeling social right now.

You can't do that. These people are your friends...possibly your only friends.

Since her divorce her other acquaintances had been mysteriously absent. Perhaps being friends with Derek the talent agent was of more value to them than being friends with Chantal the out-of-work dancer.

She frowned at herself in the mirror, taking in the fake lashes and dark, sultry make-up. What a fraud. Sighing, she stripped out of her outfit and threw on her denim shorts, white tank top and sneakers from earlier. She didn't have time to remove all of her make-up—that tedious task would have to wait for later.

Swinging her overnight bag over one shoulder, she decided against dumping it in her room first. If she found the comfort of a private room it would be unlikely she'd come back out. *Suck it up, Chantal. You've made your bed, now lie in it!*

Outside the crowd heaved, and she had to dodge the patrons who thought their ticket to the show meant they had a right to paw at her. This was *not* the dream she'd had in mind when she'd first stepped into a dance studio at the age of seven.

Her skin crawled. She wanted out of this damn filthy

bar. Perhaps a potential lawsuit was worth the risk if it meant she never had to come back.

She was midthought when she spotted Brodie, standing alone by the stairs. Where had everyone else gone? Her blood pumped harder, fuelling her limbs with nervous energy.

As always, his presence unnerved her. His broad shoulders and muscular arms were barely contained in a fitted white T-shirt; his tanned skin beckoned to be touched. His shaggy blond hair sat slightly shorter than it had used to, though the ends were still sun bleached and he wore it as though he'd spent the day windsurfing. Messy. Touchable.

But it was his eyes that always got her. Crystal green, like the colour of polished jade, they managed to seem scorching hot and ice-cold at the same time. When he looked at her it was easy to pretend the rest of the world didn't exist.

'The others have gone to the boat,' he said, motioning for her to join him. 'I didn't want you to walk on your own.'

She followed him, watching the way his butt moved beneath a pair of well-worn jeans. He'd filled out since she'd seen him last—traded his boy's body for one which was undeniably adult. She licked her lips, hating the attraction that flared in her and threatened to burn wild, like a fire out of control.

It was strange to be attracted to someone again. She hadn't felt that way in a long time…possibly not since Weeping Reef. Her marriage hadn't been about attraction—it had been about safety, security… Until that security had started to feel like walls crushing in on her.

They made their way out of the bar and into the cool night air. The breeze caught her sweat-dampened skin and caused goosebumps to ripple across her arms. She folded them tight, feeling vulnerable and exposed in the sudden quiet of the outdoors.

'You didn't have to wait,' she said, falling into step with him.

Their steps echoed in the quiet night air, their strides perfectly matched.

He turned to her and shook his head. 'Of course I did. I was worried you wouldn't make it out of the bar on your own, let alone down the street.'

The disapproving tone in his voice made her stomach twist. The last thing she needed was another overprotective man in her life.

'I can take care of myself.'

'Your bravado is admirable, but pointless. Even the smallest guy in there would have at least a head on you.'

His face softened into a smile—he never had been the kind of guy who could stay in a bad mood for long.

'Not to mention those skinny little chicken legs of yours.'

'I do *not* have chicken legs.' She gave him a shove and he barely broke stride, instead throwing his head back and laughing.

The bubble of anxiety in her chest dissolved. Brodie *always* had that effect on her. He was an irritating, lazy charmer, who talked his way through life, but he was *fun*. She often found herself smiling at him even when she wanted to be annoyed—much to her chagrin.

'No, you don't have chicken legs…not any more.' He grinned, his perfect teeth flashing in the night. 'You grew up.'

'So did you,' she said, but the words were lost as a motorcycle raced down the road.

They had eight years and a lot of issues between them. *Issues*, of course, was a code word for attraction. But *issues* sounded a little more benign and a little less like a prelude to something she would regret.

'I thought your husband would be here to watch out

for you.' He was back to being stern again. 'He should be keeping you safe.'

'I think he's keeping someone else safe these days.' She sighed. Why did all guys think it was their job to be the protector? She'd been happy to see the back of her ex-husband and his stifling, control-freak ways.

'So that means you're single?'

She nodded. 'Free as a bird and loving it.'

'All the more reason to have someone look out for you.'

Chantal bit her down on her lip and kept her mouth shut. No sense in firing him up by debating her ability to look out for herself. She wasn't stupid, her mother had made her take self-defence classes in high school, and she was quite sure she could hit a guy where it hurt most should the need arise.

They walked in silence for a moment, the thumping bass from the bar fading as they moved farther away. The yacht club glowed up ahead, with one large boat sticking out amongst a row of much smaller ones. She didn't have to ask. Of *course* he had the biggest boat there.

'Are you over-compensating?' Chantal asked, using sarcasm to hide her nervousness at being so close to him…at being alone with him.

'Huh?'

'The boat.' She pointed. 'It's rather…large.'

'You know what they say about men with large boats.' He grinned, his perfect teeth gleaming against the inky darkness.

She stifled a wicked smile. 'They have large steering wheels?'

He threw his head back and laughed again, slinging an arm around her shoulder.

The sudden closeness of him unsettled her, but his presence was wonderfully intoxicating when he wasn't waxing lyrical about her need for protection. He smelled exactly the same as she remembered: ocean spray and coconut. That scent had haunted her for months after she'd left Weeping Reef, and any time she smelled a hint of coconut it would thrust her right back onto that dance floor with him.

Her hip bumped against his with each step. The hard muscles of his arm pressed around her shoulder, making her insides curl and jump.

'It's not my personal boat. My company owns it.'

'Your company?' Chantal looked up, surprised.

Brodie was not the kind of guy to start a company; he'd never had an entrepreneurial bone in his body. In fact she distinctly remembered the time Scott had threatened to fire him for going over time on his windsurfing lessons because his students had been having so much fun. He had a generosity of spirit that didn't exactly match bottom-line profits.

'After I left Weeping Reef I bummed around for a while until I got work with a yacht charter company off the Sunshine Coast. It was a lot of fun. I got promoted, and eventually the owners offered me a stake in the company. I bought the controlling share about a year ago, when they were ready to retire.'

'And now you run a yacht tour company?'

He nodded as their conversation was interrupted by a loud shriek as they strolled onto the marina. The girls had clearly got into the champagne and were dancing on deck, with an amused Scott watching from the sidelines. Willa waved down to her and motioned for them to join the party.

Chantal's old doubts and fears crept back, their dark claws hooking into the parts of her not yet healed. She was not the person she claimed to be, and they would all know that now. They would know what a *fraud* she was.

Her breath caught in her throat, the familiar shallow breathing returning and forcing her heart rate up. She had a sudden desire to flee, to return to the dingy bar where she probably looked as if she belonged.

She didn't fit in here. Not with these classy girls and their beautiful hair. Not with Brodie, who'd made a success of himself, and not with Scott, whom she'd betrayed.

She sucked in a deep breath, her feet rooted to the ground. Panic clutched at her chest, clawing up her neck and closing its cold hands around her windpipe. She couldn't do it.

'Chantal?' Brodie looked down at her, his hand at the small of her back, pushing gently.

She bit down on her lip, shame seeping through her every limb until they were so heavy she couldn't move. *Why did you come? You're only setting yourself up to be laughed at. You're a failure.*

'Come on.' Brodie grabbed her hand and tugged her forward. 'We don't want to get left behind.'

CHAPTER THREE

BRODIE WANTED TO look anywhere but at Chantal, yet her dancing held him captive. Her undulating figure, moving perfectly to the beat, looked even more amazing than it had at the bar. In casual clothes, with her face relaxed, her limbs loose, she looked completely at ease with the world.

Unable to deal with the lust flooding his veins, he'd caved in and had a beer. The alcohol had hit him a little harder since he'd been abstaining the past few weeks. But he needed to dull the edges of his feelings—dull the roaring awareness of her. He'd hoped the uncontrollable desire to possess her had disappeared when he'd left the reef. However, it had only been dormant, waiting quietly in the background, until she'd brought it to full-colour, surround-sound, 3-D life.

When they'd first stepped onto the yacht Chantal had hesitated, almost as if she wasn't sure she should be there. But Scott had given her a friendly pat on the shoulder and a playful shove towards the girls. They'd brought her into the fold and she'd relaxed, dancing and giggling as though she'd been there all night. Every so often Brodie caught her eye: a quick glance here or there that neither of them acknowledged.

'You should get out there and dance with her.' Scott dropped down next to him, another beer in his hand.

Brodie's eyes shifted to Scott and he waited to see what

would come next. He'd harboured a lot of guilt over the way things had ended between them at Weeping Reef—not just because he'd hurt Scott, but because he'd hurt Chantal as well.

'Come on, man. You know there's no hard feelings.' Scott slapped him on the back. 'We talked about this already.'

'It's not your feelings I'm worried about.'

'Since when do you worry about anything?'

Brodie frowned. People often took his breezy attitude and laissez-faire approach to mean he didn't care about things. He knew when Scott was teasing him, but still.

'Some things are meant to be left in the past.' Some *people* were meant to be left in the past…especially when he couldn't possibly give her what she deserved. Not long-term anyway.

'You sound like a girl.' Scott laughed. 'Don't be such a wuss.'

He *was* being a wuss, hiding behind excuses. Besides, it was only a dance. How much harm could it do?

Keep telling yourself it's harmless—maybe one day you'll believe it.

Brodie pushed aside his gut feeling and joined the girls. Loud music pumped from the yacht's premium speakers and the girls cheered when he joined their little circle. His eyes caught Chantal's—a flicker of inquisitive olive as she looked him over and then turned her head so that she faced Amy.

He took a long swig of his beer, draining the bottle and setting it out of the way. Moving closer to Chantal, he brushed his hand gently over her hip as he danced. She turned, a shy smile curving on her lips. She wasn't performing now—this was her and only her. Green eyes seemed to glow amidst the smudgy black make-up… Her tanned limbs were moving subtly and effortlessly to the beat.

'Want a refill?' Brodie nodded to the empty champagne flute she'd yet to discard.

She hesitated, looking from the glass to him. Was it his imagination, or had Willa given her a little nudge with her elbow?

'Why not?' She smiled and followed him into the cabin. The music seemed to throb and pulsate around them, even at a distance from the speakers. But that was how music felt when she moved to it. It came to life.

'I'm sad to say this yacht is bigger than my apartment.' She held out her champagne flute. 'Well, my old apartment anyway.'

Brodie reached for a fresh bottle of Veuve Cliquot and wrapped his hand around the cork, easing it out with a satisfying pop. He topped up her glass, the fizzing liquid bubbling and racing towards the top a little too quickly.

She bent her head and caught the bubbles before they spilled. 'You're a terrible pourer.'

He watched, mesmerised, as the pink tip of her tongue darted out to swipe her lips. Her mouth glistened, tempting and ripe as summer fruit.

'I'm normally too busy driving the boat to be in charge of drinks. But I'll make an exception for you.'

'How kind.' She smirked and leant against the white leather sofa that curved around the wall. 'Are you always on the boats?'

'No, I have to run the business, which keeps me from being out on the water as much as I'd like. I have a townhouse on the Sunshine Coast, but it's a bit of a tourist trap up there. Sometimes I stay with the family in Brisbane, and then other times I stay on the yacht.'

'What a life.' Her voice was soft, tinged with wonder. 'You float along and stop where you feel like it.'

'It has a little more structure than that…but essentially, yeah.'

'Now, *that* sounds a little more like the Brodie I know.'

Her words needled him. He *wasn't* the surfer bum loser she'd labelled him in Weeping Reef. Sure, he might have dropped out of his degree and taken his time to find his groove, but he was a business owner now…a successful one at that.

'How's the arts world treating you?' It could have sounded like a swipe, given what he'd seen tonight, but he was genuinely interested.

She managed a stiff smile. 'Like any creative industry, it can be a little up and down.'

A perfectly generic response. Perhaps her situation was worse than he'd thought. He stayed silent, waiting for her to continue. For a moment she only nodded, her head bobbing, as if that would be enough of an answer. But he wanted more.

'I'm waiting to hear back from a big company,' she continued, her voice tight.

He suspected it wasn't true, or that she'd coloured the truth.

'Tonight was one of those fill-the-gap things. I'm sure it wasn't what you were expecting to see.'

Her eyes dipped and her lashes, thick and sultry, fanned out, casting feathery shadows against her cheekbones. She gathered herself and looked up, determined once more.

'It *wasn't* what I expected,' Brodie said, watching her face for subtle movements. Any key to whether or not she would let him in. 'But that's not to say I didn't enjoy it.'

How could he possibly have felt any other way? Watching her work that stage as if she owned the place had unsettled him to his core. A thousand years wouldn't dull that picture from his memory. Even thinking about it now heated up his skin and sent a rush of blood south, hardening him instantaneously.

'I could have done without the men ogling you.'

Her lips curved ever so slightly. 'You say that like you have some kind of claim over me.'

It was a taunt, delivered in her soft way. She hit him hardest when she used that breathy little voice of hers. It sounded like sin and punishment and all kinds of heavenly temptation rolled into one.

Brodie stepped forward, indulging himself in the sight of her widening eyes and parted lips. She didn't step back. Instead she stilled, and the air between them was charged with untameable electricity—wild and crackling and furious as a stormy ocean. She tilted her head up, looking him directly in the eye.

Brodie leant forward. 'I did see you first.'

'It doesn't work like that.' Her voice was a mere whisper, and she said it as though convincing herself. 'It's not finders keepers.'

'What is it, then?'

'It's *nothing*.'

He grabbed her wrist, his fingers wrapping around the delicate joint so that his fingertips lay over the tender flesh on the inside of her arm. He could feel her pulse hammering like a pump working at full speed, the beats furious and insistent.

'It's not nothing.'

She tried to pull her wrist back. 'It's the champagne.'

'Liar.'

A wicked smile broke out across her face as she downed her entire drink. A stray droplet escaped the corner of her mouth and she caught it with her tongue. God, he wanted to kiss her.

'It's the *champagne*.'

'Well, if you keep drinking it like that…'

'I might get myself into trouble?' She pulled a serious face, her cheeks flushed with the alcohol.

She'd looked like this the night he'd danced with her at

Weeping Reef. Chantal had always been the serious type—studious and sensible until she'd had a drink or two. Then the hardness seemed to melt away, she loosened up, and the playful side came out. If she'd been tempting before, she was damn near impossible to resist now.

'You always seem to treat trouble like it's a bad idea.' He divested her of her champagne flute before tugging her to him.

'Isn't that the definition of trouble?' Her hands hovered at his chest, barely touching him.

He shouldn't be pulling her strings the way he usually did when he wanted a girl. He liked to wind them up first. Tease them…get them to laugh. Relax their boundaries. He was treating Chantal as if he wanted to sleep with her…and he did.

He was in for a world of pain, but he couldn't stop himself.

'Bad ideas are the most fun.'

She stepped backwards, cheeks flushed, lips pursed. 'Come on—we're missing all the action out there. I want to dance.'

Only someone like Brodie would think bad ideas were fun. She could list her bad ideas like a how-to guide for stuffing up your life—have the hots for your boyfriend's BFF, pick the wrong guy to marry, lose focus on your career.

No, bad ideas were most definitely *not* fun.

Brodie was smoking hot, and it was clear that their chemistry still sizzled like nothing else, but that didn't mean she could indulge herself. He was *still* a bad idea, and she'd established that bad ideas were a thing of the past…well, once she'd got out of her current contract anyway.

If only she could tell her heart to stop thudding as if a dubstep track ran through her body, then she would be on her way to being fine. The throbbing between her legs was another matter entirely.

She stepped onto the deck, wondering for a moment if she'd dreamed herself onto his boat. The ocean had been engulfed by the night, but the air still held a salty tang. The smell reminded her of home…and of Brodie.

Shaking her head, she approached the girls. Kate extended her hand to Chantal and drew her in. She had decided almost immediately that she liked the gorgeous, witty redhead, and it was clear neither she nor Scott held any ill feelings towards her. It was a relief, all things considered.

'And where were *you*?' Willa eyed her with a salacious grin, her cheeks pink from champagne and dancing. She brushed her heavy fringe out of her eyes and swayed to the music.

'Just getting a refill.' The champagne was still fresh on her tongue…her mind was blurred pleasantly around the edges.

'Riiiight.' Willa smirked.

Chantal could feel Brodie close behind her, his hands brushing her hips every so often. Everything about the moment replicated *that* dance eight years ago. The alcohol rushed to her head, weakening the bonds of her control. The heat from his body drew her in, forcing her to him as if by magnetic force.

'I always said pretty girls shouldn't have to dance on their own,' he murmured into her ear.

'And *I* always said I would never fall for your cheesy lines.' She turned her head slightly, meaning to give him the brush-off, but his arm snaked around her waist and closed the gap between them. Her butt pressed against his pelvis and she resisted the urge to rock against him. 'Besides, I'm not on my own.'

'I know. You're with me.'

He spun her around and drew her to him. In sneakers, she could almost reach his collarbone with her lips, and she had an urge to kiss the tattoo that peeked out of his top. She was always fascinated by ink. The idea of permanence appealed to her. But life had taught her that everything was fleeting: money, success, love…

'I'm not *with* you, Brodie. You should stop confusing fantasy with reality.'

'It's hard to do when you have all that black make-up on.'

Her cheeks flamed and he laughed, holding her tight. It was all she could do to remain upright. With each knock of his hips, his knees, his thighs, her resolve weakened. Maybe one kiss wouldn't hurt—just so she could see if it was as good as she'd always imagined. Just so she could see if he tasted as amazing as he smelled.

His hand skated around her hip, a finger slipping under the hem of her tank top to trace the line of skin above her shorts. She squeezed her legs together and willed the throbbing to stop. Clearly she had a little pent-up frustration to deal with, but that wasn't an excuse to let Brodie unravel her.

Chantal spun back around and stepped out of his grip. The others had started to drift away. Kate and Scott had retired into the cabin; Amy and Jessica were finishing off the last of the bubbles and sat with their legs dangling over the edge of the boat. Willa was sitting next to them, her phone tucked between her shoulder and her ear.

'What are you going to do now, Little Miss Perfect?' Brodie's lips brushed her ear. 'It's just us.'

His fingertip traced from the base of her ear down her neck, until he plucked at the strap of her tank top. She burned all over with hot, achy, unfulfilled need. The music had been turned down but the bass still rumbled inside her, urging her to swing her hips and brush against him.

'I'm dancing.'

'You're taunting me.'

The unabashed arousal in his voice tore at the last shreds of her sanity, and with each throaty word she came further undone.

It had been so long since she'd been with anyone—so long since she'd experienced any kind of pleasure like this. Just one kiss…just one taste.

She turned, gathering all her energy to say no, but when his hands cupped her face the protest died on her lips. He came down to her with agonising slowness, and rather than crushing his mouth against hers he teased her with a feather-light touch.

'All that teasing isn't nice, is it?'

'I never teased you.' She frowned, but her body cried out for more.

'Back then your every step teased me, Chantal. You were the epitome of wanting what I couldn't have.'

His tongue flicked out against hers, his teeth tugging ever so gently on her lower lip. So close, but not enough. Nowhere near enough.

'You should have got in first.'

His green eyes glinted, the black of his pupils expanding with each heavy breath. 'I thought it wasn't finders keepers?'

'Sometimes you have to take what you want,' she whispered.

So he did.

His lips came down on hers as he thrust his hands into the tangled length of her hair, pulling her into place. She offered no resistance, opening to him as one might offer a gift. His scent invaded her, making her head swim and her knees weaken.

One large hand crept around her waist and crushed her to him. The hard length of his arousal pressed against her. Unable to stop herself, she slipped her hands under his shirt, smoothing up the chiselled flesh beneath. The feel of each stone-like ridge shot fire through her as their tongues melded. His knee nudged her thighs apart and she gasped as though she were about to come on the spot.

What happened to banishing bad choices and focusing on your career? Abs do not give you a free pass.

She jerked back, and the cool night air rushed to fill the void between them. She shook her head, though in response to what she wasn't sure. Her head should have been in the game, focusing on getting her into a proper dance company. Instead she was gallivanting around on a yacht, kissing a man she should have stayed the hell away from the first time.

'I'm sorry. That shouldn't have…' She struggled to catch her breath, emotions tangling the words in her head.

He waved his hand, ever the cool customer. 'Alcohol and sea air—it's a dangerous combination.'

The stood barely a foot apart, unmoving. The muscles corded in his neck as he swallowed, his Adam's apple bobbing, pupils flaring. He might look calm on the outside, but his eyes gave a glimpse to the storm within.

Around them the night was inky and dark. The breeze rolled past them, caressing her skin as he had done moments ago.

'Very dangerous.'

Brodie woke with a start, the feel of Chantal's lips lingering in his consciousness. Had he dreamed it? He rubbed his hands over his face, pushing his hair out of his eyes. White cotton sheets were tangled around his limbs like a python, holding him hostage lest he get out of bed and do something stupid.

Groaning, he sat up and stretched. His mouth was dry and he desperately wanted a shower. The digital clock beside his bed told him it was barely seven-thirty—why was he up at this ungodly hour? He listened to see if a noise had woken him. Were his guests up already? But the only sound that greeted him was the gentle slosh of waves against the boat and the occasional cry of a seagull.

Brodie showered, relishing the cool water on his overheated skin, and then made his way to the kitchen. He didn't drink much coffee, but there was something about being awake before eight in the morning that necessitated a little caffeine.

He fired up the luxurious silver espresso machine; it had been chosen specifically to balance the champagne tastes of the company's clientele with ease of use. Within seconds hot, dark liquid made its way into his cup and he added only the smallest splash of milk before wandering outside.

He stopped at the edge of the cabin, realising he wasn't the only early bird this morning.

Chantal stood in the middle of the deck, balancing on one leg with the other bent outwards, the sole of her foot pressed against her inner thigh, hands above her head. She stayed there for a moment before lowering her foot and bending forward until her hands were flattened to the ground, her butt high in the air. Brodie gulped, unable to tear his eyes away from the fluid movement that looked as though it should have been performed to music.

Flexibility didn't even begin to describe some of the shapes that Chantal could form with her body. Her legs were encased in the tiny black shorts, leaving miles of tanned skin to tempt him. Her hair was free flowing, the dark strands fading into a deep gold at their ends, bleached by hours in the sun.

As if she could sense him she looked up sharply and caught his eye. Unfolding herself, she gave her limbs a shake and made her way over to him.

'Enjoy the show?' A smile twitched on her lips.

'Always.'

She leant forward and breathed in the billowing tendrils of steam from his coffee. 'Got any more of that?'

He motioned for her to follow him and they walked in silence into the cabin. She climbed up onto the chrome and white leather stool at the bench near the kitchenette, her long legs dangling, swinging slightly as she propped her elbows up on the polished benchtop.

'What was that you were doing outside?'

'Yoga,' she said. 'It's part of my stretching routine—keeps me nice and limber.'

'I could see that.' And he had a feeling he would never *un*see it.

'It's good for relaxation too—helps to quieten the mind.' A flicker of emotion passed over her face, but it was gone as instantly as it had appeared. 'Are we all set to sail back to Sydney soon?'

'We sure are. Scott and Kate have plans this afternoon. I promised I'd get them back before lunchtime.' Brodie filled another cup with coffee and handed it to Chantal. 'Are you performing again tonight?'

'No, I have an audition today.' Her face brightened, a hopeful gleam washing over her eyes.

'Oh, yeah. Amy said. In Sydney, right?'

She nodded. 'This is a big one.'

'I'm sure you'll ace it.'

'Let's hope so.'

The doubt in her voice twisted in his chest. Someone with talent like hers should never be in a position to doubt herself, but she seemed less confident than he remembered. Even last night there had been a hesitancy about her that had felt new—as if she'd learned to fear in the eight years since he'd seen her last.

'How come you're not with a dance company at the moment?'

Brodie studied her, and saw the exact moment her mask slid firmly into place as if she'd flicked a switch.

'I'm waiting for the right opportunity. No sense in taking the first thing that comes along if it doesn't tick all the boxes.'

He chuckled. 'You always were one of *those* girls.'

'What's that supposed to mean?'

'You're a check boxes girl. Everything has to fit your criteria or it doesn't even come up on your radar.'

She tipped her nose up at him. 'It's called having standards.'

'It's narrow-minded.' He sipped his coffee, watching as her cheeks coloured. Her lips pursed as she contemplated her response.

'And I suppose you think it's better to drift through life unanchored by responsibility or silly things such as priorities or commitments?'

'You always thought I was such a layabout, didn't you?'

If only she knew what had brought him to the resort in the first place. Most of the kids working there had been on their gap year, looking for a little fun before hunkering down to study at university. He'd been there because he'd devoted himself entirely to taking care of his sister Lydia after a car accident had stolen her ability to walk.

His mother had pushed him to go, and in truth he'd needed the break—needed some space for himself.

'It wasn't just my opinion, Brodie. That's the kind of guy you are—fun-loving and carefree…'

'You underestimate me.' He narrowed his eyes.

'I didn't mean it as an insult.' She sighed and squeezed his hand. 'We're different people, that's all.'

He swallowed. Whatever they had in common, beneath the surface she would never see him as anyone but Brodie the lazy, talk-his-way-into-anything kid at heart. Would she?

'What are you doing for the rest of the weekend?' he asked, an idea forming. 'Do you have to go back to the bar?'

'Not until Sunday. I think they save the Saturday spot for top-billing dancers.' She rolled her eyes, as if trying to hide her embarrassment that he'd brought up her crappy job. 'I was going to hang around in the accommodation there…work on a new routine. That kind of thing.'

'Stay on the yacht with me. The gang will be back tonight and we can hang out some more.' He smiled. 'This would be better than the bar's accommodation. And safer.'

'I don't know if that's a good idea…' She sucked on her lower lip, her eyes downcast. 'I need to focus on dancing right now.'

'Well, you hardly need practice in that department. I've seen you move.' He reached out and grabbed her hand, wanting to soothe the doubt from her mind. 'Stay tonight, and if you're sick of me by the morning then I'll take you back. No hard feelings.'

'No hard feelings?' She looked up at him through curling lashes.

'None whatsoever.'

'Okay.' She nodded. 'I'll stay.'

CHAPTER FOUR

ONCE THEY WERE back in Sydney, and the rest of group had gone their separate ways, Chantal couldn't help but notice how alone she and Brodie were. Nervous energy crackled through her body, lighting up all her senses as though she were experiencing adrenaline for the first time.

It wasn't good. She needed to be calm for her audition—she *couldn't* stuff it up. If she did then she was fast running out of dance companies and productions to approach. What if she couldn't find a real job? Would she be stuck working a pole like those other women at the bar? No, she wouldn't let that happen.

She needed to focus on herself—*just* herself—no messy emotional entanglements, no betrayal, no disappointment. Just her and the stage.

Closing her eyes, she drew a long breath and held it for a moment before letting the air whoosh out. *Breathe in, hold, breathe out. Repeat.*

Staying on the yacht with Brodie was a terrible idea—she needed *all* her focus right now. And Brodie was the kind of guy who could take a woman's sanity and blow it to smithereens with a single look. He'd done it at Weeping Reef, he'd done it last night, and he would do it again.

But that kiss…

Chantal's body tingled at the memory. Brodie's kiss had been exactly what she'd thought kissing would be like as a teenager, before the reality of one too many slobbery guys had shattered the fantasy. Brodie had the kind of kiss that could make a girl's bones melt.

That's because he's had a lot of practice.

'What's with the frown?'

Brodie's voice cut through Chantal's musings. He stood above her, holding out a hand to help her up from her Lotus Position.

A pair of faded jeans hugged his strong legs and a soft white T-shirt skimmed over the muscles in his shoulders and chest. A leather cuff encircled his right wrist—it looked as though he'd worn it for years. The leather was faded and smooth, and it accentuated the muscles in his arm. But Chantal's eyes were drawn to the anchor tattoo on the inside of his forearm, as always. She had to resist the urge to reach out and trace it with her fingertip.

'Where are we going?' he asked.

'Huh?'

'Your audition. Where is it?'

'Right over there,' Chantal said, pointing across the Sydney Harbour Bridge. 'It's about ten minutes on foot.'

'Great—let's go.' Brodie turned and made his way off the yacht.

'You don't need to come with me.'

She grabbed her bag and scrambled after him, her blood pressure shooting up. Having him watch her last night had been humiliating enough. The last thing she needed was for him to witness a more serious rejection today!

'Don't you want a little moral support?'

'No.' She hitched her dancing bag higher on her shoulder and looked Brodie squarely in the eye. 'I've been doing this on my own for quite a while. I like it that way.'

'What if I want to watch?'

He said it in such a way that Chantal almost lost her footing on the jetty.

'You only get to watch when I say so.'

Her blood pulsed hot and fast, flooding her centre with an uncomfortable and entirely distracting throbbing sensation. She didn't have time to be horny. She had an audition to nail and he was getting in her way.

'Brodie, I don't have time to argue.' She waved him off. 'Can't I just meet you afterwards?'

'If you insist.' He shrugged and fell into step with her.

The sun beat down on Chantal's bare shoulders, making her skin sizzle on the outside as much as Brodie was making her sizzle on the inside. Humid air made her skin glisten and frizzed her hair. She yanked the length behind her head and fastened it with a hair tie… Anything to keep her hands busy.

They walked past other yachts, most of them matching the size of Brodie's boat. It was definitely more upscale than the place where they'd been docked last night. A family to their right boarded a boat that looked twice as big as the house Chantal had grown up in. The mother and daughter had identical long blond ponytails and carried matching designer bags.

'Do your clientele look like that?' She nodded towards the family.

'Rich?' Brodie gave them a cursory glance and shrugged. 'Yeah, I guess. People who charter a private yacht tend to have money.'

'More money than sense,' she muttered under her breath.

'It's certainly not the kind of life I had growing up, that's for sure.'

Chantal's curiosity was piqued. Brodie hadn't shared too much about his family while they'd all lived on the Whitsundays. She'd seen a picture of him with a group of younger girls whom she'd presumed to be his family. It had been pinned up on the wall in the room he'd shared with Scott. But other than that she knew little about his family, or where he was from…

'I always got the impression you were well off.'

'Why did you think that?'

She shrugged. 'I don't know… You always seemed so relaxed—so…at peace with the world. It seemed like you'd had an easy life.'

Brodie's blond brows crinkled and they walked in silence for a few minutes. Had she hurt his feelings? She hadn't intended it, but he seemed to lack the tough outer shell of someone who'd struggled their whole lives failing to keep up with everybody else. Someone like her.

'We had our ups and downs,' he said, talking slowly, as though he chose each word with care. 'My family wasn't different to anyone else's.'

'You never talked about your family much while we were working together.'

'You and I never had a serious conversation about anything.' He grinned. 'Too busy playing cat and mouse.'

'We did *not* play cat and mouse.' She shook her head, but her cheeks filled with roaring heat.

'You don't think so? I used to do anything to rile you up, to get your attention. I'd drive you crazy by teasing you about being a stuck-up ballerina.'

'And I'd try to correct you by explaining the difference between ballet and contemporary dance. But I don't think that's a game of cat and mouse.'

'Why do you think I teased you?'

They hovered under the expressway, enjoying the cool reprieve of the shade while people milled around. Sunlight sparkled on the water and laughter floated up into the air as the crowd filtered past. Everywhere people soaked up the rays, ate ice cream and held hands. The Sydney Harbour Bridge stretched out above, the Opera House in the distance, with the sun coating everything in a golden gleam.

Chantal had to admit it. As much as she found the hustle and bustle of a big city overwhelming, Sydney *was* beautiful.

'I thought you were hot.' He slung an arm around her shoulder.

'You shouldn't have thought that.'

He leant down until his lips were close to her ear. 'I *still* think you're hot.'

Caring about his opinion was a mistake, but his words made something flutter low down in her belly. She'd never wanted to be attracted to Brodie, but he had this *thing* about him. It was indescribable, intangible, invisible… but it was there.

She said, 'I think you're full of crap.'

He threw his head back and laughed. 'Prickly as ever, Chantal. Good to see some things don't change.'

'I have to get to my audition.'

She shrugged off his arm and strode in the direction of the Harbour Dance Company's building at the other end of the wharf.

You cannot stuff this up. Focus, focus, focus.

As much as she hated to admit it to herself—and she would *never* admit it to another living soul—Brodie rattled her. He was the only person who could knock her off course with such effortless efficiency. She needed a little distance from him, and tonight she would ask him to take her back to the bar. The feelings he evoked were confusing, confrontational, and she didn't have time for them.

Not now, not ever.

Perhaps if Chantal wasn't so hot when she was mad he wouldn't be tempted to tease her all the time. He loved it when she got all pink cheeked and pursed lipped. Eight years hadn't dulled or lengthened her fuse—she still lit up like a firecracker when he baited her. Hot *damn* if he didn't love it.

Up ahead, he saw her stride quicken, her full ponytail flicking with each step like the tail of an agitated cat. In all his years, through all the women he'd taken to bed, he'd never found a girl who got his pulse racing the way she did.

But he had to get it out of his head—had to get *her* out of his head. Sex with friends was a no-go zone. Normally he had enough choice that steering clear of any women he wanted to keep in his life was a piece of cake. Normally he could resist temptation… But Chantal was testing his limits.

Falling into a jog, he caught up with her. She counted the pier numbers, her gaze scanning the buildings until a soft, 'Aha!' left her lips.

'I'll be in there, but you really don't need to wait,' she said. 'I'm quite equipped to manage this on my own.'

'I've got nowhere else to be. Besides, I might spy a few hot dancers while I wait around for you.'

'Don't forget to leave a sock on the door if you get lucky,' she quipped.

Her eyes flicked over his face, her lips set into a hard line. Was it his imagination or was there a note of jealousy in her voice? *Wishful thinking.*

'You're the only one coming home with me.'

She licked her lips, the sudden dart of her tongue catching him by surprise. He hardened, the ache for her strong and familiar as ever. How was it that she could reduce him to a hormone-riddled teenage boy with the simplest of actions?

He *had* to get it out of his system—otherwise she'd haunt him forever.

'I'm coming back to the yacht with you—not coming home with you. Those two things are quite different.'

'They don't have to be different.'

'Brodie…'

Her voice warned him, as it had done in the past. *Stay away, hands off, do not get any closer.*

'Fine.' He leant down and planted a kiss on her forehead, enjoying the way she sucked in a breath. 'Good luck. I know you'll kill it.'

'Don't jinx me.' She mustered a smile and then turned towards the building marked 'Harbour Dance Company'.

He hated to see her doubt herself. She had no cause to. If the people holding the audition couldn't see her talent then they were blind. Perhaps he should follow her, just in case they needed convincing…

No. She was not his responsibility. He would wait for her, but he wouldn't get involved. He wouldn't get invested.

Brodie settled in to the café on the ground floor of the building, ordered a drink and set up at a small table by the window. Views of the pier with a backdrop of the bridge filled it. Sydney always made him feel small, but in a good way. As if he was only a tiny fleck on the face of the earth and his actions didn't matter so much in the scheme of things. As if he could be anyone he wanted to be…could sail away and no one would notice.

He envied Chantal and the freedom she had. She was beholden to no one. He, on the other hand, was stuck in the constant clashing of his desire to be his own person and his obligation to his family. He would *always* look after his sisters, but sometimes he wanted a break without feeling as though he were abandoning them. Even holidaying in Sydney was tough. What if something happened with Lydia while he was away? What if she got stuck in the house on her own and couldn't call for help?

He shoved aside the worry and reached for a newspaper, making sure to offer a charming smile to the waitress as she set down his coffee. She was cute—early twenties, blonde. But he didn't feel the usual zing of excitement when she smiled back, lingering before heading to her station. Something was definitely amiss.

Several articles and a sports section later Brodie looked up. He'd downed his coffee and then switched to green tea—which tasted like crap—and a bottle of water. A beer would have hit the spot, but he'd skipped training that morning and tomorrow's session would be hell if he didn't get his act together. Ah, discipline…it was kind of overrated.

Chantal still hadn't returned. How long had it been? Time had ticked by reluctantly, but she must have been gone an hour…maybe two. Was that a good sign? He hoped so.

The phone vibrating on the café table pulled his attention away from thoughts of Chantal. A photo of his youngest sister, Ellen, flashed up on screen. She looked so much like him. Shaggy blond hair that couldn't be controlled, light green eyes, and skin that tanned at the mere mention of sun.

'Ellie-pie, what's happening?'

'Not much.' She sighed—the universal signal that there *was*, in fact, something happening. 'Boy stuff.'

'You know how I deal with that.' Brodie frowned.

Trouble related to boys was squarely *not* in the realm of brotherly duties. Unless, of course, the solution to said boy problem involved him putting the fear of God into whichever pimply-faced rat had upset his little sister.

'Yeah, I know. I wasn't calling about that.' Pause. 'When are you coming home?'

'I only left a couple of days ago.' Not that it stopped the guilt from churning.

'I know.' She sighed again. 'Hey, can I come and stay with you when you get back?'

He smiled. 'Are the twins driving you crazy again?'

'No. Lydia's being difficult today.'

The relationship between his oldest and youngest sister had always been tense. And Lydia's mood changes seemed to affect Ellen more than anyone; she was often the one at home, taking on the role of parent when Brodie and their mother were working and the twins were out living their lives.

It might have been easier with another parental figure around, but his dad was best described as an 'absentee parent'. Even before the divorce his father had shunned responsibility, favouring activities that allowed him to 'find his creativity' over supporting his kids or his wife.

'Lydia can't help it. Her situation is tough—you know that.'

'You *always* take her side,' Ellen whined.

'No, I don't.' He sighed, pressing his fingers to his temple.

'You do—just like everyone else!' The wobble in her voice signalled that tears were imminent.

'I'm not taking sides, Ellen, and I understand you cop the brunt of it.'

That seemed to appease her. 'I want to get out of the house for a bit. And I can't go to Jamie's… We broke up.'

Oh, boy. 'Do I need to pay him a visit?'

'No. It was mutual. We weren't ready to settle down with one another.'

Not surprising—she was only nineteen. Brodie rolled his eyes. 'I'll call you when I get home. Then you can come and crash for the weekend.'

Chantal had arrived at the table, and a soft smile tugged at her lips. Was that because she'd had good news, or because she'd caught him playing big brother? He finished up his call with Ellen and shoved the phone into his pocket.

'You're still here.'

Her voice broke through the ambient noise of the café.

'Of course I'm still here. I said I would be.'

She hovered by the edge of the table, hands twisting in front of her.

'You don't need an invitation,' he said, but he stood anyway and drew back the seat next to him so she could sit down. 'How did it go?'

'I don't know. It felt good.' She shook her head and sat, tucking her feet up underneath her. 'But that doesn't always mean anything. They said they'll get back to me.'

'I'm sure you were amazing.' He reached out and grabbed her hand, giving it a soft squeeze.

'*Amazing* doesn't always cut it.'

'It doesn't?'

'No. You can't just be a great dancer—you have to look right, have the right style…' Her cheeks were stained pink and she rubbed her hands over her face. 'These are the big guns too. They didn't even open up for auditions last year.'

Her breath came out irregular—too fast, too shallow. He could see her mind whirring behind those beautiful soulful eyes. He could see the doubt painted across her face. He could imagine the words she didn't say aloud. *I hope it was enough. I hope* I *was enough.*

Instead she said, 'Some days I wonder if it's worth it.'

'Of course it's worth it.'

How could she say something like that? People would kill for her talent.

'Easy for you to say—you're not the one up there, putting yourself out for every man and his dog to judge you.'

'People judge each other every day,' Brodie pointed out. 'You don't need a stage for that.'

She smiled, her shoulders relaxing as she loosened her hair. The dark strands fell around her shoulders, golden ends glinting in the sun streaming through the café's window. 'Is that a dig at me?'

'It might be.'

He flagged down a waitress and ordered Chantal a coffee. They watched each other for a moment like two dogs circling. Wary. Charged.

'Because I think you lead a charmed life?'

'Because you don't think I work for it.' He took a long swig from his water bottle. 'I do.'

'I know you work for it. But you have to admit you seem to land on your feet, no matter what.'

'And you don't?' He raked a hand through his hair.

'No, I don't.'

She let out a hollow laugh and the sound made him want to pull her tight against him.

'You have no idea what it's been like the last few years.'

'So tell me?'

Silence. Perhaps she didn't expect him to care. Chantal paused while the waitress set down her coffee. She cradled the cup in her small hands, blowing at the steam.

When she stayed quiet he changed tactic. 'How come you never called?'

'You never called either.'

She sipped her drink and set the cup down on the table. For a moment the view of the pier had her attention, and the tension melted from her face.

'I wasn't exactly keen to share that my career was going down the gurgler. Why else would I have called?'

'Because we're friends, Chantal, despite how it ended.'

'You're right.' She nodded. 'Friends.'

God, he wanted to kiss her. She was sex on legs. Perfection.

'Friends who have the hots for each other.'

'I don't have the hots for you,' she protested, but her cheeks flamed crimson and her gaze locked onto some invisible spot on the ground.

'How about you look me in the eye when you say that?'

'Okay—fine. You're kind of a hottie.' Red, redder, reddest. She still didn't look up. 'But you're not my type.'

'What's your type?'

'Tall, dark and handsome?' she quipped with a wave of her hand. '*No* guys are my type at the moment. I have this little thing called a career that needs saving.'

'It's not that you don't have time for guys—you just don't have time for relationships.' Brodie rolled the idea around in his head. 'Maybe what you need is a little no-strings tension-reliever.'

'Is *that* what the kids are calling it these days?' She raised a brow at him and traced the edge of her coffee cup with a fingertip.

'Doesn't matter what it's called so long as it feels good.'

'I'm not a hedonist like you, Brodie. There are more important things in life than pleasure. I need my focus at the moment.'

'Perhaps… But don't you think you could do with a little pleasure right now?'

He reached out and cupped the side of her face. Their knees touched under the table and he could feel the heat radiating from her.

Her dark lashes fluttered. He wasn't going to kiss her again—not yet. She'd run scared if he pushed too hard too soon… But he would draw her in. Relax her boundaries. Give her space to let her guard drop.

Then he would have her.

CHAPTER FIVE

LATER THAT EVENING Chantal and Brodie wandered around The Rocks. To anyone else they might have looked like two people who'd been together forever. Behind the bridge the sun had set, streaking the sky with rich shades of gold, pink and red. Sydney was ready for a night out, glittering and looking its absolute best in the balmy air.

Brodie looked as though he belonged with the glamorous city crowd—as he did with any scene he joined. He had the ability to melt into a group of people no matter who they were. Rich clients, hard-working staff, children—he charmed them all. She'd seen it first hand at Weeping Reef. No wonder he'd done so well with his business.

Women were his forte. He knew exactly what to say to charm them straight out of their panties. Sometimes he could do it without saying a thing. Now she couldn't help but notice the way other women stared at him as they strolled back to the yacht. And why wouldn't they?

His hips rolled in a sensuous, languid gait. He had that loose-limbed, laid-back sexiness that was impossible to fake. You either had it or you didn't. And, *boy*, did he have it!

What is it about focus that you don't understand? Hands off, lips off, eyes off...everything off. Ugh, stop thinking about him!

'You're quiet,' he said as they returned to the boat.

The rest of the Weeping Reef crew would be joining them in an hour or so, and Chantal planned to enjoy her night off. The audition played on her mind, but if she thought about it any more she'd surely go crazy. No, tonight would be an opportunity to let her hair down and relax before she had to go back to the bar.

'My mind isn't,' Chantal muttered.

'Anything in particular bothering you?'

'Just thinking about work stuff.'

It wasn't a total lie, and she wasn't going to encourage him by revealing her inner monologue about his hotness.

'You can't be all work and no play.' He walked to the fridge on deck and pulled out a bottle of champagne, popping the cork and pouring her a glass.

'I think you have enough play for both of us.'

'I'd be happy to share it with you.'

He handed her the flute, her fingers grazing his as she grasped the stem. Goosebumps skittered across her skin and she wondered if perhaps her slinky, skin-tight dress had been a dangerous choice. She'd bought the dress after her audition because it was the exact blue-green of the ocean in the Whitsundays—a fitting choice for catching up with the old gang.

But her arms and legs were exposed to the night air, along with a portion of her back beneath the thick bands of fabric criss-crossing their way down her spine.

It would be fine. The others would arrive soon, and she'd make sure that she and Brodie weren't left alone. Piece of cake.

Yeah, right.

'So what did you do after you left the reef?' she asked, sipping her drink.

'A bit of this and that. There's not much to tell.' He shrugged, dropping down into a seat and stretching his long, muscular legs out in front of him. 'Went to university, dropped out of university, got a job sailing yachts.'

'That's it? Come on—I'm sure a lot more happened in eight years.' She dropped down next to him, resisting the desire to ease against him as he automatically slung his arm along the back of her seat.

'There was a girl.'

'Just one?' she teased, hating herself for the clutch of jealousy deep in her chest.

His eyes darkened, the pale green glowing in the dimming light. 'One relationship. It didn't end well and I don't have any desire to revisit the experience.'

'Why did you break up?' Colour her curious, but she'd never known Brodie to have a relationship with *anyone*. Unless you called repeated booty calls a relationship.

'It was a combination of things.' He shook his head, tilting his gaze up to the darkening sky. 'I was away a lot with work. I had my family to look after. She needed a *lot* of attention. Nothing more than incompatibility, pure and simple.'

'You always struck me as the attentive type.'

'No one is *that* attentive. She wanted us to be joined at the hip.' His voice tightened. 'I don't do inseparability. I need my space—the open waters and all that.'

'How did you meet?'

'She was a friend.' His mouth twisted into a grimace. 'I met her at university but we didn't get together until after I dropped out.'

'I guess she's not a friend any more?'

'No.'

'Sounds like you made the right call.'

'The right call would have been not going there in the first place.' Brodie sighed. 'Some people aren't cut out for relationships.'

It sounded like a warning. Not that she needed it. She

had no intention of getting sucked into Brodie's sex vortex the way other girls did. She knew he was a love 'em and leave 'em kind of guy… It was why she'd stayed away from him in the first place.

But she didn't exactly want a relationship right now either. Didn't that make them perfectly compatible for one night?

Heart thudding against her rib cage, she took a long swig of her champagne. Brodie's arm moved from the seat to her shoulders and his intoxicating coconut-and-sea-air smell made her mouth water.

Would it be so bad to have a little 'no-strings tension-reliever', as he'd called it? Surely she could afford to be unfocused for one day…just a night, really. Not even a whole day.

She was only working at the crappy bar tomorrow, so it wasn't as if she needed to be on her A-game. Maybe it wouldn't hurt. But could she walk away after a single night? Weeping Reef had taught her that Brodie's powers of seduction were second to none. What if he wanted more and she couldn't say no? The last thing she needed was to get sucked into a situation where she had another man trying to overpower her, trying to control her decisions.

She couldn't let that happen.

'What about you? Was it all about the dancing after you left?'

'I stayed a while longer on the resort, actually.'

After watching the Weeping Reef friendships disintegrate she'd wanted to flee. But dance school wouldn't pay for itself and she'd refused to ask her mother for anything else. It had been her time to prove what she was made of. Prove how determined she was.

'But it wasn't the same.'

'We had a great year together, didn't we?'

'We did.'

'I couldn't keep my eyes off you.' His voice was low, rough.

Chantal turned and his arm tightened around her. Her fingers ached to touch him. The now inky sky glittered with city lights. Magical. Surreal. He leant forward, his eyes drinking in every detail.

'Perv,' she said.

Her shaky laugh failed to diffuse the tension.

'I was so jealous of Scott. He had you to himself night after night.'

She tried to shrug his arm away but he held tight. 'And *you* had every other girl on the resort.'

'None of them compared to you, Chantal.' He brushed his lips against her temple, the soft kiss sending electric sensations through her. 'They didn't even come close.'

'Why didn't you say anything?'

She asked it so quietly that she couldn't be sure he'd heard it. Not till his pupils flared and his breath came in short bursts did she dare think about that night. About that *dance*.

'It was wrong being so attracted to you when you were Scott's girl.' Brodie shook his head, blond hair falling about his face.

'Is that why you left?' She reached up and brushed the strands out of his eyes.

His hand caught her wrist, turning it so he could press his lips to the tender skin on the inside. 'Of course it's why I left.'

Breathing was a struggle. Thinking was…impossible. Kissing him was all she could focus on.

'You were *everything*. All I could think about…all I could dream about.' He drew her arm around his neck and leaned in, lips at her ear. 'All I could fantasise about.'

Each word nudged her body temperature higher. Her

hand curled in the length of his hair, gripping, tugging. Resisting.

'Brodie…'

'I've wanted you from the second I saw you at that resort. You were dancing. I'd never seen anyone move like that before.'

'We shouldn't do this…' *Should we?*

His eyes were engulfed by the onyx of his pupils. 'Stay with me tonight.'

'I am staying here.'

'Stay with *me*. In my bed.'

'Brodie…' His name was a warning on her lips, but temptation spiralled out of control. Where was her resolve? Her focus?

'Just for tonight. Then tomorrow we can pretend it never happened.'

He stood and turned, waving to the rest of the Weeping Reef gang as they approached the yacht.

Chantal hadn't heard them. But with Brodie about to kiss her, a bomb might have been dropped and she wouldn't have noticed a damn thing.

'You two looked pretty cosy before,' Scott said.

The boys had separated from the girls and they hung out on the deck, port side. After dancing their feet off—and putting on quite the show—the girls were taking a break in the cabin, a fresh bottle of champagne flowing and peals of laughter piercing the night air.

'No idea what you're talking about, mate.' Brodie put on his best poker face—which, if his track record was anything to go on, was terrible.

'You're so full of it.' Scott laughed.

'You're a bit of an open book, aren't you?' said Rob Hanson, Willa's partner, in his distinctive South African accent. He eyed Brodie with an amused smile that crinkled the corners of his eyes.

Just because Scott and Rob had sorted their love-lives out it didn't given them licence to have a dig at his. Not that he *wanted* a love-life—he was happy with a gratifying and varied sex-life, thank you very much.

'Are you going to get it over with?' Scott took a swig of his beer.

Brodie rolled his eyes and looked out to the water. 'Nothing's going on.'

'Maybe not yet.' Rob smirked. 'But you're better off getting it out of your system.'

Brodie's pocket vibrated and he pulled out his phone. *Saved by the bell!* A text from Jenny—aka twin number one. She'd had a fight with twin number two and wanted a place to crash.

No can do, Jen. I'm in Sydney. Stop giving your sister a hard time.

He toyed with the phone, knowing that there would be an immediate response from his serial-texting younger sister.

'Family?' Scott asked with a knowing look. 'They still driving you crazy?'

'Are they ever?' He shook his head. 'I hope for your sake you and Kate only have boys.'

Brodie's phone vibrated again.

You always take her side.

I do not.

'Is your sister a bit of a handful?' Rob asked.

'Sisters,' Brodie corrected. 'I've got four of them—all younger.'

'Jeez.' Rob let out a low whistle. 'Your parents must have been gluttons for punishment.'

'Not really,' Scott chipped in. 'Brodie always did most of the work with them.'

'Just doing my job.' Brodie waved off the comment. He'd done what any big brother would have. His father's absence had left a gaping hole in his sisters' lives. If he hadn't looked after them who would have?

'Family comes first, but you have to find some balance,' Rob said.

Brodie shrugged. 'The rest of my life is pretty carefree. I sail when I feel like it, work on my business, cruise around the country. Meet lots of interesting people.'

'Brodie has never had any trouble meeting *interesting people*.' Scott rolled his eyes and turned to Rob. 'He used to have the girls falling at his feet when we were all at the reef.'

'It's the tatts,' Brodie replied. 'Something about a little ink makes them go crazy.'

'What's that about tattoos?' Willa wandered over and immediately tucked herself against Rob.

Rob gave her a squeeze and grinned. 'Apparently girls go gaga for Brodie's ink. What do you think, Willa?'

'I don't think it's just the ink,' she said, smirking.

'Should I be getting jealous?' There wasn't a hint of jealousy in Rob's voice, but Willa shook her head anyway. She only had eyes for Rob, anyone could see that.

The rest of the girls had filtered out of the cabin and now joined the discussion. Rob took the opportunity to make Brodie squirm.

'What do you think, Chantal? Tatts or no tatts?' His eyes glittered and he fought back a smile when Brodie shot daggers at him.

'On the right guy it looks good,' she responded carefully, her eyes flicking from Brodie to Rob and back again, as though she were trying to work out who'd instigated the suggestive discussion. 'Though looks aren't everything.'

'Aren't they?' joked Kate, flipping her long red pony-tail over one shoulder as she laughed at Scott's serious face. 'Joking!'

This time the group wasn't crashing on the yacht. Scott and Kate were staying at a hotel for the night, Amy and Jessica were going to continue the festivities at a local bar, and Willa and Rob were retiring back to their newly rented penthouse.

But what about Chantal?

'Are you sure you don't want to join us, Brodie?' Amy asked with a coy smile.

'I would *love* to party it up with you lovely ladies, but I have training tomorrow.' Brodie pulled Amy in for a friendly hug. 'Literally at the crack of dawn—and you know how much I hate mornings.'

She grinned. 'How about you, Chantal?'

Brodie held his breath. This was it. If she stayed then he would do everything in his power to make her come—over and over and over.

She shifted on her strappy tan heels and raked a hand through her long, wavy hair.

'I've got work tomorrow.' She smiled sweetly. 'I think I'm going to need all my energy for it.'

Amy stifled a smile and nodded.

The crew filtered off the boat, leaving Brodie and Chantal completely alone. She hovered by his side, refusing to look up at him. Not that it mattered where she looked, so long as it was his name on her lips.

'I hope you weren't serious about needing energy tomorrow,' he said as they waved the group off. 'You're not getting *any* sleep tonight.'

CHAPTER SIX

WAS SHE MAKING a colossal mistake? Her body seemed to think not. In fact her body acted as though it had been served up a certifiable slice of heaven, complete with whipped cream, cherries *and* sprinkles.

'Sleep is for the weak.'

His hands found her waist and pulled her close. Air rushed from her lungs with the delicious contact. His pelvis was hard against her, the ridge of his burgeoning erection pressing into her belly through the thin material of her dress.

His full lips curved into an impossibly sexy smile. 'I'm glad we're on the same page.'

'We will be if we never speak of this again.'

'Romantic,' he quipped. 'I like it.'

She ran her palms up the front of his chest, feeling the smooth cotton of his shirt glide against her skin. Each muscle in his chest was crisply defined, all hardness and athletic perfection. Her fingers hovered at the top button, tracing the outline in slow, deliberate circles.

'I don't want anything beyond one night. Clear?'

'Crystal.'

Chantal swallowed, Brodie had agreed more readily than she'd expected. But that was the kind of guy he was, the kind of life he led—easygoing, breezy, sans strings. She shouldn't be disappointed.

'Any more rules I should be aware of?' he asked, trailing feather-light kisses from her temple to her jaw.

In heels, she didn't feel quite so small next to him—though he still had a head on her. Perhaps she'd leave the heels on.

A wicked smile curved her lips. 'Ladies first.'

'Hmm…' The throaty growl was hot against her neck. 'A woman after my own heart.'

She thrust her hands into his hair and wrenched his face down to hers, slanting her mouth over his and stripping away any doubts, fears or reservations with a hot, combative kiss. He came back with equal force, his hands sliding down her back until they cupped her behind and forced her against him.

He was hard, salty and heavenly. She moaned, the sound lost between them.

A chorus of cheers and laughter from a neighbouring boat broke them apart.

A giggle bubbled up between her heavy breaths and Chantal pressed her hands to burning cheeks. 'Looks like we're putting on a bit of a show.'

'You *are* a performance artist.'

Brodie lifted her and she instinctively wrapped her legs around him, groaning as her centre made contact with the hard length beneath his jeans.

'But now it's time for a private show.'

He walked them into the cabin, through the lounge and to the bedroom. *His* bedroom. A huge bed dominated the centre of the room. It was a hell of a lot bigger than Chantal had imagined it would be on a boat. It was a bed not made for sleeping but for hot, *Kama Sutra*–referencing, scream-at-the-top-of-your-lungs sex.

Brodie turned and sat on the edge of the bed, still holding her so that she was in his lap. The friction of his jeans against the wispy material of her underwear drove her crazy. She bucked, rolling her hips to increase the pressure. His mouth came down on hers, lush and open and intoxicating.

'Dance for me,' he growled.

Cheeks burning, she pushed hard against his chest so he toppled back. She straddled him, grinding her hips in a slow circular motion. 'But it's so good here.'

'I want to watch you.'

'You only get to watch when I say so.' She echoed her words from earlier in the day, heat flooding her body and throbbing out of control.

His eyes blazed like green fire and darkness. 'I'll make it worth your while.'

'How?' The question escaped her lips before she could think, before she could reason. She needed to hear his answer. Needed to absorb the experience of being with him through her every sense.

Warm palms slid up her thighs, bunching blue material around her waist. His hand brushed her sex, sending a jolt of pleasure through her. Toying with the edge of her underwear, he traced the pattern on the lace with his fingertip.

'If you can walk, talk or function on any level tomorrow then I haven't done my job.'

Her lips trembled. It wasn't enough. She wanted detail. She wanted all of it with a greedy, hedonistic gluttony.

'More.'

'I'm going to take you to the point where you think there's nothing left and I'm going to make you beg.' His eyes were wild, his pulse throbbing in his neck. 'I'm going to make you forget any word you've ever spoken except for my name. I'm going to be the only thing you know. I'm going to be your everything.'

'Brodie…' she whispered, the throbbing between her legs ceaseless. She ached to the point of pain. It had been so long…so very long.

'Dance for me.' His voice was rough, scratched up and torn apart with desire.

She pushed back, balancing on her heels and taking a step away from the bed. Her hands trembled, and her mouth was suddenly devoid of moisture as her hips swayed to a non-existent beat.

She wasn't passionate…her dancing wasn't passionate. Hadn't that been Derek's parting shot as he'd walked out of their house for the last time?

'You're a technical dancer, Chantal, but you're all business. No passion. No one wants to watch that. You'll never make it without me.'

Her throat closed in on itself, her heart jackhammering against her ribs. This was *Brodie*—not her controlling, possessive ex-husband. Smoking hot, life-loving Brodie. She could be herself around him because tomorrow this wouldn't exist. This would never have happened.

Safe in the impermanence of their situation, she ran her hands up her body, over the curve of her bust, the ridges of her collarbones, the column of her neck, into her hair. Fingers divided the strands, shaking her hair out until it fell around her shoulders.

'God, Chantal…' Her name was a strangled plea on his lips. 'Your body is incredible.'

She reached for the hidden zip that ran down the side of her rib cage, drawing it open with agonising slowness. Cool air rushed in, tickling her exposed skin. Stepping closer to him, she pulled him into a sitting position and dragged his hands to her hips so he could feel the movement.

Her head tilted back. There was nothing but the invisible beat and his hands on her. He pulled her between his legs, thrusting the dress up over her hips. His lips made contact with the flat of her belly above the waistband of her black lacy underwear. His tongue flicked out, filled with the promise of what was to come.

She yanked the dress over her head and flung it away.

'Perfection,' he breathed, and the hot air caressed the apex of her thighs.

His hand slid up over her rib cage to clasp her naked breast. Deft fingers toyed with her already hardened nipple, wringing a low moan from the back of her throat.

'Your turn.' She reached for his shirt, unbuttoning him quickly, urgently.

'You're far too good at that,' he chuckled, blackened eyes looking up at her.

'Dance costumes—fiddly buttons are no match for *my* fingers.'

'You do have beautiful fingers.' He pulled one of her hands to his lips and kissed each fingertip in turn. 'Beautiful palms.'

His mouth was hot in the centre of her hand, tracing a line over her wrist and up to her elbow.

'Beautiful everything.'

'Don't distract me.' She pushed the shirt from his shoulders, exposing golden skin stretched tight over a wall of muscle.

The cross tattoo caught her eye. She bent to kiss it, her hands falling to his belt. She wrenched at the closure, making his hips jerk forward as she released the belt.

'Easy, girl.' He covered her hands with his as she lowered the zip.

Within seconds he was completely naked. Ink covered more of his body than she remembered. The cross on his chest had been joined by scrolling words down the side of his rib cage and another anchor lower down, with numbers surrounding it. The sharp V of muscle drew her eyes… then her hands, then her mouth.

Her fingers brushed over the hard length of him, tracing the tip before she sank to her knees and drew him into her mouth. The mixture of earthy masculine scents and the subtle taste of him intoxicated her.

'Didn't I say easy girl?' he moaned, his hands fisting in her hair. She wasn't sure if he meant to hold her in place or pull her away.

She ran her tongue along the length of him before looking up. 'I heard you. I just didn't listen.'

'Come here.'

He hauled her on top of him, tilting them both back so that she straddled his hips. The hard weight of his erection dug into her thigh.

'We've got the whole night. You're not rushing me.'

Stretching his hand back, he found the drawer beside his bed and produced a foil packet. He reached down, sheathed himself, and before she knew what was happening he thrust up into her. The sudden movement was the perfect blend of pleasure and shock…with the tiniest, most delicate hint of pain.

Strong arms held her flat against him, her breasts pushed up against his chest, her lips at his neck. Each moan shot fire through her, and each thrust of his hips bumped her most sensitive part, making her body hum. Orgasm welled within her, climbing, peaking and pushing.

His hands were in her hair again, yanking her face up to his so his lips could slant over hers. Teeth tugged at her mouth, the taste of him drawing her closer and closer to release. She ground against him. So close…so close.

'Come for me, Chantal. I want to feel you shake around me.' His voice was tight, his breath coming in hard bursts.

'Brodie…' Her voice trembled, release a hair's width away.

'Scream for me.'

And she did.

On and on and on she cried out his name, eyes clamped

shut, fists bunched in the pillow, face pressed against his neck. The bubble burst and she tumbled down, down, down. As she clamped around him he found his own release, groaning long and low into her hair.

Silence washed over them. The air was cool on their sweat-dampened skin. He held her close, clinging on as if he wanted to stay that way forever. She didn't move in case he let go.

He could officially die a happy man. The gentle weight of her comforted him. One of her legs had wound around his; her foot was tucked against his calf. As her breathing slowed he stroked her hair, breathing in the heady scent of her perfume mingled with perspiration and sex.

Beside his head her hands were still clutching the pillow. Outside, Saturday-night parties raged on, contrasting with inside, where a hazy silence had settled over them.

'That was okay, I guess,' she mumbled against his neck, chuckling when he turned to look her in the eye. 'If you like that kind of thing.'

Glossy dark strands of hair covered half her face and he pushed them aside, drinking in her drugged gaze with satisfaction. Her lips were swollen and parted, her cheeks bright pink. Tracing her lower lip with his thumb, he brought her head down for a slow, teasing kiss.

'And *do* you like that sort of thing?'

'Nah—orgasms are overrated.' She grinned, pushing herself up so she straddled his hips.

The view was pretty damn good from this angle.

'Blasphemy.'

'Total blasphemy.' She planted a kiss on the tip of his nose and traced the lines of his latest tattoo. 'This is new.'

'It's twelve months old.'

'"In the waves of change we find our true direction".'

She read the words that had been etched onto him forever. 'That's beautiful. Why that quote?'

'I thought it made me sound intelligent,' he joked, hiding his sudden vulnerability with a wink.

How did she do that? She had a homing beacon aimed straight for his most sensitive areas…and not the good kind!

She smirked. 'What's the real reason?'

'I felt like I needed a reminder that change is necessary…healthy.' He sighed, and rolled so that she came down and landed on the bed next to him.

He'd meant to move away, but her body immediately curled into his, finding the groove between his arm and his chest. It felt so damn good to have her by his side, to finally be able to wrap his arms around her without the guilt of the past. He only had one night—he might as well let himself enjoy it.

What if one night wasn't enough?

Bookings were piling up. He'd be sailing back to Queensland soon enough to bury himself in work and his family. Even if they did stretch this fiasco on for more than a night his time here had a solid end date. Normally that was what he liked. But he wasn't experiencing his usual sense of relief at their ring-fenced sleeping arrangements.

'Do you think you need to change?'

'Everyone needs to change,' he replied, running a fingertip up and down her arm.

'What do you want to change?'

He laughed, shaking his head. 'What's with the twenty questions? I thought I'd signed on for a night of steamy sex—not the Spanish Inquisition.'

'Is that so?' She reached for him, the brush of her fingertips hardening him. 'What if I'm done?'

'*I'll* say when you're done.'

Rolling on top of her, he mentally thanked the king-size bed for its endless space.

Pinned, she tilted her face up at him, a defiant glint in her eye. ‘You’re not the boss of me,’ she said.

Yeah, right. He had her exactly where he wanted her. Kissing his way down her neck, he sucked on her skin, only stopping to draw a still-hard nipple into his mouth. Her breasts were perfect: smallish, but firm, topped with bronzed peaks that were oh-so-responsive to his touch. She arched, stifling a groan. He licked, nipped, tugged until she let out the heavenly sounds of pleasure.

‘That’s it,’ he murmured against her breast. ‘Don’t keep that wonderful sound from me. I want to hear you.’

‘Bossy boots.’ Her head lolled back against the pillow. Her eyes were closed, but a wicked smile curved her lips.

‘Damn straight.’

‘We were *talking*.’ Strong fingers gripped his hair, pulling his head up so she could look down her body at him.

‘And now we’re not.’

‘Why are you so averse to talking?’

‘I’m not averse, but I prefer touching you.’ To illustrate his point he kissed a trail down to her hip, swirling his tongue over the slightly protruding bone.

‘You’re such a *guy*.’

With her hands still in his hair he made his way to the juncture of her thighs, blowing cool air on her heated skin. ‘Want me to stop?’

‘What if I say yes?’

Her voice wavered. *Victory.*

‘I’ll call your bluff.’

Delicate licks drew an anguished moan from her.

‘Stop.’

‘Okay.’ He pulled his head away but she pushed him back into place.

‘Damn you.’

He laughed against the inside of her thigh, nipping at the sensitive flesh before moving back to her sex. The honeyed scent of her made his head swim, made him want to ravish her. It wouldn't be right to push her over the edge too quickly. She would have to wait while he had his fill.

He drew the sensitive bud of her clitoris into his mouth, working her, teasing her, tasting her. Smooth legs draped over his shoulders; demanding hands pushed and pulled him into place. Chantal was clear about what she wanted, and that was exactly the way he liked it.

'Brodie…' she gasped. 'For the love of…'

'Want me to stop again?'

'No!' The tension built within her, tremors rippling through her legs. 'Please.'

He bore down, giving her what she wanted until orgasm ripped through her. This time there was no holding back. She cried out so loudly that the neighbouring boats were sure to hear.

He clutched at his drawer, grabbing another condom and burying himself in her, riding the final waves of her release as he lost himself in her pleasure.

CHAPTER SEVEN

CHANTAL AWOKE WRAPPED in Brodie arms. Her face was pushed against his bicep, which was far cosier than it should have been, considering the guy was a rock-hard tower of muscle. His even breathing soothed the thumping of her heart.

From her days at Weeping Reef she knew Brodie was a heavy sleeper. She'd tested it on more than one occasion by sneaking into his room with Scott so they could play pranks on him. Like the time they'd switched the clothes in his drawers for frilly girls' nightclothes, so that he had to wander down to Chantal's room in a pink leopard-print negligee.

Not that he'd been too upset. He'd strutted his stuff as he did every day and the girls had fallen at his feet anyway.

Biting down on her lower lip, Chantal watched his peaceful face. Full lips were curved into a slight smile; thick lashes cast shadows on his cheekbones. His shaggy blond hair managed to look magazine perfect. Damn him.

Flashes of last night came back in a rush of needy, achy feeling. Every part of her body throbbed in a totally satisfied, pleasure-overload kind of way. Brodie was as good in bed as she'd suspected, but there was a tenderness to him that had been a complete surprise. The way he'd stroked her hair, the comforting embrace in the middle of the night, the gentle sweep of his hand along her arm—she hadn't been prepared for that at *all.* If anything it would have been easier if he was cold and impersonal afterwards.

She couldn't do this with him. It had been so much more than scratching an itch. He'd pushed her limits, bringing her to sensual heights she'd never known existed. He'd stirred her curiosity. The words inked on him revealed that he was so much more than the shallow charmer she'd labelled him. How could she look into those beautiful green eyes again without wanting to learn more? To dig deeper?

It was supposed to be about sex.

It is *about sex. You don't owe him anything. You got what you wanted—now move on and focus on your career. Playtime is over.*

Careful not to wake him, Chantal extracted herself from his muscular hold. She slipped out of the bed, holding her breath as her feet touched the polished boards. It was like playing a game of Sleeping Giant—except that the giant was a hunky guy with whom she didn't want to have awkward after-sex conversation.

How was she going to get back to Newcastle for her shift at the job from hell? Cringing, she tiptoed around the room. More importantly, where the hell was her dress? She'd managed to find every single one of Brodie's clothing items from their stripping frenzy, but the little blue dress was nowhere to be seen. Normally she was a leave-nothing-behind kind of girl when it came to her clothes, but the blue dress would have to be sacrificed.

Changing slowly, and as silently as possible, Chantal pulled on the clothes she'd arrived in on the first night, grabbed her phone and slung her overnight bag over one shoulder.

Now she had to make her way to Newcastle without the aid of Brodie's boat or her car—which was still parked at the bar. Simple…*not.* A cab was out of the question, since her wallet was frighteningly lean. Perhaps she could ring one of the girls and beg for a lift?

She bit down on her lip. She hated to ask. What if they already had plans? They probably would, and she would be interrupting. The bed squeaked as Brodie turned in his sleep, spiking her heart rate. She had to get out of there.

Pushing down her discomfort, she made her way off the boat and dialled Willa's number. 'Hey, I know it's early, but I need a favour…'

Within twenty minutes she was in Willa's car and on her way to Newcastle. There would be a price to pay for Willa's generosity in giving up brunch with Rob…and it wasn't going to be monetary.

'So,' Willa began, not bothering to hide the curiosity sparkling all over her face, 'how was he?'

Chantal pretended to study an email on her phone. 'I don't know what you're talking about.'

'Oh, come on! I did *not* miss out on baked ricotta and eggs to have you BS me, Chantal.'

'Nothing happened.'

Willa chuckled. 'Then why is your face the same shade as a tomato?'

'Sunburn?' Chantal offered weakly. 'Okay—fine. I slept with him.'

'Thank you, Captain Obvious. I'd figured that out already.' Willa leant forward to watch the traffic as she merged onto the Bradfield Highway. 'I don't want confirmation—I want *details*.'

Where to begin? Images of last night flashed in front of Chantal's eyes, snippets of sounds, feelings, sensations… Her body reacted as though he were right there in front of her. Damn him!

'It was…satisfying.'

'Just satisfying?' Willa narrowed her eyes at Chantal.

'Either you dish or it's going to be a long walk to Newcastle.'

'He was amazing.'

Shaking her head, she willed her heart to stop thumping and her core to stop throbbing. She should be satiated, considering he'd woken her up twice during the night to continue wringing as many orgasms from her as possible.

'I'm sure he's had plenty of practice,' Chantal added, folding her arms across her chest.

'Don't go using that as a way to put distance between you. I can see what you're doing there.'

'I am not.'

'That's one thing I like about you, Chantal. You're a *terrible* liar.'

She huffed. Perhaps she would have been better walking. 'I don't need to put any distance between us because we agreed that it would be a one-night-only thing. Then we'd pretend it had never happened.'

'Gee, that sounds healthy.' Willa rolled her eyes.

'Why not? It's just sex—nothing more.' *I don't need any more, and I don't need him.*

'If it was just sex then why do you need to pretend it didn't happen?'

As much as she hated to admit it, Willa had a point. What was so bad about admitting that she'd had a one-night stand with Brodie?

Even thinking the words set a hard lump in her stomach. She'd been down this path before—men always started out fun, till the over-protectiveness stirred, control followed, and smothering wasn't far behind.

'Well, we don't want to upset Scott…'

'That's not it. Scott is totally head over heels for Kate. She's it for him. So I can guarantee he wouldn't care about you and Brodie hooking up.'

Why *did* she feel so funny about it? Perhaps admitting

it aloud meant it was real, and if it was real then it might happen again.

It's a slippery slope to disaster—remember that.

'Eight years is a long time to harbour feelings for someone. No wonder you're scared.'

'I'm *not* scared.' Chantal's lips pursed. 'And I have most certainly *not* been harbouring feelings for Brodie Mitchell for the last eight years.'

'I think the lady doth protest too much.' Willa stole a quick glance at Chantal, her amusement barely contained in a cheeky smile. 'You know, it *is* okay for you to like people—even annoyingly handsome men like Brodie.'

'I don't like him. I only wanted his body.' Her lip twitched.

Feelings for his body were a little easier to deal with than the possibility of feelings for him as a person. She had to shut this down right now. She did *not* have feelings for Brodie and she most certainly didn't want to start something permanent with him. It was a simple case of primitive, animalistic need. Relationships were not something on her horizon.

But no one had said anything about relationships, had they? Crap, why did it have to be so damn confusing? Head space came at a premium, and she could not afford to waste any spare energy on men, no matter how incredible their hands or mouth were.

'Uh, Chantal? I asked you a question.'

'Did you?' Great—now she'd lost her ability to even sustain basic conversation.

'Yes, I asked if you'd heard back after your audition.'

Sore point number two. 'Not yet. But it was only yesterday. They could take a little while to get back to me.'

'Do you think it went well?'

'Who the hell knows?' She sighed, rubbing her hands over her eyes. 'I can't tell any more.'

'I'm sure you'll land on your feet.' Willa reached over and squeezed her hand.

For a moment Chantal was terrified that she might cry. She hadn't allowed herself to shed any tears over her marriage or her failing career, and she didn't plan on opening the floodgates now. All that emotion was packed down tight. There would be time to cry when she'd secured herself a position with a dance company. For the time being tears were a waste of time and energy.

Thankfully Chantal was able to steer Willa to a safer topic. She was all too happy to talk about how things were going with Rob. Other people's lives were preferable talking points over the tricky, icky state of her career and her unwanted feelings towards Brodie.

Willa dropped Chantal off at the bar's parking lot, and she was almost surprised to find her car was still there. It was too crappy to steal, apparently.

Hitching her overnight bag higher on her shoulder, Chantal made her way around the back of the bar to the staff accommodation. She needed a hot shower, a cup of coffee and a lie down before she even attempted to get herself ready for another night of humiliation.

Her unit was number four. The metal number hung upside down on the door, one of its nails having rusted and fallen out. Holding her breath, she shoved the key into the lock and turned. The room didn't smell quite as bad as the bar, but the stale air still made her recoil as she entered the room.

'Home sweet home,' she muttered, dumping her bag onto the bed. *'Not.'*

The small room was almost entirely filled with an ancient-looking double bed covered in a faded floral quilt. A light flickered overhead, casting an eerie yellow glow over walls that were badly in need of a new paint job. A crack stretched down one wall, partially covered by a photo frame containing a generic scenery print. It was probably the picture that had come with the frame.

A quick peek at the bathroom revealed chipped blue tiles, a shower adorned with a torn plastic curtain and a sink that looked as though it needed a hardcore bleach application.

Chantal dropped down onto the bed and checked her phone. Nothing. What was she expecting? Brodie to be calling? Asking her to come back?

Something dark scuttled across the floor by her feet. Chantal drew her knees up to her chest and wrapped her arms around her legs.

She would not cry. She would *not* cry.

Brodie woke to the sound of his phone vibrating against the nightstand. He stretched, palm smoothing over the space next to him in the bed. The *empty* space.

Grinding a fist into his eyes, he forced the fogginess away. What time was it? He groped for his phone, fumbling with the passcode. It was a text from Scott.

Bro, I thought we were going for a run? Where are you?

Run? It was three o'clock in the afternoon. Crap, how had *that* happened?

Sorry, got caught up. Will have to reschedule.

The bed sheets were tangled around his legs and he caught a brief flash of Chantal's ocean-coloured dress peeking out from underneath his jeans in the corner of the room—a sure sign that the lavish images of losing himself in her body over and over weren't from a dream.

His phone immediately pinged with a new message.

Got caught up with what? Or should I say who?

Ugh. Where was Chantal? His feet hit the ground, thighs protesting as he stood. Yep, that was a sign of one hell of a night. He stretched, forcing his arms up overhead and pressing against the tightness in his muscles. Damn, he felt good.

He poked his head into the en-suite bathroom. No Chantal there. Padding out to the kitchen, he typed a message back to Scott.

No comment.

She wasn't in the kitchen either. Why hadn't she woken him? He wandered out onto the deck to see if she was doing any of her yoga stuff. Nope, nothing there either.

He raked a hand through his hair, coming back to the kitchen and flicking the coffee machine on. It whirred, grinding beans and then flooding the room with its delicious, fresh-brewed coffee scent.

Weak. Not that it takes a genius to figure it out...

Scott had a point. It had been bound to happen between him and Chantal. Their tension had been through the roof back then, and eight years hadn't dampened it at all. It had been a special kind of torture having Chantal back in his life...even if only for a short period of time.

Last night had been easily the best night of his life. But only because she was insanely hot and did things with her mouth that would make the most experienced of men blush. It was a conquest thing—a very long-awaited notch on his belt.

Yeah, right.

Okay, so maybe he normally woke up *hoping* the girl

had made a quick exit…if he'd even brought her back to his place. Normally he opted to go to hers, so he had control over a quick getaway.

But something about Chantal's leaving didn't sit well with him. He felt the absence of her keenly—almost as if he wasn't ready for it to be over. Understandable, since he'd been lusting after her for such a long time. He needed a little while longer to get it out of his system. Like forever.

So much for the 'hands off your mates' rule.

Frowning, he plucked his espresso cup from the coffee machine and breathed deeply. Where could she have disappeared to? Surely she hadn't gone back to that crappy bar on her own? His chest clenched, fingers tightening around the china cup.

The thought of her getting back up on that stage, dancing in front of those men… It was enough to unsettle even the most relaxed guy. He sipped the coffee, relishing the rich flavour on his tongue, but it didn't satisfy him as much as usual. After tasting Chantal all other flavours would pale in comparison, of that he was sure.

Perhaps the dance company had called her in for another audition? Not likely, since she'd only auditioned yesterday. She *couldn't* be back at that bar. How would she have got there on her own? Her car had never come back to Sydney.

His phone vibrated again, and he was about to curse Scott's name when Willa's photo flashed up.

'Hello?'

'Hey, Brodes.'

The traffic in the background told him she was calling from the road.

'I wanted to let you know I drove Chantal back to Newcastle.'

Dammit. 'When?'

'I dropped her off about an hour ago—I'm still on my way back. It's a long drive! Thought you might want to know, since I got the impression she hadn't said anything to you this morning.'

'She hadn't.'

'I don't like the idea of her staying at that place.'

He let out a sharp breath. 'Neither do I. I wouldn't have let her go…'

'That's probably why she didn't tell you.' She sighed. 'I only took her because I knew she'd find her own way if I said no. I didn't want her hitchhiking or anything like that.'

He swore under his breath. 'She makes me lose my cool, Willa.'

'She must be the only girl ever.'

He ignored the jibe. 'I'll go get her.'

'Good.'

By the time Brodie had sailed back up the coast, the sun had dipped low in the sky and his blood had reached boiling point. He wasn't sure what made him angrier: the fact that she'd left him the morning after or that she'd returned to a crappy job that was not only beneath her but a possible threat to her safety.

Okay, maybe he was overreacting, but that bar *was* shady. The guys who hung around it were rough. He could only imagine what the on-site accommodation looked like. The thought of one of those men following her after she'd finished her shift…

His fists clenched. He *had* to get her out of there.

He strode across the car park, ignoring the catcalls from a group of scantily clad girls leaning against a souped-up ute with neon lights and chrome rims. Inside, a band belted out metal music, the screaming vocals grating on his nerves.

Bypassing the growing crowd, he took the stairs up to the second floor. Would he be able to grab her before she performed or would he have to sit through the sweet torture of watching her up on that stage again?

The bass thumped deep in his chest as he climbed the stairs. Chantal wasn't on stage. Instead the crowd was cheering for an older woman wearing sparkling hearts over her nipples. Brodie squinted. Were those *tassels*? The stage was littered with a pair of silk gloves, a feather boa, and something that looked like a giant fan made of peacock feathers. The woman shook her chest, sending the tassels flying in all directions.

Find Chantal now! Otherwise she might be the next one on stage, shaking her tassels.

Two girls who sat at the bar looked as though they might be dancers. Their sparkly make-up, elaborate outfits and styled hair certainly seemed to suggest it.

'Excuse me ladies,' he said, approaching them. 'I'm looking for a friend of mine who dances here.'

'*I* can be your friend who dances here.' The blonde batted her false lashes at him, silver glitter sparkling with each blink.

'We come as a pair.' The redhead chuckled, tossing her hair over one shoulder.

'That's tempting,' he said, turning on a charming smile. 'And I'm sure you're both a lot of fun. But I need to find a girl called Chantal.'

'You can call me whatever you like, sugar.' Red winked, blowing him a kiss from her highly glossed crimson lips.

'Are you her boyfriend?' asked Blonde, tracing a lacquered finger up the length of his shirt. 'Most of the girls here don't stick to one guy. They get too jealous.'

'The guys?'

Blonde nodded. 'They start fights. You're not going to start a fight, are you?'

'I'm a lover, not a fighter.'

He watched the bartender eyeing him. The guy was old,

but his arms were covered in faded prison tattoos. Brodie directed his eyes back to the girls.

'You sure look like a lover.' Red licked her lips. 'A good one, too. But all guys go crazy for the right girl.'

'Chantal is a friend. So, have you seen her?'

'A friend? Right.' Blonde laughed. 'If she was just a friend you wouldn't be here with that puppy love face, looking for her.'

He opened his mouth to argue but snapped it shut. Trying to reason with these two would be a waste of time—time that could be better spent looking for Chantal and getting her the hell out of this hole.

'Thanks for your time, ladies.'

'Good luck, lover boy.' Red chortled as he walked away.

He stood by the bar and scanned the room. Mostly men, a few women who might or might not be dancers, muscle stationed by the stairwell and by an exit on the other side of the stage. That must be where the dancers went backstage.

He was about to attempt to get past the muscle when he spotted Chantal. In denim shorts and a white tank top, she looked dressed for the beach rather than a bar. But her face and hair were made up for the stage. She had a bag over one shoulder. Perhaps she'd already danced?

As she attempted to weave through the crowd someone stopped her. A guy much bigger than her put his hands on her arms and she tried to wriggle out of his grasp. The bouncer looked on with mild amusement, but made no attempt to step in and protect Chantal.

Brodie rushed forward, grabbing her by the arm and yanking her back against him. She yelped in surprise, but relief flooded her face when she realised it was him. She stepped back, standing partially behind him.

'Is there a problem, mate?' The guy towered over Brodie, and he saw a snake tattoo peeking out of the edge of his dark T-shirt.

'Yeah, you had your hands on my girl.' He looked the guy dead in the eye, ready to fight if it came to that.

A wave of guilt washed over him. Was this how Scott had felt that night at Weeping Reef?

He shoved the thought aside and pushed Chantal farther behind him. Nothing mattered now but getting her out safely.

'Maybe you shouldn't be letting her parade around in next to nothing, then.' He leered, exposing an aggressive gap-toothed smile. 'Some of the guys here aren't as easy-going as me.'

Brodie turned, wrapped his arm around Chantal's shoulders and steered her towards the stairs. They moved through the throng of people and he didn't let go of her. Not once.

'What are you doing here?' she asked as they exited the bar. Her brows were narrowed, and her face was streaked with conflicting emotions.

It wasn't dark yet. An orb of gold sat low on the horizon while the inky shades of night bled into the sky. Chantal hovered at the entrance of the bar, her eyes darting from the driveway to the accommodation and back to him. The red neon sign from the bar flickered at odd intervals.

'I'm saving your butt—that's what I'm doing.' He raked a hand through his hair, tremors of adrenaline still running through him. 'I'm giving you a place to stay.'

'I have a place to stay.' The defiance in her voice rang out in the night air, and her fists were balled by her sides.

'And how is it? I'm assuming you came back here after you hauled arse this morning?'

The breeze ruffled her dark hair, sending a few strands into her eyes. She blew them away. 'I did.'

'And?'

She folded her arms across her chest. 'It's serviceable.'

'And you'd take "serviceable" over a luxury yacht? Or would that just be to spite me?'

Why was he even worried? She either wanted to stay or she didn't. They weren't in a relationship. So why was the thought of her staying here alone like a stake through his gut?

Too many years playing big brother—that's all it is.

'I'm not trying to spite you, Brodie.' She sighed. 'But I don't need you following me around playing macho protector.'

'What would have happened if I hadn't been here?' He threw his hands up in the air, the mere thought of anyone harming her sending his instincts into overdrive.

'I would have handled it.'

'Oh, yeah? How?'

She waved a hand at him. 'I can look after myself, Brodie. I've done it without your help for the last eight years.'

'I would have been here the second you asked.'

Her face softened, but she didn't uncross her arms. 'But I didn't ask, did I? That's because I'm fine on my own.'

'It didn't look like you were going to be fine tonight.'

'That's *your* perception.'

How could she not see the danger? Was she actually that blind or was it all a ruse so he'd believe her strong and capable? He *did* think she was strong and capable, but the facts still stood. A huge guy would easily overpower her petite frame, no matter what skills she had. Her refusal to accept his help made him worry more.

'Only an idiot couldn't see the path that you almost went down.'

'Only *this* idiot?' She rolled her eyes, flattening her palm to her chest. 'I'm not a damsel in distress—no matter how much you fantasise about it.'

'You think I fantasise about you being in trouble?' Rage tore through him. If only she knew the fear that had coursed through him when he'd realised where she was today.

She opened her mouth to retort, but changed her mind. 'I don't think that, Brodie. But I want you to understand that this thing between us is just sex. You're not obligated to be my bodyguard.'

The words hit him like a sledge-hammer to his solar plexus. *Just sex.* Of course that was all it was. That was what they'd agreed last night... So why did he feel as if she was tearing something away from him?

'Come back to the boat.' He set a hard stare on her, challenging her. 'For *just sex.*'

'I don't want you coming back into the bar.' She loosened her arms, pursing her lips. Her eyes were blackened and heavy, her lips full. 'You don't need to rescue me.'

'Fine.'

It went against every fibre of his being, but he would have agreed to anything to get her away from the bar at that point. He would deal with the consequences next time he turned up to rescue her—because hell would freeze over before he let her put herself in danger. She could get as mad as she liked.

She eyed him warily. 'Okay, then. Let's go.'

CHAPTER EIGHT

THEY WALKED AROUND the side of the bar to the staff accommodation so she could retrieve her bag. Going back to his boat felt like giving in, which seemed spineless after her great escape that morning. But the guy from the bar *had* shaken her. His disgusting words whispered into her ear along with the sickly scent of cheap whisky and Coke had made her stomach churn. Brodie had showed up at the right time and, though she would *never* admit it, she wasn't quite sure how she would have got herself out of that situation.

But it was a slippery slope from accepting help to being controlled, and she would never go there again.

A pale yellow beam from an outside security light spilled into the tiny motel-like room, causing shadows to stretch and claw at the walls. She wanted to be here about as much as she wanted to stab herself in the eye with a stiletto. But the alternative wasn't exactly peachy. Another night on Brodie's boat…another night of searing temptation and slowly losing her mind.

True to his word, he hadn't mentioned them sleeping together, but the evening was young. Something about the way he watched her pack told her he wasn't here out of friendly concern alone.

'How many more shifts do you have?' he asked, hovering by the door.

He stayed close but didn't touch her. Still, she was fully

aware of the heat and intensity radiating off him. He wore a shirt tonight, soft white cotton with sleeves rolled up to his elbows. A thin strip of leather hung around his neck, weighted with a small silver anchor. A silver watch sat on one wrist, contrasting against his deep tan.

'I've got a month in total,' she replied. 'They're pushing for more, though.'

'You're not going to stay, are you?'

'If I don't find something else I might not have a choice.' She faced away from him, stuffing the few items she'd unpacked back into her overnight bag. 'A girl's gotta eat.'

He frowned. 'There must be something else you could do.'

'Yeah, I could wait tables or work as a checkout chick at a supermarket. No matter how bad this is, it's *still* dancing. It means I haven't given up.'

Slinging her bag over one shoulder, she walked out of the room and slammed the door shut behind her.

Silence. She sensed a begrudging acceptance from him.

'No word on the audition?'

'Not yet.'

Once on the yacht, Chantal stashed her things in the guest room, hoping it signalled to Brodie that she had no intention of sleeping with him again. Incredible as they were together, it was clear she needed to focus on her current situation. She was already taking way too much from Brodie. She couldn't rely on him, his yacht or his money. She'd made this mess—she needed to get herself out of it.

'Why don't you grab a shower and I'll get dinner on the go?' he said, already pulling a frying pan from the kitchenette cupboard.

'Are you trying to tell me I smell?' She smirked, leaning against the breakfast bar.

Soft denim stretched over the most magnificent butt she'd ever laid eyes on as he bent down. He was the perfect shape. Muscular, but not OTT bulky. Broad, masculine, powerful. She swallowed, her mouth dry and scratchy.

'If I thought you smelled I would come right out and say it.' He looked over his shoulder, blond hair falling into his eyes.

He mustn't have shaved this morning. Blond stubble peppered his strong jaw, making the lines look even sharper and more devastating. Golden hair dusted his forearms, and she knew that his chest was mostly bare except for a light smattering around his nipples and the trail from his belly button down. She couldn't get that image out of her head.

'Hurry up—before I drag you there myself.'

He said the words without turning around, and Chantal thanked her lucky stars that he didn't. The words alone were potent enough, without the cheeky smile or glint she knew would be in his eyes.

'Then you'll be in trouble.'

The steam and hot water did nothing to wash away the tension in her limbs, nor the aching between her thighs. Wasn't a shower supposed to be cleansing? The quiet sound of rushing water only gave her time to replay the most delicious parts of last night, and she stepped out onto the tiles feeling more wound up than before.

A mouth-watering scent wafted in the air as she slipped into a loose black dress, and padded barefoot into the kitchen. The table was set for two. Intimate...personal.

Two glasses held white wine the colour of pale gold. White china rimmed in silver sported a faint criss-cross pattern—simple, but undeniably luxurious. A bowl of salad sat in the middle of the table.

'Pan-fried salmon with roasted potatoes and baby carrots.' He brought two plates to the table. 'Not fancy, but it *is* healthy—and pretty darn tasty, if I do say so myself.'

'I didn't know you could cook.'

'I'm a man of many talents, Chantal.' He set the plates down and dropped into the seat across from her. 'I thought you would have figured that out by now.'

She rolled her eyes, cutting into the salmon steak and sighing at the sight of the perfectly cooked fish. 'Does it get annoying, being good at everything?'

'No.' He grinned and speared a potato.

They picked up their glasses and clinked them together. The bell-like sound rang softly in the air. Crystal glasses. *Of course they're crystal—this is a boat for rich people... not people like you.*

Chantal shoved the thought aside and sipped her wine. 'Did you do a lot of cooking at home?'

'I did, actually. I was probably the only fifteen-year-old kid who cooked dinner for the family most nights of the week.'

'Really?'

She couldn't hide her surprise. He hardly seemed like the kind of guy who would be in charge of a household. But the salmon melted on her tongue, and the tangy aromatics of a lemon and ginger marinade danced in sensational delight. He didn't cook in the way most people did, where the food was functional first and foremost. He had talent—a knack for flavour and texture.

'Yep. Mum was a nurse and she often worked afternoons and nights. The cooking was left up to me.'

'What about your dad?'

'He wasn't around.' Brodie frowned. 'Dad was an artist, and he had a lot more passion for painting than he did for his family.'

'That's sad.'

'Yeah... I was fine, but the girls really needed him—especially Lydia. She remembered him more than the twins and Ellen.' He reached for his wine, looking as though he were about to continue the thread of conversation but changing his mind at the last minute. 'What about you? Were you the house chef?'

'I can do the basics. My mum worked long hours too, so I had to fend for myself a fair bit.' She swallowed down the guilt that curled in her stomach whenever she thought about her mother. 'I can do a basic pasta…salads. That kind of thing.'

'What does your mother do?'

'She's a cleaner.' Chantal bit down on her lip, wishing the memories weren't still so vivid. 'I don't think she's ever worked less than two jobs her whole life.'

His eyes softened. Damn him. She didn't want his sympathy.

'What about your dad?'

'He left when I was ten.' She shrugged, stabbing her fork at a lettuce leaf more forcefully than she needed to.

'Siblings?'

'None. Probably sounds strange to someone with such a big family.' *Good—turn the conversation back to him.*

'Yep—four sisters and never a moment of peace.'

She envied the contented smile on his lips. It was obvious his family was important to him. She'd bet they would be close, despite his father's absence. The kind of family who had big, raucous Christmas gatherings and loads of funny traditions. So different from her. They'd been so poor at one point that her mother had wrapped her Christmas present—a Barbie doll from the local second-hand shop—in week-old newspaper. The memory stabbed at her heart, scything through the softest part of her. The part she kept under lock and key.

'It drove me nuts, growing up,' he continued. 'But I became amazingly proficient at hair braids and reading bedtime stories.'

Her stomach churned. 'You'll make a great dad one day.'

A dark shadow passed over his face. The wall dropped

down in front of him so fast and so resolutely that Chantal wondered what she'd said. A sardonic smile twitched the corner of his lips. Okay, so there *were* some things that put Brodie in a bad mood.

'I don't want the white-picket-fence deal.' He drained the rest of his wine and reached for the bottle to empty the remaining contents into his glass. 'Marriage, kids, pets… not for me. I've got enough responsibility now.'

'Cheers to that.' They clinked glasses again.

He quirked a brow. 'But you got married.'

'Just because I did it once it doesn't mean I'll do it again.' Her cheeks burned. '*That* debacle is over for good.'

The wine had loosened her limbs a little, and it seemed her tongue as well. She probably shouldn't have accepted the shot of whisky one of the other dancers had offered her before she went onstage. But she'd so desperately needed Dutch courage to force her back onstage.

'Sounds like there's a story there.'

'Maybe.' She shrugged.

Could she claw back her words? Brodie didn't need to see the ugly bits of her life…especially not after she'd gone to such efforts to hide them. Then again, did it really matter?

'I've seen you naked, remember.' He grinned.

How could she possibly forget?

'No point keeping secrets from me now.'

She took a deep breath and decided to throw caution to the wind. After all, he knew her most devastating secret: that her career had turned to crap. What harm could another failure do if it was out in the open?

'The short version is that I was young, naive and I married the wrong guy.'

'And the full version?'

'I married my agent,' she said, rolling her eyes and

taking another sip of her wine. 'What a bloody cliché. He seemed so worldly, and I was a wide-eyed baby. We met a month after I left Weeping Reef, and he promised he'd make me a star. He did—for a while—but then he started treating me like his student rather than his wife. He wanted everything his way, all the time.'

Brodie held his breath... *Dammit.* If she asked, wild horses wouldn't keep him from finding the dude and teaching him a very painful, very permanent lesson. Fists clenched, he drew in a slow breath.

'I couldn't take it. The constant criticism, the arguing...' Her olive eyes glittered and she shook her head. 'Nothing I did met his expectations—he smothered me. Pushed all my friends away until I could only rely on him. I couldn't forgive that.'

'Good.' The word came out through clenched teeth and Brodie realised his jaw had started to ache. 'A guy like that doesn't deserve your forgiveness. What an arse.'

'Yeah, *major* arse.' Her lips twisted into a grimace. 'We ended up separating, and the divorce went through about six months ago. I've been trying to find work but I keep bombing out.'

'Why do you think that is?'

'I don't know.' She shook her head, despair etched into her face. 'Maybe after being told for so long that I don't work hard enough, that I'm not disciplined enough, I've started to believe it...'

'That's complete crap and you know it.' He gripped the edge of his seat, knuckles white from lack of circulation. How could anyone not see the lengths that she went to in order to achieve her goals? She deserved every success in the world.

She managed a wan smile. 'So there you have it: the failings of the not-so-great Chantal Turner. I can't keep a career and I can't keep a man. I can't even book a goddamn dancing job without getting myself into trouble.'

'It's not your fault,' he ground out. His stomach pitched, and the need to bundle her up in his arms thrashed like a wild beast inside him.

'Oh, but it is.'

She drained another glass of wine. Was that two or three? Not that it mattered. He'd keep her safe on the boat tonight. He'd protect her.

'I've done all these things myself. My judgment—my errors.'

'You *can* ask for help.'

She shook her head, dark locks flicking around her shoulders. 'No. I got myself in trouble—I'll get myself out. Besides, I'd need to trust people. I can't do that.'

Her vulnerability shattered him. She'd worked for everything she had—chased it and made sacrifices for it. It wasn't fair that she was here, feeling as if she'd stuffed everything up. He wanted to erase the pain from her voice, smooth the tension from her limbs and barricade her from the dangers of the world.

'You can't go back to that accommodation.' It wasn't a question, and it wasn't a suggestion.

'I need to stay somewhere, Brodie. I need to find a damn supermarket and cook myself a meal.' She shook her head. 'I need to get my life together.'

He wondered if, in her head, she'd told herself that she couldn't rely on him. But he wanted her to... Against his better judgment, he *wanted* her to lean on him.

'Stay here—at least for now. That will give you time to find something else...something safer.' He grabbed her hand across the table, cursing internally when his blood pulsed hard and hot at the contact. 'I'll keep the boat docked here and you'll be close to the bar. Then we can wander around during the day. Have fun. Pretend life isn't such a pain in the butt.'

A small smile pulled at her lips as she retracted her hand from his grip. 'I don't know…'

'You don't have to trust me.'

Her eyes roamed his face before she shrugged her acceptance. 'So that's days and evenings sorted. What did you have planned for nights?'

He swallowed. It would be easy to come up with a list of things they could do at night, and most of them would make excellent use of her yoga flexibility. Hell, how would he keep his distance after what they'd shared last night? He didn't need things getting messy between them, and he certainly didn't want to do anything that would make him lose her again.

'What *about* nights? We can watch movies, chill out on the deck. Keep it PG-13.'

Totally chivalrous—he was simply being a good friend. Keeping an eye out for her. *Yeah, right.*

She smirked. 'Does PG-13 include kissing?'

'It might.'

'Heavy petting?'

'That sounds like it could lead to something a little more X-rated.'

'I want to know what kind of tricks you might try to pull—what loopholes you might use.'

'If I want something I make it happen. Loopholes or no loopholes.'

'Yes, you certainly do.' Her eyes flashed, pupils widening as she shifted in her seat.

Her foot brushed his leg under the table. Had she done it on purpose? He couldn't read her face—couldn't tell whether her flirtatious tone was meant to bait him or mock him. She pushed her plate away and leant back in her chair.

One bronzed leg crossed over the other and the hem of her dress crept up to reveal precious inches of thigh.

'But you can't blame a girl for trying to protect herself,' she said.

'Why do you think you need to protect yourself around me?'

'To make sure history doesn't repeat itself.' She stretched her arms, dragging the dress farther up her thighs. If she kept up the pace she'd be naked soon, and he'd be on his knees. Not a bad thing, given the way she'd cried his name last night.

Cut it out. You're supposed to be helping her—not plotting her future orgasms.

'No more dancing?'

'You're far too tempting on the dance floor. All the girls at the resort thought so,' she said. Her eyes focused on something distant, something lost in memory. 'You're a magnet for the ladies.'

He hadn't cared too much what the other girls thought of him. Only Chantal's opinion had stuck like a thorn in his side.

'That was then.'

'And it's not the case now?' She threw him a derisive look. 'I see the way women look at you, Brodie.'

'Are you jealous?'

'Hardly.' Her brows narrowed, pink flaring across the apples of her cheeks.

He stood, collected the dishes and carried them to the kitchen. He returned moments later with a tub of ice cream and two spoons. No bowls, which would save some washing up. It was only a bonus that they'd need to sit close to share the tub.

'Anything else off-limits?'

He opened the tub and stuck his spoon in, scooping a

small portion of the salted caramel and macadamia ice cream and shoving it into his mouth.

His eyes shut as the sensations danced on his tongue. Sweet, creamy vanilla ice cream, swirls of sticky, salty caramel, and the crunch of toasted nuts. It was heavenly.

It would taste even better if he was able to eat it off that deliciously flat stomach of hers.

Pleasure sounds came from the back of her throat as her lips wrapped around the other spoon. She dragged it out of her mouth slowly and Brodie salivated watching her. If the ice cream was delicious, then *she* was the dessert of the heavens.

'I might have to make this ice cream off-limits. I don't think I'll be able to stop myself polishing off the whole damn tub.' She sighed and dug her spoon back in. 'But we can't let it go to waste—that wouldn't be right.'

'I'll take you for a run tomorrow morning.'

He sucked another tasty morsel from his spoon, focusing on it rather than on Chantal and how her lips looked as if they were made for every kind of X-rated fantasy he'd ever had.

'That should restore some balance.'

'I don't know if I could keep up with you,' she said, tilting her head and toying with her spoon.

'You can definitely keep up.'

Were they still talking about running? She stabbed the ice cream with her spoon, leaving the silver handle sticking straight up like an antenna.

'Tell me more about your family,' she said. 'And please take that ice cream away before I eat myself into oblivion.'

He grabbed the tub, pulled out her spoon and replaced the lid before wandering into the kitchen with her close on his heels. As she climbed up onto a bar stool at the kitchen bench, her legs not quite touching the ground, he felt walls shoot up around him. *Good.* At least some of his defences remained intact. He'd been sure she'd somehow dismantled them.

'Why the sudden interest in my family?'

'I don't know.' She shrugged. 'I felt like you were a bit of a mystery while we were at the reef...and you *did* say we were friends. I know most of my other friends better than I know you.'

'I think we've had enough talking tonight.' He shut the freezer door a little more forcefully than he needed to.

Images of her naked, bending into those damn yoga positions, trailing her hair across his stomach, all invaded him with equal combative power. He wanted her again... and again and again. But they *were* friends. She'd just confirmed it. Breaking the rule once was excusable—heat of the moment and all that—but twice was playing with fire.

He couldn't afford to entangle himself in another relationship, no matter how temporary. He had his priorities all worked out: build his business, take care of his family. That was it. Simple. Straightforward. Uncomplicated.

Chantal Turner was like an addictive substance, and everyone knew the first hit was the best. He'd had his taste—time to move on. She needed to be put squarely in the friend zone.

'I'm going to bed.' He stretched his arms above his head, not missing the way her eyes lingered on him. 'Got to get up early for that run.'

'Sweet dreams.' She hopped off the bar stool, her face in an unreadable mask, and headed to her room.

'Undoubtedly,' he muttered.

The digital clock in the bedroom mocked her with each hour that passed, its red glow holding sleep at an arm's length. She tossed and turned, twisting the sheets into knots around her limbs. What was wrong with her?

Brodie refused to leave her mind alone. One minute he

was hot for her and sharing things about himself, the next he was done talking and wanted to sleep.

It's a good thing he had the guts to do what you couldn't.

Was it possible that now he'd got what he wanted, she was out of his system? That thought shouldn't have rankled, but it did—and with surprising force. Surely eight years of unrequited sexual tension couldn't be over in one night?

Why should she care?

Shaking her head, she turned over onto her side and huffed. It was clear that she'd become unhinged. Perhaps her inability to find a real job was slowly driving her insane, making her more sensitive to things that should have meant nothing. Only Brodie didn't mean nothing…did he?

The bedroom suddenly felt too confined, too tight for her to breathe. Chantal swung her legs out of the bed and stood, relishing the feeling of the smooth floorboards on her bare soles.

She padded out to the deck and tipped her face up, her breath catching at the sight of the full, ripe moon hanging in a cloudless sky dotted with stars. In Sydney the city lights illuminated everything twenty-four-seven and the stars weren't visible. She'd missed them.

Growing up in a small coastal town had meant night after night of sparkling sky—endless opportunities to place a wish on the first one that winked at her. Perhaps that was why everything was falling to pieces now? It had been a long time since she'd made a wish. She closed her eyes, but her mind couldn't seem to form a coherent thought. She knew what she wanted to wish for…didn't she? Her stomach twisted itself into a knot and her breath shortened to shallow puffs.

What if things didn't turn around? What if the dive bar was her best option? *Don't think like that, you* have *to be positive. You have to keep trying...try harder!*

Alone, she felt tears prickle her eyes. The sadness was pushing its way to the surface, mingling with her ever-present panic like blood curling in water. She needed to hang on a little while longer—long enough to get something—*anything*—which would prove she hadn't wasted her mother's sacrifices and her own hard work. Then she could deal with the bad stuff.

'What are you doing up?'

Brodie's sleep-roughened voice caught her off guard. She whirled around, blinking back the tears and pleading with herself to calm down. She didn't want him to see her like this—not when she felt she was about to fall apart at the seams.

'Are you okay?'

She nodded, unable to speak for fear that releasing words might open the floodgates of all she held back. Her breathing was so shallow and fast that the world tilted at her feet. She pressed a palm to her cheek, mentally willing him to leave her. Her face was as warm as if she'd spent the night sleeping next to an open fire, and her skin prickled uncomfortably.

'You don't look okay.' He stepped closer and captured her face in his hands, studying her with his emerald eyes.

That only made it worse. By now her palms were slick with perspiration and her stomach swished like the ocean during a storm. Tremors racked her hands and her dignity was slipping away faster than she could control it. She was drowning, and once again she was relying on him to save her.

'Hey, it's all right,' he soothed, moving his hands to her shoulders and rubbing slowly up and down her arms. 'Let's get you a glass of water.'

He pulled her against his side, wrapping an arm around her shoulder and guiding her into the cabin. Setting her down on a stool, he grabbed a glass and pressed it against the ice machine on the fridge. Loud clinking noises filled the room as the ice tumbled into the glass, followed by the glug of water from a bottle in the fridge.

Breathe in—one, two, three. Out—one, two, three.

'Drink it slowly—don't gulp.' He handed her the glass and smoothed her hair back from her face.

No doubt she looked like a crazy person, huffing and puffing like the wolf from that nursery rhyme. Her hair would be all over the place, sticking out like a mad professor's. It was only then she realised that she was practically naked, with a pair of white lace panties her only keeper of modesty. She hadn't thought it possible for her face to get any hotter, but it did.

'Thanks,' she mumbled, shaking her hair so it fell in front of her, covering her bare breasts.

She must have ditched her T-shirt while she was trying to get to sleep. Stress overheated her. Most of the time she slept in nothing at all—unless it was the dead of winter, and then she wore her favourite llama-print pyjamas. But it was warm on the boat and her body was reaching boiling point. She pressed the cool glass to her burning cheek.

You're rambling in your head—not a good sign. Calm. Down. Now.

'Do you want me to grab you something to wear?'

Brodie's voice cut into her inner monologue and she nodded mutely, switching the glass of water to her other cheek. Her whole body flamed. Shame tended to do that. This was exactly why she should have said no to the invitation to Brodie's boat in the first place! Now he knew… He knew what a mess she was. She couldn't even fall asleep without working herself up.

'Here.'

He took the glass from her hand and set it down, helping her weakened limbs into the armholes of a T-shirt and guiding her head through the neck opening.

The fabric swam on her, smoothing over her curves and giving her protection. The T-shirt was his—it smelled of him. Smelled of ocean air and soap and earthy maleness.

'Are these panic attacks a recent thing?' He leant against the bench, his face neutral.

'No, I've had them a while.' She couldn't look him in the eye.

'They suck,' he said. 'My little sister gets them pretty bad too. Water usually works for her.'

Chantal bit down on her lip, toying with the glass before taking another sip. Could she be any more humiliated right now?

'It's nothing to be ashamed of. You know that, right?'

He touched her arm, the gentle brush making her stomach flip. Her breathing slowed a little.

'Ellen gets them a lot. She's only nineteen, but she puts a lot of pressure on herself to do well. She wants to get into a performing arts school.'

'What does she do?' Curiosity piqued, she looked up.

Brodie dropped down onto the stool next to her, his knees inches from her thighs. 'She plays piano pretty damn well, if I do say so myself. I used to run her to practise when I lived at home—went to all her recitals too. She's ace.'

The pride in his voice was unmistakable. Chantal had often wondered what it would be like to have siblings—to look after someone other than herself, to worry about people all the time. She would have been a terrible sister—she couldn't even keep her own life together, let alone help anyone else.

'Then there's the twins: Jenny and Adriana. They're twenty-two, and as different as two people can be. Jenny is the loud one. She got into modelling a while ago and has done a fair bit of travelling with it. Adriana is still studying. She's going to end up being a doctor of something one day.' He smiled. 'Then Lydia is the oldest… she's twenty-four.'

His eyes darkened for a moment and she wondered if he was going to continue. His lips pulled into a flat line as he raked a hand through his hair, stopping to rub the back of his neck.

'Lydia is in a wheelchair. She was in a car accident some years ago and she was paralysed from the waist down.'

'That's awful.'

'Yeah.' A sad smiled passed over his lips. 'She wanted to be a dancer.'

Emotion ran through her—grief for this poor girl whom she didn't even know, for the sadness on Brodie's face and for what their family must have gone through. At least she could still dance. Her heart swelled. He cared so deeply about his family. For all her jokes about his carefree attitude, he was a good person.

He drew a breath, steadying his gaze on her. 'So there you go. You wanted to know something else about my family—it's not all sunshine and roses.'

'I guess we've all got our stuff to deal with.' She downed the rest of her water. 'I nearly gave up dancing once.'

'Really?' His blond brows arched.

'It wasn't long after my dad left. We didn't have a lot of money and Mum had lost her job cleaning one of the local motels.' The memory flowed through her, singeing her heart with the same scorching hurt that came every time she remembered what life had been like back then. 'She picked up cleaning work at my school. The kids used to tease me, so I told her that I wanted her to find another job…but there aren't a lot of jobs in little beach towns.'

Why was she telling him this? She hadn't told *anyone* this story—not because she was ashamed of having grown up with no money, but because she'd been so horrible to her mother. More than a decade and a half later, guilt over her behaviour lingered.

'She gave me a choice. Give up dancing and she would quit her job at the school—because that's what it was paying for. Otherwise, if I wanted to keep dancing, she had to keep working two jobs.' She squeezed her eyes shut for a moment. 'So I gave up dancing for a week.'

'You can't blame yourself that. How old were you? Ten? You were just a kid.'

'I don't think I've ever hurt her as much as I did then.' She shook her head, amazed that it felt as though a weight had been lifted from her shoulders. 'I wish I could take it back.'

'I'm sure she knows how you feel.'

'I hope so. She gave up so much for me to be able to continue dancing. She hardly ever came to my competitions or exams because she was always working, but she never complained.' She let out a hollow laugh. 'Not once.'

'She never gave up?'

'Nope.' She shook her head. 'Which means *I* can't give up.'

'Sounds like you got a lot of your tenacity from her.'

The tenderness in his voice sparked her insides, lighting up her whole body—as if he had a direct 'on' switch to her nervous system. Her hands were fluttering in her lap. The desire to reach out and touch him made her fingers tingle. If she didn't put some distance between them—and fast—she'd do something stupid.

'Thanks for the drink.'

She went to hop off her stool but Brodie's hand came down on her bare thigh. His fingers skimmed over her knee, touching the hem of the T-shirt. The touch was so light she could easily convince herself that she was imagining things. Despite her brain shouting out warnings, she didn't want this to be a dream.

'Is it wrong that I couldn't sleep because I was thinking about you?' he asked.

His bare torso was the only thing she could look at. Broad shoulders, the ripple of muscle at his abdomen, the V that dipped below his cotton pyjama bottoms. He would be naked underneath them. She could tell from the inadequate way the thin fabric concealed the length of him.

Her breath hitched, and the sudden flutter of her heart had nothing to do with panic. 'You were the one who wanted to go to sleep.'

His hand inched up, the tips of his fingers slipping under her hem of the T-shirt. Each millimetre his hand travelled stoked the fire low in her belly, stirred the tension in her centre. She pressed her thighs together, rocking gently against the stool in the hope that it would ease the need in her.

It didn't.

Nothing would ease the need except him. He was the only solution to her problem, the only cure for her ailments. In that moment she was raw. Exposing her past had opened up something within her—a cavernous hunger long buried by insecurities and fear. He'd shown her it was safe to be who she was, to open up and allow herself to be vulnerable. She wanted nothing more than to wipe away the old hurt with new pleasures. To erase the parts of herself that clung to bad memories, to be a new person.

'You were the one who wanted to figure out what loopholes I might use to make a move on you,' he said, eyes blackened with desire.

'Have you thought of any yet? Because I could use a loophole right about now.'

CHAPTER NINE

IT WAS ALL the invitation he needed. Willpower was a fragile thing, easily overridden by blazing attraction, pent-up sexual tension, and too many dirty dreams. Could he take her into his bed a second time, knowing that it wasn't going anywhere? Knowing that he wouldn't *let* it go anywhere because his life didn't have room for her?

'Brodie?'

A plump lower lip was being dragged through her teeth, and the desperation in her voice urged the increased thumping of his heart.

Even if he'd wanted to pretend he wasn't interested he didn't have the opportunity. She jumped down from her stool and stood between his legs, her hands finding the rigid muscles in his thighs, brushing the aching hardness of his erection.

'We're friends.' He pushed off his stool and moved into the kitchen, opening the freezer door and pretending to look for something.

'Friends who have the hots for each other.' She echoed his words with a cheeky smile.

The cold of the freezer wasn't making him any less hard or any less horny. In fact it had only drawn his eyes to a chilled bottle of vodka. He wrapped his hand around the neck, savouring the ice-cold glass against his heated palm. A cold shower would have been better, but getting naked might prove dangerous.

'Tell you what,' she said, reaching past him and grabbing the bottle out of his hand. 'If you can drink a shot of this off me and still not want to sleep with me, I'll let you go back to bed.'

He slammed the freezer door shut and turned, resting his back against it. 'You'll *let* me?'

'Yes.' She unscrewed the bottle. 'I'll let you. And I won't mention it in the morning—or ever again.'

'Why are you suddenly trying to seduce me with body shots when before you were more concerned about setting up barriers?' He raked a hand through his hair and tried not to think about how naked she was under his T-shirt.

'Why the psychoanalysis?' She raised a brow. 'Can't a girl change her mind?'

'I have a rule about sleeping with my friends.'

'What happened to that rule last night?' She smirked. 'You didn't seem to be too worried about rules then. Or are you afraid that you won't be able to say no after your little drink?'

She knew how to fire up his competitive streak—and she *did* have a point. He hadn't been all that worried about his rule last night. But the rule existed for a reason. Sleeping with her would be messy in both the best and worst ways. It would mean dealing with the awkward aftermath and potentially losing their friendship if things went pear-shaped. He'd made an exception for Chantal because he'd wanted to get her out of his system, but now he was caught between taking the safe route and taking what he wanted.

That backfired, didn't it? Man up—do the shot and then go to bed.

'Fine.' He grabbed the bottle from her grip and located a shot glass.

As he turned around Chantal was slowly peeling off his

T-shirt. The white lace scrap covering her sex was revealed first, then a flat bronzed plane of stomach, two perfectly formed breasts, collarbones and a long mane of dark hair as she whipped the T-shirt off. He'd need a drink now. His tongue felt dry and heavy in his mouth.

'Ready?' She hoisted herself onto the bench.

'You still have to tell me why the sudden change of heart.' With a shaking hand he poured vodka into the shot glass.

'Maybe I realised that I should be grateful for the things I have, no matter how tough it is right now.' She lay back and stared intently at a spot on the roof, lower lip between her teeth.

He'd got to her with the story about his sister. Though he was hoping she'd apply it more to cutting herself some slack and persisting with her dance career—not to mention leaving that trashy bar—rather than to jumping back into bed with him.

'And you're grateful for having sex with me?'

'I'm grateful for orgasms.' Her head tilted so she could look at him. 'It's been a long time since I let myself have any fun.'

'It *is* fun, isn't it?' He stepped closer, smoothing a hand over her stomach. 'Just a bit of fun—nothing more.'

He poured the vodka into her belly button, the excess liquid spilling out onto her stomach. She let out a sharp cry at the coldness but he dropped his head and sucked, lashing his tongue across her belly and catching the liquid before it spilled onto the bench. It burned for a second, and then a smooth warmth spread through him.

The alcohol mingled with the taste of her warm skin. He ran his tongue down to the edge of her underwear, watching the slick trail he left behind. Her fingers thrust into his hair as he snapped at the waistband with his teeth, a low groan rumbling from deep inside her. He should have pulled away then, but the vodka felt good. It softened his edges, warmed his limbs. It made it easier to forget that sleeping with her was a bad idea.

A tasty, satisfying, *perfect* bad idea.

'Don't worry—I don't expect anything.' Her voice had become rough, husky. 'A bit of fun is exactly what I need. No strings, no obligation.'

'So you're not going to fall for me?'

The scratch of her lace underwear against his tongue sent a shiver through him. He pressed his lips to the peak of her sex and was rewarded with a gasp and the sharp bite of her nails against his scalp.

'You wish.'

Smooth skin beckoned to him. Hooking a finger beneath the waistband, he peeled her underwear down to mid-thigh, trapping her legs and preventing them from opening. His lips found the bare smooth skin of her centre, pressing down with agonising slowness. A quick swipe of his tongue had her hips bucking against him.

'This is cruel…and unusual.' Her hands dug deeper into his hair, wrenching his head up. 'I can't move properly.'

'Anticipation, Chantal. Just go with it.'

He grabbed her wrist and put her hand down by her hip, holding on so she couldn't move. His other hand teased her, his thumb rubbing against the sensitive bud of her clitoris in slow, circular movements. His tongue followed, parting her so he could claim her most sensitive spot between his lips. Her movement was restricted by the underwear holding her prisoner and she writhed against him in unfulfilled need.

'Please…' she panted. Her eyes had rolled back; her mouth was slack with pleasure. Her hair trailed over the side of the bench, brushing against the kitchen cupboards as she moved.

The sight of her laid out like an extravagant dessert

was almost enough to send him over. He wanted to taste every inch of her, keep her begging while he feasted. He released her from her lacy bindings and his fingers found her hot and wet. His mouth came up, capturing a bronzed nipple as she squirmed, grinding again his hand until her cries peaked.

She shouted his name over and over, until the syllables jumbled together into an incoherent decree of passion and release. Shock waves ran through her and he withdrew his hand slowly, gently. His mouth found hers, his tongue parting her lips and bringing her back to the moment.

'Still think I'm cruel?' he murmured against her mouth, sliding a hand beneath her neck to lift her into a sitting position.

She faced him, wrapping her legs around his waist. Heat enveloped him as her hand slid down the front of his pants and stroked his erection. She caressed him—long, slow movements designed to make him want something out of reach.

'I think you've got magic hands,' he said.

Hair tickled his chest as she rested her head against him, still touching him. He pressed into her hand, gasping at the sharp flare of pleasure that forced his eyes shut.

'Brodie?'

Olive eyes met his, the black of her pupils wide. Her tongue swiped along his lower lip, the taste of her tempting him.

'I want you inside me. Now.'

Her hands tugged down his pants, exposing him to the warmth of her thighs. He lifted her from the bench and carried her to the bedroom. They landed on the bed, her body pinned beneath his, and he reached out to his drawer and withdrew a condom. Sheathing himself, he plunged into her. His mouth slanted over hers, hot, demanding. He savoured her heat and tightness until she couldn't hold on.

Her muscles clenched around him—thighs around his waist, arms around his neck. He couldn't hold back, couldn't stop the desire to drown in her warm skin and open mouth. Burying his face against her hair, he brought her close to the edge again. She shook, holding on as if she were about to fly away.

'Let go,' he whispered. 'Just let go.'

And she did. Crying, shaking, gasping. Her orgasm ripped through her with an intensity that brought on his own release within seconds. He rode her slowly, until the waves of pleasure subsided.

The realisation that she wasn't in her own bed came swiftly when morning broke. Sunlight filtered into the room—Brodie's room—and the ache between her thighs confirmed that she hadn't imagined those naughty images of them in his kitchen. It wasn't a dream—it was the mind-bending truth.

Brodie was like peanut butter ice cream with extra fudge. Decadent, tasty, hard to say no to. But, like all delicious things, he wasn't the best choice she could have made. What she needed was a steady diet of apples and focus—not ice cream and orgasms.

'Morning,' he murmured against the back of her neck.

One arm was slung over her mid-section, turned slightly to expose the edge of his anchor tattoo. She traced the outline with her fingertip. Something firm dug into her lower back. She moved under the guise of stretching her back, smiling when he groaned and pressed against her.

'Don't start what you can't finish.'

She chuckled. 'You're insatiable.'

'Says you, Miss Body Shot. I was perfectly happy sleeping on my own last night.'

'Liar.' She rolled over, catching his stubble-coated jaw with her cupped hand.

He didn't hesitate to kiss her, his tongue delving and tangling with hers. A hand found her breast, fingers tugging and teasing her nipple until she gave in and let him roll on top of her.

'Weren't we supposed to be going for a run this morning?' she asked, blinking her eyes at him with faux innocence.

'I know a few other things we can do that will burn calories.'

Apples, not ice cream.

'Worried you won't be able to keep up?'

'Ha!' He grinned. 'Like I said before, don't start what you can't finish.'

'Oh, I can finish it.' She tipped her chin up at him, giving his chest a playful shove. 'Loser makes breakfast.'

'You're on.'

Chantal regretted making the challenge a few ks into the run, when it became clear that Brodie was much better at running than she was. He jogged effortlessly alongside her, breaking into a sprint every so often to prove he could. The Newcastle coast blurred past in a haze of blue skies, bluer waters and pale sand. How was it possible to be in such a beautiful place and not be able to enjoy the scenery?

'Can we take a break?' Chantal slowed to a walk and fanned her face.

'Conceding defeat already?' He jogged on the spot, a victorious grin on his face. 'You know that means you'll be making my scrambled eggs when we get back?'

'Fine. You win.' She waved him away as she took a long swig from her water bottle. 'Looks like dancing fitness doesn't translate to running fitness.'

'No need to make excuses,' he teased, and she elbowed him.

'No need to be a smug winner.'

He reached for her water bottle, tipping it to his lips and

gulping the liquid down. Muscles worked in his neck. It was hard not to stare at how he made the most regular of actions seem inherently male.

'It's not often I get one over you, so let me have my moment. Besides, I've got a long way to go if I'm going to run a half marathon.'

Her brows furrowed. 'You're training for a marathon?'

'*Half* marathon,' he corrected.

'How far is that?'

'Just over twenty-one k.'

'Funny how you didn't tell me that when you let me challenge you to a run.' She narrowed her eyes at him. 'Cheater.'

A booming laugh erupted, startling a woman jogging past with her small dog. 'That's not cheating.'

'Why on earth do you want to run that far?'

He shrugged. 'To see if I can do it. A buddy challenged me, and you know how I am with challenges.'

'It just seems…' She took in the gleam of his tanned skin, the T-shirt that hugged his full biceps, the golden hair on his athletic legs. 'Out of character.'

'Why? Because I don't have the discipline to be a runner?' A bitter tone tainted the words.

'No, I meant because you're more of a water sports kinda guy.' She cocked her head, studying him. 'Windsurfing, sailing boats, water-skiing…that kind of thing.'

'Oh.' A smile tugged at the corner of his lips.

'I always wondered if you were half dolphin, since you spend so much time in the water.'

'Wouldn't that make me a mermaid?'

'Mer*man*,' Chantal corrected, gesturing with her water bottle.

'That's not manly.' He crossed his arms. 'What about half shark?'

'Whatever floats your boat, Mr Cheese.'

Strong hands grabbed her arms and hauled her to him. His mouth came down near her ear. Hot breath sent goosebumps skittering across her skin.

'Looks like you finally fell for my cheesy lines after all.'

Uneasy waves rocked her stomach. She'd certainly fallen for something. Her attraction to Brodie had always been physical…at least that was what she'd told herself. She was attracted to him *in spite* of his joker, take-nothing-seriously personality. At least it had *used* to be in spite of that…

Now she was the one convincing him to pour vodka on her, challenging him to a competition, teasing him about being a merman. This wasn't *her*. She was never this… relaxed.

'I haven't fallen for anything, Brodie. You're just good in bed.'

'Just sex.' His eyes avoided hers and he bent to inspect his shoelaces. 'That's all I was aiming for.'

An awkward silence settled over them. Could the exchange have felt as hollow to him as it did to her? Could he sense the fear in her voice as she tried her hardest to pull a barrier up between them?

'Let's head back,' he said, turning in the direction from which they'd come. 'I'm ready for my winner's breakfast.'

The tinkling of cutlery mingled with the rush of waves on the shoreline below. Tea light candles flickered in the gentle ocean breeze, and the smell of sea air mixed with the mouth-watering smells of steak and freshly cooked seafood.

'What's up?' Scott took a swig of his beer. 'You seem tense.'

Brodie had almost forgotten that Scott and Kate had agreed to make the trek up to Newcastle for a drink that night, at one of the beach hotels run by Brodie's friend.

Once Kate had caught wind that Chantal was staying on the boat she'd insisted they make it a double date of sorts. Having Chantal there meant he couldn't forget their run earlier that day—couldn't stop her comment swirling around in his head, kicking up all the memories and feelings he'd buried long ago.

I haven't fallen for you, Brodie. You're just good in bed.

In no possible situation should that have upset him… but he was off-kilter. Agitation flowed through him like a disruptive current, causing him to drum his fingers at the edge of the table where the group sat. Since when was being good in bed a *bad* thing?

'Maybe all this water is turning your brain to sludge.' Scott gestured towards Brodie's tall glass of mineral water. 'Why don't you have a beer?'

'The race is next week and I've reached my quota of indulgence.' He put on a fake smile and hoped that Scott had consumed enough beers not to look too hard. 'I'm winning that bet.'

The girls had gone to the bar for more refreshments. They stood side by side, giggling and chatting animatedly. Chantal's short black skirt skimmed the backs of her thighs, leaving miles of long tanned legs gleaming in the golden early-evening light. Her shoulders were barely contained in a flowing white top with small gold flowers. A small tug would be all it would take to free her, to expose her breasts to his mouth.

Brodie watched as they fended off an enthusiastic approach from a group of guys who appeared to be on a bucks' night.

'Maybe I should see if the girls need a hand,' Brodie said, frowning.

'She's got to you again, hasn't she?'

'Huh?'

Scott laughed, slapping him hard on the back. 'Oh, man, I didn't realise how bad it was. You get this look on your face when she's around—don't know how I missed it back at the reef.'

'You're full of crap.'

'*You're* an open book.' Scott's fist landed hard on his bicep. 'And when it comes to Chantal—'

'It's just sex.' *Good* sex, according to Chantal, but *just* sex.

'Yeah, and a half marathon is *just* a run.' Scott narrowed his eyes, studying Brodie in that analytical way of his.

'You know me. I don't do relationships. Surf, sand, bikinis—that's what it's all about.'

'Maybe before.' Scott shrugged. 'Doesn't explain why you look like you're about to snap the table in two because some guys are talking to her.'

Brodie looked down. Sure enough, his white-knuckled grip on the table was a little unusual. 'Says you. I thought you were going to deck me that time I danced with Kate.'

'I thought I was too. And why was that, huh?' Scott chuckled. 'Anyway, I'm not letting you get away with changing the subject. You helped me and now it's my turn to help you.'

'I don't need help.' Brodie let go of the table and ran his palms down the front of his jeans.

'You don't want help, but you damn well need it.'

The girls arrived back at the table, champagne in hand, plus a beer for Scott and another mineral water for Brodie.

'How does it feel, being a teetotaller?' Kate asked, flipping her long red hair over one shoulder.

'It's temporary. I don't think I could handle it long-term.' Brodie twisted the cap on his bottle, waiting for the rush of bubbles to die down before removing it. 'But temporarily it's okay. I can handle temporary things.'

Scott kicked him under the table and rolled his eyes. Okay, so maybe subtlety wasn't his strong suit. Nervous energy coursed through him, making the words in his head stumble and trip over one another. Kate eyed him curiously and Chantal pretended to be deeply involved in something on her phone.

Brodie contemplated smoothing things over, but his own phone vibrated against the table. Home.

'Hello?'

'Hey, Brodie.' The voice of his youngest sister, Ellen, came through the line. Her voice was pinched—a sure-fire sign that she was about a hair's breadth away from flipping out about something.

'What's up, Ellie-pie?'

'It's Lydia, she's had a down day. She won't eat her dinner. Mum's at work, but she said I had to make sure Lydia eats.'

The words ran into one another, and the wobble in her voice twisted like a knife in his stomach.

'Where are the twins?'

Sniffle. 'Jenny's at a party and Adriana hasn't come home from uni.'

'Put Lydia on the phone. I'll get her to eat.'

Within moments he'd convinced his sister to have at least a salad, even if she didn't want a full meal. It was hard for all of them to look after Lydia on her down days. There were times when she point-blank refused food and water for hours on end…sometimes days. He remembered a particularly bad patch when she'd ended up so dehydrated he'd had to rush her to the emergency ward. All she'd wanted was her dad—but of course they hadn't been able to get hold of him. Typical.

Perhaps he should sail home early. It was hard for him to be away. Normally he spent more time in the office running his business than on a boat. This was the longest he'd been away for some time. His stomach curled.

He hung up the phone, receiving a text almost immediately from Ellen with THANK YOU! xx in big capital letters. He loved his sisters more than anything, and right now he felt as if he was being a terrible big brother by taking time off for himself.

'Family emergency sorted,' he said, forcing a jovial tone as he returned to the table.

Chantal sipped her champagne, watching him quietly. 'Everything okay?'

'Fine.'

He looked out to the picture-perfect view of the beach slowly being drowned in darkness. Vulnerability wasn't something he did well—he didn't want her to see that he was anything but his usual cool, calm self. 'Just sex' didn't involve feelings or spilling your guts about family stuff… no more than he had already, anyway. In his defence, that had been to comfort her—not because he'd needed to get it off his chest.

'I should probably head off,' Chantal said, downing the rest of her drink and reaching out to give Kate a friendly hug. 'Thanks for the company.'

'Are you still dancing at the bar?' Scott asked, looking from her to Brodie and back again.

'Yep—I still need to make a living, don't I?' She seemed more comfortable about it than she had previously, there was light at the end of the tunnel. Her contract would run out eventually, and Brodie would make sure she didn't sign on for more work there.

'Don't let the creeps get you down,' Kate said.

'Creeps?' Brodie asked, his protective sensors going off.

'It's nothing.' Chantal shot Kate a look. 'You've seen the place. The clientele isn't exactly the picture of genteel politeness.'

'I'll meet you out the front when you finish,' Brodie said.

Chantal shook her head, shooting him a warning look as if to remind him of their argument last night. 'I'll be fine.'

'I'll meet you out the front.'

CHAPTER TEN

THOUGH SUMMER HAD drawn to a close a few weeks back, the air still hung heavy with humidity. Brodie stood by the railing outside the bar, waiting for Chantal to appear. He'd spent a good five minutes deciding whether or not to go in, but the temptation of hauling her off the stage had been too much to bear, and he didn't want to show her he was having doubts about his feelings towards the temporary nature of their arrangement.

Instead he waited outside, fending off requests for cigarettes, wishing that somehow Chantal had wriggled her way out of the contract. He wasted the time away by texting Ellen, hoping that she didn't hold his absence against him.

'I'm with someone.'

Chantal's voice caught him by surprise. He whipped around and saw her backing away from a big guy whose tank top said 'Team Bogan'. The guy looked at Brodie, sizing him up.

'See.' Chantal gestured to Brodie. 'This is my boyfriend—Axl.'

Brodie raised a brow. *Axl...really?* The guy lumbered away, distracted by a group of girls who didn't appear to have boyfriends waiting for them. Chantal used the opportunity to jog over to him, and sling her arm around his waist.

'Axl was the best you could do?' He shook his head. 'Never picked you for a Guns N' Roses fan.'

'Sorry.' She laughed, holding on to him as they made their way out of the bar's parking lot. 'The band was playing one of their songs as I was walking out. Mum used to listen to them all the time when I was young.'

'Better than the music *I* listened to growing up. Mum was a huge country fan—I hated it.'

Stars winked at them from the inky sky. Away from the hustle and bustle of Sydney the darkness wasn't diluted by the glow from skyscrapers and headlights. It reminded him of home—of the outdoorsy beauty of Queensland he'd grown to love after returning home from Weeping Reef.

'Have you talked to the guy who runs the bar about skipping out early?'

Chantal shook her head. 'No, and I haven't heard back about my audition yet, so I'm not giving up a paying job if there isn't something else to go to.'

'I'll lend you some money.'

'Over my dead body.' She tucked close against him as they walked, melting into him though her tone still revealed a touch of hesitation. 'It's kind of you to offer but I don't take loans—especially when I'm unsure how long it will take me to pay it back.'

'I know you're good for it.'

'Doesn't matter. I'll finish out this contract, see where I am, and figure out my next move.'

'Why are you so against asking for help?' he asked drily.

'I don't need charity.'

They walked through the yacht club and down to where his boat was docked. On board, they sat on the cosy leather-lined seat that curved around the deck. Chantal found a spot next to him, sitting with her head and shoulders resting against his chest. He draped his arm over her and skimmed his fingers along her stomach. It was frighteningly intimate and comfortable. *Familiar.*

'Haven't you heard the saying *Many hands make light work*?'

'Some of those hands get burned,' she said. 'I prefer doing things on my own. That's how it was growing up and I like my independence. Nothing wrong with that.'

'There's a difference between being independent and being stubborn to the point of self-detriment.'

'Asking for help hasn't ever got me anywhere to date. I trust the wrong people.'

'Do you think it's wrong to trust *me*?'

'I trust you as much as I'll ever trust anyone, but I'm still my own person. I do my own thing. That's why this isn't anything but two friends enjoying one another while it lasts.'

'Right.'

Raucous laughter floated on the breeze from a neighbouring boat. Chantal shifted against him, stroking his knuckles with her fingertips. It was a light touch, casual in its intimacy, and yet it flooded him with awareness. She was far from being out of his system. If anything, she'd burrowed herself deep without even trying. Without wanting to.

He couldn't be falling for her—not when he had a life and a family in Queensland to get back to and she had a dream to follow. Different worlds. Disconnected goals. They were wrong, wrong, *wrong.*

'Was everything really okay with your family today?'

A lump lodged in his throat. He didn't want to talk about that now—not when Chantal had made it clear that there was nothing real between them. But then he would be a hypocrite, wouldn't he? He couldn't berate her for not accepting help if she was willing to lend an ear and he didn't take it.

'Nothing major. Lydia was having a bad day. It happens every so often.' He rested his cheek against the top of her head, breathing in the scent of her faded flowery perfume and his coconut shampoo in her hair. 'Ellen was on her own, trying to deal with it. But she's only a kid herself—she needed help.'

'Ellen's the youngest, right?'

'Yeah. She's a good kid—they all are.' He swallowed against the lump in his throat. 'After the accident I was the one who looked after Lydia on a day-to-day basis. She listens to me. Whereas she's big sister to the other girls and yet feels like she can't do anything for them because of her paraplegia.'

'I bet she's grateful she had a big brother to take care of her.'

'She would have preferred to have Dad around. If that didn't make him come home nothing would. But the world didn't stop turning because she couldn't walk any more.' He sighed. 'Mum still had to bring home the bacon…the girls still had to get to school. I was the one who made sure she got to her appointments, made sure she did her exercises, helped her while she was still adjusting to her wheelchair.'

'That must have been tough.' Her hand curled into his and she snuggled farther down against him.

'It's hard to be away from them. Mum's always working, and Dad just…' He shook his head. 'The guy can barely manage a call on their birthdays. He'll disappear for months at a time, then show up out of the blue—usually because he needs money.'

'Where does he disappear to?'

'Who knows? He's a painter, the creative type, and he always seems to be off somewhere unreachable. Then he comes back, tries to make amends with Mum, and it goes well for a while until he asks for money.' Brodie cursed under his breath. 'Every time it happens he breaks the girls' hearts all over again…Mum's included.'

'And your mum's okay with him coming and going?'

'Not really—she did divorce him after all. But she puts her feelings for him before the girls.' Brodie laughed, the sound sharp and hollow. 'See? I told you my family wasn't picture perfect.'

'You don't have to be the parent. You do know that, right?'

But he did have to. Whether he liked it or not, *he* was responsible for looking after those girls. They relied on him—on his advice, on his life experience, on his care. Especially Lydia.

'You shouldn't feel guilty for taking a little time away,' she continued. 'You have to live your own life.'

'I *am* living my own life. I'm here, away from home, seeing my friends and spending time with you.'

'And you feel guilty as all hell, don't you?'

How could she read him like that? Silky hair brushed against his cheek. Her body was warm beneath his hands. How could she read him as though they were far more than friends who happened to be having very casual, very *temporary* sex?

'I have a sense of obligation to my family. What kind of person would I be if I didn't care?'

'I'm not saying you should stop caring. But there are varying levels—it's not all or nothing.' She pushed up, leaning out of his grip. 'Your dad is the one who needs to step up, here—he needs to commit to being a father.'

'Only when hell freezes over.'

'Have you ever talked to him about it?'

'No point.' He shook his head, tightening his grip on her.

In that moment she anchored him. Her questions were digging deep within him. Unlocking the emotion he'd tried to keep buried, allowing him to feel angry about his father.

To see that he'd been suppressing the hurt in order to be a rock for his sisters and his mother.

'Why? Do you think he deserves to shirk his responsibilities and have you pick up the pieces?'

'Of course not. But that doesn't mean I can let the girls go without.'

'No, but maybe you're in a position to try and push your father in the right direction.' She sighed. 'It might allow you to have a little more breathing room…to have the life that you want.'

'I have everything I want.' He gestured to the air. 'Got my boat, got my business. I don't want anything else.'

'Don't you?'

Pink flashed in front of his eyes as her tongue darted out to moisten her lips. She played with the ends of her hair, twirling the strands into a bun and then letting them spiral out around her shoulders.

'Is that all you want out of life?'

Wrapping her arms around herself, she shivered. Tiny ridges of goosebumps patterned her skin.

'Let's go inside. I don't want you getting sick.' He held out a hand and she took it without hesitation. 'Although maybe that would be a good way to get you out of that contract.'

'I'm not getting out of the contract.' She followed him to the kitchen, perching herself on a bar stool. 'I have a sense of obligation too, you know.'

'There's no doubt in my mind about *that*.'

'Why do you say it like that?'

'Your career before everything else. I have no doubt it's the most important thing in your life.'

'It is.' She tilted her head, watching him as he flicked on the coffee machine and pulled two cups from the cupboard. 'What's wrong with that?'

'I think your career is like my family. It's important… sometimes *too* important.'

'So you agree you need space from your family?' She grinned, swinging her legs.

'That's about as much agreement as you'll get from me.'

'You're so stubborn!'

'Ha! You should take a look in the mirror some time.'

The coffee machine hissed, steam billowing out of the nozzle in coils of white condensation. Black liquid ran into the cups, filling the air with a rich, roasted scent. He splashed milk into the first cup and handed it to Chantal. A grin spread over her lips and she blew on the steam, waiting for him to make the first move.

She wore the black skirt and white top she'd had on at drinks earlier that evening, but she'd ditched her shoes and jewellery. The gold threads in her top glinted under the light, making it seem as if she were glowing. It wasn't possible for her to look any more at home on the boat. He wondered what it would be like if they both tossed their obligations overboard and set sail. They had a boat—he had money. It could be the two of them. Together. Alone.

What is it about 'just sex' that you don't understand? She doesn't want you like that. You're just a body. A good lay.

'Are we going to keep dancing around like this or are you going to invite me to bed?'

She looked over the edge of her cup, the white porcelain barely hiding a cheeky smile. Her dark lashes fluttered and warm pink heat spread through her cheeks.

'Who's insatiable now?'

'Time's ticking. I want to enjoy this arrangement while I still can.'

It doesn't have to stop.

The words teetered on the edge of his tongue, willing his lips to open so they could pour out. But he couldn't let them. Instead he walked around to the other side of the breakfast bar and pulled her into his arms. His lips crushed down on hers, seeking out the hot, open delight of her mouth. The taste of fresh coffee mingled with the honeyed sweetness of her.

'As you wish.'

Chantal woke to the sound of something vibrating, but the haze of slumber refused to release her. Groggy, she pushed herself into a sitting position, smiling as Brodie reached for her in his sleep. Fingertips brushed her thigh and he sighed, rolling over. Blond lashes threw feathered shadows across his cheekbones and his full lips melted into a gentle smile.

'You look so damn innocent,' she muttered, brushing a lock of hair from his forehead. He didn't stir. 'But I know better.'

The vibrating stopped and a loud ping signalled a text message. Removing Brodie's hand from her leg, she set off in search of her phone. It wasn't in the bedroom, though everything else of hers appeared to be—a lacy thong, matching bra, white and gold top, stretchy black skirt.

A laugh bubbled in her throat. Her clothes were strewn so far around the room it looked almost staged. But her aching limbs told the truth. They'd spent another amazing, pulse-racing, heart-fluttering, boundary-breaking night together.

Danger! Emotions approaching—full speed ahead.

It was just sex…wasn't it? She could stop any time. *Spoken like a true addict, Turner.*

Huffing, she stomped out to the kitchen. She didn't want to be having thoughts like this. Brodie was a bit of fun. A friend, yes, but nothing more. She couldn't let it be any more…not when he'd already shown that he had the same protective urges as her ex. No matter how well intentioned he was, she would *not* let herself be smothered again.

A flashing blue light caught her attention. One new voicemail. It had better not be the bar, pushing her to extend her contract. She'd officially be admitting defeat if she signed with them for another month. Then again, it wasn't as if she had other offers to consider, and this thing with Brodie had to come to an end. He'd be sailing home at some point, and she couldn't exactly stow away on his boat to avoid her problems. No, she needed an apartment, a job…a *better* job. She needed her independence back.

She tapped in her password and dialled the voicemail number. Her pulse shot up as the caller introduced himself as being from the Harbour Dance Company. They wanted her to come in for a chat about the company and a second audition. She hadn't flunked it!

By the time she hung up the phone Brodie had ambled into the kitchen. Cotton pyjama pants hung low on his hips. A trail of blond hair dipped below the waistband. He was a god—a tattooed, tanned, six-pack-adorned god.

'Good news?'

'How could you tell?' She put her phone back on the table and bounded over to him, throwing her arms around his neck.

'Your greetings are usually a little less enthusiastic than this,' he said, chuckling, and lifted her up so that her legs instinctively wrapped around his waist. 'Not to mention you were bouncing around so much I thought you'd been stung by a jellyfish.'

'They want a second audition!' She didn't have time to counter his teasing. She was so brimming with relief that she had to let it out.

'Why wouldn't they? You're pretty damn fantastic.' He backed her up against the breakfast bar, bringing his mouth down to hers. 'So that means we'll be heading back to Sydney?'

'*I'll* be heading back to Sydney. The audition isn't till the end of the week, and you're taking off then…aren't you?'

He hesitated, the jovial grin slipping from his lips as he avoided her eyes. 'Yeah, I'll be heading back soon.'

Had he been thinking about staying? For *her*? That was too confusing a thought to process, so she pushed a hand through his hair and kissed the tip of his nose.

'No more swanning around on yachts for me.'

'No.'

'All good things must come to an end, as they say.' She wished the cheerful tone of her voice mirrored her thoughts. But the words had as much substance as fairy floss.

What was wrong with her? This was *Brodie*. Beach bum. Playboy. Dreamer. Drifter. Flake.

Only he wasn't any of those things in reality. He was a successful businessman. A friend, a great cook, a family man, the best sex of her life. He was complex, layered, and not at all as she'd labelled him. Could it get any worse?

'We should celebrate,' he said, cutting through her thoughts by setting her down. 'How about I take you out on the water and we'll have lunch?'

'I have to be back for a shift tonight, but that would be great.'

'Of course,' he said, a hint of bitterness tainting his voice. 'How could I forget about the bar?'

'Don't start, Brodie…it won't go on forever.' She wasn't going to let that scummy bar ruin their celebration.

'Why don't you have a shower and I'll get us underway.'

'Are you trying to tell me I smell again?' She shoved him in the shoulder and his smile returned…almost.

'You smell like sex.'

'Gee, I wonder why.' She rolled her eyes and skipped off towards his room.

Some time later she emerged, having spent longer than usual showering. Water helped her to think. She often did her best problem-solving under the steady stream of a showerhead. Unfortunately today seemed to be an exception to the rule. No solution to her confusion about Brodie had materialised. She was *still* stuck between wanting to enjoy their time for what it was and the niggling feeling that perhaps it was more than she wanted to admit.

Dangerous thoughts... Remember what happened last time you gave in. Remember the smothering you didn't see coming until it was too late.

She wandered to the upper area of the boat, spotting Brodie standing at the wheel and looking as though he'd been born to do exactly that. Wind whipped through his hair, tossing the blond strands around his face as the boat moved. Blond stubble had thickened along his chiselled jaw, roughening his usually charming face into something sexier and more masculine.

'Clean as a whistle,' she announced, stepping down into the driving area of the boat. 'Can I join you at the wheel, Captain?'

'You may.'

'Wow, there are a lot of dials.' Chantal hadn't yet been up to this area of the boat. It looked like the cockpit of a plane.

'It's a fairly sophisticated piece of machinery. A slight step up from your average tugboat.' He winked.

'It feels like you're free up here, doesn't it?'

The sparkling blue of the ocean stretched for miles around, and the sun glinted off the waves like a scattering of tiny diamonds.

'That's what I love most about it. I can think out here.'

A shadow crossed over his face. 'It's like I have no problems at all.'

'Do you ever wonder what would happen if you sailed away and never came back?'

'Are you trying to tell me something?' His smile didn't ring true, the crinkle not quite reaching his eyes.

'I'm serious. Don't you think it would be great to go somewhere new? Start over?' That sounded like the most appealing idea she'd ever come up with. A fresh start. No baggage. A clean slate unmarked by her previous mistakes.

He shrugged. 'Yeah, I think about it for five seconds and then I realise what a stupid idea it is.'

'Why?'

'I couldn't leave my family.'

'Even if it was the thing you wanted to do most in the world?'

'It would take something pretty spectacular to make me seriously consider it. To date, nothing has come close.'

Chantal bit down on her lip, hating herself for allowing his words to sting. He was clearly drawing a line in the sand, defining their relationship...or lack thereof. She should be happy. He'd absolved her of any guilt about leaving him at the end of the week. But the words cut into her as real and painful as any blade.

'Doesn't hurt to fantasise,' she said wistfully.

'Sometimes it does.' He looked as though he were about to continue but his face changed suddenly. 'We're going to stop soon, but you might want to head portside in a minute.'

Chantal looked from left to right. 'Portside?'

'Sorry—boat-speak.' Brodie pointed to a section of the railing to his left. 'Stand over there.'

'You're not going to tip me overboard, are you?'

He smirked. 'Don't tempt me.'

Chantal went to the railing, holding on to the metal bar with both hands. 'What am I looking for?'

'You'll know it when you see it.'

Beautiful as the view was, she couldn't see anything much. They were clearly approaching land, but the fuzzy green mounds still looked a while away. She shielded her eyes with her hand, searching.

Something glimmered below the water—a shadow. Holy crap, was that a *shark*? Moments later the water broke, and a group of a dozen dolphins raced alongside the boat in a blur of grey and splashing blue.

'Did you see that?' Chantal shouted, leaning over the railing to watch the majestic creatures leap out of the water over and over.

They were so sleek. So fast and playful.

'Careful!' Brodie called out with a smile on his face. 'Don't fall in.'

'There's so many of them.'

She watched, mesmerised by the fluid way the dolphins moved—as if they were trying to keep up with the boat. Their smooth bodies sliced through the water, their beaked faces appearing to smile. They looked joyful. Uninhibited.

Chantal could feel the heat of Brodie's gaze on her, boring holes through the thin layer of her ankle-length dress. Right now his boat was the most amazing place in the world. How would she ever leave it at the end of the week?

CHAPTER ELEVEN

SEEING CHANTAL'S FACE when she discovered the dolphins had melted his insides. The sparkle in her eye, her squeak of delight, the way she'd hung over the railing as though she was desperate to jump into the water with them...it had been too much.

After the dolphins had moved on he'd steered them to Nelson Bay and moored in the spot normally reserved for one of the dolphin and whale-watching companies. After ordering Chantal off to the shower that morning he'd called in a favour with a friend who ran the mooring services for the Port Stephens region. Now they had a couple of hours for lunch before he'd need to leave the area and head back to Newcastle.

A spread of smoked salmon, bagels with cream cheese and fresh fruit covered the table that sat in front of the curved leather and wood seat. He'd also popped a bottle of champagne, which sat in a silver ice bucket.

'Did you know the dolphins were going to be there?' Chantal asked, taking a hearty bite out of a bagel. Cream cheese spilled forward, coating her upper lip, and her pink tongue darted out to capture it.

He remembered her obsession with bagels back from when they were at Weeping Reef together. Despite being slim as a rail, she'd devoured the doughy delights every morning for breakfast. Always with cream cheese. God, he had to stop looking at her mouth. She dived in for another bite, her eyes fluttering shut as she savoured the flavour.

'You never know for sure. But there is a group of dolphins who live in the area, so it's common to see them.' He took a swig of his water.

'They live here?'

'Not specifically in Nelson Bay, but in the general Port Stephens area. It's a big pod too—about eighty dolphins, I think.'

'Wow.' She sighed. 'They're so beautiful. I've always wanted to do one of those swim-with-the-dolphins things.'

'They're a lot of fun. The bottlenecks especially—they're very playful.'

Her eyes widened. 'You've done it? I'm so jealous.'

'Yeah.' Brodie nodded, a memory flickering. 'We did it as kids once...me and Lydia. Before her accident.'

For a moment he wondered if she would dig further, ask about Lydia's accident. Instead she said, 'What do they feel like?'

'They're smooth—kind of rubbery.'

'What do they eat?'

He laughed, taken by her intense curiosity. 'Fish, squid...that kind of thing.'

Lying back on her chair, she kicked her legs out and crossed her ankles. A contented sigh escaped her lips. 'I'm so full. That salmon was amazing.'

'You're welcome.'

She turned her head, shielding her eyes with her hand. 'This is the best celebration I could have asked for... although it's not a done deal. I might flunk the next audition.'

'Always thinking positive—that's what I like about you,' he teased.

'Nothing wrong with being realistic.' She sighed. 'I'm

trying to protect myself, I guess. I don't want to be disappointed if I don't get it.'

'If they want a second audition then they obviously saw something they liked.'

'That's true.' She twirled a strand of hair around one finger.

'You're immensely talented—you know that, right?' He chewed on his own bagel, concentrating on the food so that he could hide the conflicting emotions doing battle within him.

'Let's just hope the Harbour Dance Company agree with you.' She paused. 'I've had fun staying on the boat.'

He'd hoped to hear *with you* emerge from her lips, but she stopped short. *Stop waiting to hear that she's fallen for you. She hasn't.*

'I've had *fun* too.'

He half-heartedly waggled his brows and she swatted at him, laughing.

'I don't just mean the sex, Brodie. I mean I've had fun… hanging out.'

'Hanging out? What are we? Teenagers?' he teased.

She shook her head. 'Way to make a girl feel awkward. Can't a friend give another friend a compliment?'

Friend. There it was again—the invisible barrier between them. He'd broken his rule by sleeping with her in the first place. Funny thing was, that rule had always been in place to preserve the friendship, so that when he rejected any serious advances the other person wouldn't get hurt. He'd never counted on it going the other way—not when he had his priorities sorted out and they certainly didn't include a serious relationship.

'I prefer my compliments to be of the physical variety.'

'You're not nearly as sleazy as you try to be,' she said.

'I'm not *trying* to be anything.' It came out way too defensive. Why didn't he just hold up a flag that said *Emotional sore point. Proceed with caution.*

'Yes, you are. You're hell-bent on being the casual, laid-back, cool-as-a-cucumber fun-time guy.'

'You seemed to believe I *was* that guy.'

'I didn't know you then.' Her olive eyes glowed in the bright afternoon light, the golden edges of her hair glinting like precious metal. 'But I do now.'

'You know what I want you to know.'

'No way.' Her lips pursed. 'You sailed a yacht out here to show me dolphins—you packed a champagne lunch for me. All because I got a second audition—not even a proper job. That's not a fun-time guy.'

'What is it, then?'

He was giving her a chance to be honest, to open up to him. But the shutters went down over her eyes and colour seeped into her cheeks. Her hands folded into a neat parcel in her lap. Shutdown mode enabled.

'You're a good person, Brodie. I wish we'd got to be real friends sooner.'

There was that F-word again. If he heard it come out of her mouth one more time he was going to throw something. Clearly he was going out of his mind. Girls didn't rattle him—that wasn't how he acted. On the scale of annoyance, girl problems ranked somewhere between lining up at the supermarket and typos. In other words it fell into the bundle of crap he didn't care about.

'We should probably head back.' He pushed up from his chair, feeling the burn of the afternoon sun on his legs. 'Don't want to make you late for work.'

'Yeah, that thorn in my side.' She sighed.

She followed him around as he prepared the boat to return to Newcastle. Her anxious energy irritated him—partially because he felt she had no reason to be anxious, and partially because it made him want to bundle her up and kiss her until she relaxed. The woman had an emotional stronghold over him that was both dangerous and stupid. He already had four women to take care of—five if he counted his mother. He didn't need a sixth.

'You don't need to pick me up from the bar tonight,' she said once they were back at the helm, with the boat cruising out of the marina.

'I'll be there.' No way he'd let her walk back to the boat on her own.

'I can stay at the accommodation, if you like.'

'You're welcome to stay on the boat until I have to sail back. That hasn't changed.'

He didn't look at her, but her nervousness permeated the air. She knew he was angry with her. He had to keep his emotions in check.

'I want you to stay.'

'Okay.' She put her hand over his. 'Thanks.'

Don't grab her hand...don't grab her hand. 'No worries.'

'I'll be happy when I finish up at the bar. It's certainly been a learning experience.' She let out a small laugh. 'Although the crowd is a bit rough for my liking.'

'A *bit*?' He stole a glance at her and regretted it immediately. Make-up-free, hair flowing, she looked young and vulnerable. *You're weak, Mitchell, absolutely weak.*

'Okay, a lot. It wouldn't be so bad if the guys weren't so handsy.'

'What do you mean, *handsy*?'

'You know—some guys seem to think by buying a few drinks they can have free handling of the dancers.' She rolled her eyes. 'Pigs.'

White-hot rage brewed in his stomach. 'Dammit, Chantal. Why didn't you tell me?'

'Because it's not your problem—it's *mine.*' She spoke

calmly, but she crossed her arms and stepped backwards. 'Besides, last time you came into the bar you flipped out.'

'Of course I did!' He fought to wrangle the frustration and anger warring inside him. 'It's like you refuse to look after yourself just to prove a point.'

'I'm not trying to prove a point.' She gritted her teeth. 'Anyway, I had a word with them and told them to back off.'

'Jeez, you had *a word* with them? I'm sure that will make *all* the difference.' He shook his head, gritting his teeth at the thought of these grubby morons touching her. 'You need to tell me these things.'

'I don't *need* to tell you anything.' Her eyes flashed like two green flames. Her lips were pressed into a flat line and her breath came in short, irritated stutters. 'It's not your job to protect me.'

'What if they attacked you? What if you stayed at the accommodation and they followed you?' Nausea rocked his stomach. If anything ever happened to her...

'You're not my knight in shining armour, Brodie.' She spoke through gritted teeth, her hands balled by her sides. 'I can look after myself. Don't you get that?'

'All I see is someone who's too damn stubborn to ask for help.'

She folded her arms across her chest. The air pulsed around her as she narrowed her eyes at him. 'Independence is important to me.'

'At the cost of intelligence, it seems.'

'Oh, that's rich coming from you.'

'What the hell is *that* supposed to mean?' His blood boiled. He couldn't remember the last time he'd felt this... this *everything*. Emotions collided inside him, strong and flying at full speed.

'You won't live your life because you think it's your job to take care of every tiny thing for your family. You live in guilt because your father left but you won't even confront him about it. You're scared.'

'I'm not scared.'

'Yes, you *are*.' She jabbed a finger at him.

With her composure out of the window, Chantal let frustration and anger flow out of her unchecked.

'You won't let yourself feel anything for anyone outside your family.'

'Oh, and that's as bad as dancing at some skanky bar where you're not safe?' He shook his head. 'Yeah—real smart.'

'Dancing at that bar might seem stupid to you, but I need to make it on my own. I will *not* let someone else tell me what to do.' *Least of all someone who's supposed to be a 'no-strings tension-reliever'.*

'Who would try, Chantal? It's clear you won't listen to anyone else. You're so goddamn bull-headed.'

'Try looking in a mirror some time.'

In a rush, tears welled up with the force of a tidal wave. She had to get out. *Now!*

She flew down the stairs to the lower deck and didn't stop until she reached the kitchen. Her chest heaved, and she was dragging in each breath as though it resisted her with the force of an army. Cheeks burning, she felt the toxic warmth seeping down her neck and closing around her windpipe. She would *not* have a meltdown in front of him…not again.

The smooth marble bench was cool against her palms. Was he coming after her? *And who would sail the boat then? Idiot. Of course he's not coming after you.*

Twisting the kitchen tap with a shaking hand, she bent down to splash some water onto her face before filling a glass. Brodie's yacht had made her feel free when they'd sailed out of Newcastle that morning, but now…now it was as if the walls were closing in, crushing her, trapping her. She sipped, savouring the sensation of the cold liquid slipping down the back of her throat.

It was time to end things with Brodie. Chantal only ever got mad when she cared—she only ever lost her temper when something important was on the line. Even when Scott had left Weeping Reef she hadn't been angry…just guilty because it had all ended so suddenly and because of her inability to control herself. But she'd known deep down that Scott wasn't the man for her.

What did that say about Brodie and the way she was feeling now?

It's nothing. You had a great time with him, he provided you a nice place to stay, but now it's back to reality. No more messing around. You've got an audition to nail and a job to finish.

When they arrived back at Newcastle, Brodie didn't materialise on the lower deck. Chantal decided to avoid him by getting ready for her shift. Smoky shadow made her eyes look wide and alluring…a clear gloss played up her natural pout. The make-up gave her something to hide behind—another persona to help her get through the shift. The patrons of the bar saw only the image she wanted them to see, not the real her.

But Brodie had seen the real her. The scared girl with too-high expectations, a faltering career and a predisposition for panic attacks. Appealing stuff.

She bit down on her lip so hard the metallic tang of blood seeped onto her tongue. She couldn't afford to lose it now. A second audition with the Harbour Dance Company was a sign that she was heading in the right direction. A sign that perhaps everything would turn out the way she wanted it to. Or did she want more than that?

Her packed bags sat by the kitchen bench. How long had she been living out of a bag now? Too long. The rest of her belongings had been stashed at her mother's place, with a few extra essentials in the back of her car…if it was still in the bar's car park after all this time.

Oddly, she didn't care. Numbness had taken over the anger, smoothing down the edges of her emotions until she felt smooth and cold. Closed off…the way she preferred it.

Hoisting her bag over her shoulder, she slipped her feet into a pair of ballet flats and made her way onto the deck. Brodie's voice floated down from the upper level. He was talking to one of his sisters. A smile tugged at the corner of her lips. He had a certain tone for his sisters. Tough, and yet so full of love it made her heart ache. No one spoke to *her* like that—not even her mother.

Should she bid him a formal goodbye? Thank him for giving her a place to stay? Probably.

Instead she left, heading towards the bar with a hard knot rocking the pit of her stomach. *Keep going...one foot in front of the other. You need distance and so does he.*

She was doing the right thing. Staying would only be prolonging the inevitable breakdown of their relationship… whatever *that* was. She didn't know how to label it.

At some point he'd been a mere acquaintance, a secret crush. Then a friend. Then a friend with benefits… And now?

She squeezed her eyes shut, willing away the persistent thumping at the base of her skull. Dancing tonight would be tough, but she had to get through it. Light was most certainly at the end of the tunnel…so long as she kept Brodie out of her head.

'What's wrong, Brodes? You sound upset.' Lydia's voice floated through the phone, her concern twisting something sharp in his chest.

'I'm fine. It's the sound of relaxation. You know how long it's been since I took a holiday.'

'Yeah.' She laughed. 'You work too hard. You don't sound relaxed, though.'

'It's nothing.'

'Swear?'

He gritted his teeth. He'd never sworn on a lie to any one of his sisters and he wasn't about to start now. Perhaps if he didn't say anything she'd get bored and move on.

Lydia audibly smirked into the silence. 'What's her name?'

Damn. 'Her name doesn't matter.'

'Oh, come on. I don't get to do the boy thing much how about a little vicarious living?'

She said it with such calm acceptance that he wanted to hang up the phone and get to her in any way possible. It wasn't fair that she didn't have a boyfriend simply because she couldn't walk. Although with the way Chantal had left him with a permanent imbalance perhaps it was a good thing.

'Her name is Chantal. She's a friend.'

'But you want more?'

'No, I don't. We agreed to keep things…friendly.' His brow creased. He was so *not* talking about this with his little sister.

'Do you love her?'

He hesitated. 'Of course not. I only have enough love for you guys… There's only so many women a guy can have in his life before he goes crazy.'

Lydia huffed and he could practically see her rolling her green eyes at him. 'You sound like Dad.'

There was a scary image. *I take care of you girls. I don't run away from my family when the whim takes me.*

'When was the last time you heard from Dad?'

'Touché,' Lydia said with a sigh. 'Why won't you be more than friends with Chantal?'

'We're not having this conversation, Lyds.'

'But—'

'Not. Having. This. Conversation.'

'OMG, you're *so* boring.'

He could hear the laughter in her voice and he thanked the heavens that she was having a better day today.

'I miss you.'

'I miss you too.' There was a slight pause on the other end of the line. 'I *would* like it if you got married one day.'

'Marriage isn't for me.' He shook his head, wondering how on earth he'd got roped into talking about relationships. 'Besides, you already have three sisters. You don't need another one.'

'But I might not get married and I'd like to be in a wedding. Why wouldn't you want to do it?'

Brodie swallowed the lump in his throat at the thought of all the things he took for granted. Why wouldn't he want to do it? Did he even *know* why? He told himself he didn't have room in his life for a relationship…but then again Chantal was different from his ex. She wasn't clingy or needy…quite the opposite! He'd sworn off long-term relationships because he knew he'd have to choose between them and his family. What if he'd been wrong? What if he *could* have both?

'You'll get married one day, Lyds. Not until I've checked the guy out, though. I'll need to make sure he's good enough for you.'

She laughed. 'You'd better not scare any potential husbands away.'

'Watch me.'

He hung up the phone and made a mental note to pop in and see Lydia as soon as he got back to Queensland. Perhaps he'd head back earlier than planned. It wasn't as if Chantal would be coming back to the boat after their argument. Without her he didn't have a reason to stay.

And where would *she* stay? A cold tremor ran the length

of his spine, settling in the pit of his stomach. The bar accommodation wasn't safe, he believed that even more now after what she'd told him today. He'd noted the single lock on the door while Chantal had packed her bags in front of him. That door needed at least another five locks before it became remotely secure. Not that the cheap wood door would withstand a well-aimed kick or the swing of a crowbar…

He dropped onto a sun lounger and put his head in his hands. How had it gone downhill so quickly? One minute they were out on the ocean, racing the dolphins, and the next they were yelling at one another. That was definitely not in the vein of their friends-with-benefits arrangement.

Maybe he could convince her to let him pay for a hotel room. There was a suitable beach resort down the road from the bar. It wasn't anything fancy, but it would be more secure than her room. He could give her a couple hundred bucks, make sure she was safe, and then leave her the hell alone.

Would she take the money from him? Not likely, but he had to try. The thought of anything happening to her filled him with cold, hard dread. He cared about her. She was a friend—of *course* he cared about her. That was normal, wasn't it?

He paced the length of the helm, his muscles tightening with each agitated step. Chantal valued her independence, that was for sure, but he had a right to step in if she was endangering herself. It was his duty…as a friend.

Jogging down the stairs to the lower deck, he went on the hunt for his wallet and phone. She was gone. Her bags were nowhere to be found and the bedroom was so tidy it was as if she'd never been there. But her presence hung in the air like perfume—sweet and memory-triggering. All the scraps of lace that had littered the floor after their various escapades had been removed, and the small pile of her jewellery on his bedside table had vanished too.

He snatched up his keys from the hook on his bedroom wall and jammed his wallet into the pocket of his shorts. She was going to be royally pissed at him trying to buy her a room, but he didn't care. Having her angry at him was better than any of the other alternatives. She'd have to deal with her anger. He wasn't going to take no for an answer.

CHAPTER TWELVE

BACKSTAGE AT THE BAR, Chantal tried to psych herself up for her performance. Truth was she wanted to run away with her tail between her legs and never come back. But she was a professional, a trooper. She never backed down.

Part of her wanted to get out there on that stage to prove a point. Brodie had treated her as if she was made of crystal—as if she'd break with the slightest knock. But she didn't break. She'd been through her share of tough times and she *always* kept going. No matter what.

'Don't look so down, honey.' A blonde girl in a sparkling corset pouted at her. 'If I had natural boobs like that *I* wouldn't be frowning.'

Chantal instinctively crossed her arms over her chest. 'I'm fine.'

'Is this your first time dancing?'

'No, not at all.' Did she look *that* nervous? Hell, what had Brodie done to her? She was wound up tighter than a spring.

'It'll be okay.' The blonde nodded and gave her shoulder a light pat. The woman's long silver nails glinted like tiny blades. 'Don't let the audience frighten you. They're big old lugs. Only here for the tits and the booze, never mind that fabulous dancing we all do.'

Chantal couldn't help but smile. The blonde gave a little shimmy, flicking the black fringe edging her corset back and forth. Her stockings stopped at mid-thigh, biting into her generous flesh, and she wore black gloves that stretched up over her elbows. She looked at ease with herself...with what she was doing.

'Just have fun. Leave your worries behind!' She sang the last few words, twirling and shaking her ample booty.

'I think I need to take a leaf out of your book,' Chantal said, smiling.

'Good idea. I always get a little tipsy before I dance.' The blonde leaned in conspiratorially. 'A couple of shots of tequila. *Boom!* Loose hips.'

Chantal practised her routine in the small space next to the mirror-lined bench. Sure, this wasn't the best place on earth, and it wasn't what she wanted for her career, but she could get through it. To hell with Brodie. She'd be fine and she didn't need anyone else to take care of her. She *would* stand on her own two feet.

The dancer before her gyrated on stage, using the pole to complete some gravity-defying tricks. The audience roared, catcalls and wolf-whistles drowning out all but the heavy thump of the bass. Then it was her turn. She peeked out as the other dancer finished up. The crowd had swelled considerably since she'd first arrived.

Then she spotted Brodie. He was unmistakable. Sitting in the front row, arms folded across his chest, biceps on display...most likely on purpose. The blood drained from her face and her confidence followed it until the world tilted beneath her feet.

What the hell was he doing here?

Her music started but her feet were rooted to the ground. Someone shoved her in the back and she stumbled a little as she walked on stage. The audience didn't seem to notice. They cheered and hooted as she swung her hips, pivoting on one foot with a dainty flick of her hair. Under Brodie's intense stare she might as well have been naked. His eyes seemed to penetrate her, seeing all that she wanted to conceal.

He didn't smile, and his eyes certainly didn't sparkle the way they normally did. Had *she* turned him into this hardened lump? Where was the free and easy Brodie she'd fallen for?

And had she really fallen for him…even after everything that had happened today?

Confusion made her head fuzzy, the thoughts clashing in her mind. It was nothing—just a fling. She shook her head, trying to dislodge the warring emotions.

The steps of her choreography eluded her, but she had to keep going. Close to the edge of the stage she felt a hand brush by her—not Brodie's. A portly man with a heavy beard and mean eyes leered up at her. Her skin crawled and she backed away, still clinging to her stage presence though she was sure she'd never danced so terribly in all her life.

Brodie had leant over to the man, his face red and indecipherable words falling from his lips. For a moment she would have sworn a fight would break out, but it didn't. The bass thumped at odd intervals with the pounding in her head…everything unravelled. Fast.

She rushed off stage before her time was up, ducking her head at the curious stares of the other dancers and ignoring the cutting remarks from the manager as she scuffed her feet into her sneakers and grabbed her keys.

Outside the change room people swarmed the crowded space of the bar, the smell of beer and body odour making the air heavy and thick. Swallowing against the nausea, she pushed through, swatting away invasive hands and avoiding lingering stares. If she didn't get outside… Well, it wouldn't be pretty.

Brodie had got up from his chair. Chantal spotted him in her peripheral vision but didn't stop. This was all his fault! He shouldn't have come here thinking he could distract her, making her look like an idiot in front of all these people. As much as she didn't care about their opinions, she was still dancing. Forgetting her choreography was *unforgivable.*

'Chantal!'

How could she have let herself fall for him? The way he'd acted tonight *proved* he was the wrong guy for her. He was just like her ex: over-protective…ready to smother her.

She headed towards the stairs, running down them as fast as she could while dodging two people kissing up against the wall. Downstairs a heavy metal band thrashed about on stage, the drummer's double kicks resonating through her, the beat reverberating right down to her bones.

She stumbled outside, tripping over a pair of feet in her desperation for escape. The cool air rushed into her mouth, was trapped where her throat was closing in. She gasped, sucking the air in greedily and forcing each breath down like a pill without water. How could she have forgotten her choreography? *How?* She balled her shaking hands, wishing she could crawl into a crack in the ground and disappear forever.

'Chantal!' Brodie's voice rang out in the car park, muted by the music from inside the bar. 'Wait—'

The deep rumble of a motorcycle raced past and drowned out the rest of his words. For a moment she kept walking, each purposeful step slamming into the ground. What would happen if she kept going? Tempting as it was, she couldn't quit—she couldn't. Not when things were turning around.

'I'm trying to protect you.' His voice carried on the night air.

Chantal whirled around, her body tense, like a snake about to strike. She locked her arms down by her sides. 'You distracted me up there. I forgot my steps because I couldn't concentrate on anything but whether or not you were going to start a fight.'

'I'm here to make sure you're safe—not to distract you.' His brows pulled down, a crease forming in his forehead. 'I only wanted to make sure you had somewhere safe to stay.'

'I'm not coming back to the boat.'

He shook his head. 'I was planning to pay for a hotel room for you. I'm thinking about your best interests.'

For some reason his words cut right through her chest, making her head pound and her stomach turn. Safety…protection…best interests. These were all words she'd heard before—the vocabulary of a control freak.

'Why don't you trust me, Chantal?'

'You told me I didn't *have* to trust you.' Her voice wobbled and she cringed. 'That was part of the deal.'

His eyes flashed; his mouth pulled into a grim line. 'I thought you'd change your mind.'

'I haven't.'

He raked a hand through his hair, the blond strands falling straight back into place over his eyes. He'd come straight from the boat, still wearing his shorts and boat shoes from their trip to Nelson Bay. The black ink of his anchor tattoo peeked out from the rolled-up sleeve of a crisp blue shirt. Damn him for looking so utterly delectable when she wanted nothing more than to throw her shoe at his head.

What had happened to the laid-back Brodie she knew? Did all guys turn into 'me Tarzan, you Jane' types as soon as you slept with them?

'Have you changed your mind about *anything*?' He stepped forward, folding his arms across his chest.

'Like whether or not I should finish my contract here?' She shrugged, hoping she looked as though she cared a lot less than she did. 'I'm a professional dancer. I can't quit.'

'That wasn't what I was talking about.'

'What *are* you talking about, then, Brodie? Because I sure as hell have no idea.'

His jaw twitched, and the muscles in his neck corded as he drew a long breath. 'What about your desire to do everything on your own?'

'That's how I *need* to do it.'

At least that was what she'd believed most of her life. But somehow she didn't feel so convinced any more. *Remember what happened when you got married... You trusted him and look how* that *turned out. Mum did it all on her own—you can too.*

'Why?' He took the last few steps towards her until there was no space between them and his hands gripped her shoulders. '*Why* do you think you need to do everything on your own?'

'Because it's safer that way.' She shut her eyes, wishing her brain would stop registering the scent of him and firing up all the parts she needed to stay quiet at the moment. 'I'm sick of being a charity case. I want to do something on my own that I can be proud of. I *need* it.'

'You can be independent without pushing away everyone who feels something for you.'

Blood rushed in her ears. The roaring made it hard to think straight. 'Are you trying to tell me *you* feel something for me?'

That was exactly what he was saying, wasn't it? He *did* have feelings for her. Why would he keep chasing her if he didn't?

'What if I do?'

'That would go against our agreement.' Her olive-green eyes were wide, like two shimmering moons, begging him not to continue.

If he admitted to caring about her and she rejected him what would happen next? He'd never see her again. The thought of a life without her seemed pointless. Colourless. Dull.

'We're supposed to be friends,' she whispered.

'We are.'

'That's all I have room for. I don't want a relationship right now. I want to get my career sorted. I've worked my whole life for this. I'm not stopping now.'

'You do know you can have more than one thing in life, don't you?' He couldn't help the words coming out with a derisive tone. How could she be so narrow-minded?

Hypocrite.

'Can you? I thought family was *your* one thing.'

She stepped backwards and he let her slip out of his grip.

'Someone told me I was too scared to invest in anyone outside my family. Maybe that person was right.'

'No. Family should come first for you.' Chantal shook her head. 'Go back to Queensland, Brodie. Go home.'

'Who's scared now?' He hated himself for the waver in his voice. She'd managed to do what no other woman ever had—she'd made him feel something. She'd made him want to stay.

'*I* am, Brodie. I'm scared.' She looked at him with a blank face. 'I'm scared for my career, so that's what I'm focusing on right now. Please don't follow me.'

With that she turned and left him standing in the middle of the parking lot. Her silhouette faded into the night and every nerve ending in his body fired, telling him to go after her. But she'd made it clear her life had no room for a relationship. No room for him.

If she wasn't going to let him in there was no point hanging around. He was stupid to have even tried. Of course she wanted nothing more from him. How had he fallen into that trap? *He* was supposed to walk away—it was what he always did.

'You're a goddamn idiot,' he muttered, unsure if he were talking to himself or to her.

By Friday, Brodie was ready to sail home. His travel bag was packed, but he hadn't been able to convince himself to go. Instead he'd headed back to Sydney, in the hope that a change of scenery could pull him out of his incredible funk.

The view from the boat should have cured any bad feelings he had, and the sunlight sparkling off the water and the girls in their tiny shorts and tank tops was his definition of nirvana. Not today, though.

Humid air clung to his sweat-drenched body. He'd hoped going for a run would allow him to burn off the agitated energy that had kept him awake the last few nights. It hadn't. Since then he'd called the office, video chatted with the family, and run until his legs trembled. *Now what?*

The shower beckoned. He stripped, hoping the rush of cool water against his sizzling skin might ease the confusing thoughts in his head. But the normally soothing sound of water against tiles gave him space to think…something he needed like a hole in the head.

He was officially broken.

A noise caught his attention. The vibration of his phone against the benchtop, sounding like insects buzzing. Who would be calling him? The guy who managed his office had already told him to butt out until his holiday was officially up. Apparently things were running like clockwork, and he'd told Brodie he sounded as if he hadn't had any rest at all.

Brodie rubbed his eyes and tilted his face up to the spray. Exhaustion weighed down his limbs. No wonder… He was pretty sure he'd seen each hour tick over on his clock last night.

What if Chantal was calling?

He wrenched at the taps, shutting off the water, and stepped out of the shower. He grabbed a towel and wrapped it around his waist, checking the ID flashing up on his phone. Of course it wasn't her. She'd made it damn clear there was nothing between them. That didn't stop the way his body sprang to action at the thought of her contacting him.

Pathetic.

'Hello?'

'Hey, man.' Scott's voice boomed over the line. 'Want to grab a drink?'

The last thing he wanted was to see Scott face to face. His friend would know in an instant that things had gone south. 'I'm actually having a little time out at the moment.'

'You're back in Queensland?'

'No, not yet.' He'd been so rattled by the encounter with Chantal that he'd hightailed it back up the coast to Sydney without telling *anyone*. Not even Scott.

'Everything okay?'

'Nothing major,' he lied, padding to his bedroom.

'Work problems?'

He paused, unsure how much he wanted to reveal. But Scott's pushing meant he knew something was up. 'Not exactly.'

A chuckle came down the line. 'Let me guess—it starts with C and ends with L.'

'Spelling was never my strong suit.' He tried to make light of Scott's words but it sounded hollow, even to him.

'What happened?'

'I don't know. One minute it was fine—*we* were fine—and the next…' He dropped down onto the bed and rubbed his temple with his free hand. 'It was supposed to be convenient. Fun.'

'Love is anything *but* convenient,' Scott said sagely.

'I didn't say I loved her.'

'Didn't need to. Why else would you be hiding out?'

Scott had a point. He'd run like a scared little kid, tail between his legs, all because she'd drawn the line at sex. In what universe would he be upset by *that*? It was guilt-free—for once *he* didn't have to be the bad guy.

'I don't know if I love her.'

'Are you feeling miserable?'

'Yes.'

'Miserable' was probably a few notches down from the aching in his chest that had appeared when he'd sailed out of Newcastle that morning.

'Confused?'

'Hell, yeah.'

'Lost?' Scott didn't bother waiting for an answer. 'That's what love feels like.'

'It blows.'

Scott laughed. 'It only blows before you sort things out. Then it's pretty bloody amazing. Kinda funny how the tables have turned.'

'I'm not laughing.'

He wanted to throw something—anything that might help him release some of the deadening weight in his limbs.

'So what's your plan of attack?'

'Plan?'

'To get Chantal back. Jeez—keep up, Brodie.'

And there was the rub. 'It's hard to get someone back if you didn't have them in the first place.'

'Did you tell her how you felt?' Scott sounded as though he were explaining something to a dumb animal for the tenth time.

'Well, no.'

'Did you even try?'

Brodie groaned inwardly, this was *way* out of his comfort zone. He was used to being the one giving advice—as he'd done with Scott not that long ago. Why couldn't he seem to sort out his own situation?

'I kind of went a little…caveman.'

'Wow—and you're wondering why she didn't give you anything?'

'She didn't want it. I could tell.' He remembered the look in her eyes, almost as if she was pleading with him to leave.

'She's got a thing about being independent—you can't change that.' Scott sighed. 'She needs her space.'

'I know.'

He rubbed a hand over his face. Of course she wanted to be her own person, but that didn't stop him wanting to protect her. Was it completely hopeless?

'How did I screw it up so bad?'

'Is she worth the pain?'

'Yes.'

The word slipped out before he'd even had time to weigh up possible answers. Uttering that one little word had released the tension from his neck and lifted the heaviness from his shoulders. Was it possible that he was in *love* with Chantal Turner?

'What should I do?'

'Aren't *you* supposed to be the lady whisperer?' Scott teased.

'I'm lost, man. She makes me question everything and I've got no clue what to do next.'

'What do you do when you wipe out?'

Brodie smiled—he could always count on Scott to put something in *his* terms. 'Are you trying to tell me I need to give it another go?'

'I'm not trying to tell you—I *am* telling you. I know Chantal is tough. You need to let her know how you feel—she's not great with ambiguity.'

'What do I say?'

'You'll figure it out. But I would start with an apology. There's no excuse for going caveman.'

Brodie put the phone down and stared at it long and hard. He would figure it out… But having Chantal meant sacrificing other things. To be with her he would need to be away from his family more. He couldn't expect her to drop her dreams of being a dancer and move to Queensland with him.

If this thing between him and Chantal was going to work then other things needed to change too.

He reached for the phone and sucked in a huge breath, dialling his father's number quickly, before he could change his mind.

CHAPTER THIRTEEN

HIGHWAY SCENERY BLURRED past as Sydney faded away in Chantal's rearview mirror. Her old car struggled to keep up with the speed limit, but she was moving…and that was all that mattered.

Last night she'd stood tall in the face of criticism from the bar manager, keeping her head high and knowing that she would make it through to the end of the contract like the professional she was. Knowing that, no matter how dire her situation, she was supporting herself.

Thoughts of Brodie were insistent, but she cranked up the music to drown them out.

After spending the morning at her audition for the Harbour Dance Company she'd gone looking for a cheap apartment to rent. Luck must have been on her side. A tiny one-bedroom place had been vacant for a few weeks and the owner was desperate to get someone in. As she'd signed the paperwork a call had come from the dance company, congratulating her on a successful audition.

Now she was on her way to visit her mother and collect all the boxes she'd stored there. Everything had turned out the way she'd wanted it to—once her bar contract was over it would all be perfect. So why didn't she have a sense of accomplishment and relief?

Brodie.

He'd been the only thing on her mind since she'd walked

away. It had barely been three days and already there was a gaping hole in her life where he'd inserted himself in their short time together. She missed his cheeky smile, the way his arms felt as they squeezed her against him, his lips. The unmanageable desire that materialised whenever he was around. How could she have let herself fall so hard? So quickly and so deeply?

Her childhood home came into view as Chantal rounded the corner at Beach Road, where blue water lined the quiet coast of Batemans Bay. *Home sweet home.*

The roads were empty. Most of the tourists from Canberra would have gone home by now. Work would be slow for her mum…the motels and self-contained units that dotted the shoreline wouldn't need extra cleaning services now that summer was over. Hopefully she still had a gig with the local high school to at least cover rent and bills. Though there would be little left over after the essentials were covered.

Chantal pulled into the parking bay of the apartment block and killed the engine. Stepping out of the car, she smiled at the way the number on their letterbox still hung at a funny angle and the squat garden gnome she'd given her mother one Christmas still guarded the steps up to their second-floor apartment.

The stairs were rickety beneath her feet, and the railing's paintwork peeled off in rough chunks. She was certain it had been white at one point—now it looked closer to the colour of pale custard. The doorbell trilled and footsteps immediately sounded from within the front room. Her mother appeared and ushered Chantal inside with brisk familiarity.

'You should have called. I would have put afternoon tea on.' Her mother enveloped her in a quick hug.

Frances Turner's affection was like everything else she did: quick, efficient and with minimal fuss. She'd never been overly demonstrative while Chantal was growing up, but age had softened her edges.

'No need,' Chantal said, smiling and waving her hand. 'I'm here to visit you—not to eat.'

It was more that she hadn't wanted her mother to feel obligated to go out and buy biscuits, or the fancy tea she liked to drink when Chantal came over. It was easy to see where her desire to keep up appearances had come from.

'Sit, sit…'

Frances gestured to the couch—a tattered floral two-seater that had yellowed with age. Chantal remembered using the back of it as a substitute *barre* while practising for her ballet exams.

'How are you?'

'I'm good.' She smiled brightly, pulling her lips up into a curve and hoping her mother didn't look too closely. 'I got a call this morning. I'm joining the Harbour Dance Company.'

Frances clapped her hands together. 'I *knew* you could do it, baby girl.'

'Thanks, Mum.'

'Why the sad face?' Frances studied her with olive-green eyes identical to hers. Nothing got past those eyes. 'What's going on?'

'Oh, it's nothing,' Chantal said, but she couldn't force the tremble from her voice. 'Boy problems.'

'Derek's not giving you trouble again, is he?' Her thin lips pulled into a flat line. Her mother had hated Derek from day one—something Chantal should have paid more attention to.

'No, Derek is long gone.' She rolled her eyes. 'I've been spending some time with an old friend. It got…confusing.'

'How so?' Frances motioned for Chantal to follow her into the kitchen.

Yellow floral linoleum covered the floor, matching the

painted yellow dining chairs and the small round dining table. The kitchen was her favourite part of the unit—it was kind of garish and dated, but it had the heart of a good home.

She traced her fingertip along the length of a photo on the wall. Chantal stood with her mother, wearing a jazz dance costume they'd stayed up till midnight sequinning the night before a competition. She had a gap-toothed grin and her mother looked exhausted. She didn't remember her mother looking that way at the time. All she'd cared about was the trophy clutched in her young hand.

Guilt scythed through her.

'He doesn't get me and I don't get him. We're different people.'

'But you liked him enough to spend time with him?' Frances twisted the tap, holding the kettle under the running water with her other hand.

'I did.' *I do...*

'And you think it's not good to be different?' Her mother threw her a look she'd seen a lot growing up. She called it the *Get off your high horse* look.

'It's not that. It's just…' How could she explain it? 'He wanted to do everything for me. And I'm capable of doing things myself. I *want* to do things myself. I don't need some knight in shining armour to rescue me.'

Her mother would be the one person who would understand. She'd stood on her own two feet since Chantal's father had walked out. She knew what it meant to be independent—what it meant to achieve things on your own.

'And that bothers you?'

'It does. It's like he can't understand that I need to fix my own problems.' She sighed. 'I want to be able to say that I made my way without any hand-outs.'

'Accepting help is not the same as accepting a handout, Chantal. There's no gold medal for struggling through life on your own.'

The kettle whistled, cutting into their conversation with a loud screech. Frances lifted it from the stove and poured the piping hot water into two mugs with pictures of cats all over them.

'I know that.'

'Don't you think I would have accepted some help if it was available when you were growing up?'

The question rattled Chantal. 'But you used to tell me that it was us against the world and we had to work hard.'

'I wanted you to be strong, baby girl. I wanted you to be tough.' She dropped the teabags into the bin and handed a mug to Chantal. 'Sometimes being strong means knowing when you can't do it on your own. Accepting help doesn't make you weak.'

They moved to the table, and Chantal was glad to be sitting on something solid. Her knees had turned to jelly, and her breath was escaping her lungs in a long whoosh. Her mother had tipped all her long-held beliefs on their head.

'I would have *killed* for someone to come along and offer a hand when you were younger.' Frances blew on the curling steam from the tea. 'Though I feel like I did a pretty good job with you, considering.'

A smile tugged at the corners of Chantal's lips. 'Would it be conceited if I agree?'

'Not at all.' Frances reached across the small table and patted the back of her hand.

'I've stuffed up, haven't I?'

Realisation flooded her, running across her nerves until her whole body was alight with the knowledge that she'd thrown away something important. Something special.

Brodie.

She didn't want to have him back in her life. She didn't want to love him.

But she did.

She'd known it was more than sex from the first time she'd woken up in his arms. But it hadn't been until she'd stood at the edge of his boat, with the freedom of the open waters dancing in her hair, looking down at the dolphins, that she'd realised how much he would do for her. That he wanted to show her what she was missing out on by being so narrow-minded.

And what had she done to return the favour? She'd picked a fight with him…refused to let him in. She'd told him to go. No matter how much time passed, she'd never forget the hurt written on his face when she'd told him not to come after her.

How could she possibly fix it?

'Nothing is irreversible, baby girl.'

Could she let herself believe that? Would she be able to handle the rejection if the damage was too much? Funny how a few weeks ago the thought of another dance company rejecting her had been her driving force. Now her victory seemed hollow without Brodie in her life. She loved dance—it was in her blood—but a world without him seemed…hopeless. Grey.

'I need to get my stuff. I've got an apartment in Sydney now.' Her voice was hollow, her movements stiff and jerky, as if she were being directed by puppet strings.

'Go to him, Chantal. The stuff can wait. *Things* can wait.' Frances stood and gave Chantal a gentle shove towards the front door. 'He might not.'

'I don't know how to get to him.' There were too many variables…too many things to deal with. What if he'd already left for Queensland?

'Find a way—you always do.'

Chantal surprised her mother by pulling her in for a big hug—a *real* hug. Planting a kiss on her cheek, she grabbed her bag and headed for the front door. Canberra airport was the closest airport that would allow her to fly to Brisbane, but it was a two-hour drive away. She didn't even know the name of his company.

Her sneakers hit the steps in quick succession and didn't slow as she raced towards her car.

'Call me when you find him!' Frances called out.

'I will.'

She slammed the door too hard in her haste, the sound ringing out like a shot. Was she *doing* this?

Chantal bit down on her lip and looked at her mobile phone in its holder on the inside of her windscreen. There was one person who could help her. She had no idea if his number was still the same, or if he would protect Brodie rather than talk to her. But she had to try.

As she paused for a red light Chantal tapped the screen and dialled a number.

'Hello?' Scott's voice echoed through the car.

'Scott, it's Chantal. I'm hoping you can help me…'

Brodie stood in the helm, staring blankly out at the harbour. The moored boats were lined up in tidy rows, the *Princess 56* blending into the Sydney scene better than it had in Newcastle. He couldn't be anywhere on the boat without remembering Chantal.

Was she back in the city by now? Doubt rooted him to the deck. Not because he didn't believe in his feelings for her, but because he had no idea if she would ever reciprocate. He couldn't remember a time when a girl had left him so strung out…except for the Weeping Reef situation with Chantal the first time around.

Chantal: two. Brodie: zero.

Giggling came from a couple walking past the boat—the sound of two people in love. He looked away, focusing on the dials in the cockpit. He knew he should sail home, but something had stopped him from preparing the yacht.

The beautiful views and the freedom of sailing felt wasted without Chantal. No matter how opulent the scenery, it was marked by her absence.

He turned his phone over in his hands. He could call her, invite her for a drink. Apologise for pushing too hard. Then what?

Those three little words hung over him like a dead weight. Three. Little. Words.

They changed everything. He'd never loved any woman before—he hadn't thought he had any love left over after his family had taken their share. But she seemed to pull emotion from him that he'd never even known existed. It had forced him to do things he'd never thought he could… like confront his father.

The *Princess 56* was waiting for him, ready and willing. It sat there patiently, needing him only to make a decision. He could either find out where Chantal was or he could sail home.

No, he wasn't going home without her.

Scott was right—he *had* to try again. He *had* to be sure there wasn't a chance for them. His attraction to her had always been more than he'd admitted. More than her gorgeous legs, her dancing, the sex. It was something so frighteningly intense and real that he'd been unable to process it until it was too late.

Brodie was about to pick up his phone to dial her number when it buzzed. Lydia's smiling face flashed up on the screen.

'Hey, Lyds.'

'Hey, Brodie.' There was hesitation in his sister's voice. 'So…Dad called.'

'He did?' Something lifted in Brodie's chest. His father had ended their call earlier with a promise to get in touch with the girls more often, though Brodie still had his doubts. 'What did he say?'

'He's coming to visit,' Lydia replied. 'Well, he *says* that, but we'll see.'

'Would you *like* him to visit?'

'Yeah, I guess.' She hesitated. 'It would be good to see him.'

He sincerely hoped his father lived up to his promise. He'd got a sense that his father's attitude had changed—there'd seemed to be something more receptive about him that had been lacking in the past. Something down in his gut told him that their conversation had been a shifting point for the older man—a reality check that his family needed him. That his daughters needed him.

Brodie could get by on his own, but he had plans to make Chantal a part of his life more permanently—and that meant he couldn't always play the role of pseudo father. The girls needed to know they could rely on their real father as well. Hopefully this was the beginning of all that.

Lydia caught his attention by launching into a new problem—something to do with Ellen and how she was trying to mother her, even though she was the youngest sibling. But Brodie was no longer listening.

A figure hovered nearby on the jetty. Long legs, long dark hair.

Chantal.

'Brodie, are you listening to me?'

Lydia's indignant tone brought his attention back to the call. 'Sorry, Lyds. I have to go.'

He stepped out onto the upper deck and tried to get a better look at the figure. Was it really her?

'But I need your *help*.' His sister sounded as though she were about to cry. 'That's *why* I called you.'

'I'll help you. But I need to do something for me first.'

She sniffled. 'What's more important than talking to your sister?'

He jogged over to the stairs, taking them as quickly as his legs would allow. 'Love.'

'Is this about that girl?' Lydia asked, her voice returning to normal.

'It is.'

'You *love* her?'

'I do, Lyds. I'm going to ask her if she loves me back.'

'Dibs on being the maid of honour,' Lydia said. 'Call me later. Tell me *everything*.'

'I promise.'

Brodie rushed to the jetty and looked around. Late afternoon had given way to early evening and the sun was lowering itself into the water along the horizon. Autumn had started weeks ago but it had only now taken on its first chill of the year, and the cool air prickled his exposed forearms.

People milled about, stopping to take photos of the yachts. Dodging a father towing two small children, Brodie jogged to where he'd seen the figure standing. He couldn't locate Chantal amongst the swarming tourist crowd.

The girl with dark hair had disappeared—had it even been her?

He walked up past the yacht club entrance, past the other boats, until he neared the hotel that sprawled along the water's edge.

He was going crazy. His imagination was playing him for a fool. Why would she come to him when he'd stuffed things up? He hadn't even been able to tell her that he loved her. She deserved better than that.

He headed back to the boat, turning his phone over in his hands. His thumb hovered over the unlock button, ready to dial her number. As he walked across the boarding ramp and raked a hand through his hair he stopped to rub the tense muscles in his neck.

'Brodie?'

Chantal walked out from the cabin, hands knotted in front of her. Long dark strands tumbled around her shoulders, the messy waves scattered by the gentle breeze. A skirt with blue and green shades bleeding into one another swirled around her ankles with each step. A long gold chain weighted by a blue stone glinted around her neck. She looked like a mermaid…a siren. A fantasy.

'What are you doing here?' he asked, his heart hammering against his ribs.

'I thought you'd gone back to Queensland.'

She bundled her hair over one shoulder, toying with the ends as he'd noticed her doing whenever she was anxious. He noticed everything about her now.

'I was supposed to.'

'Why did you stay?'

Light flickered across her face—a ray of hopefulness that dug deep into his chest.

'Unfinished business.'

'With who?'

The question emerged so quietly it might have come from his imagination. But her lips had moved; her eyes were burning into his.

'With you, Chantal. Why do you have to make everything so hard?'

A smile tugged at the corner of her lips. 'I'm difficult, I guess.'

'You are.'

He rubbed at the back of his neck, wishing that his body would calm down so he could be in control of the conversation. Instead his central nervous system conspired against him by sending off signals left, right and centre. There was something about the mere presence of her that had him crackling with electricity. Those parts of him had been dead before her.

'I'm sorry I pushed you away.' She drew a deep breath.

'I'm sorry I wouldn't let you help. I've been afraid of letting anyone close—not just after my divorce but for a long time.'

'You do seem to have trouble accepting help…'

What if he didn't accept her apology? It would be her own fault. She'd been stubborn as a bull from day one, determined to keep a wall between her and the outside world. Only now she wanted to tear down anything standing between her and Brodie. She wanted to remove all barriers—even the ones that had been there so long that they had cemented themselves in.

'I'm working on it,' she said solemnly, swallowing against a rising tide of emotion. 'I thought that I needed to do everything on my own because that's what my mother did. I wanted to be strong…to be my own person.'

He rubbed a hand along his jaw. 'It's a lonely way to live.'

'It is.' She nodded. 'I've been so concerned with making everyone think I was leading this successful life that I put no time into my reality. I only cared about my career, and I almost lost the best thing that ever happened to me.'

'Which is…?' His green eyes reached hers, the burning stare making her knees shake and her limbs quiver.

'You, Brodie. You're an amazing friend, and I lost you once because I refused to acknowledge my feelings. I'm not doing it again.'

She stepped towards him, resisting the urge to reach out and flatten her palms against the soft cotton shirt covering his chest.

'I don't want your friendship, Chantal.' He ground the words out, his teeth gritted, jaw tense.

Her breath hitched. The flight response was tugging against her desire to fight. *No!* She'd come too far to turn away—she could make him see how much she cared. She could make him see that she could change. That she *had* changed already, thanks to him.

'You asked me that night if I felt something for you.' Memories flickered: the sensation of dancing in his arms. The scents. The heat. The intoxicating attraction. 'I never had the chance to answer and then you were gone. I spent eight years convincing myself I'd made an error of judgment. I'd got caught up in the emotion. But I *did* feel something.'

'And now?'

'I want you in my life, Brodie. I want to sail away with you. I *want* your friendship, but I want more than that too.' She squeezed her eyes closed for a moment so she would have the courage to speak again. 'I love you.'

In the silence of waiting for his reaction she'd never felt so vulnerable in her life. No matter how many stages she'd performed on, no matter how much rejection she'd faced before—this was it. She was at a turning point, at the edge of falling into something wonderful. Her breath caught in her throat.

'I'll protect you even when you don't think you need it—I can't help that.' His voice caught, the scratch edge telling her that he was fighting for control too. 'But I'll support you in being your own person.'

She nodded, her breath caught in her throat.

'I'll help you with everything. I will *always* be there for you.'

She sucked on her lower lip, her mind screaming out for her to touch him. But she didn't want to stop his words, didn't want to risk ruining things with him again. If only he would say those words back to her.

I love you.

'I'll make you part of my crazy needy family.' He reached forward and drew her close. 'But I know now that I don't need to be your knight in shining armour. I pushed too hard at the bar. I understand that you need your independence. So I propose that we be our own people… together.'

'Oh, Brodie.' Relief coursed through her, buckling her knees so she sagged against him. The warmth of his body relaxed her, calmed her.

'As much as I love my family, I want to be my own person too. You made me see that. I'm going to put my own needs first for a change—and that starts with loving you.'

She looked up at him, catching his mouth as it came down to hers. The taste of him sent her senses into a spin, the gentle pressure of his lips making her feel as if she'd come home. His tongue met with hers, all the relief and desire and love exploding within her like New Year's fireworks. This was it—this was how life was meant to be.

She broke away from the kiss. 'What needs might they be?'

'Specific needs,' he whispered against her ear, his warm breath sending a shiver down her spine. 'Needs that can only be met by stubborn brunette dancers who like to practise yoga.'

'I might know someone who fits the bill.' She ran her hand under his T-shirt and pressed against the hard muscles in his stomach, as if memorising every ridge and detail of him. 'But she's pretty busy these days. I heard a rumour that she finally made it into a dance company.'

His eyes lit up and he hoisted her up in the air. 'You did?'

The harbour lights blurred as he spun them around. The sky darkened as each moment passed. Somehow it felt as though the universe was cementing their decision to be together.

'I did.' She laughed as he brought her back down. Solid ground would never feel the same again.

'I never had any doubts.'

'You were the only one.' She shot him a rueful smile.

'Not true.' He cupped her face with his hands and pressed another exploratory kiss to her lips. 'But you *do* need a little help with the constant doubt.'

'Are you testing me?'

'Maybe.' A sly smile pulled at his lips.

'Well, I accept your help.' She jabbed a finger into the centre of his chest, unable to conceal a grin. 'So there.'

'Chantal, I need to be able to help you. I need to be part of your life in a way that no one else can. I'll give you everything you deserve. I'll do everything I can to give you the life you want.'

The thumping of his heart reverberated against her ear.

'I'm going to run the business from Sydney.'

'Can you do that?' Her head jerked up.

'That's the best bit about being the boss.' He grinned. 'I can do whatever I like.'

'But what about your family?'

'I put a call in to my father. He's going to start sharing the load with me.' A flash of vulnerability streaked across Brodie's eyes. ''Bout time.'

'Really? That's wonderful.'

'Besides, Queensland is only a state away, and I'm sure you'll need a break at some point. I'll have to split my time across the two states but I know I can manage it.' He chuckled. 'Besides, the girls will be desperate to meet you.'

'I'd love to meet *them*. I never had what you had growing up. I know your family isn't perfect, but I've never been part of a family like that before.'

The idea was frightening—what if his sisters hated her?

'They'll love you. I know it.' He stroked her hair, pressing his lips to her forehead. 'But you were right to point out that I hide behind my family responsibilities. I *have* been hiding.'

She smiled against his chest. 'You can't hide any more.'

'I don't want to. I love you, Chantal.'

He spoke into her hair, his arms tight around her shoulders, his hand caressing her back.

Music wafted over the night air from the boat next to them.

Brodie wrapped his arms around her waist, moving her to the music. 'And I always said pretty girls shouldn't have to dance on their own.'

'I won't dance on my own ever again.'

* * * * *

THE SPY WHO TAMED ME

KELLY HUNTER

For my wonderful editor, Joanne Grant.
Thanks for your patience.

CHAPTER ONE

ROWAN FARRINGDON DREADED Sunday dinners with her parents. The tradition was a new one, instated exactly one month after her parents had retired and bought themselves a gleaming glory of a house that has all the showiness of a museum and no warmth whatsoever. Even the floral arrangements were formal.

She'd made a mistake two months ago, when she'd turned up with an armful of scented overblown cream- and butter-coloured roses and had had them relegated to the laundry sink—doubtless to be tossed out at her mother's earliest convenience.

She hadn't made that mistake again.

For some reason her mother loved this house, and insisted that Rowan—as her only child and heir—love the house as well.

Never going to happen.

Rowan's hurried 'I'm well set up already, Mum. Sell the house. Spend every last penny you have before you go, I really won't mind...' probably hadn't been the most politically sensible thought ever voiced, but Rowan had meant every word of it.

To say that Rowan and her mother neither knew nor understood each other was something of an understatement.

Four people graced the enormous round table at this particular evening's formal dinner. Rowan's mother, father, grandfather, and herself. Presumably the round table gave the impression that everyone sitting at it was of equal importance, but the actual conversation around the table told a different story.

Rowan shared a glance with her grandfather as her father launched into yet another monologue that revolved around dining with dignitaries and very important people she'd never heard of. Both her parents had been Army in her younger years, and had made the switch to foreign ambassador postings later on. They'd led the expat life for most of their lives, while Rowan had been largely left behind with her grandfather. His job hadn't exactly been geared towards the raising of children either—he'd been an Army general—but he'd never once left her behind and she loved him all the more for it.

Rowan's phone buzzed once from its pocket in her handbag, sitting on the side table where she'd put it when she arrived, and Rowan winced. She knew what was coming.

'I thought I asked you to turn that off?' her mother told her coolly, her almond-brown eyes hard with displeasure.

People often thought brown eyes were soft, liquid and lovely.

Not all of them.

'You know I can't.' Rowan rose. 'Excuse me. I have to take that.'

She took her phone and the information on it out into the hall and returned a minute or so later. She crossed to her bag and slung it over her shoulder.

'You're leaving?' Her mother's voice was flat with accusation rather than disappointment.

Rowan nodded.

'Trouble?' asked her grandfather.

'I'm covering for one of the other directors this week, while he's out of the country. One of his agents has just emerged from deep cover. We're bringing him in.'

'We barely see you any more,' her mother offered next—never mind that before they'd retired they'd barely seen her at all.

'You barely saw her during her childhood,' her grandfather told his daughter bluntly. 'At least when Rowan leaves at a moment's notice she gives us an explanation.'

There was enough truth in those words to make her mother's lips draw tight. Enough of a sting in them to make Rowan's memories clamour for attention.

'But it's my *birthday*,' Rowan had once said to her mother as her parents had headed out through the door, their travel bags rolling behind them like obedient pets. 'Grandfather made cake. He *made* it for us.'

'I'm sorry, dear,' her mother had said. 'Needs must.'

'But you've only been here one day,' she'd said to her father once, and had received a stern lecture on tolerance and duty for her efforts.

'Where are you going?'

She'd stopped asking that one. To this day she didn't think she'd ever received a truthful answer. The take-home message had always been that they were going somewhere important and that Rowan wasn't welcome.

'You need to toughen up,' her parents had told her over and over—and toughen up she had.

That her mother now wanted a different type of relationship with her only child concerned Rowan not at all.

'I'm sorry. I have to go.'

'Your grandfather's not getting any younger, Rowan. You could do more for him.'

Her mother's salvo had been designed to hurt, but Rowan just smiled politely and let it land on barren ground somewhere left of its target. Rowan saw her grandfather at least twice a week, and called him every other day and then some.

Not that her mother knew that.

Nor did Rowan feel the urge to enlighten her.

'You'd like this agent who's just arrived,' she told her grandfather, for she knew he'd be interested. 'He's been causing utter mayhem with very limited resources.'

'Is he ex-Army?'

'No, he's one of ours from the ground up. Very creative.'

Ten to one that the next time she called her grandfather he'd know who she was talking about. He might be long retired, but he still had impressive contacts.

'Yes, yes, Rowan. We *know* your job's important,' her mother said waspishly, and Rowan turned towards the immaculately coiffured woman who'd given birth to her.

For a woman who'd presumably had to fight the same gender battles that Rowan still fought, her mother appeared singularly unimpressed by Rowan's successes and the position she now held within the Australian Secret Intelligence Service.

'Enjoy your meal.' She managed a kiss for both her parents. 'I brought apple cobbler for dessert.'

'Did you make it yourself?'

One more barb from a mother who'd barely lifted a hand in the kitchen her entire life—such was the privileged expat existence she'd led.

'No. A friend of mine made it because I paid her to. It's her grandmother's recipe, passed down through the generations. I hope you like it.'

Dismissing her mother, she crossed next to her grandfather and placed a soft kiss on his cheek.

Her phone pinged again and Rowan straightened. 'Time to go.'

'I suppose that's your driver?' her mother said sarcastically. 'He's a little impatient.'

'No, he's just letting me know that he's here.'

'Maybe you'll see your way to staying for the entire meal next month. If I even bother to continue with these dinners.'

'Your call, Mother.' Rowan glanced towards her father, who'd sat uncharacteristically silent throughout the exchange. 'Are *you* displeased with me as well?'

Her father said nothing. Ever the diplomat.

'You know, Mother...both of you, come to think of it...just once you might want to try being proud of me and the position I hold instead of continually criticising my choices. Just once. Maybe then I'd give you the time of day you so clearly expect.'

And that, thought Rowan grimly, was the end of Sunday dinner with her parents.

Her grandfather stood, always the gentleman, and accompanied her into the hall and to the front door while her parents stayed behind. It wasn't his house—it was her mother's immaculate mausoleum—but it would never occur to her to afford her daughter the same kind of courtesy she'd spent a lifetime offering to others.

Her mother had been a well-respected foreign ambassador, for heaven's sake. Marissa Farringdon-Stuart *knew* how to honour others.

'Don't mind her,' Rowan's grandfather said gently.

'She's getting worse.'

'She's losing her grip on what's acceptable behaviour and what's not. Early onset dementia.'

'Nice try, old man, but I know what dementia is and what it's not.'

What her mother dispensed had nothing to do with dementia—it was carefully calculated vitriol.

'She's jealous, and some of that's my doing,' her grandfather said gruffly. 'I never had time for her. I learned from that mistake and made sure I had time for you. Plus, you've done extremely well in your chosen profession. Your mother's competitive. That irks her too.'

'And my father? What's *his* beef with me?'

'Who'd know?' There was no love lost between her grandfather and the man his daughter had chosen to marry. 'He's an idiot. Too much noble blood and not enough brain cells.'

'I'll call you tomorrow,' she murmured.

'You look beautiful this evening,' her grandfather told her gruffly.

'Flatterer.'

Rowan tried to look her best for Sunday dinner—her mother expected it—but there was no escaping the fact that her eyes were unfashionably slanted, her mouth was too wide and her ears stuck out rather a lot, no matter what she did with her hair. In the end she'd cut her hair pixie-short and to hell with her ears.

She could look 'interesting', at a pinch.

Give her half an hour and the right kind of make-up and she could even look arresting.

But she would never be beautiful.

'Take the apple cobbler home with you when you go.

Ask for it. She'll only toss it the first chance she gets, and I had Maddy make it especially for you. Extra cinnamon.'

'I'll save you some.'

'I'll hold you to it.' Rowan embraced her increasingly fragile grandfather. 'See you Wednesday?'

He nodded. 'And bring me carnage, politics or intrigue.'

Rowan stepped from the house and headed towards the waiting vehicle. 'You can be sure of that.'

CHAPTER TWO

HE'D MISSED BIRTHDAYS, two Christmases and two New Year's Eves, but he hadn't missed his sister's wedding. That had to count for something.

So he'd been slightly late and utterly filthy? His sister Lena had still slotted him into her wedding party without a moment's hesitation, before turning back to the celebrant and marrying his best friend, Trig—Adrian Sinclair.

That had been several hours ago now. The wedding dinner plates had long since been cleared away and the dancing was now in full flow beside the lazy snake of an Aussie river, with spotlit red gums soaring into the night sky. Jared had tried to be there in spirit as well as in body. He'd smiled until his jaw ached. He'd danced with the bride and he'd teased the groom. He'd stood until he couldn't stand any more, and then he'd sat beneath one of the big old gum trees, his back to the bark, and let the party happen around him.

It had to be mid-evening by now—with many of the guests gearing up to kick on well into the night. Jared, on the other hand, could feel the adrenalin seeping out of his body and leaving a bone-deep exhaustion in its wake. He needed to find a bed and lie in it for a few days, weeks, months… He needed to find a place to be, a place to stay.

Damon had offered the beach house, and, yeah, maybe that would work for a few days. But people had a habit of dropping by the beach house, and what Jared really wanted was to be alone.

He watched with faint interest as Trig headed his way with a woman in tow. She'd arrived about an hour ago and hadn't seemed the slightest bit perturbed that she'd missed the wedding ceremony or the food. Not a guest, he surmised. He didn't quite know *what* she was.

Immaculately dressed—he'd give her that. All class, with slender legs and a pair of high-heeled shoes that he figured had cost a small fortune. Both his sisters had gone through an expensive shoe phase. He recognised the look of them, even if he couldn't recognise the brand.

The shoes stopped in front of him and he looked up, his head resting against the tree trunk, steadying him, holding him.

Up close, he could see that the slender athletic form he'd been admiring had more miles on it than he'd thought. Up close, he could see that whoever had put this woman's face together had had one hell of a liking for the unusual. She had a wide, lush mouth that tilted up at the edges, and wide-set eyes that tilted up at the edges too. Her nose was small. Her brown hair was short and boyish. Her ears weren't big, but maybe—just maybe—they stuck out a little.

Together, her features made up a whole that was too odd to be classically beautiful and too arresting to be ignored.

'Jared, I want you to meet Rowan Farringdon,' Trig

said. 'The new Head of Counter-Surveillance, Section Five.'

Section Five. Jared tried to get his brain to work. Section Five was Eastern Europe, and when he'd left two years ago it had been headed up by Old Man Evans. Hard to say if she was going to be an ally Jared could use or not.

Probably not.

'Your reputation precedes you, Mr West.'

Her voice came at him gravel-rough, with just enough honey at the edges to keep things interesting. She bent lower; she had to if she wanted to get a good look at his face.

'You're not as pretty as I'd been led to expect.'

'Give me time. Bruises fade.'

She smiled at him then, careless and casual, and that smile…

That smile was a weapon.

'Your sister suggested that you might want a lift up to the house. I have a car here.'

He'd noticed it. Black. Sleek. Probably armour-plated.

'Why all the security for a wedding?' He'd noticed them—of course he had. Fully a quarter of the guests here tonight were Special Forces and plenty of them were packing. As was the woman standing in front of him.

'You know the answer to that one, cowboy.' She smiled again, more gently this time. 'We're here for you.'

'You're not my section head.'

'And for that I am truly grateful. You've made quite a mess. *Bravo.* But the fact remains that we're here to take you to Canberra and make sure nothing untoward happens to you along the way.'

'Give me the weekend and I'll go willingly.'

'Mr West…' It was a murmur shot through with indulgence. 'We're giving you tonight, and for that you should be grateful. You were due back two years ago.'

'Sorry I'm late.' Jared shot her a lazy grin, just to see if it would annoy her. 'You're young for a director.'

'I'm forty years old and cunning as an outhouse rat.'

She was ten years older than him.

'Like I said…'

Her laugh came low and unfettered and slid straight into the number one spot in the list of things he needed to make this woman do again.

'Don't underestimate me, Mr West. And I won't underestimate you.'

'Call me Jared,' he murmured, and then he caught Trig's sudden alertness and switched his attention to his oldest friend—who was now his brand-new brother-in-law.

'Jared…'

Trig looked faintly amused—or was it resigned? Maybe Trig had ESP, or maybe he'd simply known Jared so long that he could read every twitch, but somehow Trig had sensed his interest in this section head with the funny face and the whisky voice and the smile that was a weapon.

'No.'

'Yes.'

'Really bad idea.'

'I've had worse.' Jared turned his attention back to the director and smiled.

Rowan Farringdon wasn't slow on the uptake. 'Listen to your friend, Mr West. I'd chew you up and spit you out before breakfast.'

'I wouldn't complain.'

'Oh, but you would.'

Did the woman's lips *never* stop tilting towards a smile?

'If I get in that car with you am I going to end up at the farmhouse or in debrief?'

'At the farmhouse for tonight. I give you my word. You don't have to be in debrief until ten past nine tomorrow morning.'

'Any idea what they plan to do with me after that?'

Her expression grew guarded and in that moment he got a glimpse of the razor-sharp politicking that could make a woman section head at forty.

'I dare say that'll depend on the way you play your cards from here on in. You *can* play? Right?'

He was handsomer than she'd expected, thought Rowan—and she'd expected a lot. His body was big, and brutally honed for fighting, and the close-cropped black hair on his head only added to his formidable air. In contrast, his face could have graced billboards or movie screens, and his mouth had a ripeness to it that would leave lovers dreaming for just one more taste. Great jawline and cheekbones—and eyes that had seemed soft and liquid-bright whenever he looked at his sister, but were sharp and assessing now.

This was the man who'd singlehandedly destroyed a hundred-billion-dollar illegal arms empire. Singlehandedly exposed a line of rot within the anti-terrorism unit he'd worked for that had stretched all the way to a sub-director's chair. The fallout had been spectacular, and there was fierce debate as to whether there was still more to come—whether he'd withheld information… saved the best until last.

She would have.

'Mr West, let me drive you up to the house and have a doctor take a look at you. My men are taking bets on how many ribs you've broken and whether or not you've lost your hearing. Odds are three to one at the moment that you're simply a very good lip-reader.'

'They just want to look at my lips.' Jared West let his lips curve into that lazy smile again. 'I get that a lot.'

'I'm sure you do. And I'm sure you use it to your best advantage.' She let her gaze linger on the lips in question, because they really *were* that good, but after a slow count to three she stopped and snapped her gaze back to his eyes. *Control.* She had it and she fully intended to keep it. 'The fact remains that we'd like someone to take a look at you.'

'Is that an order?'

'Do you take them?'

He smiled again. 'From you—I might.'

'You could use a Taser on him?' Trig suggested. 'That might work.'

'I could, but he looks rough enough already. If I killed him there'd be paperwork.'

'Director, would you mind if I had a word with the groom in private?' asked West.

He tried to make the words sound like a request—he did give her that. But he expected her to grant his request. That much was very clear.

Rowan wasn't going anywhere until she'd figured out his health status.

'Try over by the river,' she suggested. 'It's private there.'

'It's private here.'

'Mr West.' Gloves off, then, and to hell with protecting his ego. 'How about you stand up and prove to my people that you can still walk?'

His chin came out. His gaze was all fierce challenge—no weakness in it at all.

'I can walk.'

'I'd like to see that.'

But he didn't get up.

Pride was a bitch.

'See that he gets to the house. We've a doctor waiting for him.'

Rowan didn't wait for Trig's reply before heading towards her car. She knew what it was going to cost West to get moving again. She'd been monitoring his movements ever since Antonov's super-yacht had blown up. The trail of destruction he'd left in his wake and his relentless drive to get home in time for his sister's wedding had been truly spectacular. No sleep for the past fifty hours and he was beyond exhausted—his body was struggling to hold him upright.

The only thing *keeping* him upright was willpower.

This was a man who'd been streamed for command from the moment he'd taken his first special intelligence service entry exam. He'd excelled at every position they'd ever given him. And if you counted his time with Antonov as solo dark ops work, he'd excelled at that too. She'd been expecting a pretty face atop a fierce intellect—a will of iron and a predisposition towards making trouble.

She wasn't disappointed.

'Great walk,' Jared murmured as he watched her walk away, all confidence and sway. And he still liked her ears.

'*Can* you walk?' Trig wasn't going to be distracted.

'I think so. I just can't get up.'

Trig held out his arm and Jared grasped it—high near the elbow, a climber's grip. Next minute he was standing, and gasping, trying not to pass out or throw up or both. Two harsh breaths after that Lena materialised beside him, swathed in wedding dress white, with her hand wrapped around his other upper arm to keep him balanced.

'You're heading up to the house?' she wanted to know.

'In a bit.' There was the small matter of having to get there on his own two feet to consider first.

He *could* walk.

Couldn't he?

'Use the bed in the master bedroom.'

'You mean *your* bed?' Their wedding bed? *Unlikely.* 'Yeah—no. Pretty dress. Maybe you should step back a bit.'

She didn't, and he bit down hard on his nausea. Lena never had been inclined to do as she was told. She was a lot like him in that regard. Instead she stepped up into his space, put a hand to his cheek and studied him with worried eyes.

'You look awful. Like you've been through hell to get here. Tell me you're not going back?'

'I can't tell you that, Lena.'

She got that stubborn set about her jaw that boded well for no one.

'Got some cleaning up to do,' he offered gruffly. 'Nothing too strenuous.'

'Do you still have a job?'

'Could be I'm not flavour of the month.'

Trig snorted.

'What did the director say?' asked Lena next.

'That we're leaving tomorrow.'

'Did she tell you that there's a doctor waiting up at the house to check you over? She called for one two minutes after she laid eyes on you.'

'Women *will* fuss.'

'Don't you dare lay that line on me. Or on her, for that matter. If I'd walked into *your* wedding looking like you do you'd have dragged me to the hospital two minutes after I arrived.'

'I'm going,' he muttered. 'Stop looking at me as if I'll break.'

'I had a *year* of people looking at me like that.'

'*I* didn't look at you like that,' he protested faintly.

'Yeah, because *you weren't here*.'

'I'm here now. Lena.'

It sounded like a plea. It *was* a plea. For mercy. For absolution. And she really needed to step away from him soon—before he ruined her dress.

'I'm going. I'll find a bed. Do whatever the good doctor says.' He covered her hand with his own and leaned into her touch. A moment of weakness—a tell for those watching. And there were plenty watching this little exchange. 'I'm going. I was just enjoying the party, that's all.'

He took one breath and then another. Stepped forward.

And the world went black.

CHAPTER THREE

'STUBBORN, ISN'T HE?' Rowan said to the hovering bride, in an attempt to put her at ease, while a local doctor recently persuaded to make house calls ordered the groom and one of her agents to lay Jared West on his back on the bed.

The bedroom décor was a mix of rainbow meeting Venetian chic, and the unconscious Jared looked decidedly out of place in it—never mind his hastily cobbled together wedding attire. Once a wolf, always a wolf… no matter what clothes he wore.

'You have no idea,' Lena said glumly. 'I should have let you escort him to hospital the minute he got here.'

Jared's eyelids lifted mere millimetres—just long enough for him to glare at them momentarily before they lowered again.

'What's his name?' asked the doctor.

'Jared West,' said Lena. 'Pain in the arse *extraordinaire*.'

The doctor grabbed a small flashlight and bent towards the patient. 'Jared? You with me?'

Jared grunted what might have been a yes.

'I'm going to check your pupils for responsiveness to light. This won't hurt.'

'Not concussed. Concussion was three days ago. I'm over it,' Jared mumbled, but he proceeded to co-operate.

'Glad to hear it. Does that diagnosis come with a medical degree as well?'

'Comes with experience.'

'Is he always this argumentative?' Rowan asked Lena from the end of the bed.

'Yeah, that's him. He prefers to call it persuasion.'

'Got any bumps on the head?' the doctor asked his newest patient.

'Couple.'

Jared let the doctor examine them.

'What about your neck? Any stiffness there? Movement okay?'

Jared had his eyes closed when he answered. 'My neck's okay. Shoulder's wrecked.'

So much for the busted eardrums theory, thought Rowan with a sliver of relief. If Jared could answer the doc's quiet questions without watching the older man's lips, he wasn't deaf.

'You're not deaf,' she said, and was rewarded by the faintest curve of Jared's lips. 'There goes a week's wages for at least half of my agents.'

'Yeah, but the other half will be richer for it.'

'What's he like when he really smiles?' Rowan asked.

Maybe it wasn't an entirely appropriate question to voice, but it never hurt to be well informed and armed for the battles ahead.

'I haven't seen it for a while,' Lena said. 'But historically it tends to be pretty lethal. Nations fall. Angels weep. That sort of thing.'

'Amen,' Jared mumbled.

'See, if he wasn't all beat up I'd thump that arrogance out of him,' offered Lena. 'Because I love him.'

Her eyes filled with tears and she turned away before her brother could open *his* eyes and see them.

The doctor picked it up, though, and his next words were soothing. 'He's conscious, he's coherent—'

'No blood coming out of any orifices. I'm perfect... Got any painkillers?' the patient said next.

'For what?'

'Ribs.'

'Sit up and let's have a look at them.'

Jared moved to a sitting position on the edge of the bed with a little help from Trig. He also accepted help when it came to the removal of his borrowed suit jacket, but he unbuttoned the shirt beneath it himself.

He took his time, but Rowan figured that the delay had more to do with Jared's current lack of fine motor skills than with any real desire to delay the process. Finally the shirt came off, to reveal a sweat-stained bandage held in place with silver electrician's tape.

'I dislocated my shoulder at one point as well. But I got it back in.'

'Yourself?'

'A bathtub helped.'

'Jared, can you raise your arms above your head?'

'Last time I tried that I woke up two hours later, face-down on the deck.'

'When was that?'

'Three days ago.'

'Any additional problems since then?'

'A crucifying lack of sleep.'

'Jared, I'm going to check your lungs and heart. Then you're going to raise your arms for me while I do it all again, and then you're going to lie back down while I examine your ribs more thoroughly.'

Jared nodded.

Rowan tried to afford the man some privacy, but it was hard not to stare at the spectacular bruising that bloomed across his sculpted chest as the doctor unwound the bandage. He'd taken a beating, this man. And then some.

The doctor listened to his lungs and heart with a stethoscope and then poked and prodded around his stomach and lower still while everyone else stood and watched. And then, as the patient began to raise his arms and the doctor began to press on his ribs, he passed out again.

'May as well keep going,' said the doctor as he caught him and eased him back onto the bed with impressive nonchalance.

Jared came round moments later but stayed right where he was, encouraged to do so by the doctor's hand on his shoulder.

The examination continued and the doctor finally made comment. 'Without access to X-rays, I'm thinking he has four substantially cracked ribs.'

'Show-off,' muttered Lena, her voice ragged with worry. 'What else?'

'Soft tissue damage—as you can see. Probably some compression damage. Do we know what hit him?'

'We know there was a series of explosions on board a yacht, and we can reasonably assume that Jared was thrown around by them. He also drove a truck through a warehouse wall and rolled a four-wheel drive in the desert.'

That was all the detail a civilian doctor needed.

'All of which happened two to three days ago.' She looked at the physician. 'He's been travelling ever since. Does he need a hospital?'

'No,' said West. Conscious again. 'I've already been to one.'

Not by my reckoning. 'Where?'

'In…um…' His voice drifted off. 'Might have been Budapest. X-rays. Strobe lights. Everything. They gave me pills.'

'Sure it wasn't a disco?' she offered dryly.

'I like you,' he said.

'Can you remember the name of the pills?' the doctor asked.

Jared snorted. 'No. They were good, though. Kept the packet for future reference. Pocket.'

The doctor leaned down and rifled through the shirt on the floor, pulling out a small container. 'How many did they give you?'

'Five.'

'Two to three days ago, yes? It says here one a day. Where are the other two? And don't tell me you doubled up on them.'

So the patient said nothing.

'What are they?' asked Lena.

'Cocaine derivative. Explains his ability to keep going, perhaps. And why he's crashing so heavily now.'

'Yep,' Jared muttered. 'Sleep.'

And then abruptly he tried to sit up again, with limited success.

'Why are there strawberries? Am I in the bridal suite?'

'No,' Lena told him. 'You're in the spare room.'

Jared subsided somewhat, but kept eyeing the strawberries warily. 'And those? Growing in the giant stripy teacup?'

'What about them?'

'Why?' His voice conveyed vast layers of confusion and a complete inability to comprehend such a thing.

'Her house, her rules,' offered Rowan. 'Don't over-think it.'

His eyes opened to slits. 'Does *your* spare room have strawberries in it?'

'I don't have any room to spare.'

'You probably let people crash in your room instead.' His lips quirked. 'I like it.'

'Jared,' said Lena sternly. 'Director on deck, remember? Less flirting—more respect.'

'Why are you still here?' Jared asked. 'Shouldn't you be at your wedding reception? All I'm doing right now is going to bed.' His voice softened. 'It's okay. *I'm* okay. I made it here, didn't I? Don't make me regret the effort.'

'If you need a hospital, Jared, and you're lying about having been to one already, I swear on my new husband's soul that I will make you regret it.'

'She's vicious,' Jared told his best friend. 'I hope you factored that in?'

The groom smiled, wide and warm. 'Get some rest.'

'I would if you left.'

The bride and groom made their exit, with Lena glancing back over her shoulder and warning her errant brother to be good just before the door closed behind them.

Only then did Jared allow his face to reset into a grimace of pain. 'Hey, Doc? About those painkillers…'

'On a scale of one to ten—one being zero and ten being unbearable—how much pain are you in?'

'If I lie perfectly still I can get it down to about a seven.'

The doctor told him to stay in bed and rummaged through his black medical bag for two little blue pills. He got a glass of water to wash them down with.

'This is going to knock you out. You may shower in the morning when you wake. No sudden movements. Preferably no more boat explosions or motor vehicle incidents.'

He looked at the patient and expanded his list.

'No surfing, boxing, skydiving or martial arts training. No weights, rock-climbing or kayaking. Getting the picture?'

'Loud and clear.'

'Gentle swimming...floating, paddling. Pretend you're three again. Shouldn't be too hard, by the sound of it.'

Rowan *liked* this elderly smalltown doctor.

'Listen to what your body is telling you and you might just come out of this in better shape than you deserve.'

Rowan liked this doctor a *lot*. 'You're not looking for casual work on an as-needed basis, are you? Because your bedside manner could really work for us.'

'I'm two years away from retirement and I've seen everything I want to see and then some when it comes to medical emergencies. I don't need to see any more of those.'

Pity.

'Hey, Doc...' the patient mumbled. 'Do you think she's got a funny face? I think so. But I really like it.'

The doctor sighed. 'That'll be the painkillers kicking in.'

'Great voice too,' Jared told them next. 'Makes me think of sex. Does it make *you* think of sex?'

'Son, you need to get some rest. Stop fighting it.'

The doctor slid Rowan a glance, his smirk in no way hidden.

'You might want to leave before he proposes.'

'I might want to hear it for blackmail purposes.' Come to think of it, she might just want to hear it for her own selfish reasons.

But it was a moot point. The man on the bed was already asleep.

'Do we have the all-clear to fly him elsewhere in the morning?'

The doctor nodded. 'Get him X-rayed as soon as you can…keep him hydrated, keep an eye on him.'

'Thank you for your co-operation.'

'Not a problem—no matter what my wife says. Always a pleasure to help our special intelligence service.' The doctor smiled his charmingly distinguished smile. 'Who do I bill?'

Jared woke in a bed that didn't rock with the rhythm of the ocean. It wasn't his bed—he knew that much. His bed for the past two years had been a narrow bunk beside the engine room of Antonov's super-yacht. It had been a floating fortress, locked down so hard that no one had been able to get near it undetected, and it had been more than capable of sinking anything that tried.

His bed hadn't been soft, like this one, and his bunkroom sure as hell hadn't contained a chest of drawers beneath a wooden window. Was that a pot full of *strawberries* sitting on top of it? He thought he remembered being puzzled by them last night as well. Because…*why*?

He opened his eyes a little more, turned his head and discovered lime-coloured sheets and a floral magenta and green comforter. If this was a motel he was clearly in the lollipop suite—but he didn't think this *was* a motel.

He rolled over onto his back and winced at the pain that seared through his body. There'd been a doctor at some point last night. The doctor had told him that his estimate of two cracked ribs had been a little under. There'd been pills last night too, and then there'd been blessed oblivion.

He was at Lena's farmhouse. He remembered now.

And he could use a couple more of those painkillers.

He heard a door open and then footsteps that seemed to stop at the end of the bed. He opened his eyes a little more. *Pretty* was his first thought. *Funny* was his next.

It was the woman from last night. He remembered her mouth and her ears. He didn't remember her eyes being quite such a tawny vivid gold.

'You awake?'

He also remembered her voice. His body heartily approved of her voice. 'Mmm…'

She wasn't just any woman. She was a director of counter-intelligence and he was in deep trouble. She wore a white collared shirt, dark grey trousers and a thin silver-coloured necklace that looked as if it would break the minute someone tugged on it. She was older than him by a few years and then some, and he was attracted to her, aware of her, in a way that he hadn't been aware of a woman for a very long time.

'We met last night,' he offered, in a voice still thick with sleep.

'So we did.'

No rings on her wedding finger. No rings anywhere on those slender, expertly manicured fingers.

'Not sure I remember who you are, though. Memory's a little fuzzy.'

Could be he was winding her up—just a little. Could be he wanted to see if her eyes would flash with irritation at having to introduce herself again, section director being such a forgettable position and all.

But her eyes did not flash with irritation. Instead, crinkles formed at the edges of them as she smiled, slow and sure. 'Oh, you poor darling man. I knew you were confused last night, but I didn't know you were *that* far gone. I'm your sister's wedding caterer.'

'I see.'

He really *didn't* see.

'You don't remember begging me to give you a lift to the nearest motel?' She looked so guileless. Damn, she was good. 'Because I did. Take you to the nearest motel, I mean. But the night manager took one look at you and remembered that he didn't have any vacancies. I was a little sceptical, but he was very certain. He figured you were either going to puke all over the room or die in your sleep, or both, and apparently that's bad for business. Also, you had no ID. He didn't like that either.'

Jared smiled. He had no idea where she was going with this story, but he figured he might as well let her run with it. Or maybe he just liked hearing her voice.

'What happened after that?'

'I offered to take you to the hospital.' She leaned her forearms over the slatted wooden bed-end. 'To which you said an emphatic no. You then told me I had the sexiest mouth you'd ever seen.'

'I did?' He might have thought it. He didn't think he'd *said* it.

'I was swearing at you at the time. Trust me, I was surprised too.'

Jared let his gaze slide to her mouth, all shapely and tilted at the corners as if she was always ready to smile. "You shouldn't have been that surprised.'

'And *then…*' she said, and followed those words with a very long pause. 'Then you said that if I gave you a bed for the night you'd give me an orgasm I would never forget.'

'I— *What?*'

'I know. An offer too good to refuse, right? I mean… I have this mouth, you have that face… I think you've cracked a rib or four, but we could have worked around them. So I brought you here and offered you coffee, but you said if it wasn't Turkish you didn't want it. That's when I got my first inkling that we might not be soul mates.'

We might not be wha—?

He was almost awake, and thoroughly confused, and, okay, he might have offered her a good time at some point—it wasn't beyond the realms of possibility—and the coffee line sounded like him, but still…

'And then you told me that the ripples in my hair reminded you of deep ocean waves—in the moonlight, no less—and I figured we might just be soul mates after all. I've been wrong before.'

'I did *not* say that. I would *never* say that. Your hair's too short for ripples. It's unrippleable.'

'I gave you a glass of milk and three prescription painkillers and you groaned your gratitude. It was a deep and growly groan. Very sexy. I still had faint hope of an exemplary orgasm. Ninety seconds later you were asleep.'

She was better at this game than he was. He was playing injured, for starters. But maybe, just maybe, she was the better player.

'You can stop now, Director. I know who you are.'

'Of course you do.' She shot him a very level gaze. 'You need to stop playing me for a fool, Mr West. You need to stop looking at my mouth. And then you need to pay attention to what I'm about to say.'

He eased into a sitting position, wincing as he slung his legs over the side of the bed. At least he still had his trousers on. He remembered bandages too, but maybe they'd been coming off rather than going on. Either way, they were nowhere to be seen. Neither were any of his other clothes. Possibly because they'd been filthy.

He eyed the suitcase in the corner with interest. 'I'm listening.'

'You need to know that there's no record that you were working for us during your time with Antonov. No one's going to claim you as their dark pony. You're on your own.'

That got his attention. He dragged his gaze from the suitcase back to the section director standing at the end of the bed. 'So you're throwing me under a bus?'

These things happened when you came back covered in filth rather than glory.

'I'm sorry,' she murmured, but she didn't deny it.

'I want to talk to my handler.'

'Then talk. Because right now the closest thing you have to a handler is me.'

'No offence, but I don't know you.'

'No offence taken, but I do hope there's *someone* in-house that you're willing to talk to. I'll be in your sister's kitchen, Mr West. As for you, it's time to get dressed. My people are almost ready to leave and you're coming with us.'

'I am?'

'Yes. Either willingly or not.' She smiled gently. 'We don't care.'

'You know, they never mentioned that in the brochure.'

This time she laughed. 'Maybe you should have read the fine print.'

If Jared had figured to slip quietly out of the farmhouse unnoticed, he'd been sadly mistaken. A big breakfast cook-up was in progress by the time he emerged from the bedroom, with his brother, Damon, wielding the tongs and his sister Poppy presiding over the flipping of fried eggs. The director was there too, sitting on a stool, sipping coffee and reading something on her computer, looking for all the world as if she had a place in his family—as if she was comfortable there.

He headed for the coffee machine. Looked at it and sighed. It was shiny, spanking new, and he had no idea what half the knobs on it did. 'Does this do double-shot espresso?'

'Only if you ask nicely,' said Damon's very pregnant wife.

Ruby was her name, and Jared eyed the bright green bow atop her head warily. She opened the lid of the coffee container and the aroma of freshly ground beans assaulted his nose and sent him straight back to a little coffee house in Istanbul.

Ruby obligingly waved the container beneath his nose. 'We can put this in a pot and make it Turkish-style, if that's your preference?'

'I'm beginning to understand why Damon married you.'

'You mean, it didn't instantly dawn on you?'

'Um...' Why was his world suddenly so full of beautiful smart-mouthed women? 'Turkish coffee would be great. I can make it.'

Ruby favoured him with a pretty smile. Jared risked a glance in Damon's direction before taking a careful step back. He liked women with pretty smiles. *He did.* He'd never before been scared of one, but there was a first time for everything.

'I...uh...I'm sorry I couldn't make it back for your wedding.'

'Play your cards right and you can be Damon's plus-one at the birth.'

Oh, dear God. She was probably joking. Hopefully she was joking. But he figured a change of subject wouldn't hurt. 'Anyone seen the newly happily married couple this morning?'

'They're still in bed.'

Jared winced. There was another image he really didn't want in his head.

'You don't approve?' asked Poppy.

'I do approve. I just don't want to think about it.'

'Very healthy,' his new sister-in-law murmured.

'If I whimper will you back off?'

'I didn't think terrorist-hunters whimpered.'

'This one does.'

He shuffled around to the kitchen side of the bench,

opened a couple of cupboards before finding a saucepan and dumping some water in it. Surprisingly, Ruby carefully shook a damn near perfect amount of ground coffee into it before putting the coffee tin back on the counter.

'How are you feeling?' asked Poppy.

'Good.' As if a rhinoceros had rolled on him. 'Peachy.'

And then Poppy was beside him, worming her way beneath his arm and hugging him carefully, and he closed his eyes and rested his cheek on her head as he gathered her in—because it *was* good to be home, and they had no idea how much he'd missed this, missed them, and for what?

He'd brought down the Antonov operation. So what? Another arms dealer would take Antonov's place. He'd exposed a few moles in high places, but he'd be a fool to think he'd exposed them all. He *knew* he hadn't exposed them all.

He opened his eyes to find Rowan Farringdon staring at him with puzzled eyes. He knew he was showing his weakness for family but he just didn't care any more. He closed his eyes and hugged Poppy tighter.

'Do I get one of those?'

The voice came from the doorway. Jared opened his eyes and looked straight at Lena. She looked well, if a little tousled, and her pretty floral sundress suited her. She looked happy.

'If you want,' he offered gruffly.

'I do want.'

Lena started towards him, a slight hitch in her step—no way was he going to call it a limp—and then he had his arms full of Lena and Poppy both.

'Got to do something to take that look off your face,' said Lena.

'What look?'

'The faraway one. You need to come back to us, Jare.'

'I *am* back.'

Lena stared at him intently for what felt like a very long time before silently shaking her head and stepping away and turning towards the director.

'When does he have to leave?'

'Five minutes ago.'

Poppy's big blue eyes were grave. 'How much trouble are you in?'

'Don't care.'

'Will you stay working for them?'

'Don't know.'

Poppy didn't care that they were having this conversation in front of Rowan Farringdon. Neither did Jared.

'Do you want to?'

He didn't answer. He didn't know.

Damon shoved a dripping bacon and egg sandwich in his hand. Jared extricated himself from Poppy and bit into it with relief. He didn't need a plate—he was an old hand at eating on the go.

'Ready when you are, Director.'

'I haven't finished my coffee yet.' *You haven't even had yours*, her look said. *I'm cutting you a break, here. Take it and shut the hell up.*

He shut the hell up.

He bit into his sandwich more slowly this time. Coffee appeared and he reached for it gratefully. One minute passed. Two minutes. They left him alone. They asked no more questions.

And then two suited men darkened the doorway and Rowan Farringdon shut her little silver computer and stood up.

'Agent West,' one of them said, and there was a measure of respect in the man's voice that Jared had never heard before. 'It's time to go.'

CHAPTER FOUR

ROWAN'S OFFICE WAS the same as the offices that housed the other five section directors. Large, as befitting her position, it also had a small apartment tucked in behind it, for when she worked around the clock and needed to freshen up with a shower and a change of clothes—or, indeed, catch a couple of hours' sleep after coming off a thirty-six-hour shift.

Jared wasn't strictly her responsibility any more. In all good conscience Rowan could have left him to Corbin to break or to fix. But she, like everyone else in the building, was uncommonly interested in whatever further information he might have to divulge.

Not that Jared West seemed inclined to divulge anything at all—at least not to Corbin.

Rowan gave yesterday's recording of Jared's debrief one last scathing glance before leaning back in her desk chair and tilting her head from one side to the other in an effort to ease the tension in her neck. It was only Tuesday morning, but she felt as if she'd been here for ever.

She reached for her headset and put it on. 'Sam, have Agent West see me as soon as he's out of debrief.'

Some people in this building wanted to hear a real debrief, not the fairytale version that Jared was out there spinning—and as of this morning Rowan had been given the task of earning his trust and breaking him open.

If she could.

Jared didn't get out of debrief until midday Wednesday, and if he never again saw the inside of that little white room with its one-way mirror it would still be too soon.

Rowan Farringdon's request caught up with him two minutes later. Five minutes after that he was standing in her outer office, staring at a lionfish in a wall-sized fish tank while her plump and pretty assistant buzzed him in.

He liked it that she didn't keep him waiting. He liked it that she stayed seated behind her desk, because it reinforced their respective positions within the service. They weren't equals here. He didn't expect them to be.

He stood before her desk, feet slightly apart, hands behind his back, and waited while she looked him over in silence. The bruises on his face combined purple with a sickly shade of yellow. He wondered if she thought him any prettier.

She got more arresting every time he saw her. Today she wore dark grey tailored trousers and a fitted shirt that had two layers—the inside layer a soft-looking dove-grey cotton, the outside layer a fine white silk. She looked comfortable in her clothes, her skin and her surroundings. Power suited her.

And Jared...Jared had *always* been attracted to power.

She gave him approximately three seconds to settle before looking up from her paperwork and getting to the point. 'Mr West, your debrief is a joke. Everyone knows it; not everyone's happy about it. Who *do* you intend to confide in?'

No one.

'I want to talk to my handler,' he said instead. 'I told Corbin that. I've told you this before as well. How many times do I have to say it?'

'I'm sorry.' She looked momentarily torn. 'Serrin's dead. He's been dead for two months.'

Jared kept his shoulders square and his face stony. This blow wouldn't break him. He was just…tired. Tired of all the games. Tired of dealing on his own and making mistakes that cost other people too much.

'Was it me? Did I leave him exposed?'

'Yours wasn't the only dark operation on Serrin's books. He came unstuck elsewhere.'

One less stain for Jared's soul. Assuming she was telling the truth.

She tilted her head to one side, her eyes searching and her smile oddly compassionate. 'Jared, things would go a lot easier if you could bring yourself to trust me.'

'I really don't do trust.'

'I know. I've read your file. Very few people are even allowed into your life, never mind privy to your thoughts. Your mother died giving birth to your brother. You're fiercely protective of your sisters, not so much your father or your brother, who you blame—just a little—for your mother's death. The only other emotional attachment you've ever made in your thirty years of living is to Trig Sinclair. You accepted *him* into your family unit when you were five.'

She still wasn't wearing any rings on those expertly manicured fingers.

'Here's the problem,' she continued. 'A lot of people around here think that you haven't quite finished exposing Antonov's reach. A lot of people want to help you finish what you started. So here are my questions, given that you're disinclined to share details. What are you waiting for? What do you need?'

A break, he wanted to say. *Absolution*. But he doubted she could give him either. 'I need to go to Belarus,' he said instead. Would she do it? Belarus was within her jurisdiction—her part of the world to monitor. 'Just for a few days. Corbin won't send me and I don't know why.'

She laughed, and it was still one of the nicest sounds he'd ever heard. 'Jared, have you *seen* your latest psych report?'

He hadn't seen it. Chances were he wasn't *going* to see it. 'What does it say?'

'That you have attachment issues, delusions of autonomy and a well-developed death wish. Corbin's not going to send you to Belarus. He's going to have a hard time sending you to the bathroom alone. All those sharp edges.'

'I am *not* suicidal.'

'Tell me what you want done in Belarus and I'll put someone on it. Discreetly. You can run them from here.'

'I don't work that way.'

'No? Maybe you should.'

She stood and headed for the door, but he wasn't ready for this interview to be over, and he hadn't yet let go of the rough edges he'd acquired after two years playing thug for Antonov.

He shot out his hand to keep the door closed and got up in her face.

Up close, he saw her eyes had little flecks of chocolate-brown in amongst the amber. He could smell the fresh lemon scent of her hair, feel the puff of her breath against his lips, and he knew that he was too close, that his lips were far too close to hers. Another inch and he'd be tasting her—and he wanted to. God. He wanted to fall into this woman and take his own sweet time climbing back out, and it didn't matter that she was a section head or that his behaviour was way out of line. Maybe he'd forgotten what normal behaviour was. Meet a woman, like a woman, ask her on a date. Maybe he should start there.

'Have dinner with me.'

'*That's* your next play?'

Nice to know he could surprise her. 'Why not?' He could feel the warmth in her, sense the steel in her, and he wanted both. 'You can toy with me. Mentor me. Discipline me. I'm young. Impulsive. Smitten.'

'I'm not.'

'Could be why I like you.' He eased back, just a fraction, and watched for signs of arousal in her—the faint flush of her skin or the hitch of her breath—but he didn't find any. Just a soul-deep caution that matched his own.

'You need to back off, Agent West.'

'How about I take you to lunch? I promise to behave.'

'No.' She pushed her knuckles into his injured ribs—not hard, but a warning nonetheless. 'You're out of line.'

'Would you hurt me?' He leaned into her hand. 'I don't think you would.'

'I'd rather not have to. Doesn't mean I won't, Mr West—'

'Call me Jared. Call me by my name.' He hadn't answered to his real name for such a long time—two years or thereabouts. He'd been Jimmy. Jimmy Bead. 'Just—use my name. The way you did before. I want to hear people say it.'

'Is your last name not enough?'

'First name's better.'

'Why?'

'There's more *me* in it.'

'Jared—'

'Yeah. That's the one.'

He stepped back all the way this time, and gave her the room she deserved. Her hand fell away and he felt the loss of warmth as if someone had dipped him in the Atlantic. He had a feeling that his psych report hadn't covered half of what was wrong with him at the moment.

Or maybe it had.

'If I say that my next question is for your benefit as well as mine, will you believe me?' she asked quietly.

He ran a hand through his hair. He'd been doing that of late too, and it wasn't something he'd ever done before—either as Jared or as JB...Jimmy Bead. 'What's the question?'

'Do you know who you're hunting? Antonov's last insider... Do you know who it is?'

'I— No. I think it's a director, but I don't know who it is. If I could have nailed a bullseye to his forehead I'd have done it.'

'That much I *do* believe.'

'Get me to Belarus,' he begged.

'No. Not yet. You need to rest. Take some leave. No one's going to send you back out into the field in the condition you're in. Get some sleep and let your body heal and *then* we'll talk again. And, Jared...?'

'That's me,' he muttered, and there was a joke in there somewhere, though it was probably on him.

'Welcome back.'

CHAPTER FIVE

THE WEST FAMILY beach house sat on the edge of a long stretch of unpatrolled beach in northern New South Wales. Jared's brother had bought the sprawling house several years ago, with the intention of making it his home, but that hadn't happened yet and all four West siblings tended to treat it as their own personal place of sanctuary and of rest. Although preferably not all at once.

Lena and Trig's big old farmhouse was a twenty-minute drive away, although given how much time they'd spent at the beach house with Jared this week he could be forgiven for thinking them homeless.

They were supposed to be on their honeymoon, for heaven's sake. A honeymoon that Lena had said they'd cut short because there was no place like home.

Jared hoped, for the umpteenth time, that they hadn't cut it short because they'd wanted to keep an eye on *him*. They kept making excuses to drop by. Lena in particular wouldn't stop *hovering*—which was rich, given how much she hated it whenever someone did that to her.

She had already been by this morning. She'd skipped out to the shops, because apparently Jared needed more food in the fridge, but she'd left Trig behind with Jared.

Trig was currently out on the deck, examining his parachute, because apparently they were doing a jump just as soon as Jared's ribs had healed.

Without physical challenge in his life, Jared got cranky, Trig had informed him blithely. And they needed to fix that.

Apparently a lot of things about Jared needed fixing.

Jared glared afresh at the psych report in his hand. *His* psych report, fresh off the back of his debrief. A normal person probably wouldn't have asked his brother to swipe a psych report from the secure ASIS databanks, but to Jared's way of thinking that was what genius younger brothers were for.

It had been three days since Rowan Farringdon had called him in to her office and asked him what he needed in order to finish the job. Three days and now he was on leave for two weeks—thinking about his future, trying to settle into the 'now' and going quietly out of his mind.

'Who writes these delusional masterpieces anyway?' he asked Trig.

'Psychiatrists.' Trig looked up from the parachute spread out before him, eyes narrowed as he took in Jared's scowl. 'Stop obsessing.'

'I'm not obsessing. I'm disagreeing with the evaluation.'

'You shouldn't *have* the evaluation. No disagreeing with that.'

'Apparently I have an Oedipal complex.'

'Your mother's dead, dude. How can you be in love with her?'

'Could be I'm in love with a ghost. A perfect memory.'

'*Was* she perfect?'

Jared thought back to what little he could remember. His mother's wild curly black hair and the deep blue eyes that both he and his sister Lena had inherited. Her patience with her wayward children and her fierce defence of them when anyone else tried to discipline them.

'Yes.'

'You know that if you *do* have an Oedipal complex you're going to have to bond with your father in order to get over it?'

'Bite me.'

'Okay—not ready.'

'*She* said that the last emotional attachment I made was you.'

'Who said?'

'Rowan Farringdon.'

'Ah.'

'What do you mean, "ah"?'

'Are you ready for that beer? I'm *really* ready for a beer.'

'What do you think of her?'

'Who?'

Jared just looked at him.

Trig abandoned his parachute inspection and headed across the huge open entertaining area towards the kitchen.

He pulled out two beers, twisted the tops off and padded back out to the deck area that Jared had made his own.

'She's the first female section head in thirty years,' Trig said as he passed Jared a beer. 'I think she has connections, ambition, and a mind made for taking people apart and reshaping them to her purpose. That's not a criticism, by the way, it's respect. She's older than you, Jare.'

'So?'

'Oedipus?'

'I am *not* looking for a mother figure. Don't make me shoot you. Lena would *not* be pleased.'

'Neither would I.'

'I asked her to have dinner with me.'

'Bet *that* went down a treat.'

'I almost kissed her.' He was rubbing his hand over his lips just thinking about it. 'Wanted to.'

'You want my thoughts on that?' Trig offered warily.

'Only if you're not going to call me psychologically maladjusted, three kinds of stupid, and pathologically unable to take direction.'

'Or you could just be in need of sex.'

'You think I should have sex with her?'

'No, I think you should have sex with someone else.'

'Who?'

'Has that ever been a problem for you before? What about Bridie?'

'Too nice. I want her to be married by now, with a kid on the ground and one on the way.' He caught Trig staring at him strangely and shrugged. 'It's what she wanted.'

'Simone?'

'Too soft. What if I break her?'

'Simone's brother?'

Jared felt his lips twitch. 'The psych report says I'm heterosexual.'

'Yeah, 'cause we're believing that now.' Trig took a long swig of his beer. 'You said you wanted someone who wouldn't break. Just putting it out there…'

'I want a *woman* who won't break, and I've found one. Gorgeous, whip-smart and powerful. And—if I'm reading her right—interested.'

'Yeah…nothing at all to do with you having information she wants.'

'There is that. Still… Makes for interesting conversation.'

And then his phone beeped. He fished it out of his pocket and looked at the message.

'Trouble?'

'Hopefully. Director Farringdon's coming here bright and early Monday morning. For what reason, she doesn't say.'

'Hnh…' offered Trig after a very long pause.

'Probably something to do with Antonov's last mole that I haven't uncovered yet. Probably nothing to do with sex at all. Still…'

Jared was nothing if not adaptable, and he'd take his opportunities as they came.

'Don't do it, my friend,' Trig told him.

'You keep saying that.'

'Think of the complications.'

'She gets what she wants. I get what I want. There *are* none.'

'What about in the long run? How would it affect your career if you had a relationship with her? How would it affect hers?'

'Not sure I have a career left, to be honest. Not sure I want one.'

'And hers?'

'Guess we'd find out.'

Trig's troubled gaze rested on him. 'Jare, do you *ever*

think about what your short-term decisions might cost people in the long run?'

'All the time. I know I've screwed up. Lena getting wounded under my command and now never being able to have kids of her own. That's on me.'

'No. I don't think that. Lena doesn't think that way either. We were in the wrong place at the wrong time. It happens. And we're all still alive.'

'Then you're talking about the lengths I went to to get Antonov? And the fact that he and two others are now dead? That wasn't my intention.'

Trig grew uncharacteristically silent. 'What happened?' he asked finally.

'I had enough information to bring his entire operation down and I needed one more name for my own satisfaction. In reality I probably had enough dirt on him to bring him down six months ago, but I wanted that one last name so much. And then your wedding invitation landed and I decided that enough was enough. I was leaving—first chance I got. Two days later an old business associate of Antonov's turned up with a new grudge and enough C-4 to blow up a battleship—and I let him do just that while I went and got the kid and the nurse and took off.'

'And your problem with that is…?'

'I wanted revenge and I got it. Not sure I wanted it that way. Antonov wasn't all bad. He was different things to different people. He had a son he loved. A sister he'd sacrificed all contact with to protect. Those other dead men—they had families back in Belarus. They sent money back all the time.'

'They're not dead by *your* hand, Jare.'

'Then why do my hands feel so bloody?'

'I don't know. God complex? You are *not* responsible for all the bad things that happen in this world.'

'But I *am* responsible for my actions, and I should be able to foresee some of the consequences. Isn't that what you're trying to tell me when it comes to my interest in Rowan Farringdon?'

'All I'm saying is talk to the woman first—before embarking on the seduction campaign. Women are easy for you—God knows why.'

'Money, looks, renegade status and genius.'

'Like I said, God knows why. And you do *not* need the downfall of the first female section director in thirty years on your already overburdened conscience.'

'She's smarter than that.'

'How do you know? Will you be reading *her* psych report next?'

'Do you think she has one?'

Jared felt the edges of his lips lift. A small smile, but a smile nonetheless. It was good to finally talk to someone freely. Someone who knew him inside out and didn't hold back.

'Doesn't matter. Even if she does, I'm going to ban Damon from getting it for you.'

'You wouldn't.'

'Oh, but I would.'

'Would what?' asked Lena, stepping from the house onto the deck. ''Cause it sounds vaguely threatening.'

'Your brother wants to read Rowan Farringdon's psych report. Among other things.'

'Seems only fair,' Jared murmured. 'She's read mine.'

'Are you *still* smarting about that idiotic psych report?' she asked, and Jared grinned outright this time.

Injury and near death hadn't softened Lena—they'd

simply made her blunter…and surprisingly more affectionate, he decided as she engulfed him from his shoulders up in a fierce hug.

'Where is it?' she murmured. 'Hand it over. I'm going to barbecue it. By the way, I stopped by the fishing co-op and bought barramundi and king prawns. And because I love you both I'm going to cook them up for dinner. You two can unpack the car, make the salads, pour me some wine and make encouraging remarks about my cooking.'

It was good to be home, Jared thought.

Maybe it would be enough.

Monday morning couldn't come around quickly enough for Jared. He'd swum in Damon's pool and in the surf, and nobly restrained himself from getting the windsurfer out. He'd gone with Lena and Trig to one of their favourite local watering holes on the Saturday night and reacquainted himself with old friends as they'd watched whatever game had been on the big sports screen. Flanked by the two people he trusted most, he'd even managed to relax.

But that had been Saturday. By Sunday afternoon Trig and Lena had retired to their farmhouse, and Jared had been rattling around by himself and trying to *stay* relaxed. He hadn't been sleeping well. He missed the rise and fall of the ocean beneath him. Maybe he needed to investigate yacht ownership.

By Monday morning he'd made enquiries on three oceangoing vessels, and the need to *do* something thrummed through him at a low-level burn.

He hauled himself out of the pool and reached for a towel. His body was still various shades of black and blue, with a few cuts and scrapes besides, but other than that he was in good shape. Antonov had kept his crew fighting fit, and there'd been ocean all around them. Regular diving to examine the hull… Swimming…

Maybe Jared should take up marathon swimming now that he was home.

The doorbell rang and he ditched the towel and headed towards it. He opened it and stepped aside to let Rowan Farringdon in.

'Pretty shirt,' he told her, and it was.

The burnt-orange band of colour across the bottom of it suited her. The rest of it was white, and the inch-wide shoulder straps showed off more body tone than he'd expected from someone who sat in a director's chair. The crisp white trousers she had on rested easy over her rear—not too tight, but not baggy either. *Comfortable*. He hadn't expected this woman to look quite so comfortable in casual clothes.

And still maintain her air of authority.

Her gaze swept the open-plan living area and the pool beyond before returning to him.

Jared offered up a lazy grin by way of reward for her attention. 'Would you like pancakes? I'm having pancakes.'

'Is this a variation on dinner?'

Her voice came at him dry as dust and laced with amusement.

'Could be. But it's also breakfast time, and as a good host I'm offering you some. You've come all this way. It's the least I can do.'

'I've been in Brisbane,' she said. 'You're a detour—not the main destination.'

'I'm crushed.' He led her through to the open-plan

kitchen that backed on to the living area and the pool. 'You take your coffee black, right?'

Her coffee at the farmhouse had been black.

She nodded. 'With one.'

He diligently added sugar to her cup. 'I hope you like Turkish? Lena found it for me in town on Saturday. It's good. I had to promise not to mainline it.'

He lit a flame beneath the skillet and waited for it to get hot. He poured her some coffee and set it in front of her. Added butter to the pan and enjoyed the faint sizzle as he pushed it around with a knife. He added the batter next, before turning back to face her.

'What did you want to see me about?'

'Do you always do two things at once?'

'Keeps me from climbing the walls.'

She smiled at that. 'Say you came across some information that connected a now-deceased illegal arms dealer to a respected worldwide charity organisation...'

'In what capacity?'

'They fed Antonov money and within six months he quadrupled it for them.'

'Did they know who they were dealing with?'

'Does it matter?' She eyed him curiously. 'Do *you* think it matters?'

'Yes. Intent matters. Maybe they didn't know who he was or what he did. Maybe they were naive.'

'The charity's intention was to make money. They succeeded well beyond what any regulated money market could ever do for them. Hard to believe that they thought their investment strategy legitimate, but let's ignore that for a moment. What might Antonov's intention have been?'

'What was the charity?'

'They fund medical research.'

Jared frowned and glanced back to see if the pancake batter in the pan had bubbled up yet. Nope.

'When it came to arms dealing Antonov was a cold-hearted businessman who dealt with the highest bidder and cared nothing for cause,' he offered. 'At first glance no one would mistake him for a philanthropist.'

But Rowan Farringdon would already know that from the reports other people had done on the man. She wanted more. She wanted to know if Jared had ever seen into Antonov's head.

'He was also father to a very sick son. I could see him helping out some research foundation in the hope that their research might some day benefit his kid.'

'They say you played chess with the man?'

Jared nodded.

'Did you win?'

'I grew up with a brother and sisters with genius IQs. They used to play each other and sometimes I'd play the winner. Occasionally I even managed to hold my own. Antonov was bright, but he wasn't that bright. His main asset was his ruthlessness. I gave him a good game and I usually made sure he won. Are you going to shut down the charity?'

'That's not my call. Did you drink with him too? Play catch with his kid?'

'Yes,' Jared muttered roughly. 'I did.'

'Yet you still brought him down?'

It was time to turn the pancakes. 'I let him be brought down by someone else, yes.'

'And the fallout was extreme. Antonov and two others dead. The boy—Celik—fatherless now, and returned to his high-class whore of a mother. New players fighting over Antonov's turf. Tell me, Jared—do you sleep?'

'Do *you*?' He tried to keep his voice low and his temper in check. 'What do you want from me? A confession that I have regrets? Yeah, I do. Would I have gone about things differently if I'd known some of the things that I know now? Yes. But what's done is done and I sleep better for it.'

'I don't think you sleep much at all.'

She was too observant.

'I didn't kill them. That was never my intent. Intent is important.' It was all he had left. 'What's *your* background, Rowan? Why do you sit in a director's chair? What's *your* intent?'

'How about you call me Director?'

'In a workplace situation that requires it, I solemnly swear that I will never call you anything else.'

'You really *are* used to getting your own way, aren't you?'

'Firstborn child,' he murmured. 'It's in my file. What about you? Any brothers or sisters?'

'No. My parents were diplomats—children really didn't fit their career plans, so they made do with one. I was raised by my grandfather. He was an Army general.'

'How'd you get your director's chair?'

'Drive, forward-planning and connections. I decided I wanted to run my own covert operations team when I was fifteen.'

'If I told you that I joined the secret intelligence service with all the forethought of an adrenalin junkie in need of his next fix would you smack me?'

'Yes. Please tell me you planned at least *some* of this?'

Jared grinned at her censure. She was a strategist—no question. *His* skills ran more to being pointed in the right direction and doing what was needed. He'd had no problem with his approach whatsoever at first. Right up until he'd realised that he no longer had complete trust in the people doing the pointing. And then life had got increasingly difficult.

'You *could* smack me. We'll see how we go. I might even like it.'

'The way I read it, you have a certain innate…'

'Charm?'

'Cunning,' she corrected. 'A wariness that stems from your lack of trust in others. And you have no small amount of luck. You're tenacious and a natural-born leader. Corbin has a vacant sub-director's chair. He's put you up for consideration.'

Jared set his coffee down abruptly. 'What are my chances of getting it?'

'Corbin's pushing hard. A few of the other directors have questioned your maturity and your ability to plan ahead. No one's blocked you outright yet. That's down to Corbin's political clout, by the way—not yours. You've done no political manoeuvring whatsoever for over two years.'

'Been a little busy elsewhere…'

'We know.' Rowan watched him steadily. 'Do you want it?'

The pancakes were ready. He fished two plates from the cupboard, loaded hers up and took it to the counter. He pushed the sugar bowl towards her and swiftly quartered a couple of lemons. He added more butter to the pan. More pancake mix.

'I don't know.'

'Where do you see yourself in five years?'

'If I'd known this was a job interview I'd have worn a shirt.'

She let her gaze drop to his chest, but it was hard to tell whether she was admiring his physique or cataloguing the bruises on it.

'You could always put one on now.'

'How *do* you sleep?' he asked abruptly. 'How do you smile when people go down and don't get up and it was your call that put them there?'

'You're talking about your sister getting shot?'

'I'm talking about dead men and belief. How do you know that you're doing the right thing? How do you know when you've chosen the lesser of two evils?'

'Intel helps.'

There was a hint of sorrow in her words that commanded his attention.

'Arrogance helps. You have to *want* to take control and believe that you're the best-equipped person to do so.'

'Maybe I *did* believe that I was the person best equipped to take down Antonov two years ago,' he offered raggedly. 'The one with the most determination. The one with the burning desire to do so. Not sure I believe it now.'

He'd opened up to her this much—he might as well let her see the rest of it.

'I can't settle. I don't sleep. I feel like I'm peeling out of my own skin half the time. I came back for the wedding. I forced things into play so that I could be home in time for that. I've left loose threads that I need to go back and tie up and now you want to put me in a manager's chair? I can't do it. I don't belong in a chair. I'm no manager and I can't stand paperwork. All I want to do is clean up my mess.'

'And how would you do that?'

'I need to know what's happening with Celik—Antonov's kid. I promised him he'd be okay. I need to get to Belarus and put something in play there that *might* lead us to the last of Antonov's moles within ASIS. I need to get to the families of the other two dead men and see how they're situated. I need to finish this so I can sleep.'

'You came back too soon.'

'I had to.'

'You put family first.'

'I always will. You can't be too surprised by that. It's all I've ever done.'

He turned the burner off, took hold of the skillet and tipped the pancakes onto his plate. He sat down opposite where she'd been sitting and reached for the sugar.

He ignored her when she slipped in between him and the corner of the kitchen bench, one elbow on the bench as she studied him intently.

Had she squeezed in between him and another person at a bar, in an effort to get served, he wouldn't have thought anything of her proximity. But there was a lot of room at this breakfast bar and she wasn't currently using any of it.

'What are you doing?' he asked warily.

'May I try something?'

'I don't know whether to say yes or no.'

She reached out and slid the back of her hand up his cheek and towards his temple…a soft caress that made his breath hitch and his body stiffen against the utter pleasure of it. Her hand didn't stop there and soon her fingers were in his hair, scraping gently across his scalp, making his eyes close and his body tremble.

'You're touch-starved.'

Her whisky voice rippled across his senses.

'We see it sometimes in those who've held themselves apart, those who've gone too deeply undercover for too long. I thought I saw a hint of it the other day in your sister's kitchen, and then again in my office. You weren't looking for it. You thought yourself attracted to *me*.'

'I *am* attracted to you. How much more obvious do you want me to be?'

He caught her wrist, then deliberately brought her hand back to the counter before releasing her. He wasn't going to act the Neanderthal the way he had the other day. He just wasn't.

'Move over,' she said, and reached across the bench for her plate of pancakes and her utensils.

When she sat down beside him she let her lower leg rest against his, pinching his footrest instead of using hers.

'Touch doesn't always have to be sexual. Sometimes it's about comfort and connection.'

'Are you *mentoring* me?'

'You did say I could. Are you objecting?'

'Yes,' he said firmly, and glared when she patted him on the forearm. 'And don't mother me either. Don't need one—don't want one. Don't call *me* Oedipus.'

She smiled like a Madonna. 'I challenge you to stay in casual body contact with me for five minutes and see if it relaxes you any. If it works we'll get you a puppy.'

'Don't want a puppy, Ro.' He gave her his full wattage smile. 'I want a *girl*.'

'And I thought you wanted *me*. How are your ribs?'

'Better.'

'The doctor said it would take weeks for them to fully heal.'

'Almost better.'

'It's probably too soon for you to be playing contact sport as a way of encountering touch. There's massage…?'

Her leg was already sliding against his as he moved his own leg around. 'The frustration would kill me.'

'Self-massage beforehand?'

'Wouldn't help.'

'Maybe you could take dance classes? Start with a waltz…finish at the tango?'

'No partner.'

'The dance teacher would be your partner.'

'You're really serious about this touch thing, aren't you?'

'Are you feeling more relaxed than you were a minute ago?'

Surprisingly, he was.

'Might not be about touch, though. Might be proximity to *you*. You could stay the night. There could be dinner out on the deck. A swim this afternoon. I could teach you how to kite surf.'

He wasn't allowed to, on account of his ribs, but that wouldn't stop him teaching someone else.

'Wouldn't I have to learn how to surf first?'

'Oh, Ro… *No.* You don't surf? Do you know what this means?'

'That we may not be soul mates after all?'

'It means you're missing out on one of life's great pleasures. Now I *have* to teach you how to surf.'

'You mean right after you teach me how to swim?'

For a moment he thought she was serious, and then she smiled and he knew she was playing him. 'You can swim. The General would have made sure of it.'

She laughed at that. 'And then there was canoeing and sailing—diving and the rest. I swear that man should have joined the Navy, not the Army.'

He liked hearing those kinds of things from her, liked having her around.

'Can you stay? We *could* swim or surf—the offer's there. You *could* stay the night—there's plenty of bedrooms. We *could* go out to dinner. There could be fresh seafood and bright stars in the sky. A playful breeze. There could be body contact and relaxation. I'm all for it.'

'My flight leaves at midday. This is a work-day for me.'

'There's always next weekend. You could come back.'

Her leg rocked gently against his. 'You're very tempting. You already know this, so it's not as if I'm telling you anything new. But you're not in a good place right now, and I'm trying to figure out what I *need* to do for you in a work capacity and what I *might* be able to offer you in a private one. The answer to that second question being that if I know what's good for me I'll offer you nothing.'

'We could try friendship?' he offered. 'Something simple. I'd like simple.'

'You'd need to stop hitting on me. And—given that I have at least *some* self-awareness—I'd need to stop flirting with you too.'

Rowan smiled ruefully and turned her attention to the eating of her pancakes. They ate in companionable silence, and by the time Rowan had finished her pancakes and drunk her coffee Jared was feeling more at ease.

'Get a massage,' she told him as she stood to leave. 'Go hug people. Use the beach and concentrate on the physical sensation of the waves breaking over you and the sun on your skin. Hold your hand over your heart and breathe. Concentrate on sensory details when you want to give your brain a rest.'

'You're giving me coping mechanisms for *anxiety*?'

'You asked me how I cope with some of the decisions I've had to make over the years. I'm telling you what has helped me.'

'Sex.'

Jared rubbed his hand across the back of his neck and tried to explain his thought processes before Rowan decided that he was hitting on her again.

'Trig said I needed sex.'

'It's not a bad idea—provided that your partner knows what you're having sex for.'

'I'm pretty sure that telling someone I'm touch-starved and over-anxious and therefore need to have sex isn't going to fly.'

'Oh, I don't know… With *your* face and body?' She leaned across the counter for her black leather satchel. 'It might.'

'Are you flirting again?'

'I hope not.' She stood up and slung the satchel over her shoulder. 'Time for me to go.'

'Yeah.' He didn't want her to go. 'Do you need any more on Antonov?'

'No. That wasn't the main reason I came here and you know it. I wanted to check up on you—see how you were tracking. I'm supposed to be gaining your trust, and that's hard to do when you're nowhere in my vicinity. I was also very curious as to whether you want that sub-director's chair.'

'Director—' He knew she'd notice the name-change. He hoped she knew that he was replying to the chair now and not just to her. 'I don't want a promotion. I can't think about that right now. If you want me to do what I do best, cancel my leave and get me to Belarus. Let me clean up my mess.'

She looked at him hard.

He waited.

Finally, she nodded. 'Belarus it is, then.'

'When?'

'Any objection to coming with me now?'

'None at all.'

'In that case pack what you need and put on a shirt.'

Jared shot her a brilliant smile as he stood to do her bidding. Or his bidding. Either way, he thoroughly approved of the direction this beautiful friendship was going in.

'Hey, Ro? The touch thing? I think it's working.'

'Nothing at all to do with getting your own way?'

'Oh, you noticed that?'

She spared him a very level glance. 'I'm setting you loose in Belarus for two reasons. One: I want that final head to roll and I have my own thoughts as to who it is—I just don't quite have enough to nail him yet, and with your help maybe we'll get there. Two: you're not recuperating here in your brother's beach house...you're drowning, and I have rope that might save you. I suggest you grab it.'

CHAPTER SIX

By the time they touched down in the capital Rowan had done a whole lot of touching, brushing against and just plain standing close to Jared West, and the extended contact was beginning to take a toll on her senses. She liked the smell of him and the feel of him.

Everyone liked the sight of him. He'd changed into a business suit and he wore it to perfection. It gave him an air of authority and added a couple more years to his thirty. His wristwatch signalled the kind of wealth that got handed down from generation to generation. His grandfather, according to the records, had made a fortune in shipping, and his father had taken it into the investment banking arena and quadrupled it. Between Jared, his siblings and his elders, they had property on every continent and in most major cities.

For Jared to choose working for secret intelligence over all the other options available to him had been an unusual move. For him not to want to advance through the ranks now was more unusual still. She didn't know what drove him—beyond family loyalty and wanting to clean up his mess.

'Jared?' she said as they stepped from the airport terminal and headed towards a waiting car. 'Don't make me regret my belief in you.'

He glanced her way, his gaze strangely searching. 'What is it about me that you believe in?'

'I believe that you want to see this through.' She nodded to Jeffers, her driver, who had opened the door as she approached, sparing only a glance for Jared.

Jared settled in beside her. Jeffers handed her a tablet and she took it and opened up her information stream. Jared didn't ask anything else. He let her get on with it and looked out of the window, deep in his own thoughts.

It wasn't until they were back in the corridors of Section that he spoke again. 'How soon can I leave?'

'I'll need to bring you into my section and under my jurisdiction first. At the moment you're Corbin's.'

'Will Corbin be a problem?'

'We're about to find out.'

They'd reached her office and Sam looked up, her cool gaze encompassing them both.

'Director. Agent West.'

'Mr West needs to book a flight to wherever it is he's going. I'll leave him with you.'

But Jared followed her to her door instead of taking his cue. 'Don't I get to listen in on your courtesy call?'

'No. Try not to annoy Sam too much, Mr West. She's perfectly capable of sending you to Belarus via Antarctica.'

'I'll keep that in mind,' he murmured.

She smiled encouragingly and shut the door on him with no little satisfaction. Back in her domain, back in control, and out of range of that killer smile and perfect body. He was hard on the senses, Jared West. Hard on the mind.

She wasn't game to examine her confidence.

* * *

Rowan's conversation with George Corbin didn't begin well.

'You can't have him,' he said curtly when she put her request to him. 'He's on medical leave.'

'He's back, he's bored, and I need him for a job.'

'Consulting?'

'Fieldwork.' She knew damn well that her decision to send Jared back into the field wasn't going to go down a treat. No need to mention that the job was Antonov-related.

'You're crazier than I thought.'

'Will you release him or not? He doesn't want your sub-director's chair, by the way.'

'Maybe I never expected him to take it in the first place.'

She could hear the older director's exasperation, loud and clear.

'Maybe all I'm trying to do is get him looking towards a future in which Antonov's reach *isn't* his entire focus. Get him thinking about how to come out of this current situation with his career intact. Maybe I simply don't like watching one of our best and brightest break.'

'He won't break. He'll do what's asked of him.'

'Says who? Him? Or you? He's not physically fit. He's not mentally ready. What makes you think that if you send him out now he'll even return? What makes you think he won't end up in pieces?'

'He'll come back when he's due back—and it won't be in a body bag.' She could picture Corbin's cold grey eyes and his tightly drawn lips. 'Do I need to call in favours?'

'I don't *owe* you any favours.'

'In that case I'll owe *you*.'

She could practically hear the older man calculating what he might demand of her. Nothing good.

Eventually he spoke again. 'You can have him—but my objections are going on record.'

'Thanks, George. That's exactly what I wanted to hear.'

Corbin hung up.

Rowan put the phone down, closed her eyes, and banged her head against the padded leather headrest of her chair a couple of times.

That had been so *not* what she'd wanted to hear.

If Jared didn't come through with the name of that final mole she was screwed.

Several hours later Rowan had managed to wade her way through most of her work for the day. Tomorrow's schedule was in place, Sam was finishing up, and the only memo sheet left on her desk was the one regarding Jared's impending travel arrangements.

He was booked to go via Warsaw with his first flight leaving at four-forty a.m. He was scheduled to return four days after he got there. Six days in total—not nearly long enough for him to pay his respects to two dead men's families, check on a kid in the Netherlands, and go after the name of Antonov's final mole. His arrangements were flawed from the beginning.

Not a good start.

'Agent West wanted to know what time you usually leave the office,' Sam said as she shut down her computer and secured her desk drawers with the thoroughness with which one might secure a safe.

'What did you tell him?'

'She said I should be able to catch you about now.'

The office door was open. How Jared had managed to appear framed in it without either her or Sam hearing him was a testament to how quietly he could move.

She nodded to him, eyeing the carry-bag draped over his shoulder and the white plastic shopping bag that dangled from one hand. The plastic bag smelled strongly of chilli, basil, lemongrass and curry.

'You told her I'd be back with food, right?' he asked Sam.

'I was just about to mention it.' Sam turned her blandest gaze on Rowan. 'I didn't say you'd eat it.'

'Is this a variation on *Will you have dinner with me?*' Rowan asked him.

'Or I can eat and you can watch,' he offered with a sinner's smile. 'I'm hungry.'

'Apparently you're also very fragile—I've been hearing that all day. This had better not be your version of the Last Supper.'

'If it was I'd have chosen the lobster instead of the duck.'

Not for a second did he let her see whether her words had got to him. And then his gaze skidded to her mouth and hers went to his for more than a count of three.

Damn. Rowan dragged her gaze back to the rest of his face and motioned him into her office.

'See you in the morning, Sam.'

Sam nodded and left without another word. Jared walked past Rowan and headed straight over to the panelled bookcase that doubled as a door that led through to her private apartment. He knew how to open it and didn't wait to be invited inside—just strode on through.

Perhaps he expected her to follow.

Warily, she did.

Rowan didn't use the apartment often. She kept a few changes of clothes there, a few emergency toiletries in the bathroom cupboard. Sometimes she ate there. But not often.

'You know the layout of my office and you know my favourite food. What else do you know?' she asked as she leaned against the doorframe and watched him make himself at home.

'Have you eaten since you ate my pancakes this morning?'

She hadn't.

'That's what I thought.'

He found plates in the cupboard and cutlery in the drawer. He fished napkins from the bag and she let him, more focused on his economy of movement in such a small kitchenette space than on his words.

'I bought a boat today.'

'What kind of boat?'

'An oceangoing yacht.'

'Do you miss Antonov's yacht?'

'That was a floating fortress, not a yacht. I don't miss it specifically. I *do* miss being at sea.'

'You work in Canberra. How often are you going to use this yacht?'

'Not as often as I'd like, but I won't be the only one using it. Lena went halves on it with me.'

'That must be nice.'

She didn't mean for him to stop serving up the food—heaven forbid—but he paused long enough to slide her an enquiring glance.

'Having siblings to share things with,' she elaborated. 'Do you have a favourite sibling?'

'Lena's closest to me in age. Closest to me overall.'

And Lena had just married Jared's best friend.

'Lena followed you and Adrian Sinclair into the service. You made a good, reliable team, the three of you. You led, and mostly they followed. And then Lena got shot while the three of you were checking out an abandoned biological weapons factory in East Timor.'

Jared's lips tightened.

'Adrian stayed to look after her. You, on the other hand, went rogue, trying to pin down who was responsible for hurting your sister.'

'I had a handler. I didn't go rogue. Serrin knew what I was doing.'

'I've read Serrin's notes,' she countered mildly. 'Frankly, they made me wonder who was running who.'

'Still not rogue. I worked within the framework that was there.'

He handed her a plate piled high with red curry duck, plain rice and Asian greens.

'Where's the wine?' she asked.

'You don't drink.' He said it with utter confidence.

'We really *are* going to have to stop letting your brother use our database as his personal information library.'

Jared smiled and shoved a forkful of food into his mouth. Rowan looked at her plate and headed for the little table in the room. She walked over to it, pulled out a chair and kicked another one out for him. He joined her moments later.

Corbin's words of warning slid insidiously through her mind. *Don't bury him. Don't send this man to his death.*

She didn't want to. 'What's in Belarus?'

'Churches, city squares, a fine fear of the Motherland and a man Antonov wanted to impress.'

'A man Antonov wanted to *impress*?' The only people she could think of who might fit that particular criteria would be hellishly hard to access. Rebel leaders and legitimate ones. People of power. 'Does this man have a name?'

'Ro, you haven't even tried your duck. It's really good.'

'Do you know how to find him?'

'Yes.'

'And then what?'

'I think he knows who Antonov's main mole within Section is.'

'Assuming you're right, you still have to get that information out of him.'

Jared said nothing.

'Are you going to bring him in?'

'Wasn't planning on it.'

'It's an option.'

'Given who he is, it's really not.'

Something to chew on… 'Does your sister know that you're going back out there? Does Sinclair?'

'No.' Jared kept right on eating.

Rowan nudged his foot with hers. 'Will you tell them before you go?'

'Wouldn't want to worry them.'

'Withholding your whereabouts from them isn't going to make them worry any *less*. I thought you'd have learned that lesson by now?'

Jared scowled. 'I'll phone them from the airport. Satisfied?'

'Beats having Sinclair and your sister contacting *me*

for your whereabouts. I'm all for delegating my excess workload. You're on record for this trip, by the way. Check your inbox. You're liaising with a new informant on my behalf.'

Jared's scowl had morphed into something a whole lot more thoughtful. Rowan studied his face—the refined masculine beauty of it, the cuts and bruises that hadn't quite faded from it. She was risking her neck for this man and she still didn't really know why.

Take a deep ops agent, fresh from two years in the field, driven by a personal vendetta and deep feelings of failure and responsibility, one who had a dislike of authority and a bad case of alienation and expect him to be a team player?

No. A team player he wasn't.

The best Rowan could do was give him the space he needed to get the job done and hope that there were pieces of him to pick up afterwards.

'Jared, are you up to this?'

'Yes.'

She wanted to believe him.

'Yes,' he repeated. 'I know you've probably had to convince, connive and bury my psych report in order to get me back out there this fast, but I won't let you down. Trust me.'

She nodded—because it was a more positive response than telling him to please stay alive.

She took a couple of mouthfuls of the curry. 'The duck *is* good.'

'Yeah.'

They finished the rest of their meal in silence. It wasn't a companionable silence—more like a heavy, expectant waiting. Jared cleaned up. Rowan helped. His shoulder brushed against hers—the chambray of his shirt soft and well-worn against the bare skin of her shoulder—and her nipples pebbled tightly beneath her bra. She had a jacket somewhere. Wouldn't hurt to put it on and get the hell gone from here before the mind-melting awareness between them turned into hot, sweaty sex.

'If I was ten years older would you take my attraction to you more seriously?' he asked.

So much for ignoring the elephant in the room.

'It's not the age difference.' *Nothing but the truth.* 'Given your experience with life, loss and the demands of intelligence work, you'd be a good match for me. Your body in its prime would just be a bonus.'

'Is there someone else in your life?'

'No.' *Not for years.*

'Who *do* you get intimate with?'

'Since the director's chair? No one.'

'Well, that can't be healthy. How long do you plan on *keeping* the chair?'

'It's hard to say. It was my end-game. I got here a little sooner than expected. Now I'm regrouping. Starting to plan ahead.'

Next thing she knew she'd be revealing that sometimes she questioned what had driven her to this and whether the power she now wielded had been worth the sacrifice. The gruelling hours and the responsibility. Always having to watch her back on account of the power games people played. She could count on one hand the number of people she truly trusted.

Even Jared trusted more people than she did.

'You could set your sights on the top job,' he said. 'Run the division.'

'I could. That's likely to depend on the mistakes I

make in this job and the never-ending politics. Are you going to be a mistake on my résumé?'

'No.' He held her gaze. 'That's not the plan.'

'Then what *is* the plan? You come in here this evening, bearing food—'

'People eat in this building all the time.'

'Yes, in the twenty-four-hour cafeteria.'

'Never seen a director eating in there yet. You could have asked me and my duck to leave.'

'And I will—but not before you give me the name of your informant.'

'And what will you give me in return?'

'Permission to leave the room *and* the country.'

'I want a kiss.'

Nothing but challenge in the rough purr of his voice and speculation in his eyes.

'Because *that's* not going to undermine my authority at all?' she offered dryly.

'You're a little hung up on authority, Ro.'

'It comes with the territory.'

'Last chance,' he offered. 'You want a name; I want a kiss. Think of it as a trust-building exercise.'

'Or blackmail?'

'A freely given exchange,' he countered smoothly.

'If you don't return—if you crash and burn or simply decide that your attention is needed elsewhere—my head is going to roll unless I have something to bargain with. I'm trusting you to do your job, and I have precious little reason for doing so other than gut instinct. I want the name of your informant and I want you back here in six days—free of all Antonov baggage, clear-headed and fit to work.'

'*Then* do I get my kiss?'

'Then you gain my trust—and, for what it's worth, my respect. Finish the job, Jared. And then we'll talk relationships and sex.'

CHAPTER SEVEN

JARED STARTED WITH money for the families first. Local currency and plenty of it. Their dead loved one had had an insurance policy, courtesy of their employer, he told the head of each family. Blood money—nothing more than a Band-Aid applied to his conscience and a couple of years' financial security for the families—but he had to believe that it would help. Money always helped—stained red or not.

He went after Yegor Veselov next, who was in Singapore. It took him another day to get to him and extract the information he required, and by then he'd missed his scheduled flight back to Australia.

His new director was *not* going to be impressed.

He rang Sam instead. 'Tell her I missed my flight.'

'Oh, no. You can tell her yourself.'

He guessed he didn't have to identify himself.

There was a click, two rings, and he almost hung up—like a kid on a prank call. Instead he waited.

'Jared?' his director offered curtly. 'This better be good.'

He gave her the name of another director and smiled mirthlessly when the first words out of her mouth were 'I knew it.'

'You're sexy when you're smug.'

'Does that line *ever* work for you?'

'I've never used it before. It's a first.'

'In that case I'll attempt to feel flattered. Is our informative friend in travelling shape? Can you bring him in to testify against our man?'

'Doesn't seem wise. He's currently dining with an Eastern Bloc president. Or aren't we caring about that?'

'I guess we're caring,' she said. 'So, have you tied up all your other loose ends?'

'I still need to check on the kid. I need another couple of days.'

'No, you need to prove yourself reliable and be back here when you said you would be. That's non-negotiable.'

'Even though I've given you a name?'

'That name is going to need your weight behind it. Is there any reason you need to see this kid in the flesh?' she countered flatly.

Besides wanting to see Celik for himself and gauge the child's wellbeing…?

'He's being monitored by the Dutch authorities,' she offered next. 'Check up on him that way, and if you're still not satisfied I'll send you to the Netherlands to see him—no question.'

'I'm already halfway there.'

'I'm sending you the contact details for the Dutch who are monitoring him. Call them. And then, in the interest of your future career and my current one, get back here.'

'Is that an order?'

'You don't take orders, so let me put it another way. You asked for my co-operation and trust and I gave them to you. How about you goddamn *earn* it?'

* * *

Jared walked with new purpose and confidence. He wasn't fixed, by any means—he still slept far less than any man should, and indecision still plagued him—but there was no denying that a weight had lifted from his shoulders now that he'd finally finished what he set out to do. Expose the rot in the counter-intelligence organisation he worked for—all the way back to the roots. Maybe now he could rest and get his life back. Figure out what it was he wanted now.

Apart from that kiss.

Director Rowan Farringdon sat at her desk and watched him approach, her eyes sharp and assessing. Probably looking for signs of weakness or fatigue, injury or distress. It didn't sit well with him that she was most likely sitting there trying to assess his needs. On the one hand he drew comfort from her concern. On the other hand it made him feel somehow...*less*.

Less worthy, maybe.

Less capable than he was.

'I'm back,' he said by way of greeting. 'What did you do with the information I gave you?'

'I sent it to the top.'

'Will they be able to get rid of him? With your information and mine, is it enough?'

'I put together a solid case. I believe it'll be enough. Have you had any sleep?'

'I slept on the plane.' More or less. Mostly less.

'In that case you're wanted upstairs. Management wants a word.'

'That's a level of management I've never been introduced to. Any tips?'

'Yes. Try to impress them.'

She stood and came around her big glossy table, crossed the room to where he was standing with his feet slightly apart and his hands behind his back. She stood a good head shorter than him, even in shoes with medium heels. Today she wore a steel-grey dress with a geometrical pattern on the front in pewter and bronze. Professional and classy. Beautiful lean muscles and some very nice curves.

He wanted very badly to have earned the trust she'd placed in him.

He thought he might have.

He wanted very badly to trust that she'd made the right call when it came to him not going to check on the kid.

'Jared,' she murmured. 'My face is up here.'

'I know.' He got there eventually and smiled—because he wanted to.

'Thank you for coming back on time and in one piece,' she said. 'I'm impressed.'

'Did you doubt me?'

'Yes.'

And then she stepped up into his space, slid her hand around his neck and fitted her lips to his.

It was a quiet kiss—neither tentative nor bold. A very welcome kiss. He tried not to frighten her, tried not to let his hunger show… Except that one second he had his desire under control and his hands behind his back and the next moment he had his hands either side of her face and his longing could no longer be denied.

He coaxed her mouth open and she responded with an intrusion both accomplished and welcome. She tasted of passion and perfection and he groaned his pleasure, for it was a taste he hadn't known he craved until this moment.

He tilted his head and deepened the kiss, unleashed his hunger for her just a little bit and felt her match it.

And, *oh*, the intensity she brought to everything she did—to the feeding of her need and his. He loved it.

Testing her, he unleashed a little more, and her eyes swept closed even as her mouth opened greedily. Careful, considered exploration turned into surrender after that as he offered up *his* kind of hunger—the kind with a hard and dangerous edge. *His* brand of possession—desperate and all-encompassing. And Ro…Rowan Farringdon…his director…was right there with him.

Revelling.

As if she'd been made for him.

He had her backed against the table moments later, because all he could think was that there was so much more of her to explore and he wanted his mouth on every last bit of it—no self-restraint left. Only then did she wrench her mouth from his with a gasp and put her hand to his chest to stop him.

Not that it stopped the tremor that ripped through him.

'Are you eating with anyone this evening?' he muttered roughly.

'I'm working late.'

'After that?'

'What? No offer to bring dinner here?'

'I want you gone from this place.'

He wanted equal footing and he wouldn't get it here.

'I want to take you back at my place, or the beach house—anywhere that's private. I want to be in you, over you, under you, touching you for a good long while, and I want to make good on any promises I made to you that first night at my sister's wedding.'

A slow smile lit her eyes at that. 'You never made any.'

'Make 'em up.'

Her mouth joined the smiling caper then—a generous curve that he desperately needed to explore some more.

'You're wanted upstairs,' she murmured. 'I'll be finished here by ten p.m. and I'll be back at six tomorrow morning. I'll need food at some point, and I'll need a bed to sleep in. You can pick me up at five past ten from the steps outside the entrance to the building.'

'You don't mind people here knowing who you're going home with?'

'It'll be a problem, yes. How about we let the others choke on it?'

'Dangerous...' He liked it.

'Nothing I can't handle.'

'Have they give you permission to seduce me?'

'They've given me permission to use whatever means necessary to gain your trust and co-operation. Not that I need to sleep with you to do that. Let's not mistake work for willingness.'

'*Are* you willing, Ro?'

'What do you think?'

He waited until he'd reached the door before looking back. She was still leaning against the desk, still wholly focused on him. He wondered if his lips looked as kiss-blown as hers.

'How many hours of sleep do you need?'

She held his gaze and the smile she sent him was full of promise.

'In any one night? Six.'

Jared was used to men in suits looking him over and not liking what they saw. He was used to them seeing him as either a threat or a weapon to be used against others. He usually enjoyed a certain measure of respect—and when he'd been in Antonov's service fear. Lust—he got that too.

Utter indifference was new to him.

The man standing behind the desk was reptilian—cold and imposing to look at. Pale grey eyes and greying black hair…that rare mix of colour that came out of nowhere and stayed in the mind like a thorn. He was in his fifties, at a guess. Big-bodied, well-honed and powerful. Imposing.

'You hand me the head of one of my directors on a plate and yet you've no ambition to succeed him?'

The man's voice matched his looks. Cold. Precise.

'You don't like the rules so you either bend them or outright break them. You've no wish to remake them, apparently, and you're about to start screwing one of my best directors. Tell me, West, what would *you* do with you?'

'Probably move me on.'

'To where, exactly?'

'A place where section rules don't apply.'

'Why would you even think such a place exists?'

'They always exist.'

The head of the service smiled mirthlessly. 'If you could put together a team for this place where normal rules don't apply, who would you choose?'

'Adrian Sinclair and my sister Lena.'

'Sinclair I approve of. But your sister's performance record is unremarkable and her injuries are extensive. What would you do with her?'

The man had no idea of Lena's determination or her fierce loyalty to family.

Jared didn't bother explaining it to him—just ran through the rest of his list. 'My brother, Damon. My sister Poppy.'

'You've no problem with leading them into danger? Your psych report suggests otherwise.'

'They'd follow me there regardless. May as well make it easier on them.'

'Who else?'

'That's it.'

'Not Rowan Farringdon?'

'She'd limit me. Rein me in.'

'If you let her, yes.'

'Not really my thing.'

'You were doing well until then.'

'You need to find someone who cares.' *May as well come clean.* 'I want Antonov's last mole gone and then I really don't know what I want. I don't like being used, lied to, and finding myself on my own when I come in from fieldwork that *you* authorised.'

Not for a second did the older man look contrite.

'Should you agree to head up this team you'll report directly either to me or to the woman whose desk you passed on the way into this office.'

'Your secretary?'

'She's not a secretary.'

'Then what is she, exactly?'

'My confidante. My partner in all things. My conscience, at times, as I am hers. Vera stays in the outer office because she says it keeps her more connected to section politics than she would be if she held equal title to me. Her choice, and I respect her for it. Vulnerability and accessibility are powerful weapons.'

Not what he'd been expecting—and the older man knew it.

'Every system can be exploited, Mr West. Patriarchy, especially.'

Now *there* was an argument. He wondered what the woman he'd just kissed would think of it. Whether the lesser status would satisfy her. He didn't think so, frankly.

'How would you expect me to trust you *or* your associate? How would I know that the information you'd be feeding me was good?'

'You'd get your team to double-check it. I would have a checking mechanism in place as well. Everyone wins.' The older man's cold grey eyes narrowed. 'I expect you to put together a black ops crew and run them in a manner that will get the job done—*any* job done. You're being groomed, Mr West, for this chair, no less—in about ten years' time, all going well, it will be yours. If you're not inclined towards this outcome you may tender your resignation from the department on your way out.'

'Do I get time to think about it?'

'If you need time to think about it you're not the right man for the job.'

Jared smiled grimly. 'I don't believe that.'

'Tell me, Mr West, do you question *everything*?'

'Do *you*?'

This time he won from the man a smile that might have been genuine.

'If you have a job for me in the here and now I'll look at the brief,' Jared told him. 'I'll make the acquaintance of your partner. I'll approach the people I trust and see if they're willing to go where I lead. And I will let you know, after that, whether I can be what you need.'

Jared didn't consider his stance out of line, considering what the older man was asking of him. And if it was—well, maybe it *was* time to leave.

CHAPTER EIGHT

HE WAS WAITING for her when she stepped from the building and started down the stairs to the footpath. Rowan quickened her step and tried to ignore the acceleration of her heartbeat. His car was sleek, black, expensive, and parked in a no standing zone—and he leaned against the gleaming paintwork as if he had all the time in the world.

He wore battered jeans, a shirt with a collar and a black leather jacket, and he'd look like every muscled guy she'd ever seen in the movies but for the sheer beauty of his face and the fierce intelligence in those midnight-blue eyes. Two of his younger siblings had genius IQs. Jared had been tested too, in his younger years, and those tests had been re-analysed again recently. There was some reason to believe that Jared had screwed those tests up deliberately.

Brains, brawn, an ingrained disrespect for authority, a taste for revenge and utter loyalty to his family. As a director, Rowan had no idea how to handle him. As a woman she had an unhealthy desire to get under his skin and become important to him in ways they'd both regret.

Not exactly a comfortable headspace to be in.

He opened the car door for her as she approached, and she slid him a careless smile and got in.

'Where are we going?' she asked when he took the driver's seat.

'Some place nice.'

'Some place neutral?'

'My father keeps an apartment here for family use. I haven't been in it for over two years and I probably haven't stayed there for close to five years. Is that neutral enough for you?'

'I guess we'll see.' She gave tacit agreement to the plan. 'How far away is it?'

'It's in a hotel complex near here. There are several restaurants to choose from— or, if you prefer, Room Service. You'll have immediate access to other people should you decide to leave the privacy of the apartment. There's a concierge who can call you a taxi if you need one.'

'Am I going to need one?'

'I don't know. Either way, you'll have a swift and easy exit available.'

'Thank you.'

She leaned back against the leather seat and closed her eyes. Her last meeting of the day had been difficult. Jockeying with other section heads for project priority was always taxing. When it came to having dinner with Jared, she'd barely had time to think beyond the fact that she'd agreed to it. That he'd gone ahead and taken the time to plan the evening carefully, with both her physical and emotional comfort in mind, was a very welcome bonus.

'How did your meeting with the management go?'

'It threw up some…unexpected career opportunities.'

He could have said more but he lapsed into silence

and Rowan didn't push him. Sharing information didn't come easily to this man. Trust had to be built slowly.

She opened her eyes and looked in his direction, instantly captivated by the play of shadows across the hard lines of his face and those perfectly formed lips. He was so very beautiful to look at. She doubted she'd ever tire of doing so.

'I patted a puppy this afternoon,' he offered next, with a wry smile in her direction. 'It wasn't *my* puppy, mind, but I figured it counted as far as taking your advice was concerned. Do *you* have any pets, Ro?'

'My grandfather has a tortoise. Apparently I'll inherit.'

He laughed—and *there* was a sound to make a woman sit up and take notice, for it was a good laugh. Rich and rolling. Infectious.

The hotel he took her to looked unimposing from the outside—nothing more than a single set of oversized wooden doors with a black-suited doorman attending them—but the inside was a different matter altogether. Anyone would be able to see this place was on the seven-star side of exclusive the minute they stepped through the doors. Assuming you were allowed through the doors at all.

Jared had to hand the doorman a plastic swipe card and then face a camera and be photo-IDd. Rowan had to be IDd as well, for this hotel clearly took the security of their guests and visitors extremely seriously.

'Your family keeps an apartment here and no one uses it?' she asked as they stepped into a gilt-edged lift with bronze handrails and mirrors. The kind of lift a princess or a president might be acquainted with.

'My grandfather bought it. My father keeps it mainly for sentimental reasons, I think. Occasionally he uses it to impress. Doesn't mean he doesn't profit from it. We have an agreement with the hotel whereby they have the authority to put guests in the suite when we're not using it.'

The apartment he took her to was a three-bedroom penthouse, complete with a ten-person dining table, a bar, and an exquisitely furnished lounge area. It was the kind of suite that foreign dignitaries and heads of state stayed in. It was the kind of hotel that afforded its guests several extra layers of security.

'This do?' Jared asked as he shut the door behind them.

'Yes!' Opulence, privacy, and service at their fingertips. 'You knew it would impress.'

'No. I just hoped it would fit our needs. I have no idea what would impress you.'

'Loyalty. Intelligence. Self-awareness. I'm impressed.'

For a fleeting moment he looked boyishly pleased, and then he shrugged and added a few more words to the mix. 'Vengeful, destructive, inaccessible…'

'Trifles,' she said. 'You'll grow out of it.'

He laughed at her words, his eyes warm and his expression boyishly unguarded. 'We'll see.' He crossed to the bar. 'What can I get you to drink?'

'Cool, clear, bubble-infested water.'

'Do you *ever* drink alcohol?'

'Occasionally. I don't dislike it. It's more a matter of being permanently on call.'

'That's a strong service ethic you have there, Ro.'

Maybe he meant it as a criticism—she didn't know. 'Plenty of people have one.'

He nodded and handed her the room service menu, then tucked in shoulder to shoulder with her while she read it. She didn't push him away. He felt good and smelled better, the faintly woodsy tang of his aftershave teasing her senses.

'Veal for me,' she decided after careful perusal. 'With the creamy fennel sauce and greens—and I absolutely *do* want the wattle-seed and bush honey *crème brûlée* afterwards.'

'I'm having the rib-eye,' he said. 'With fries, cracked pepper, salad to make it look healthy, and a beer to wash it down with. I'm a simple soul. And I'm not on call.'

He picked up the hotel phone and put the order through.

'Someone's coming to sort out the dining area and bring bread and tapas for us,' he offered when he'd finished.

'Good service.'

'Always is.'

She cocked her head to one side. 'You're used to this level of wealth?'

'I don't need it,' he said with a shrug. 'I can exist on a lot less. But, yes. I was born into wealth. I've never wanted for playthings. What about you?'

'I'm used to less.'

He crossed to the entertainment console and moments later the soft strains of a well-played acoustic guitar filled the room. A little bit Spanish…a little bit alternative.

'Your choice?' she asked.

'Probably Damon's—although I recognise who's playing. Sounds of my youth.'

'Do those youthful memories relax you? The ones you had before ASIS?'

'Yes. There are good memories there. My teenage

years were good ones. I thought myself invincible and thought that the world revolved around my every whim. Because it did.'

'See? Told you—you'll grow out of things.'

This man could have done anything. Been anything. Yet here he was.

'Why did you join ASIS?'

'I think I was looking for a cause. A way to combine adrenalin-junked-up dangerous activities with righteousness.'

'What did your father say to that decision?'

'Nothing.' Jared shrugged. 'It's not that we don't get on. We just never saw much of him after my mother's death. Damon and Poppy got the worst end of that stick. They barely know the man at all.'

'Do they care?'

Jared shrugged. 'Can't speak for them, but I like to hope that even if our father wasn't around much while they were growing up they didn't miss out on having family who loved and cared for them. Lena's good at binding people together. Love, concern, support—just being there for people in the day-to-day. She's bossy as all hell, mind—and so was I. But the four of us kids held together as a family. We still hold, even though we're scattered across the globe.'

'I'm glad you have them.'

'Trig's a part of the family too. I've been thinking about something he said the other day. A question he asked me. You and me…if we get together…how will that affect your career? Are you looking to me to enhance it?'

He crossed to the bar, poured himself a Scotch and stared down at it, frowning.

'Because I have to tell you, Ro, that I'm considering finishing up with special intelligence altogether—so if you have some notion that you and I could team up at some point…be some kind of power couple within the organisation…I'm not on board with it.'

It had been a long time since someone had managed to shock her so thoroughly, and it must have shown on her face because Jared suddenly grinned.

'A *power couple*?' she echoed flatly. 'In what way?'

'Management offered me a black ops crew of my own choosing—provided I also chose you for your expertise and experience. They spoke of grooming me for the top job. Your name was mentioned. In a partnership. A working one. A personal one. I felt as if they were handing you to me on a plate.'

It took a lot to make Rowan lose her cool, but she was getting there. She sipped at her water and set it carefully on the bar-top while she tried to stem the angry tirade of words that wanted to spew forth.

'If you want to stop working for Section, then stop.' She kept her voice level and her gaze steady. *Good job, Rowan.* 'Believe me when I say that whoring myself out to you—or anyone else—in order to gain power is *not* on my list of things to do. If I want more power I'll damn well go after it on my own, thank you.'

Okay, now she was getting snappy.

'You have vastly underestimated my self-respect.'

'You're sexy when you're riled.' Jared smiled again, his big body relaxing infinitesimally.

She speared him with her meanest glare. 'No. You *don't* get a free pass on this. You *believed* them. You thought I was *in* on it.'

'I never said that.' His mouth hardened. 'I told you

what they said and then I told you what I was thinking. There's a difference.'

'And now you know what *I* think.'

'Exactly.' He lifted his glass and drained it. When his voice came again it was raspy. 'I still want to know you, Ro. It feels good to explore your boundaries.'

A knock sounded on the door, accompanied by a softly spoken 'Room Service…'

He crossed to the door and let in a man and a woman in black and white service uniform. Rowan watched in muddled silence as the two attendants set silver-domed serving trays on the table before crossing to the sideboard and opening it to reveal everything a well-dressed dinner table would ever need. Thirty seconds, tops, and the table had been expertly set for two and a candelabra lit.

'Your main meals will be with you in fifteen minutes,' the older man informed them with a smile, and then left.

'You can leave any time,' Jared offered quietly, but Rowan took a steadying breath, crossed to the table and took a seat instead.

'I'm hungry. I need to eat and relax and I like your company. Will you join me?'

'And make small talk?'

'You could always try telling me about yourself,' she murmured as he took the seat opposite, candlelight and shadows making him even more beautiful.

'When I was eight I wanted to be a submariner,' he said as he reached for the bread. 'When I die I want to be fed to the fishes.'

'Do you think about dying a lot?'

'I think about surviving more.' He broke his bread, put it in his mouth and chewed.

'When I was eight I wanted to be a foreign correspondent news reporter,' she offered.

'Seriously?'

'Yes. I grew up an only child in a very serious household where news ran twenty-four-seven. Foreign correspondents were my rock stars. I guess you had to be there.'

'Chances are I wouldn't have stayed there. I like being outdoors—anything to do with water and swimming in the rain.'

'Is this a song?'

'Feel free to add your own verse,' he offered generously.

'I like scalding hot showers, with multiple shower heads.'

'Hedonist.'

Their conversation continued, sporadic and easy, as they ate their way through plates of truly excellent appetisers.

The fact that Jared *wanted* to be open and honest with Rowan didn't mean that it came effortlessly to him. It had been years since he'd last shared pieces of himself with anyone, even if she *did* make it easy for him.

And then their main meals arrived, and he tried not to let the silence ratchet up his tension again. Every scrape of cutlery on a plate fed his senses. Every taste and touch—every glance—branded straight through his skin to enflame the beast beneath.

When she pushed her plate aside at the end of the meal and leaned back in her chair to study him he was hard-pressed not to start trembling, his need to reach out and take was so big.

'Ro…'

He wished his voice worked better, but all he could manage was a gravel-scrape across the vowel. He needed to lose himself in sensation, sink so deeply into it that there was no thought for anything but pleasure, no thought of anything but sex. No room for memories, no way to screw up.

'How do you like your sex?'

And she looked at him with those all-seeing eyes and just knew where he was going with this.

'Soft and sweet not really going to cut it for you?' she asked.

'No. And I don't want to break anything. You, especially.'

'I'm hungry,' she murmured. 'It's been a while for me. If we do this, I don't mind getting a little reckless.'

She was saying all the right words, and her delivery was malt-whisky-smooth. Then again, she'd read his psych report.

'I'm trying to be honest here.' And maybe—just maybe—he was trying to avert disaster. 'I'm touch-starved, apparently. And I'm hungry for you. I've been sitting here fighting the need to reach for you. And it's *big*, this need, and I'm struggling to control it. If we start this… If you want to… I need to know that you'll be okay if I get a little greedy.'

He needed more from her than a simple touch, more than a simple caress, and he didn't know where this would take them or how it would end.

'I usually lead during sex—I take control. But—'

The thought of bringing two years' worth of abstinence to the table and not being able to control himself…

She stood and crossed to the bar, poured him another whisky and brought it to the table, leaning into him and brushing her breasts against his shoulder as she did so. She threaded her fingers through his hair and he closed his eyes on an indrawn breath, unable to do much more than ride the spark of heat that shot from head to groin.

'There is another way we could do this,' she whispered. 'A way to take all that fear of breaking things right out of the equation. Shall I tie you up, Jared? Would that help?'

One hand was still in his hair and the other was tracing a slow trail around his neck. He swallowed hard and nodded as a tremor ripped straight through him.

'Yes.'

She kissed him then, slow and careful—until he framed her face with his hands and let the hunger lick through him.

'Get up,' she whispered, so he did.

And somehow they made it to the bedroom without breaking anything.

She undressed him and kept his tie in her hand. He knew that silk was strong—he'd trusted his life to it on more than one occasion—but if she thought one necktie was going to hold him she was mistaken.

The knot she used to bind his hands together in front of him was impressive.

'On your back, on the bed, arms above your head,' she said next, and then crossed the room and reached for the thick silk rope that held the curtains back.

That was more like it…

He groaned, his dignity in tatters, because…*yes*.

She tied his hands to the bedhead—the very centre of the bedhead—and she had to straddle him and lean all over him to do it. Or maybe she didn't have to. Either way, he wasn't complaining. He twisted beneath her, seeking skin with his lips—the soft inner skin of her upper thigh—and tasted salt and sweetness, felt the give in her as she momentarily melted against him, the strength in her as she redoubled her efforts to secure his hands.

The scent of her…he breathed it in. Skin—he wanted more of it. She obliged by lifting her dress up over her body to reveal two lacy scraps of underwear and then she leaned forward again, so that the skin across her ribs was within reach of his lips, and sighed her approval when he went there, and then higher, to the underswell of her breasts. Higher still as she pushed the lace of her bra aside and gave him access to her nipple. He took his time with that, played her soft and sweet, until finally he clamped down and sucked hard, deeply satisfied by the dark flare that lit her eyes. Yes, she'd take more of that.

And then she pulled away and leaned over him again, testing the strength of the ties by curling her hands around his wrists and pulling until the cords drew tight. She trailed her hands along his arms and over his shoulders, slid her body down his and went to work on him. Mapping him with her hands and with her lips, every ridge and valley, she explored him until he was little more than a straining, moaning mess.

'Good?' she whispered.

'Yes.'

And then she blanketed him with her body and started kissing him, languid, messy, got-all-the-time-in-the-world kisses, while her body learned the shape of his and how best she'd fit against it. She kissed him until he was iron-hard and straining for release, slick with promise... He hadn't come from just the touch of a body against his since he was a teenager, but tonight he thought he might.

Would.

If she didn't stop.

His kisses grew harder and more biting—a warning, in the same way his bucking up against her, unseating her, was a warning.

'Rowan,' he growled, and strained at the ties that bound him. 'Don't you make me come like this. I won't forgive you.'

'Relax.' She slid off him, taking away the heat and the warmth of skin on skin, her eyes assessing. 'What do you want next?' Her fingers teased him and he bucked again. 'Ask.'

'Want your mouth on me,' he rasped. 'Want my tongue buried inside you.' He wanted his sex dirty, filthy and glorious, and he wanted Rowan as unhinged as he was.

She did it with a whimper—swivelled around and settled over him—and he'd never felt the lack of hands more as she held herself above him, barely letting him lick at her, let alone feast.

'More.'

She gave it, little by little, and he tried to be delicate with her even as his hunger roared, and then she lapped at him, and flicked her tongue over his crown, and that was the end of any restraint he might have conjured.

There. Right there. Flicking and sucking. And there was nothing else in his world but the taste of her as he feasted. Rowan's scent, Rowan's taste, Rowan's whimpers. *Ro...* Her name was a litany inside his head, and when her mouth came off him with a gasp, and she rested her face against the crease of his pelvis and started swearing, he knew she was close to orgasm.

She came on his tongue, and every muscle in his body was strung so tight he could hardly breathe. He needed his own release the same way he needed air, but not yet… He was nowhere near ready to end this yet.

And then she was turning around again, lining him up and taking him in in tiny increments, and that was exactly the way he wanted her—he wanted to feel everything. The burn in his shoulders, the tug of her teeth scraping against the underside of his jaw, his breath leaving his body on a groan as he thrust up into her.

He'd have had her on her back by now if he hadn't been restrained. He'd have been out of control, too hard for her to handle, too far gone to hold back. But this…

This was exquisite.

She sat up, hands to his chest, and with her eyes never leaving his face steadied herself and used what little weight she had to push his body back against the bed. She scraped her nails across his nipple, paused with one of them between the nails of her finger and thumb, and then pinched it hard. The stab of pain hit his brain like an aphrodisiac.

'So full of you,' she whispered. 'You're everywhere. And I'm almost there again.'

He snapped up into her and was rewarded by another bolt of pain, courtesy of her fingertips digging into his ribs.

This time it did nothing but drag him further out of himself and into that place where only sensation existed.

'You still with me?'

He had to concentrate in order to understand her words.

'Yes.'

'You still want this?'

'Don't you stop now. Don't.'

'Do you want to come now? Like this? Tied up and on your back? So you can only take what I'm willing to give? Is this the kind of sex you need tonight?'

Heaven help him, it was.

'Yes.'

The sounds she made as she started to move mirrored his own…pleasure and pain and utterly intoxicating. And then she leaned back a little more, set up a little roll of her hips on each downward stroke, closed her eyes and went to town.

And that was the end of him.

CHAPTER NINE

ROWAN WOKE BEFORE DAWN. Her body knew her routine as well as her brain did. The hard and heavy weight against her side was Jared West, and his eyes opened to slits when she began to extricate herself from him.

At some point not long after his second orgasm she'd untied him. It had come as no surprise at all to her that he'd immediately gathered her to him and slid into her again, his mouth on hers, slow and coaxing, his hands everywhere, reverent and gentle. Still all about skin on skin… He hadn't seemed to be able to get enough, but his gaze had been sated and slumberous as he'd brought her to orgasm this time with nothing more than his fingers and the feel of him. And he had followed moments later, cursing and shuddering and making her feel more cherished and wanted than she'd ever been.

He was quite something.

Rowan pressed a kiss to the curve of his shoulder in a silent thank you and he smiled just a little bit, his eyes drifting closed again.

'Time for me to get gone,' she murmured. She still needed to shower and drop by her place for another set of clothes before she went to work. 'Go back to sleep.'

'I'll take you home,' he mumbled, still all sleep-mussed and relaxed.

'Stay. I'll grab a taxi.'

'I'm taking you wherever you want to go. Don't argue.'

It was hard to argue with a sleep-sweet man. 'Stubborn.'

'I like to call it determined.'

She trailed her fingers over his outstretched arm and watched his body respond as if he'd been made for her touch. Heady stuff, but it wasn't real. The state he was in at the moment he'd respond that way to anyone with half a clue about the kind of release he needed. She shouldn't read anything into it.

'May I shower here?' she asked him.

'You don't need to ask.' His eyes had opened to slits again. 'Did you read anywhere that I'm not a morning person?'

'No, but I'm observant.'

'Coffee, Ro. Coffee's the solution.'

'Or you could go back to sleep?'

She patted his hand and slipped from the bed.

The bathroom was full of the kind of expensive shower gels and moisturisers that Ro adored. The shower rose was as big as a dinner plate and delivered enough pressure to make her groan. She felt well used this morning, a little tender in places as she sluiced up and washed away the remnants of last night's lovemaking.

She looked in the mirror once she'd finished and saw a slight woman with small breasts, slender hips, and a funny face that had always been unique rather than beautiful. She leaned closer and looked into her eyes and felt every single one of her forty years. No make-up, just pale porcelain skin and lines of responsibility etched around her eyes and between her brows.

Too old for him, a nagging voice whispered, and she couldn't silence it.

She was too caught up in her work to have any sort of meaningful relationship. Last night…Jared West… she'd known what he'd needed, that was all, and she'd offered a mutually beneficial exchange, seeing as their wants and needs had coincided.

Why, then, did last night feel like such a precious gift?

He was up and moving when she came out of the bathroom wearing yesterday's clothes and a dusting of make-up. He had his jeans on and his shirt in hand and he smiled and slipped past her on his way to the bathroom.

'Give me five minutes,' he murmured.

She should leave.

Instead she headed for the kitchenette and finished what he'd started when it came to the making of coffee. It wasn't going to be particularly *good* coffee, mind, but the little machine was doing its best and she was grateful for it.

Jared joined her a few minutes later, and the expression of pure appreciation on his face would have been gratifying indeed had it been directed at her rather than at the beverage.

'Thanks,' he muttered when she pushed the mug towards him.

'My pleasure.' She smiled wryly. 'How do you feel this morning?'

He took his time answering. 'Quiet. Empty. I slept. You? How do *you* feel?'

Rowan held steady under the sudden intensity of his gaze. 'Responsible,' she offered truthfully. 'Wary.'

She watched his gaze harden.

'You don't need to be either of those things.'

'Grateful,' she said next, and sipped her coffee and studied him over the rim of the mug. He was pretty when he scowled. 'Grateful for your trust.'

He ran his hand through his hair and for a moment he looked so lost.

'I'm not—' he began. 'I'm not always like that in bed.'

'What are you usually like?'

'Dominant.'

'Sometimes people switch.'

He didn't look convinced. 'Not me. Not often. Ro… last night was all about me, and I'm sorry, because it shouldn't have been. What do *you* want out of this? What do *you* need?'

Now it was Rowan's turn to feel lost and uncertain. 'I don't know what I want from you, or what I'm likely to need. I enjoy your company. Your body.' And, truth be told, she enjoyed his current vulnerability.

His gaze skated to her bare upper arm. 'I know it's a little late, but what about pregnancy?'

'I have long-term contraception in place.' A lot of agents did.

'I figured,' he muttered. 'Still should have checked.'

'It wasn't just your responsibility.'

'Yeah.' He ran his hand through his hair—that nervous gesture of his again. 'Things are different with you in the mix. I'm getting that loud and clear.'

'Is that a bad thing?'

He set his coffee down abruptly, took hers from her suddenly nerveless fingers as well. And then he framed her face and kissed her, and she felt the hunger and the desperation in him all the way to her soul. By the time he pulled back they were both breathing hard and her hunger was probably a match for his.

'No, it's not bad at all,' he muttered roughly. 'You scare the hell out of me. *I* scare the hell out of me. But I want more of this. Whatever this is.' He pulled back. 'I'm going to make some decisions today—career and lifestyle-altering decisions. I hope you'll bear with me. I hope you'll still want me.'

'Jared—' She badly wanted to see his confidence return, along with devilry and laughter. She wanted life for him, and peace. 'I think that's a given.'

Jared sat at his temporary desk in the open-plan cubicle that was meant to be an office and stared at the two identical reports he'd just handwritten. He'd given them everything that he'd held back the first time. Every person who'd come looking for Antonov's wares during his time with the man, every name he knew, the connections he'd fathomed, the business framework the now-deceased arms dealer had built. Handwritten—all of it. Not a copy in existence. No cards left to play any more.

He was finished.

Management had asked him for a decision yesterday and he'd stalled them. Turned out he hadn't needed much more time in order to make his decision after all. He didn't have anything to pack—his desk was empty. He didn't have anything to wipe from the computer in front of him because in the short time he'd been back he'd never used it. Save to open emails and ignore them.

He made his way up to the management office he'd been in yesterday and stopped ten feet in front of the secretary-who-wasn't-a-secretary, waiting for her to acknowledge him.

He didn't have to wait long.

'Jared.' She sounded cautious beneath the overlay of pleasant. She looked as if she knew his answer already and was simply waiting for him to voice it.

'I have a report for you. It discloses the information I gathered during my time with Antonov. I hope it's useful.'

She didn't even look at the sheaf of papers he placed on the table. 'So you're leaving us?'

'Yes. I like the woman you chose for me. I'm flattered that you think I could ever partner with her to run the division. I'd learn a lot from her, I think. And from you.' He nodded towards the door on the left. 'And from him. I respect what you do here and the skills required to do it. But the wellbeing of my family will always come first with me and every last one of my siblings is in a good place at the moment, living good lives that they've created for themselves. I don't want to cut myself off from them and I don't want to lure them into the shadow world you're offering. My resignation is at the end of the report.'

She regarded him solemnly. 'It's true, this life is not for everyone. We appreciate you considering it.' She looked at the report. 'Would you be willing to consult with us on occasion?'

'If it's only my skills you want, yes. If you want access to the resources the rest of my family has access to, then no.'

'I'll make a note. Thank you for the report. Your resignation is effective immediately. Is there anything else?'

'No.' He made to take his leave.

'Mr West? If you're dropping by Section Five on your way out, tell Director Farringdon I'd like to see her when she has a moment.'

'Of course.' He hesitated. 'Has anyone ever sat in the top job by themselves?'

'Of course they have.' She smiled slightly. 'And may again.'

Rowan was on a conference call when he went to see her, according to Sam.

'How long will she be?'

'They're just getting started.'

'I only need a minute.'

'Not possible.' Sam eyed his duffel bag with suspicion. 'Going somewhere?'

'To pick up a yacht and then to my brother's beach house. I'm done here. I resigned this morning. I need one minute with her. I want to drop something on her desk. She doesn't even have to break her call.'

'You're welcome to leave whatever it is with me.'

'I'd rather hand-deliver it. C'mon, Sam. One last indulgence and then you'll never have to indulge me again.'

'Uh-huh?' she said dryly. 'I'll see you in. Don't talk if she's sitting at her desk with headphones on. Fair warning.'

'I won't.'

Sam opened the door to the inner sanctum for him and he walked in and saw her sitting behind the desk, headset in place and her desk covered in papers. The expression on her face was a captivating combination of intense focus and serenity—as if this world was one she enjoyed…as if she'd been shaped for it.

She'd told him she'd been working towards it since she was in her teens.

Jared smiled a little at the eyebrow she raised in his direction. He withdrew the second copy of his report and held it up for her perusal before setting it on her desk, picking up her pen and scribbling on it that there were only two such reports in existence and that Management had the other one.

She read the words, nodded, and kept right on listening. *Later?* she scribbled on a memo pad, and he shook his head.

Beach house for me, he scribbled back, and then, belatedly remembering, *Management wants to see you when you're free.*

She frowned at him then, and spoke into the headset speaker. 'Yes, Clayton. I understand.'

He took one more look at her, just in case it was the last one he ever got of her in her workplace element.

He memorised her face.

And then he left.

It took Jared until Friday to get his new yacht to its new home at the marina near the beach house. Five days of putting the craft through its paces and rediscovering the beauty of Australia's eastern coastline as seen from the Pacific. Five days of the sun on his face and shoulders and the spray of the ocean sandpapering his skin.

There had been two storm fronts and he'd revelled in the challenge of them. He'd slept better for being tossed around and catching snippets of sleep whenever he could…far better than he'd slept in any bed lately—with the exception of the bed he'd slept in with Rowan.

He'd slept after she'd tied him up and slaked her thirst for him and his for her.

He'd slept heart to heart and skin to skin with her name on his lips.

Her name was still echoing in his head and in his heart, deep in his psyche. Altering his perceptions. Changing his way of thinking about things. He'd left a message on her phone, telling her where he was going, what he was doing, and saying that he'd be in touch with her again once he'd docked. He'd invited her to the beach house, if she wasn't doing anything this weekend.

He didn't want to hear her say no. The little bird of hope in his chest just didn't want to hear it. So he hadn't rung again.

When he docked mid-morning on Friday, he didn't interrupt Rowan's work-day by calling. He let the little bird keep right on fluttering and called Lena instead, asked her if she wanted to meet him at the marina and take a look at their new purchase. He knew it for a token question because he knew full well she'd be there within the hour—her curiosity wouldn't have it any other way.

If he was lucky she'd bring lunch.

She came by the swift red speedboat that Jared had forgotten she possessed. It had been a present from Trig, and Jared had got into trouble once for stealing it.

He smiled at the memory as Lena tossed a rope up to him with a cheerful 'Looking good, brother.'

Lena looked beautiful and carefree, sun-browned and happy. She handed him a bright red Esky next, and then put her hand up for him to haul her aboard.

He laughed. 'Wait for the ladder.'

'I don't need a ladder—just give me your hand.'

'With my ribs? Hell, no. You look heavy.'

'I'm a lightweight these days, I shall have you know,' she protested. 'My husband can carry me easily. You're just getting careful in your old age.'

'Had to happen some time. I'm also world-weary and jaded—and as of three days ago unemployed.'

'Good thing you're independently wealthy, then.'

He set the ladder over the side, and only when she'd reached the top did he offer his hand and some of his strength to help her board.

'Nice,' she said, looking around the little craft. 'I thought you said it was second-hand?'

'It is. Although I don't think the previous owners ever actually sailed it anywhere.'

'Good for them.' Lena grinned. 'Better for us.' She headed for the hatch and leaned down to look inside. 'Dear God, it's *mustard*!'

'It's soothing.'

'You're joking.' She started down the hatch. 'Damon's wife, Ruby, has the most amazing eye for colour. I say we let her loose on it.'

'Isn't she a little busy right now? With a baby coming?'

'Okay, you're right, I'll do it myself. Maybe Ruby and the baby can help. You realise that I fully intend to be the mad aunt who leads that child astray every chance I get? He'll have West genes to contend with—shouldn't be too hard.'

'He?'

'Or she. I have no preference. I just want a beautiful healthy baby for them.'

'You're not—? You don't—? I mean…'

He had no idea how to ask his next question, but Lena took pity on him.

'Am I jealous?' She nodded, but her wry smile held no bitterness. 'A little. I'm kind of still coming to terms with the fact that no child will ever carry my blood, but there are other options. Adoption. Surrogacy. Even fostering. I met a twelve-year-old boy in hospital last year when I was there. He's still there. The rest of his immediate family died in the same car accident that damaged his pelvis and legs.'

'You want to take him on?'

'Thinking about it. He's a sweet kid. Never gives up. He'd fit right in.'

'Does he have any other family?'

'A grandmother on his maternal side who loves him dearly. But her resources are limited.'

'Would she give him up?'

'I don't know that I'd even ask that of either of them. I'm thinking more along the lines of encompassing them both.'

'Where does she live?'

'Byron. That's the beauty of it. She wouldn't necessarily have to relocate. If we can show that between us we have all Tom's rehabilitation, schooling, social and emotional needs covered we could bring him home from hospital.' She shoved her sunglasses atop her head and fixed him with a penetrating stare. 'What do you think?'

'I think that if anyone can make it work, you can.'

He'd stood in front of the head of special intelligence only a few days ago and the older man, upon hearing Lena's name, had questioned what she would bring to a team in her current state.

Heart. She would have brought that.

'Management asked me to put together a black ops

team the other day. If I'd have done so you'd have been in it. No—correction. I'd have asked you to be in it.'

Her smile faded.

'I turned the offer down. Didn't want it. Would you have wanted it?'

She looked at him for a long time and then slowly shook her head. 'No. Once upon a time, hell yes. But, no—not any more.'

'Then I guess I did the right thing.'

'I guess you did.'

She studied him intently, as if she couldn't quite get a good read on him, and it shattered him to know how closed-off he'd become these past two years—even to family.

'So how does it feel to be free of it?'

He looked out over the ocean and thought of the days he'd just experienced. The stirrings of a new beginning in them…and a woman he'd never forget.

'Feels good.'

Lena's smile was blinding and her hug was fierce, and then she fell back and let him find his footing when it came to all the pesky emotions running through him.

'Lunch? I need to investigate the mustard colour further. And the fittings. Bring the Esky.'

She disappeared down the hatch completely this time, and all he heard then was her voice—no visual to go with it—but it made him laugh regardless.

'Seriously?' Her voice had risen an octave. 'You bought a yacht with purple floral curtains?'

'Told you the owners weren't sailors.'

'Yes, but you've been sailing this poor wee boat for how long? And you haven't yet taken them *down* yet?'

'I've been preoccupied.'

He hadn't actually registered them as offensive—just unnecessary—and with the absence of anywhere to toss them… He started down the steps and found half the curtains and their strings already on the ground.

'You'd better not be touching my half. I like them.'

'You do not.'

The rest of them were down before he even had the food on the bench and his sister stood, hands on her hips, surveying the interior of the yacht—which admittedly seemed much brighter now.

'Much better. I'm even warming to the mustard leather. At least the walls are white.'

Not everywhere. 'Bedrooms are that way,' he said with a tilt of his head—and waited for her reaction.

She looked. 'Oh, for the love of— Someone skinned a spotted cow and draped it all over your bedroom.'

'You mean *your* bedroom. I took the other one.'

'Oh, no. No way. She who paid her half first gets first choice of the bedrooms.'

She opened the door to the other bedroom and Jared didn't have to wait long at all for her screech.

That bedroom had purple and mustard walls with black and white hatbox trim. And a lime-green shag pile carpet. The second bedroom was awesome.

'This isn't a yacht—it's a sideshow palace,' she said, turning to flick him a quick grin. 'I can't believe you bought it.'

'It had been on the market for a while. Do you love it? I love it.'

'We're getting Ruby in. This is beyond me. I know my limits.'

There were a lot of limits in place these days. Many of them learned the hard way.

'She sails well,' he said of the yacht. 'Like an angel.'

'What a *good* girl. Does she sail *now*?'

And that was how they ended up moored off Green Island, swimming from boat to beach, later that afternoon.

Lena lay in the shallows, content to be buffeted by gentle waves. Jared sat next to her and wondered at the inner peace that he'd somehow found between one day and the next. Walking away from his job. Sleeping with a woman he'd connected with on a level that had left him wrung out and craving more.

'What do you think of Rowan Farringdon?'

Lena lifted her head to look at him. 'In what capacity?'

'For me.'

Long black lashes swept down over her sister's eyes. 'Well, she's not dumb.'

'But?'

'Is it even possible for someone in her position to have a decent relationship? A sharing and caring one, with someone who's not involved in that world any more?'

'I don't know.'

'Is that the kind of relationship you even want?'

He shrugged and she splashed him with water—a great swathe of it, driven by her outstretched arm.

'You need to get in touch with your feelings,' his sister told him.

'Says the woman who spent ten years ignoring her own feelings, when it came to who *she* loved.'

'So I'm slow? Not exactly a newsflash.'

'You're not slow.'

It was an old scold that went way back to when schoolwork had come so easily to him and his younger siblings but Lena had had to work hard for every mark she received. She'd despaired of her inadequacies, and sometimes she still did.

'Wash your mouth out.'

She grinned at him, more mermaid in that moment than human soul. 'I missed you,' she murmured. 'I'm glad you're back, and I'm selfish enough to like the fact that you've quit a job that would have swallowed you whole. I like it that you're finally showing more than a passing interest in a woman, even if I'm not entirely sure she's going to be able to give you what you need.'

'What *do* I need?'

'Someone who can be there for you the way you'd be there for them. It's a big ask. Because I know full well the lengths you'll go to for the people you love.'

Jared stared out over the blue sky and the darker blue of the ocean. 'I like her. There's something about her.'

'So keep me posted?'

'That'd be telling.'

'Yes.'

He didn't have to turn to see the smirk on her face.

'Yes, it would.'

CHAPTER TEN

ROWAN TOOK THE weekend off. She'd worked the last three weekends in a row and she was entitled to some down time. She headed for the airport, got on a plane, and three hours later touched down at a little regional airport in northern New South Wales.

And found Jared waiting for her.

Oh, she could get used to this.

He was good at making a woman feel special.

Offer her a crooked smile and a searching glance and the job was done.

'Where are we going?' she asked, and it was good to know that she hadn't had to organise anything about this weekend beyond turning up to it.

'Beach house tonight. Sailing tomorrow. Lena's for late-afternoon drinks when we get back, and then beach house again on Saturday night. How does that work for you?'

"Beautifully.' It sounded a whole lot like heaven.

'Do you have to be anywhere on Sunday?' he asked.

'I did have an invite to Sunday dinner with my parents, but I cancelled on them.'

'Is that going to cause a problem?'

'I get the feeling they were expecting it. My parents

recently retired and they're feeling invisible. They're searching for meaning within their new life, people to fill it, but I can't be there for them the way they want me to be. Except for my grandfather, I don't really do family.'

'Why not?'

'Because there isn't any.'

He fell silent after that, and so did she as they headed towards a four-wheel drive tabletop ute, with fishing rod racks and surfboard racks gracing its roof.

'I'm glad you came,' he said as he stowed her carry-on bag in the back and opened the door for her.

'So am I.'

'I'd kiss you, but I want to get you home first.'

'Is this a control thing?'

He smiled down at her, slow and sweet. 'It's a once-I-start-I-don't-aim-to-stop thing.'

Maybe it came naturally to him, or maybe he'd had a lifetime's practice, but this man knew instinctively how to make her feel like the most precious person in the world.

And Rowan loved him for it.

Jared figured that asking Rowan how her working week had gone was off-limits. He told her what his family was up to, what he'd been up to, and that took five minutes. He made a late supper for them out of mussels and broth and chunky bits of bread and her eyes warmed even as she demolished it.

'Are you on call?' he asked, and she shook her head around a mouth full of food.

No.

'White wine?'

Yes.

He'd been seducing women since his late teens. Confidently. Effortlessly.

This was different.

'Beds and bedrooms are down the hall.' Not exactly the smoothest introduction to their potential sleeping arrangements. 'There's plenty of them.'

'I'm thinking yours.'

Well, all righty, then.

But he didn't rush to get her there. He wanted to take his time.

They headed for the deck after dinner, and maybe Rowan guessed that it was one of his favourite places and maybe she didn't, but in the end they had the big-screen television out there as well, along with enough pillows, cushions and deckchair mats to sleep twenty.

Open-air movie night, and the movie Rowan chose for them to watch was a spy one. They rewrote it as they watched, and Rowan laughed and drank another glass of wine, and pretty soon it was going on for one a.m. and her head was resting on his chest and her eyes were closed and her breathing was regular and deep.

Jared knew what bone-deep tiredness felt like and he had a sneaking suspicion that Rowan was no stranger to it either. He turned off the big screen and the lights and let the stars shine down on them. He dragged pillows towards them, pulled a cover over, tucked her into his side until they fitted together like pieces of a puzzle, and followed her into oblivion.

And the little bird inside his chest—it was singing.

Rowan woke before dawn—it was just her way. She'd been doing it for too many years to adjust easily to waking at a later time.

This time, however, she woke to a sea of pillows and blankets, the sky overhead, and a warm weight at her side was—Jared West. And he was a possessive bastard, even in his sleep, if the hand splayed over her heart was any indication. He hadn't pressured her into anything last night. In fact he'd given her what she'd needed. A place to unwind from the pressures of a hellish week, permission to lie back and breathe.

She might have wanted soul-stealing sexual relations, but he'd given her exactly what she'd needed.

She rolled onto her stomach and moments later he followed, awake and tracing gentle fingers down her spine.

'Did you sleep well?' he murmured.

'Mmm.'

'Want to not sleep any more?'

'Mmm.'

How was that even a question, given that his lips were following his fingers down her spine, soft and dragging and wholly reverent? A breaking dawn and the promise of lovemaking. She arched back against him, helpless in her longing for him.

'Want you to be in me.'

He savoured her—there was no other word for it—and she surrendered to the blinding pleasure and the warmth.

He curled his hands around her thighs once he'd finished exploring every dip of her back. He lifted her to his mouth and for a while she thought he might be a sex god. And then he released her, and then blanketed her again as he slid into her, slow and easy, and then she could have sworn he was a sex god.

He rode her slowly, teased and tormented, built a

stairway to the sky for her. She climbed every step of it. And in the light of a new day they climaxed together.

This wasn't sex as she knew it.

This was different.

'Children,' Rowan said to Jared later that afternoon, over a meal of barbecued ocean perch and mixed salad, served on plastic plates on the deck of Jared's yacht. 'What's your view on them?'

'I like them,' he told her. 'Got nothing against them. Not sure I want any.'

'You're young yet. This is only to be expected. Do you envision them anywhere in your future?

'What if I get it wrong?' He gestured with his fork, barefoot and expansive, looking ever more carefree. 'If I fall down on the parenting job the child wears it. Parenthood requires careful consideration.'

Indeed it did.

'What about you?' he asked. 'Do *you* want children?'

'My parents are really bad role models. My grandfather, by his own admission, was neglectful of my mother, and my mother continued the tradition. I figure that if I remain childless the cycle will stop.'

'And I figure that for bull. Do you *want* children? If you had a loving family to raise them in…a village full of caring people to help you…would you want them then?'

Her hesitation told him many things.

'I'd still have to make a lot of lifestyle changes,' she murmured. 'And I'm getting a little old for child-bearing.'

A valid point—but not insurmountable, by his reckoning.

'And I've never really met a man I've felt a compelling urge to have children *with*,' she added quietly. 'I don't know what kind of parent I'd make. What about my job? You know the hours I keep. It took me five days and two IOUs to get this weekend off.'

Jared frowned.

'I gave up on the idea of motherhood when I got the directorship,' she told him. 'I know you don't think that the age gap between us matters, but maybe my ambivalence when it comes to having children *will* matter to you.'

'You're pushing me away?'

'No.' She looked troubled for the first time that weekend. 'I'm letting you in. Telling you about the hopes and dreams I still harbour, as well as the ones I've let go of.'

Jared digested that, as she'd meant him to all along, and then he looked out over the ocean and realised that fatherhood held no appeal for him if the woman by his side didn't want to be a mother. It was one of the more easy decisions he'd made in quite some time.

'How do you feel about being an aunt?'

'I would make a really good aunt,' she told him solemnly. 'Alas, I have no siblings.'

'I have three. And one very pregnant sister-in-law. I figure that if I get in good with her she might let me borrow the kid from time to time. You could tag along.'

Her eyes warmed. 'You're kind of perfect. Don't let anyone ever tell you any different.'

They made it to Lena's for drinks that afternoon, but only just.

And it wasn't because of sailing boats and contrary winds.

Rowan left late Sunday night, and Jared let her be for three days while he tinkered with the yacht.

He wasn't the only one feeling the tyranny of distance when it came to relationships. Trig was back at work in Canberra—a mere twelve-hour drive from the farmhouse—and although his sister was fiercely independent, there was no denying that Lena was missing her husband.

'We could go visit them,' she said on Wednesday afternoon over the phone. 'Do you still have your private pilot's licence?'

'I haven't flown for two years. I'll need a review.'

'Good thing I kept mine up to date, then.'

'Brat. Do we still have a plane?'

'We do.'

'Does it go?' Keeping the Cessna flight-ready had once been *his* task—back before Antonov.

'Of course it goes. What good are toys if you can't use them?' Lena paused. 'So what do you think? Want to go to Canberra? Because I think midweek visits to people we care about are important.'

'I think you're right.'

Rowan liked Thursdays—and never more so than when a blue-eyed devil rang her at six-thirty, while she was still at work, and asked her to dinner that night.

'Why aren't you at the beach house?' she wanted to know.

'Lena decided to implement a must-see-Trig-midweek-and-have-dinner-with-him policy. She also has a plane, so we flew down.'

'You people…'

'You're not going to talk carbon footprints, are you?'

'No, I was going to stick with a comment about obscene wealth instead, but I've changed my mind. It's good to hear from you.'

'And dinner this evening? I know it's short notice.'

It was. Rowan eyed the number of case updates still open on her taskbar, all of which needed to be read and signed off on. Tonight.

'What if I bring dinner to you?' he said into her silence. 'How late do you have to work?'

'Can you give me another hour and a half? After which time I will be well and truly ready to leave.'

'You want me to pick you up?'

'Or you could meet me at my place with food in hand. There would be huge brownie points earned. Enormous. There could be vanilla bean and shaved chocolate ice cream for dessert.'

'Do I need to bring the ice cream as well?'

'No, there's some in the freezer.'

'I'll meet you there,' he said. And hung up.

There was a lot to be said for walking towards the glass-walled lobby of her apartment block and finding a beautiful man waiting for her with a bag full of takeaway food dangling from his fingers.

She watched those fingers tighten as she walked towards him, watched him catalogue everything about her—from the shoes she wore to the colour of her lipstick.

She wondered if he saw what she saw. A woman of average height and mediocre looks. A woman who—on a personal level—people rarely waited around for.

The closer she got the better he looked. The smell of delicious food wafted towards her, mixing and mingling with the faintest scent of *him* as she leaned in to brush her lips against his face, first one cheek and then the other.

His gaze lingered on her lips for a satisfyingly long time after she drew back, the thrumming stillness of his body a sign that he'd liked her greeting a lot.

He liked her lips—she remembered that.

Gave thanks for that.

They got in the elevator and she pressed the button for the top floor. He didn't crowd her. He just watched.

'Come on in,' she murmured when finally she opened the door to her apartment, more than a little curious as to what he would make of her home.

Neutral colours for the walls and a pale wooden floor, richer caramels and ivory colours for the bigger furniture items. No knick-knacks…a couple of family photos. She liked colour, and had added it in the form of cushions and throw rugs, the textures soft and inviting. The views from the windows were of the surrounding cityscape and nothing special. None of it was special.

This place hadn't been designed with looking outward in mind. This place was for curling up in, intimate and engulfing. The hotel apartment he'd taken her to had been bigger and better outfitted.

'It isn't much. One bedroom, a couple of bathrooms, one study and this space. I've never—'

He followed her through to the kitchen and set the food on the counter. 'Never what?'

She was for ever revealing her innermost thoughts to him. 'I don't entertain here much.'

'It's your cave,' he murmured. 'I get it. And I'm flattered that I got an invitation. No pressure, okay? You want me to leave—just show me the door.'

'I don't want you to leave.' And it wasn't just because

the food containers he'd started lining up on the kitchenette bench held so much promise. 'Is that pork belly with plum sauce on the side, green beans and mashed potatoes from my second favourite restaurant?'

She might have been guilty of telling him about the dish on the weekend and waxing lyrical.

'It is. When did you last eat?'

Rowan rubbed at the frown between her eyes. 'Maybe around eleven?'

'And you started when? Six?'

She nodded, and he speared her with a penetrating glance.

'Work. Sleep. Eat. Play. *Balance*, Ro. Haven't you ever heard of it?'

'Says the man who up until a couple of weeks ago lived his work twenty-four-seven. Undercover.'

'And I have learned my lesson.'

She dumped a handful of serving spoons on the counter and he picked one up and started dishing food out.

'More potato?'

'Yes. Always yes to that question. How long are you here for?'

'We'll leave again tomorrow night and take Trig with us for the weekend. You too, if you want?'

Rowan hesitated. Much as she wanted to, her dance card was already full. 'Sorry. I'm on call. And I have a date with an octogenarian.'

'Your grandfather?'

'You should meet him. I think you'd like him.'

Jared stilled, and then carefully, casually, continued serving.

'I saw that hesitation,' she murmured. 'Too soon to talk of having you meet my favourite person?'

'No, I— It wasn't that.' It was as close to a mumble as he ever got. 'You said I should meet him and I instantly thought yes. Which gave me pause—because normally there *is* a pause while I try to figure out how to say no thanks.'

'You probably only want to meet him because he's a retired general who owns a pet tortoise called Veronica.'

'Veronica, huh?'

'You should probably compliment the General on her superbly patterned shell. He's very proud of her.'

'I have absolutely no idea whether you're setting me up or not.' His smile warmed her. 'But I like it. Where are we eating? Bench or table?'

'Table.'

He really was deliciously easy to accommodate. They sat and ate, and Rowan tried not to bolt her food, but it was so good, and— *Oh*.

'What would you like to drink?' So much for her skills as a hostess.

'Relax. I'll get it.'

He came back with soda water for both of them and she looked at the drinks and grimaced in embarrassment. Soda water, still water or milk had been his only choices.

'I really wasn't expecting you tonight. If I had I would have magically arranged for my fridge to be fuller.'

He smiled, slow and contented. 'I really don't care if your fridge is full or not.'

So there was that, and his apparent ease with her living arrangements, and a slow-building heat that made her wonder whether it would be appropriate to push her meal aside, crawl across the table and feast on *him*.

Instead, she chose small talk. 'What have you been up to?'

'Racing speedboats and thinking about my future. Last time I decided on a career path I didn't think of anything beyond superficialities.'

'All the pretty toys?' she murmured.

'Exactly.' He speared a pork square and offered it to her—and who was she to refuse? 'These days I'm older, wiser and more searching. I want to feel useful. Money isn't a necessity. I thrive on adrenalin and I'm narrowing down options.'

'What kind of options?'

'Banking. The family business. It'd make my father happy and the stock exchange pit might suit me.'

She studied him in silence.

'No comment?'

'Maybe as a short-term career option, sure…'

His smile turned wry. 'You think I'd get bored?'

'You said it yourself. You're not money-focused. You need a cause.'

'I had a cause once. It was corrupt.'

'Not all of it.'

'Enough to give me pause. I don't want to go to work each day and have to decide who's going to betray me today and who's not. I don't know how you do it. The politics and the conniving. The lack of loyalty.'

'It's not that bad. The politics and the conniving—I'm good at it. As for the loyalty… Well…' Maybe she was simply used to rolling with betrayal. 'I know what you could do,' she began. 'What about something along the lines of what your brother does? Cyber information acquisition? Ask him who's hiring.'

Jared eyed her with a frown. 'Not my thrill.'

'What about physical retrieval?'

'Of what?'

'Anything. Do your homework when it comes to who wants what and why. Pick and choose your jobs carefully. You call the shots.'

He stared at her for a good long while. 'Maybe.'

'It'd suit your lifestyle.'

'And what lifestyle is that?'

'Plenty of action, plenty of travel. No time to get bored because every job would be different.'

'And if I wanted to forgo the travel and stick a little closer to home?'

'Is that what you want?'

He'd surprised her. *Again*. But then, when had he ever not?

'Yeah. My gut says it's time to settle down. Choose a place and make it home.'

'And what does your gut say about you flying in to have takeaway dinner with a woman who can't even keep a meal in her house?'

'My gut says the food's good and yours is the company I want.' His voice had gone all raspy. 'I wanted to see you, Ro. Touch base. Something like that.'

She was still waiting for the other shoe to drop.

'Touch base or just touch? Are you having trouble sleeping again?' Maybe that was why he was here. Maybe he needed the kind of release she'd given him at the apartment.

'I'm sleeping well enough.' His voice had husked out. 'I don't need you to tie me up.'

'Really not a problem if you did.' She put it out there. 'I enjoyed it.'

Hell, she'd *loved* it.

He shrugged again—only this time it was an invitation if ever she'd seen one.

'Not this time.' His eyes had gone dark. 'Stop trying to give me what you think I came here for, Ro. Stop trying to fix me as if I'm broken. Nor is it your job to direct me towards a solution. Otherwise I'm going to start thinking you're still at work.'

'*How* am I directing you?' she asked indignantly. 'I've done no directing at all tonight!'

'No? Then why is the focus all on me and my problems? On what I might need and how I might arrange my life? I didn't bring those topics up, Ro. You did. You're still looking at me as if I'm one of your problems to be solved.'

'No.' Was he right? *Was* she still in work mode? 'I—Maybe I—'

'Yes?' he enquired silkily.

Well, hell. Rowan sat back in her chair and stared at him. Had she still been in work mode? Half of her trying to figure out what he needed so that she could provide support? The other half assuming that he couldn't possibly be there simply because he'd wanted her company. Just her company—nothing more.

'I'm interested in you and I make no apology for some of my questions,' she offered finally. 'How else will I know what's going on in your life if I don't ask? But maybe I do need to ease out of work mode a little more—stop trying to offer up solutions and just…relax now that I'm home. It'll happen. The relaxation part. Any minute now. I'm almost sure of it.'

'Uh-huh?' He loaded up his fork with potato. 'Eat your dinner, Rowan. And then we'll set about seeing what it takes to get you to unwind.'

Rowan filled her mouth with food—it seemed like the best course of action—and at some point during the meal Jared's leg kicked into hers and stayed there.

Not unwinding.

He told her about Lena and Ruby ganging up on him and insisting that mustard was not an appropriate colour for the interior of a yacht. He made her laugh, but he looked at her with an intensity that made it impossible to relax. How was a person supposed to relax into *that*?

'Would you like ice cream now?' she asked when they'd cleared their plates. 'I'll just get—'

'No, you won't. Stay.' He eyed her sternly and took the plates to the dishwasher. 'Do you even *want* ice cream after that? Or is it just something else to offer your guest?'

'I sometimes have ice cream after dinner.'

'Do you want some tonight?'

She was tempted to prove him wrong and say yes—but she'd be lying. She didn't have to stay sitting at the table like a lump, though. It was *her* kitchen. The least she could do was help tidy it.

But he blocked her way and there was pure challenge in his eyes when he murmured, 'It's done, Rowan, and it really doesn't need any final check-up.'

'You think I'm a control freak?'

'I think we're about to find out. Would you like me to tell you what kind of sex I'd like tonight?'

'Um…' Could be a test. 'Your call.'

'Good answer.' He was advancing on her, backing her against the wall, boxing her in with his arms either side of her and his body heat licking at her senses. 'If you want me to leave, tell me now.'

The best answer to that was silence.

'I want to make you forget your own name tonight,' he murmured. 'You good with that?'

'Well, you can try. Are you waiting for permission?'

Her tone would probably have been a lot more challenging had he not been dragging his lips over her neck at the time. Because all she could manage as his tongue got in on the act was a whimper.

By the time he got around to kissing her lips she had her eyes closed and her hands palms to the wall for fear of burying them in his hair and directing him where she wanted him to go. And then he coaxed her shirt up over her head, and when her arms fell they fell to his shoulders.

He didn't need any direction when it came to getting his shirt off, or her trousers either. No direction at all as he picked her up as if she weighed next to nothing, his hands on her buttocks, his strong fingers curling under and around to tease at the edges of her panties.

She was so wet for him. The minute he touched her he would know, if he didn't already, that all he had to do was put his hands on her and she was halfway to gone.

And then his fingers skated across the slick she was making for him, and he growled and slammed her back into the wall, coaxing her legs to open around him—and, *oh*, that worked for her. She spread her legs wider, rocking up into that teasing hardness, letting him know in no uncertain terms that she would like more of that.

'Please…' she whispered into his mouth as she wound her arms around his neck and held on.

Denim rasped against her as she ground up onto him—hard.

'Please. I won't break. Anything you want.'

She wanted to feel his thickness inside her so that she

didn't have to clench around nothing. She wanted the burn that came of trying to swallow him whole.

And then he took her to the counter, hooked his fingers through her panties and pulled them off. He unzipped himself next and pushed his boxers down. He took himself in hand, his eyes almost black as he breached her—just a little. Nothing more than a promise that soon…soon he would fill her up.

He opened her mouth with his thumb next. She sucked it in and got it good and wet before pulling back to nip at the knuckle. *There. All done. Good job.*

He was still toying with her, not giving her nearly enough of his length, and he toyed with her some more as he put his thumb to her centre and rubbed, finding exactly the right spot.

She bit her lip to stop herself from keening, but some sound escaped and his gaze, which had been fixed elsewhere, met hers.

'There? Is that good?'

He knew it was.

His next kiss was filthy—all grazing teeth and demanding tongue.

She was riding the ragged edge of desperation, and he knew she wanted more, but he made her wait even as he built her slowly, inexorably towards climax.

She slapped one hand behind her on the counter for leverage, the better to lift her hips up and forward. Greedy…so greedy…for more pressure from his thumb and an inch or seven more. It wasn't as if he didn't have them to give.

He slid into her a little more—huge, hard and so welcome she could hardly stand it. Almost there…almost.

'What do you want?'

His rumbled words licked at her as she bucked forward and she gained another inch of him, and then cried out her frustration when he wouldn't let her have any more.

But she wasn't going to direct him this time. She didn't always have to call the shots. Sometimes she wanted more than anything to ditch that responsibility and have someone call them for her.

'Anything,' she whispered. 'Whatever you want.'

'Good.' He sheathed himself all the way inside her with one mercifully hard thrust. 'Come.'

CHAPTER ELEVEN

ROWAN WOKE TO a warm and touch-happy man in her bed and didn't mind his presence at all. Not the circle of his arms or his sleepy good morning. Not the way he kept one hand on her stomach even as he rolled over to check his phone.

'What time do you have to be at work?' he mumbled.

She muttered something about six o'clock and pulled his phone towards her so that she could see the time more clearly. She groaned—six o'clock being forty minutes away and all.

'I've got to get up. What time are you and the gang heading back today? Because you're welcome to stay here this morning. Just lock up on your way out.'

'You know what I remember best about my mother?' he said as he pulled her to him and placcd a kiss on her temple. 'Whenever my father had to leave for work, be it for a day or for a fortnight, she always got up and saw him off, and he always left smiling. Even back then I liked her priorities.'

Rowan remembered back to those days in far-flung countries when her parents hadn't even bothered to tell her where they were going. She'd simply wake to an amah or the housekeeper telling her they were gone

Could be why Rowan liked her job so much nowadays. Knowing where people were and what they were doing just flat-out *worked* for her on a psychological level. That kind of information was important to her. It made her feel secure.

'Was she a stay-at-home mum, your mum?'

'Depends on your definition. Companies used to come to her with their figures for analysis. She was a mathematician—an incredibly bright one. I think that's where we all got our smarts from.'

'She sounds like a remarkable woman.'

'Life is full of them.' He turned his head, his eyes as penetrating as any laser. 'You're one.'

'Trust me—I am not that smart.'

'You're a driven, focused, impressively networked problem-solver. And you know I'm more than halfway gone on you. And now we need to get out of this bed before I derail all your good intentions when it comes to you being on time for work.'

Rowan slid out of bed with a light in her heart. She shared her toiletries and her shower with him and smirked her satisfaction when he emerged, hair still spiky and wet, smelling faintly of ginger and roses. She ground beans and made coffee with the sinfully expensive machine that had been a fortieth birthday present to herself, and watched his eyes glaze over when he lifted the steaming black brew to his lips.

This man practically turned into a biddable little lamb in exchange for a morning cup of coffee.

Something to remember.

By the time he was on his second cup she was almost ready to walk out through the door. 'You'll lock up behind you?'

He nodded and set the cup down. 'So… Me coming here to see you during the week. You coming up to the beach house when you can. Is that going to work for you? Because if it does…if you want to try to build some kind of ongoing relationship with me…I'm all for it.'

'An exclusive relationship?'

'I don't share.' His eyes flashed hot with temper. 'We do this and you're mine and no one else's. And I'm yours.'

'Yes.'

She wanted to crawl into his lap and stay there for a week. Gorge herself stupid on him and let him feast on her. She wanted this man and all that he was offering. There would be spats with him, because he wasn't a malleable soul and neither was she. There was a good chance that she would want more than he could give.

But she contented herself with kissing him slow and sweet and savouring this moment of pure happiness. 'Yes,' she whispered. 'Yes, I think that would work.'

CHAPTER TWELVE

ON WEDNESDAY THE following week Jared got a phone call from Damon. He and Damon didn't really *do* social calls, so his brother's quiet 'Hey, how you tracking?' caught his attention, regardless of the innocuous words.

'Yeah, good. Better than I was.'

'And your ribs? They're good now too?'

Okay, now his brother was getting weird.

Jared strode past the pool on his way to the big double doors that led out onto the deck overlooking the ocean. 'Yeah, they're fine. What's going on?'

'You at the beach house?'

'Yeah. Why? You need it for something?'

'Need you to get something out of the safe for me. I'll call you back in five minutes.'

'Better make it ten. I know that safe, but damned if I can remember the password.'

'You break it—you buy it. Search your memory, brother. I know you have one.'

'You always have to do things the hard way,' Jared grumbled.

'Good to hear you bitching again. I've missed it.'

Damon rang off.

Jared sighed, put the phone back in its cradle and

padded down the long hallway to Damon's study. He'd barely set foot in it since he'd been here. Mostly he used the kitchen, the pool and the beach that beckoned so brightly. He was taking it easy. Feeling his way in this new life and trying not to demand too much from the woman he wanted to be with.

Jared remembered the combination to the safe the moment he looked at it. His brain was good for stuff like that. He scooped up the phone, the computer and the power cords sitting in the safe and took them out to the kitchen and plugged them in. There was nothing else in the safe. This was it.

He made himself a rare roast beef sandwich—tomato, lettuce and pickle included—in the two minutes he had left before Damon rang again. His brother was excruciatingly punctual. If Damon said he'd call back in five minutes, he meant five minutes.

He was mid-bite of his sandwich when one of the 'safe' phones rang. Damon and his insistence on black market phones that couldn't be traced… Mind you, they were useful.

'You know that phone you left in Seb's toiletries bag at the wedding?' Damon began when Jared picked up, referring to their sister Poppy's partner.

'I thought that was *your* toiletries bag?'

'Nope. It was Seb's. Luckily he's a sharing, caring kind of guy and he told me about it. I brought it home with me and I've been keeping it charged. I figured if you wanted it you'd ask for it.'

'Thanks.' Jared eyed his sandwich longingly before putting it down. 'It has information on it that I didn't feel like sharing.'

'Someone called the phone last night.'

'Say *what*?'

'You sound surprised.'

'Only one person ever used that number. And he's dead.'

'It's Antonov's kid, from what I can gather. I'm going to play the messages for you now. First one's just a hang-up call—didn't leave a message,' Damon said. 'The second one's more interesting.'

Damon did something to the phone at his end and Antonov's seven-year-old son's voice came on the line.

'JB? Jimmy? You said to call you if I ever got in trouble, so I'm calling,' the boy said in his native Russian. 'My mother doesn't want me. She thought I'd come with money but there isn't any. And my father's friends don't believe her, and she's scared because they're saying that my father owed them and now she owes them and they're really bad men. She says I'm too sick and that I'm more trouble than I'm worth and that she can't protect me. She doesn't want me.' The boy's voice broke. 'She never did.'

Jared slumped against the counter and closed his eyes against the wash of remorse that slid through him like poison. Antonov's little boy had always been his weak spot when it had come to bringing Antonov's operations to a halt. *What would happen to the sick little boy with Antonov in prison and a mother who'd been nowhere in the picture and didn't want to be?* Only Antonov had died, which had changed the equation again. Celik's mother had become the boy's next of kin and Celik had been shipped off to her.

'You still there?' asked Damon.

'Yeah,' he rasped in a voice that wasn't his. 'I'm listening.'

'This next one came in a couple of hours after the second message.'

Jared waited to hear what the boy had had to say this time.

'You promised I'd be okay. I'm not okay. *Please*,' Celik begged. 'You promised my father that if anything bad ever happened to him you'd look after me. I *heard* you. Can you come and get me?'

The message ended and once again no one spoke.

And then Damon cleared his throat. 'Did you really promise that?'

'Yeah.' His brother hadn't *been* there. 'Yes, I did.'

'I love you, man, and I know you move mountains—you've been my hero ever since I was a kid, think Superman—but how the *hell* do you intend to make good on that promise?'

'I *can* make good on it.' Jared's hands might be trembling but he had to believe it. 'Can you trace the calls?'

'The calls track back to a canal house in Amsterdam and all three of them came in overnight—my time. Truth be told, I didn't check that phone for messages when I first got up. I didn't even look at the phone until after lunch. It's been silent. I've only being paying cursory attention to it.'

'I never asked you to check for messages. I didn't think there'd *be* any.'

'So what's your plan?'

'Go and get him.' Nothing else he could do.

'You need any help with that?'

He was going to need a great *deal* of help with that. Not to mention some kind of real plan. 'Don't you have a pregnant wife to be with?'

'Just saying that I'm right here if you need anything

by way of information or assistance. I don't have to be there in order to help you. Have computer will cyber-travel, man. If you're planning a covert extraction…if you're aiming to disappear the boy out from under everyone's noses…don't count me out. Count me in.'

'I— Thanks.'

He'd always left Damon out of the loop when it came to the work he'd performed. He'd always left Damon out of the loop, *period*. If Jared were to hazard a guess he'd say that he'd always thought of Damon as too young and unpredictable to take part in any wild scheme he and Lena had dreamed up as teenagers. But his brother wasn't that kid any more.

Courtesy of that damned psych report, Jared now had more than a passing acquaintance with the slights he'd bestowed on his younger brother over the years and the underlying reasons for them.

Damon alive. Their mother dead.

Resentment.

'Yeah. I could probably use your help if you want in,' he muttered gruffly. 'Celik Antonov is a sweet kid. A *good* kid. He doesn't deserve this.'

'Do you have a plan for once you have him?'

'Antonov has a sister. He set her up with an alias and enough money for a simple life twenty years ago and then he left her to it. No contact whatsoever until three months ago, when a Romanian woman contacted him about donating a kidney to his son. A kidney with a high chance of being a match for the kid. Her name was Sophia and Antonov had her on speaker phone. He cut her off. And then he broke down and wept.'

And then the story had come out.

'Did she give the kid the kidney?'

'She never called again.'

'What makes you think she'll take the boy?'

'She offered him her kidney.'

'Do you know where to find her?'

'No, but I know she's a schoolteacher in a small village in Romania and that she's childless. Also that she was worked over by thugs when she was twelve and Antonov was eighteen. Antonov had got on the wrong side of some dangerous people and that was their warning to him. Care to do a bit of sleuthing?'

'Sophia…schoolteacher…Romania…childless and her age,' Damon replied dryly. 'Good thing I'm brilliant.'

'Ah, modesty. Guess it runs in the family. Call me when you have something.'

'You taking anyone with you when you go to get him?'

'Wasn't planning on it.'

'Will you tell Trig where you're going? Or Lena? *Anyone?*'

'Are you insinuating that I need to share more with the family?'

'*Yes*. Save yourself a repeat of Lena going after you. Again. Because she will—and she'll drag us all into it.'

'Consider them told.'

Somewhere in the past two years Jared had lost control of his family entirely. Something to rectify. Eventually…

'Hey, Damon?' Jared considered his next question carefully. 'I'm going to need a handler on this job. I need someone to plan ahead with. Someone to talk me through the options once I'm on the ground and steer me in the direction that's safest for the kid… Would you do it?'

'Are you asking me?'

There was something in Damon's voice that sounded a whole lot like hope. Willingness—that was in there too. Need, even.

'Yeah, I'm asking you. And I know exactly what kind of responsibility it entails, so if you don't want—'

'I'll do it,' his brother said gruffly. 'Who better, right? It's not as if I'd want anyone else doing it.'

'Okay.' Jared cleared his throat. 'Okay, thanks.'

This family.

There was silence then, while their relationship settled into new territory, and then Jared took a deep breath. 'This Amsterdam canal house? Where do I find it?'

'I'll send you directions. You going to ring the kid?'

'You going to give me the number?'

The answer to both was yes.

Rowan hated it when someone else's plan went awry and landed on *her* desk. She'd been keeping tabs on Antonov's son from a distance, touching base with the officials responsible for placing the boy with his mother. So far she didn't think much of their decisions. 'Set and forget' being their preference.

The child's mother was a high-class courtesan who'd held Antonov's attention long enough to beget him a child. He'd paid her handsomely for her trouble and she'd given up the child without a backward glance.

That was then.

These days Celik's mother worked even more selectively, operating out of her own home in the middle of Amsterdam. She wasn't a criminal, and she enjoyed a comfortable standard of living. She didn't take drugs and didn't drink to excess. On paper, sending Celik Antonov to live with his birth mother once his father was dead had seemed like an obvious solution.

Until one started factoring in the late arms dealer's enemies and alliances.

The boy's mother was smart, but she was currently beset by vultures she didn't have the resources to deal with. She was out of her league.

It was time to do something.

Rowan sighed and reached for the phone.

She waited until the man that she and all the other directors answered to picked up. She needed to cover all bases with this one—her own base included.

'Sir, I have the latest report on Celik Antonov in front of me. I'd like permission to bring Jared West back in on the case in an advisory capacity. He knows the child and he understands the situation. I'd like to run certain scenarios on relocation for the child past him.'

Her request was reasonable. She was just doing her job. But there was more to her request than that.

'I also think Jared would want to be notified of this. It was his case. His fallout.'

And Jared would see it as his problem to fix.

There was silence on the other end, and then that dry, deep voice spoke. 'Jared, eh?'

'Yes, sir.' She'd known that the use of Jared's first name wouldn't go unnoticed. She wanted full disclosure on this. 'I'm intimate with him. This is the one case within my portfolio that I would share with him—with your permission.'

Rowan's palms were sweaty. Not only was a child's wellbeing at stake, so too was her fledgling romantic relationship. It wouldn't sit well with Jared that she had fresh information on Celik that she hadn't passed on to him. She *needed* a yes from Management on this.

'Sir…?'

Could be there had been a whole lot of pleading in that one little prompt. Could be she'd just altered the course of her own career irrevocably.

'Do it,' he said, and hung up.

Rowan slumped back in her chair and ran a clammy palm down over her face in relief.

One down. One to go.

Rowan put a call through to Jared next, knowing full well that he wasn't going to like hearing that the child's situation needed a rethink.

But all she got was an answering machine.

CHAPTER THIRTEEN

JARED ARRIVED IN Amsterdam and made the city his own. Bicycle- and pedestrian-friendly, creatively organised and full of water, the city appealed to him. The watercraft weren't like the ones he'd grown up with, and the canals were a rats' maze, but the place was beautiful and free-wheeling and it appealed to him on a visceral level.

He'd have liked to see Celik grow up here in safety, but that wouldn't happen so long as Antonov's parasites kept after him. Celik's perceived inheritance was the magnet, but the authorities had frozen it. No one could get to it. Not Celik's mother—bless her non-maternal soul—not Antonov's debtors, nor his creditors. That money wasn't going anywhere.

Two years ago he wouldn't have hesitated to go in and take the child, with no one any the wiser. These days his world was not nearly so black and white.

Undercover work had shown him the many facets of every situation. Likewise, Rowan's approach to problem-solving took into account and tried to balance many different needs. Celik had a mother—a woman who had taken him in—and before Jared put any plan for the boy in motion he needed to talk to her and take her needs into consideration.

Jared *wasn't* going into this guns blazing.

He thought Rowan would approve.

Getting to see Celik's mother was easy.

Damon invented an obscenely wealthy, fully verified background for him and booked him an appointment. Two hours, four-thirty to six-thirty p.m., cash only.

Damon's wicked sense of humour at work, but it gave him a cover persona and a trail leading nowhere should anyone decide to investigate.

Damon had invented another persona for Jared as well. In this one he was a highly skilled government operative, specialising in witness protection. It was this second persona that Jared had to sell to Celik's mother in order for any of their plans to work.

He was here to lie, scheme, to light a fire and destroy a little property, and kidnap a child and possibly the child's mother as well.

Every one of those activities should have given him pause.

And they didn't.

Needs must.

He had a plan, finessed by Damon, and he was running with it.

At four-thirty p.m. exactly Jared entered a narrow street paved with cobblestones and walked towards house number twenty-three. The entrance door was flanked by flowerpots filled with colourful blooms. An ornate wrought-iron railing guided visitors up the three steps to the deep red door with its brass lion knocker. The house itself stood three storeys tall—one of Amsterdam's historic 'Gentleman's Houses', abutting one of Amsterdam's oldest canals. Prime real estate, carefully tended and exclusive.

He rang the bell, and was surprised when Celik's mother opened the door herself.

He knew what she looked like from the photos Damon had sent him. He'd been expecting polish and he got it. She was a very beautiful woman in her late twenties, with a face that had an innocence to it that couldn't possibly be real, given her profession. But she had a kind of vulnerability—and her smile was sweet as she asked him his name and then stood back to let him in, waiting until the door had closed behind him.

She led him into a small sitting room filled with deep armchairs and elegant furnishings before asking him for more formal identification.

'A driver's licence, if you please, or a passport.'

He handed her the passport Damon had secured for him and she took a photo of it with her phone and presumably sent it somewhere, presumably for safekeeping.

Not a foolish woman, by any means.

'Precautions,' she said, with another sweet smile. 'Should you become a regular patron, this part of the afternoon can, of course, be dispensed with. My name is whatever you want it to be this evening. Would you care for a drink?'

'I'm really not here for what you think I'm here for.'

He pulled out the second set of credentials and handed them over and watched her innocent expression fade, to be replaced by sharp-eyed consideration.

'I'm here in collaboration with Dutch and Russian officials. I work for an organisation that relocates certain individuals—if that's what they need. I'm here to offer you and your son entry into a witness protection programme.'

Would she do it? He had a plan in place, just in case she said yes.

But neither he nor Damon had judged it likely.

'No.' He watched in silence as her pretty face contorted into a mask of pain and frustration. 'Yes, I requested help, but this is *not* what I want!'

He and Damon had judged correctly.

'Witness *protection*?' she continued angrily. 'Why should I give up my life here when this was never the arrangement? I bore that man a child, yes. A sick child that I couldn't care for. The child's father paid me to go away and stay away—and I *did*. That child upstairs was three days old when I walked away from him. I have the paperwork to prove it. I made no claim on him, or on any fortune he might some day inherit. I have paperwork for that as well. But does anyone care? No! "You're his mother," they said. "He's your problem now—*you* deal with it."'

Not a lot of maternal instinct in that heart.

'Look, he's a sweet kid. He's soft. He has this *innocence*...' she continued. 'How *that* happened, given that father of his, I have no idea. But I can't protect the boy from who he is and what his late father owes. I don't have access to the money his father's business associates want. I don't have the weapons they want. I was never in Antonov's confidence. But these people...they don't want to hear that.'

'You fear for your safety?'

'Yes!'

'I'm offering you and your son a chance to leave this place and start afresh. Somewhere Antonov's debtors won't find you.'

'Take the boy—yes. If he goes away my problems

will disappear. Take him. Please. And leave me out of it. I have a life here—and it's a good one.'

'If that's what you want…' He'd been counting on it. 'I require your signature and your co-operation when it comes to getting the child away from the property without being seen. Your son will have a new identity and a new life without you in it. One that precludes any contact with you in future years.'

'Take him.' She spoke with no hesitation. 'Keep him safe if you can. Let him grow to become his own man—there's freedom in that, and choice. He could go to school, make friends with other children. I tried to get him to make friends, but he's too used to being with adults…he's never been anything but home-schooled.' She shook her head. 'The child thinks he's too sick for regular school. He's not. He was home-schooled because of his father's protectiveness and paranoia.'

'Under the circumstances, I guess the paranoia was warranted.'

'All I'm saying is that if he stops being Antonov's son Celik can go to school. He can choose who he wants to be.' She looked sad suddenly. 'He won't get the chance to start over if he stays with me.'

'You *do* carc about him?'

'No! Not enough to change my life. There's a difference between wanting someone to have a chance and caring about them.'

'Do you need more time to make a decision?'

She shook her head and turned away. 'No. Take him now. Take him away. I don't care.'

'Do you like yellow tulips?'

Her gaze met his in the mirror above the mantelpiece

as she poured herself a shot glass full of cognac and swallowed it. 'They're a little common.'

'Once a year, on this date, you'll receive a bunch of yellow tulips. A message, if you will, that your son is alive and well.'

Once upon a time Jared would never have thought to offer anyone that kind of solace. These days he better understood that some situations could be beyond a person's capacity to deal with them.

'You really don't have to do that.'

'I'll do it once. Should you refuse the delivery, you won't get any others.'

'Will you take the boy with you now?'

'Before six this evening—yes.'

'You have my thanks.' She shrugged, elegant, unapologetic, and whimsical again now that her life had been rearranged to her liking. She crossed to the window and drew the curtains aside. 'They watch my house all the time now. Two from below. One from a house across the canal. There may be more.'

'There *are* more. But I've got this. May I see the boy now?'

'Take the stairs to the top floor. He's in the room on the left. You can't miss it. His tutor is with him.' She shot him a wry smile. 'It's school time.'

Jared climbed the stairs, opened the first door to the left and watched the solemn-eyed little boy's face light up with relief.

'Jimmy!'

'Hey there, champ. How's it going?' was all he had time to say before his arms were full of boy.

'And you are…?' enquired the steel-haired matron sitting at a desk filled with books.

'Just passing through.' Jared smiled his most charming smile and watched the older woman's eyes start to thaw. He looked down at Celik next and shot the boy a grin. 'According to your mother you have five minutes of school left before we can break you out of here and go have some fun,' he said in Russian.

'Schooling is important,' the teacher said, clearly having no trouble at all understanding Jared's somewhat thick northern Russia accent. And then she offered them both a smile. 'But maybe today we will finish early, no? Maybe just this once.'

By the time darkness fell Jared and Celik were in the basement of the old canal house and Jared was busy removing the narrow window that sat just above the waterline from its hinges.

'Remember what I told you.' Jared crouched down and held the boy's gaze. 'We're going through the window and then we're going for a swim using scuba gear. It's just like the snorkelling gear you used to use, only better.'

'Like what you used when you checked the hull for bombs. You showed me.'

'Exactly like that. But it's going to be dark underwater and you won't be able to see much.'

'And I'm going to be clipped to you.'

'That's right. And we'll only be this far under the water.' Jared's spread his arms about a meter or so wide and then shortened it to half that before lengthening the distance again. 'So the moment you want to go to the surface you tug on my arm and up we go. Got that?'

The boy nodded.

'And what does this mean?' Jared continued the drill,

commanding the little boy's attention with his voice and eyes as he made the universal sign for okay with his fingers.

'It means I'm okay.'

'When we come up to the surface—and we will a few times—that's the signal I want to see. It'll tell me that you're ready to go back under again. Okay? Make the sign.'

He held up his own curled fingers as an example. Celik made the sign and Jared nodded.

'Good. Are you ready?'

The boy nodded enthusiastically, and Jared picked him up and stood him on the bench he'd placed below the window. They watched together as a long, many-seated, shallow-bottomed tourist boat stalled right in front of the little window. The pilot would slip overboard and then the boat would catch fire and provide them with some smoke and cover. Bless Damon and his remote management skills.

'Remember when I told you that a boat was going to help hide us while we slide out the window and into the water? That's the boat. And it's going to blow up now.'

Celik's eyes grew big and round.

Yeah, not a sentence a seven-year-old boy heard every day… Not even Antonov's son.

The explosion was a good one. The boat went up in flames, accompanied by a roil of black smoke. Jared took the window out and hoisted himself through it and into the inky black water, and then motioned for Celik to come. It helped that the boy could swim like a fish and looked upon this as an adventure. It also helped that one of Antonov's thugs had shown him as a six-year-old how scuba gear worked and had let the boy play around with it in a swimming pool before Antonov had put a stop to it.

The scuba gear he'd set in place earlier was still there. Less than thirty seconds later they were two feet underwater and swimming away from the blaze. Jared kept them close to the side of the canal and brought them to the surface beneath the shadows of the nearest bridge. He wanted to see that okay sign.

The kid was like an eel in the water, and when Jared gave him the sign the kid nodded vigorously, wrapped an arm around his neck and signalled right back.

So under they went again.

Two more times they surfaced, and soon enough came upon a row of houseboat hulls. Jared started counting them off. Six—and then a sharp right into an adjoining canal.

They were halfway through the turn when another boom sounded—a boom that shook the water. That didn't bode well. Forward progress suddenly became a whole lot more difficult, with water flowing swiftly in the opposite direction, and Jared clung with all his strength to the canal wall.

That secondary explosion was neither his nor Damon's doing.

Something to worry about.

Their last crawl along the side of the houseboat hulls took as much time as the rest of the swim put together, but eventually they surfaced again. Every muscle in Jared's arms and shoulders was screaming with the weight of Celik and the drag of the water.

This time they'd surfaced next to a ladder that was half hidden between a houseboat and the canal wall.

Jared wasted no time in getting the scuba gear off them and sending Celik up the ladder first.

'There's a towel waiting for you. Grab it and get warm.'

Moments later they were in the bowels of a comfortably shabby tourist houseboat and Jared was turning lights on.

'Are we good?'

Celik nodded, his eyes bright and his hair sticking up in tufts. 'Did we lose them? The bad men?'

'Yes. Jump in the shower and get warmed up while I put some soup on. Then I'm going to tell you a story about a little boy who never knew he had an aunt. An aunt who loved him very much, even though they'd never met. An aunt who wanted nothing more than to meet this little boy named Celik and help him to grow up healthy and happy and strong. Do you like the sound of that story?

Celik nodded.

'Good. Because next time I tell it I'm going to add speedboats, aeroplanes, sleepy mice and penguins.'

Rowan stood in front of the stern-faced grey-eyed man and stared down at a picture of what had once been an elegant Amsterdam canal house and was now little more than a pile of rubble, courtesy of some kind of explosion or bomb. The owner of the house—one Cerise Fallon—had not been injured in the explosion, but according to her there had been two others in the house at the time of the incident. A client, whose details had been lost along with her phone, and her seven-year-old son.

The next picture in the pile showed a picture of a beautiful woman standing in darkness, staring up at her burning house, her face lit by the nearby flames. Her tears looked convincing.

‘Two days ago you asked me if you could brief Jared West on a situation involving Antonov’s son,’ said Rowan’s boss. ‘Know anything about this?’

‘No, sir. I know nothing about this.’

‘You expect me to believe that?’

‘I never briefed Jared. I haven’t been able to get hold of him. Have they found any bodies yet? Her son? The body of the client?’

‘Not yet.’

‘Then how do we know this isn’t something that the Dutch authorities set up in order to spirit the child away? With the mother’s full co-operation?’

‘We don’t.’

‘Do we know what caused the explosion?’

‘From what we can gather a boat caught fire outside the house. And then someone shot a grenade into a first floor window. There’s a Dutch forensics and recovery team working on it now.’

‘A grenade?’ Rowan winced.

‘Was it West?’ he asked again.

‘I don’t know.’ Nothing but the truth.

‘You said you hadn’t been able to contact him. How many times did you try?’

‘I called his number immediately after I spoke to yo about the case two days ago. My assistant has been try ing to get hold of him ever since.’

‘And your inability to reach him didn’t make yo suspicious?’

‘He’s just bought a yacht. I thought—’ Rowan stoppe There was no point continuing.

‘You presumed?’

'Yes, sir, I presumed to know where he was.'

'Get him in here, Director. Preferably tonight. Make me believe that Jared West had nothing to do with this.'

'Yes, sir, I'll try.'

When Rowan still couldn't raise Jared she called his sister.

'Rowan!'

Lena sounded pleased to hear from her. Lazy Saturday afternoon drinks down by the river last weekend had a lot to answer for.

'You'd better make it Director Farringdon, Lena. This isn't a social call. I'm looking for Jared.'

'He took the boat out storm-chasing,' Lena offered, a whole lot more carefully. 'He does that.'

'Are you prepared to swear to that in court?'

Silence.

'If I send the coastguards out looking for him are they going to find him?'

More silence.

'Is there *any* chance at all that he can put in an appearance down here before tomorrow morning?'

'How about I get him to call you?' said Lena.

And Rowan felt her heart break, just a little bit, because any faint hope she'd had that Jared wasn't involved in this was rapidly dwindling.

'That's really not going to be good enough.'

'I'm sure he'll do his best.'

'Thanks.' Rowan hung up.

She was pretty sure he'd already done it.

Three days later there were still no bodies and Jared still hadn't called. On the fourth day the authorities advised that two bodies had been found. One as yet unidentified male and Celik Antonov.

For the first time in her career Rowan stopped all calls, sat back in her fancy leather chair and tried to remember how to breathe.

Sam stood in the doorway, her expression uncertain. 'Director, shall I send Jared West's identification details to the Dutch authorities?'

'No.' It was barely a croak. 'Let them do the work. We flag nothing. We have no knowledge of this. And, Sam? Cancel my appointments for the afternoon. I think I'm just going to go…home.'

She felt a sting in her eyes as Sam nodded and shut the door behind her. She *wouldn't* let tears fall here, in this place. It wasn't professional.

Think, Rowan. Think about this. Nothing was certain…even the child's supposed death.

Theory one: the Dutch authorities had spirited Celik Antonov away somewhere and were misleading them all. Oh, she liked that theory.

Theory two: young Celik had indeed lost his life, bu the unidentified body was not Jared's. Rowan hated thi theory, but it was better than the third.

Theory three: Jared was dead. Celik—dead. And wrong call by her—back when Jared had wanted to g check on the boy—had contributed to their downfall.

If that was indeed Jared lying there in a body bag.. *If* it was.

So Jared had gone to see the boy—what then? Wha had gone wrong?'

Rowan wrapped her arms tightly around her middl and tried not to rock back and forth. She couldn't *be* thi bereft. It wasn't possible. How could she have fallen s hard and so fast for Jared West when she'd only had the tiniest taste of him? A handful of stolen nights and a couple of meals—that was all. Intense when they were together, but it wasn't as if they'd been sharing each other's lives for a dozen years or more.

She hadn't been witness to his life for very long at all.

She couldn't be in love with him. She just couldn't.

Trembling, she picked up the phone and dialled a number that she'd memorised days ago. 'Lena?'

'Rowan?' She sounded uncertain. 'I mean, Director…'

'Yes. They're saying that Celik Antonov is dead and that an unidentified male died with him. They're saying they have the bodies.' Rowan barely recognised the sound of her own voice. 'Tell me that you know where Jared is. Tell me you've spoken to him.'

'I've spoken to him,' Lena said instantly.

Rowan choked on a moan.

'Rowan? Director Farringdon? Do you hear me? I spoke to Jared not two hours ago. Whoever they have in that body bag, it's not my brother. I *know* this.'

Rowan couldn't speak. Her eyes were on fire and her throat kept trying to close. She couldn't breathe.

'Rowan, *talk* to me.'

'No one's—no one can find him.'

'He does that. I couldn't find him once for almost two years. I'm going to kill him. I told him to contact you. I *told* him.'

'No—it's—' She tried to pull herself together and couldn't.

'Director—?'

'I'll let you go.' A feeble end to a misguided phone call. 'I have another call coming in.'

Liar.

Desolation warred with relief as Rowan put the phone gently back in its cradle and then put her head in both hands and dug her fingers into her scalp until it hurt. Lena said she'd spoken to Jared, and Rowan believed her. He was alive.

He just hadn't seen fit to return her calls.

She made herself small and quiet—found that place deep down inside where she'd retreated so often as a child, that little dark hole where she could put herself back together again, piece by piece, until she was whole again.

Jared was alive. That was a block right there to build upon. Jared was alive and all she had to do now was sort out her private feelings for him and keep them separate from what was required of her professionally.

The Dutch were saying they had bodies. What good was it going to do anyone if she went sleuthing and discovered that this was a fabrication? What good would it do to confront Jared as to his whereabouts these past few days? Did she really want to know? Occasionally it was preferable simply to remain ignorant.

She'd know anyway. The minute she saw him again she'd know whether or not he'd had anything to do with Celik's demise or disappearance.

She'd send him that report about the two bodies, and if that didn't get him in here, spitting fire and glaring daggers…if that didn't get him roaring at her for not letting him go check on the boy two weeks earlier…

As for the rest of her relationship with him…

Deep down inside she started to curl in on herself again—so little spine, so weak and pathetic.

No need to be in love with a man she'd only known a few weeks.

No need to mourn the loss of a connection that had never been there in the first place.

He didn't trust her, and maybe she didn't trust him, and without at least some level of trust there was nothing worth having.

She'd needed him to call her this week and share something. His actions, his whereabouts. She'd have even gratefully accepted the briefest of calls just to let her know that he was still breathing.

But no.

He'd offered nothing.

ared flew into Canberra dead tired but determined to ee Rowan. Damon had forwarded him the press release from the Dutch, citing Celik and an unknown male dead, ase closed and no more questions.

Celik's mother had probably told them of his involvement by now, but that was all they knew. Jared had told hem nothing, so whatever game they were playing… e wasn't in on it. No one knew where Celik was now. As far as Jared was concerned no one ever needed to.

He took a taxi to the ASIS building and talked his way past the front desk. His presence *had* been requested y the director of Section Five after all.

Several days ago now.

Rowan's trusty assistant sat at the outer desk as usual, eadphones on and fingers flying across the keyboard. made his silent approach easier, and he was almost pon her before she looked up from her work. Her eyes idened at first, and then narrowed alarmingly. No welcome in them whatsoever as she slid her headphones off and stared at him in silence.

'Hey, Sam. Is she in?'

'If by *she* you mean Director Farringdon, then, no. Not in.'

Okay, maybe he should try that again. 'May I make an appointment to see the director, please?'

'Sweet manners, but you'll still have to wait your turn. How about—?' Sam turned her attention back to her computer screen. 'Friday week?'

'Seriously? She left a message saying she wanted to see me.'

'That was last week, when she was being hauled over the coals for a stunt some fool pulled in Amsterdam. Two dead, apparently.'

Jared scowled. 'I've seen the report.'

'Have you, now? And yet it still took you three days to put in an appearance? Where have you been, Mr West?'

'Busy.'

'Aren't we all? The director's not here and she no longer needs to see you. I'll let her know you've been in. She slipped her headphones back on, dismissing him. 'You know the way out. You've walked it enough.'

Yes, he should have called her. He'd been somewher in Poland when Damon had relayed her first messag He'd thought about calling her and lying outright, bu that hadn't sat well with him. He'd thought about cal ing her and coming clean, but he honestly hadn't know what she would do with the information.

She was a director for the Australian Secret Inte ligence Service. She'd have been obliged to hand th information over to them. She couldn't tell them what she didn't know.

Surely she would know that he'd been protecting her?

Surely she could see that a new start had been imperative for Celik and that someone had to organise it and that the best man for the job had been him?

Surely…

And even if they did have differences of opinion when it came to the way he'd handled the situation, surely she'd hear him out?

Wouldn't she?

He had every confidence in her ability to bring a thoughtful, rational approach with her to their current predicament. That was why he was currently pacing the pavement outside her apartment block like a downtrodden preacher without an audience.

He saw her drive past and into the car park beneath the building. He knew he was in trouble when she walked back out of the driveway and started towards him. She looked older tonight, in the shadows of the evening. As if her own light had dimmed in the week since he'd last seen her.

It had only been a week.

Okay, a week and a half—and he'd got here as soon as he could.

She stopped in front of him and simply stood there and looked at him—and the tilt of her lips might have been a smile but for the complete lack of a smile behind them.

He tucked his hands in his pockets and tried not to worry.

'You're looking good,' she said. 'You always do.'

Okay, he had no idea where she was going with this. Nowhere good. 'I got here as soon as I could.'

'You heard about Celik Antonov's death?'

'I heard about his supposed death. Not sure I believe it,' he offered carefully, and watched as what little light she had left went out altogether.

'I tried to call you,' she said quietly. 'I was hoping to bring you in on the case before the situation worsened. I thought you'd want in on it. Did you not get my messages?'

'They caught up with me a couple of days back.' He opted for the half-truth, knowing as the words spilled from his lips that his explanation wouldn't satisfy her.

'And the reason they didn't catch up with you before then…?'

'I switched phones and left the old phone at home.'

At least that was the truth. He hadn't known that Rowan had been trying to contact him practically from the moment he'd left for Europe.

'I should have called you sooner, though. I just wasn't altogether sure who I'd get. The woman I have a relationship with or the ASIS director.'

'Something we might have discussed had you rung,' she said bleakly. 'Why couldn't you have given me that opportunity? Do you trust me that little?'

'I was trying to *protect* you.'

'In that case, keep up the good work. Go home, Jared. And if you don't have one of those go wherever it is that you go when you don't want to be found.'

'Rowan, please. Hear me out.'

'No. I don't want to hear what you have to say. Not in relation to any case that has just been closed. Not in relation to anything else.'

'We have a *relationship*,' he insisted.

'No. A relationship requires some small measure of trust and respect for the other person's feelings. We had sex.'

'We had more than that.'

'I thought you were dead.'

Okay, so there *was* that…

'I go into work and have a report come in on Celik Antonov's situation. I immediately ask for permission to bring you in on it. I call and you don't answer. Two days later I get hauled over the coals for a situation that I know nothing about and I try to call you again. Still no answer. And then it gets worse. I get a report over my desk that Celik and an unidentified man are dead. I sit there and I wonder, and I try not to fall apart. Finally I call your sister and tell her that I haven't heard from you, that I have this report on my desk. And she *knows* what I'm thinking without me having to say a word and she throws me a bone… She tells me that you're not dead—and at least that's something, right? You're *alive*.' Her voice cracked. 'That was two days ago.'

'Ro—'

'No! Do you have *any* idea how I felt? One phone call, Jared. You could have told me you were in Antarctica and I wouldn't have pushed you for anything else. But you never made the call. You didn't trust me with *any* information at all. How do you think that made me feel?'

'Rowan, let's take this inside.' He was shaking. 'Let me explain.'

But she went toe to toe with him instead. 'What's to explain? You don't trust me. You left me and I didn't even know where you'd gone. Where—in any of this—is your consideration for my feelings for *you*? Anywhere? Because I can't see it.'

'I can do better. I *will*. There won't *be* another situation like the one we were just in. We can do this, Rowan—please. I'm sorry.'

'I'm sorry too. Because I so badly wanted to believe in us. But you don't get to diminish me like that—make me feel as if I barely exist.'

The tears that spilled down her cheeks gutted him.

'I won't let you.'

'Rowan, don't—

'*No!* Go away, Jared. I don't want to hear it. I'm sorry, but we're done.'

CHAPTER FOURTEEN

RIGHTEOUS ANGER MIGHT have helped Rowan hang together long enough to do what had had to be done, but it didn't make for good company. She spent one night locked in misery and the next day and night functioning on autopilot, wishing Jared West would disappear from her memory—only it wasn't happening.

He'd put in another appearance at Section and she'd immediately kicked him over to Corbin, who'd questioned him about the Amsterdam incident.

Not surprisingly, Jared had denied all involvement.

She'd watched the interview from behind a one-way mirror, along with the steely-eyed man who oversaw all the sections, and at the end of the interview he'd turned to her and asked if she believed the story West was spinning.

'Do you?' she'd asked quietly, but hadn't waited for his answer.

She cut her work-day short and went to see her grandfather.

He was in his garden, as usual, pampering runner beans, dahlias, and his fifty-year-old tortoise, Veronica. He smiled when he saw her.

'Granddaughter.' The smile dimmed somewhat when

he got a good look at her. 'What gives? Because you are three hours and one day early for our dinner date.'

'It's been a hard week. I wanted to touch base with my favourite tortoise.'

She spared a glance for her grandfather's pond. Yep, there she was. Half out of the pond, neck at full stretch, and beady eyes trained on the latest goings-on. Nothing escaped Veronica.

'Problem at work?'

'There was. But it's been resolved.'

'To your satisfaction?'

'To the satisfaction of some.'

'But not you?'

'Can't have everything.' She'd learned that as a child. 'Do you think I have abandonment issues?'

Her grandfather's eyes narrowed. 'That's quite a question...'

'Are you likely to need tea, coffee or any other fortifying beverage before giving me an answer?'

'Tea and cake might help it along some.'

He gathered up his walking stick and headed inside and Rowan followed. Not until they were both settled at the little kitchen table by the window did he return to the question.

'Who let you down?'

'A man. A young, impulsive one.'

'A good man?'

'Yes.' It was true, even though the word burned on her tongue. 'In many ways...yes. He's a little reckless.'

'You're a little cautious.'

'I'm not cautious at all. I just like to plan ahead and cover my bases.'

He smiled slightly. 'And everyone else's.'

Okay, maybe he had a point. 'Remember how I mentioned that we were bringing someone in from deep undercover? His name's Jared West and he's the one I'm having trouble with.'

'In a personal sense or a professional one?'

Rowan sipped at her coffee. 'Both. Although he no longer works for ASIS. He finished up a couple of weeks ago—as soon as his debrief was done.'

'How long was he undercover for?'

'Two years. He was in the employ of an international arms dealer.'

'Antonov?' Her grandfather huffed a dry laugh. 'He brought down the Antonov operation?'

'Yes. And left Antonov's son exposed. The boy was placed with his mother, but she couldn't cope with the legacy Antonov left behind. I think Jared relocated the child. Put him somewhere safe. That's what I'd like to think. But I don't know.'

Rowan shrugged and traced doodles on the tablecloth with her fingertip.

'I got too close to him, Grandfather. I let myself care for the man and then he went no contact. He just...disappeared without a word and I didn't know where he was.' Her heart thumped hard. 'I *hate* that.'

'I know you do. Did Jared West have a reason for going no contact?'

'You mean besides not wanting anyone to know what he was up to?'

'Plausible deniability, Rowan. You know how it's done. This way you know nothing. And you continue to know nothing.'

'And then there's what would be best for the child. I

know it was playing on his mind. The child needed witness protection. A new life. We could have arranged it.'

'Although possibly not to Jared West's satisfaction,' her grandfather said dryly.

'Possibly not.'

Her grandfather regarded her solemnly. 'Did he know that you might react badly to not knowing where he was? Did you tell him about your upbringing in those early years?'

'I— No. I don't really talk about that.'

'Maybe you should.'

Rowan picked up her coffee mug and took a deep gulp. 'So I'm asking again,' she continued doggedly. 'In this case, given what I've told you, do you think I have abandonment issues?'

'Yes. You developed them as a child and for a time you let them rule you. But you're not a child now.'

'I sent him away.'

'So get him back.'

'I suggested he stay away.'

'Can a person not admit that they were wrong?'

'*Was* I wrong?'

'Rowan. I'm not all-knowing and all-seeing, no matter how wise I like to think I am. Only you can answer that one.'

Jared hadn't given up. He never gave up when he wanted something badly enough. He figured it would come as no surprise to the director that he would give her a couple of days to cool off and then he'd be back. With food that might tempt her to stop and take a bite. With another apology—a bigger one—and an explanation if she wanted it. With promises if she wanted those, and every intention of keeping them.

He kept his word.

She saw him the minute she walked away from the ASIS building at nine p.m. Hard not to, given that he was standing there leaning against his car. She'd agreed to give him five minutes of her time. Or Sam had agreed on Rowan's behalf. Either way, she headed towards him without hesitation.

'I probably have half an hour left in me before my brain gives up in exhaustion,' she said quietly. 'Would you like to join me at the Marble Bar?'

It was a white-collar work haunt, connected to an international hotel chain, and it was just around the corner. The booths were private and the lights were low. They could have a relatively private conversation there—of a sort.

'Sure.'

He opened the car door for her, wanting nothing more than to gather her up, wrap his arms around her and bury his head in the curve of her neck and stay there until she softened. Her body would remember him. He could coax capitulation from her, he was sure.

Instead he kept his manners in place and tried to ignore the silent simmer between them as they made their way to the bar and found a booth and placed their drinks order. Decaf coffee for them both. He added a couple of side dishes for good measure. Lamb pieces in a yoghurt sauce. Rice balls.

'I made a promise,' he began. 'To a seven-year-old. When the world around us was burning I promised that I would look out for him and I have. I will continue to look out for him from afar. I'd rather you didn't ask, but if you do I *will* tell you everything.'

'I'm not asking.' She held his gaze. 'The case is closed.'

'Which kind of just leaves the promises I want to make to you going forward.'

He watched as tears gathered in her eyes and threatened to fall. She looked utterly miserable, and so far away from him in that moment that she broke his heart.

'Don't cry. Don't. I can't stand it.'

'Talk,' she said raggedly. 'I'm listening now. I wasn't the last time I saw you.'

Where to start?

'I should have told you I was heading off and wouldn't be in contact for a while. I thought the less you knew of my movements last week the better, but clearly that isn't going to work for us.'

'I used to wake up all the time when I was small. New country, big house with staff, and my parents would be gone. No one ever told me anything. I used to feel so invisible. I still react badly to feeling invisible.'

'I have *never* thought of you as invisible. I walk into a room and you're the one I look for. As for those bodies that the Dutch claim exist… That was *never* part of my plan. I knew you'd be wondering what had gone on with the boy and I thought to protect you by telling you nothing. I knew you were looking for me and I still didn't call. I would have called had I known what I know now. If ever there's a next time, I will call. There can be ground rules. Never leave without saying goodbye. Never stay away without getting in touch. Never let you think that I don't love you. Because I love you so much.'

He'd always thought that those simple little words of love would be hard for him to say.

They weren't.

'I love you.'

'You do?' She curled her hand around her coffee cup and wouldn't look at him. 'You could have anyone.'

'Good—because I choose you.'

'Someone beautiful.'

'You *are* beautiful. And don't say I could have someone young, who'd want to give me a family. I know what I want. From the moment I saw you that was me gone. Please, Rowan. Give me another chance.'

'Okay.'

He could barely hear her.

'You kind of had me at *I made a promise to a seven-year-old.* And you kept it.'

Finally she looked up at him and he allowed himself to hope.

'Would you like to take this somewhere more private? My place?'

'Or my place here? You haven't seen that one yet. Or the apartment? Wherever you feel the most comfortable.'

'My place. Or— No. There's no food in the fridge.'

'Do we care? Are we caring about that?'

'Not even ice cream. I ate it in one sitting. When I thought you were dead.'

'Perfectly reasonable.' He had sisters. He could handle this.

'I cursed you to straight to hell.'

'Harsh, but fair.'

'You do realise the power balance will tumble back and forward between us all the time?'

He smiled at that. 'I'm looking forward to it.'

'And my work—we're going to need some ground rules when it comes to what I can discuss.'

'I can understand that. I'm good with that. I have a couple of ongoing projects that I won't discuss either. We can *do* this. We just need to keep the communication lines open when it comes to what we can't discuss. I can tell you I'm off to visit the penguins in Antarctica every now and then. Call you from an iceberg.'

He spun some money on the table, more than enough to cover the drinks they'd ordered, and stood.

'I really need to hold you now. And we need to take it somewhere private, because my self-control is all but shot.'

She came around to his side and pressed up against him.

He'd never known a woman's touch that could both soothe and inflame him until this touch. He never wanted any other woman at his side but this one.

'My place is closest,' she whispered. 'We could go there, and I could gather the courage to stand naked before you and tell you that I love you right back.'

'Good plan.'

They made it outside and to the car door before he gave in to temptation and kissed her.

'You have no idea how much I admire your forward-thinking right now.'

'And then you can get naked too—I can help you with that—and then you can tell me you love me again.' She smiled dulcetly. 'And make me believe it.'

CHAPTER FIFTEEN

THE LITTLE YACHT rode the waves with panache, even if the interior cushions *were* still the colour of mustard. Rowan had the wheel, and Jared trimmed the sails, and together they made the craft skim through the Pacific like a hot knife through butter.

Put Rowan and Jared together and they could usually conquer anything. This they had discovered in the six months they'd been together.

It had been the happiest, most adventurous and fulfilling six months of her life.

Jared's siblings had accepted her without question, even if she was ten years older than Jared and destined to remain childless. Jared's choice—Jared's business. They trusted him, as she trusted him, to do right by all of them.

He was that kind of man.

He'd taken on two more retrieval jobs since Celik, with Rowan's full knowledge and unofficial support. Rowan had been his muse and Damon had been his handler during the runs. Jared had called her every day and talked about penguins and icecaps. He'd returned bearing fresh scars and seeking her touch, and she was no longer worried that she wasn't the one for him.

Not when every glance and every touch confirmed it.

Three times now Rowan had asked Management if she could call him in on a case. They'd let her bring him up to date and together they'd brainstormed. On one turbulent occasion he'd even gone into the field and fixed it.

Yes, she'd been worried. Yes, she'd handed over case management to Corbin on that one. But she'd been Corbin's shadow and there'd been security and reassurance in knowing that she had every detail of his whereabouts and actions at her fingertips.

Action and thought. They could slice and dice these two elements every which way and still manage to make things work.

'Hey, Jared? Where are we going?' she called as he tightened the mainsail and she adjusted their course.

'East.' He could still be insanely fuzzy when it came to details. 'We'll just tack our way out.'

'Yes, but *why*?' If they kept going east they'd end up in Chile.

'The wind, Ro, the *wind*! Think of the ride back in on the turnaround.'

And then there was the fun in him. The daredevil with the mile-wide grin and eyes the colour of the ocean.

She had a proposal for him.

'Hey, Jared? I had a talk with Management yesterday and they offered me a new position. Complete autonomy. Black operations. Specialist team.'

'Really?' Suddenly the sail snapped tight and he tied it off and made his way back to her. 'What was your answer?'

'I declined the offer and gave them a counter-offer to consider.'

His arms came around her from behind, crossing over her waist, making her feel treasured.

'This is why I love you,' he murmured. 'What did you tell them?'

'That I wanted to finish up in my position and go freelance. Or a part-time position. And that I would bring my own carefully selected team to the table with me when required.'

Jared leaned forward so that he could see her face. 'You *what*?'

'I know. Most beautiful counter-offer ever. They accepted it.'

'But—your career… The one you've dreamed about since you were a teenager. The one you've worked all your life towards.'

'I had a look at where else there was left for me to go and I didn't much care for the view. The career I have now has got me to the point where I can name my own terms. There's nothing more I want from it. I'm on two months' notice.'

'Are you sure?'

'Very sure.'

'And this team of yours? Who does that involve?'

'I mentioned no names and they didn't ask. I made no promises whatsoever on your behalf. Still…if you're interested…I'm thinking three, maybe four jobs per year. Specialist retrieval jobs that need our combined touch. It'd let us be selective. It'd give me more time for you. And this.'

'I'm in.' His arms tightened around her. 'Ro, are you sure?'

'I'm sure. I don't want to see you on Wednesday

nights and weekends any more. I'm greedier than that. I want more.'

'Where do you want to live?'

'On the beach,' she said instantly, for she'd fallen in love with it. 'Somewhere near here—close to Lena and Trig and to Damon's beach house. This is the place for us.'

'What about your grandfather?'

'He loves it here. I think he could be persuaded to visit regularly.'

'And your parents?'

'I figure we'd see them less often.' She tried to accommodate them—she did try. But there was still a lot of distance to bridge. 'I have some money saved. I can sell my apartment. I can put in my fair share and then we can do a budget and go looking.'

'Always with the details…' But he was smiling when he said it. 'I'm in. I am *so* in.'

'There's one more thing.'

'I'm listening.'

She took a deep breath and put it out there. Not a little thing. A really big thing that would need serious consideration and discussion.

'Want to make a baby with me?'

Time stopped. Wind rattled the sails and the little boat shuddered. There could be no turning back from this.

He wanted to. She could see it in his face and she had never felt so much happiness. No matter what happened when it came to babies, and the likelihood of them, she would always have this moment and this decision.

'Yes,' he growled, and bent.

The next thing she knew she'd been upended over

Jared's shoulder and was staring at his faded-jeans-clad, wholly delectable ass.

'Now. Right now.' Jared West—man of action. 'Let's do this.'

And she was laughing even as she caught hold of the stair railings and resisted his downward motion. 'But, Jared, don't you want to think about this for more than two seconds?'

'Don't need to.'

'I'm older. It might not work.'

'Then we'll die trying.'

'And then there's the genius genes. If our child turns out to be super-smart, that's *your* responsibility.'

'No problem. I'll farm him out to Damon.'

'Him? *Him?*'

'Or her. *Them.*'

Her man was nothing if not adaptable, and they were *doing* this. Jared *wanted* this. She had her answer.

'So we're doing this now?'

'Yes!'

Oh, hell yes.

But it simply wasn't in her nature to make it easy on him. 'But, Jared, what about this pretty boat? The wheel, the sails, the *wind*?'

'It's good,' he said. 'It's all good. Trust me.'

And she did.

EPILOGUE

THE WALLS WERE round and the furnishings were soft
A posy of lavender sat in a cheerful yellow vase in the
corner. There were two beds in the room and Jared ha
already pushed them together to make a big one. It wa
the latest and greatest in the private hospital's maternit
wing—overnight rooms for new families. Theirs eve
had a sliding door leading out to a tiny private court
yard surrounded by screening hedges and featuring
bird bath complete with inquisitive sparrows.

Up until recently soothing whale music had echoe
through the room, but the music had been stopped a
Rowan's request. Any more whales and she was goin
to reach for the nearest harpoon, she'd said

His daughter—the one snugged in tightly to Rowan'
chest—didn't know about whales, lavender or hospita
rooms yet, and maybe she wouldn't remember this roo
full of aunties and uncles and one sleeping cousin, bu
they were all here. Every one of Jared's siblings and thei
partners was here to celebrate the latest, littlest additio
to their family group and Jared was grateful.

Yesterday's labour had been hard and long. Rowa
had been exhausted and Jared had been more so, thor
oughly traumatised by all the things about birth that h

couldn't control and a midwife who'd reassured him that everything was going exactly as it should. All that pain and the pushing—exactly as it should have been. Heaven help them all.

And then Rowan had delivered a sticky and squalling baby girl and Jared had taken one look at her and fallen in love all over again. Seven pounds and eight ounces of little baby girl. His to love, treasure and honour. No setbacks for either baby or mother.

The midwife had placed the baby skin to skin atop her mother's heart and Rowan had looked up, her eyes shining, and said, 'C'mere…'

And now he was done. So enamoured of his girls that he had barely been able to see daylight when it had arrived this morning. And if his family teased him about the expression of wonder currently stuck on his face, then so be it. They didn't *know*.

Okay, Damon knew. Damon and Ruby had a son on the ground—a laughing little guy who had taken his first wobbly steps not two days ago. Maybe they knew this feeling better than he did. Still…

Those two…right there on the bed…the beautiful woman with the funny face and the ears that maybe stuck out just a little, and the baby girl with her eyes currently fixed on her daddy's shirt…they were his world.

Poppy and Seb were going to wait a while when it came to children. Damon and Ruby were planning another one. Lena and Trig—Lena for whom children were no longer an option—currently had the care and feeding of a twelve-year-old boy.

Jared had looked to Lena with faint apology in his eyes when she'd first come into the room, with Trig not far behind, but she'd taken one look at him and launched herself at him, hugging him as much in warning as in love.

'Don't,' she'd said. 'Don't you dare spoil this moment with whatever guilt trip is in your head. You let me celebrate your little girl. Because I am going to celebrate this one, Jare. For *all* of us. I'm going to celebrate hard.'

Yeah… As far as family was concerned, his little girl had landed in a special one.

'So, this is…' He looked to Rowan and grinned foolishly. 'Mine.'

'What are you going to call her?' asked Lena.

'Damona,' said Damon instantly as he cradled his sleeping Thomas in his arms. 'Got a nice ring to it.'

'Stay away from Shakespeare,' Poppy—full name Ophelia—told him earnestly. 'And hallucinogenic flower names—stay away from those too.'

'I always liked your name,' Lena said to Poppy. 'It's pretty.'

'They might want a shrub name, in keeping with Rowan's,' offered Poppy's partner, Seb. 'Willow? Or Bay?'

'Pomona?' Poppy said. 'Meaning apple. She's also the Roman goddess of fruit.'

'Stay away from the fruit,' Jared's best friend, Trig told him, and struggled to keep a straight face. 'In fac stay away from all the food groups. Honey, Ginger, Margarita…'

'Don't you listen to them, sweetheart,' said Rowan covering the little girl's ears. 'They're all mad. I'll explain how *that* happened when you get older.'

Jared smirked and pushed the dozens of pillows surrounding Rowan aside so that he could slip in besid her on the bed. 'Tell me when they get too much and I'll move them on,' he murmured.

'I heard that,' said Lena. 'And you can try, but I'm not leaving until this baby has a name. Look at her—she's so perfect. She reminds me of—' Lena stopped and her eyes sought Jared's. 'A perfect little girl,' she finished softly. 'Rowan, what *are* you going to call her?'

'Jared and I had a deal. If the baby was a boy I got to choose the name. If we had a girl it was Jared's choice.' Laughing, dancing eyes turned towards him. 'You should put your family out of their misery.'

'I'm enjoying their misery,' he said, but he touched the pad of his thumb to his daughter's tiny head and then awkwardly cleared his throat. 'So…I…uh—it's a family name. Everybody: meet Claire…Claire Elizabeth Farringdon West. After our mother.'

Nothing but silence followed.

'Is everyone okay with that?' he asked gruffly.

Lena nodded and promptly burst into tears. Poppy soon followed.

'It's good,' said Damon, who'd never known their mother.

Damon's wife, Ruby, stepped close and silently put her arms around him and Thomas and both. 'Feels right.'

And then the midwife came in and took one look at all the teary-eyed visitors. Her steely gaze fell next on mother and baby. 'What's all this?'

'We just named her,' Rowan said. 'Meet Claire Elizabeth.'

'A fine name it is,' said the midwife. 'And all the crying is because…?'

'Because it's perfect,' said Lena as more tears threatened to fall.

'That's it for visiting hour,' said the midwife in a no-nonsense voice and opened the door wide, looking more than capable of pushing people through it should anyone dissent. 'This lovely family have had a hard night—all three of them. They need their rest.'

But Lena moved forward before she went out, her eyes faintly pleading as she caught Rowan's gaze. 'May I touch her?'

'Would you like to hold her?' offered Rowan.

So far only Jared had held her, apart from Rowan.

'No! I—I… Not yet. I just—' Lena stroked the tiny head and then pressed a kiss to the baby's crown. 'Okay, I'm done.'

'Hey, Claire?' Jared rumbled softly. 'That was your aunt. She's probably going to teach you how to skydive.'

'And terrify your father,' Lena said. 'Consider it my gift to you.'

The midwife cleared her throat and Lena straightened.

'Congratulations. She's so beautiful—and so lucky to have you as parents. I know you'll be good.'

They all filtered out and the door closed behind them, leaving Jared and Rowan alone with their newborn.

'Have I told you how much I love you yet today?' he murmured as he settled back in beside Rowan.

'Yes.'

Good job.

'And I love *you*.'

'That's good to hear.'

He would never tire of hearing those words, or of needing this woman's love. He reached out and touched Claire's tiny hand, captivated all over again as his little girl wrapped tiny fingers around his big one and held on tight.

'Do you think she'd like to hear a story?'

'What about?'

'I have an extensive repertoire. Explosions, escapes, hair-raising adventures, espionage…'

'You should probably start small.'

Rowan looked ever so slightly incredulous, and he oved it that he could still put that look there. Never dull, this life of theirs. And right here, right now, it had never been more perfect.

'You want me to tell her about Veronica the tortoise nd the garden hose?'

'It's a little raunchy for a newborn.' Rowan's smile aid it all. 'Tell her the one about the sun in the sky, the lippery slide and the dancing penguins first.'

* * * * *